Liza Perrat

Wolfsangel

D1260065

TRISKELE BOOKS

Cover design: JD Smith.

Published by Perrat Publishing.

All enquiries to info@lizaperrat.com

First printing, 2013.

ISBN 978-2-9541681-2-8

To my beloved father, Stanley Southan.
Sorry you didn't get to read this one;
I think you would have enjoyed it.

When you go to war as a boy you have a great illusion of immortality. Other people get killed, not you. Then when you are badly wounded the first time you lose that illusion and you know it can happen to you.

Ernest Hemingway

Céleste Primrose
8th June 2012

1

We gather in the cemetery, before the ossuary, with the straggle of other remaining survivors and their families. Our heads dipped, the mayor begins his memorial speech to commemorate the tragedy that became a legend around these parts; the evil that part of me still believes was the result of my own reckless actions.

There isn't a region in France that didn't pay the price of war with the blood of its children, but here in the village of Lucie-sur-Vionne one can truly contemplate the depths to which the pure devilry of man was cast.

The chill of last winter stole my husband, and though my extended family are with me, I feel lonely without him by my side, remembering the fateful afternoon that has tormented me for sixty-eight years — the sickening odour of charred flesh, the smoke parching my throat, the green-brown blur of the woods as I fled the clomp of German boots. My fingertips skitter across the scar on my left arm, eternal reminder of that inconceivable climb, then the free-fall of an unstrung puppet, and the certainty that I too would die any second.

My conscience might have been soothed if I'd been punished; if I'd had to pay somehow, but by then there was barely a soul left to sit in judgement.

Perhaps that's why I chose to become a midwife, bringing new lives into a world from which I'd taken so many. Or, as my mother claimed, the birthing skills were simply in my blood.

I glance across at my granddaughter, who wears the bone angel necklace these days. She's gripping the pendant between her thumb and forefinger as I used to; as countless kinswomen of L'Auberge des Anges did before us. I touch the spot where it once lay against my own breast, feeling its warmth as if I were still wearing the little sculpture.

I wonder again if my daughter and granddaughter truly understand what that heirloom endured with me through those years of the occupation. Can they grasp the comfort, the strength it gave me? I doubt it. You'd have to live through a thing like that to really know how it was.

My eyes slide down the list of names engraved on the ossuary's marble plaque, their cries, curses and laughter chiming in my ears as if it were yesterday.

The breeze catches the perfume of lilacs and splays the velvety heads of the red roses, like opened hearts, as the mayor concludes his sombre speech. We stand in silence for a minute, remembering those who never got the chance to grow old — loved ones who perished for our freedom.

From beside the row of the oldest, grandest headstones, the band strikes up *La Marseillaise*, the trumpets drowning out shrill birdsong and the low hum of a passing tractor.

We trudge out of the cemetery and head along the woodland path to the Vionne River for a picnic lunch, as we do every year. It's part of the ritual.

Ip, ip trills a bird. *Ga, ga* cackles another. A dragonfly hovers over a seam of current that folds the waters of the river across stones, ferns and errant flower heads. The Vionne displays her illusion of tranquillity, though I know, better than most, that it has claimed victims — witches of the Dark Ages punished by drowning, and the children who perished two centuries ago, for whom a stone memorial cross sits on the ridge.

I think of the others who died here — those who have no such memorial; not the slightest trace, for rain and snow have long since washed away the bloodstains. I have always wondered who found them and where they were buried, and if it weren't for a dog-eared sepia photograph gathering dust in a secreted wooden box, I might convince myself they had never existed.

After the picnic, my daughter offers to drive me home to the farm. No, thank you very much, I tell her, I'm only eighty-nine, still quite capable of walking back to L'Auberge.

L'Auberge des Anges, haven for weary travellers, orphans and refugees, which has withstood centuries of plague, revolution and war, reclines on the crest of the slope like a solid matriarch. I shuffle through the wooden gateway, the sun flinging its warmth across the cobbled courtyard, the pink puffs of cherry blossom and the white backsides of rabbits bobbing through the orchard.

My daughter fancies herself as an artist and as I negotiate the uneven cobbles, I dodge the collection of sculptures she has fashioned from scrap metal, waste and discarded objects — effigies of our loved ones who never came home. The official document confirming their deaths didn't arrive until 1948 but it seemed we'd already mourned them for a lifetime.

Curious travellers who have heard of the tragedy stop off in Lucie-sur-Vionne on their way south, or west to the Atlantic coast, for summer holidays. Once they've toured the legendary site they find their way up here to L'Auberge des Anges, and wander amongst my daughter's sculptures. They ask us who the people were, and they want to know about Max, as they admire his paintings in the gallery.

I climb the steps, wincing as another barb pierces my frail shell. It appears from nowhere, this guilt I claimed from the smouldering wake of that evil reprisal. I know it will shadow me for days, weeks or months. Then, as winter seems to have settled forever, spring arrives, and my self-reproach will vanish for a time, only to return to the same dark nooks of my mind, the cycle beginning again.

No one ever knew for certain why they marched into Lucie-sur-Vionne that hot June morning of 1944, but it is a crime I have never been able to forget. Nor can I forgive. Least of all myself.

Céleste Roussel
Summer – Autumn 1943

2

'Stop dawdling, Célestine,' Maman said with her usual scowl.

I squeezed into the trap beside our boxed goods and Gingembre clopped down the hill to la place de l'Eglise. Beneath the lemony-green sky, dew glistened across stripes of vines and ripening wheat and oats. Sunflowers turned us a soulful brown eye and the orchards were a coloured patchwork of cherries, plums and peaches.

The village square of Lucie-sur-Vionne was always busy on market mornings with clouds of squawking chickens, bicycles loaded with baskets and wagons laden with urns of milk. Père Emmanuel cradled his bible and nodded greetings to members of his congregation. Men leaned against doorways, smoking, patients hurried to and from the surgery of Dr. Laforge, and the red flag with its black swastika flapped from the window of the Town Hall like some great bloodstain.

My brother Patrick took Gingembre's reins and led the horse through women balancing trays of bread and pastries, stalls piled with fruit and vegetables, meats and cheeses. In the shade of the lime trees, Patrick slid off his beret as he greeted his friend, Olivier, and Gingembre drank from the fountain with the other horses.

The newspaper kiosk beside Saint Antoine's church was, as usual, selling single-sheet bulletins informing us of the Germans' version of the war's progress. People walked by saluting the poster images that were stuck to the church wall, of a kindly, smiling Marshal Pétain, and schoolchildren chanted the song they'd been made to sing since the occupation — *Maréchal nous voilà!*

'They only sing like that to impress the Germans,' Maman said. She nodded towards the soldiers standing on each corner of the square, guns nestled in the crooks of elbows, bored looks on their pale faces. Another group sat on the terrace of Au Cochon Tué bar enjoying croissants and real coffee. Yet more wandered through the stalls buying whatever trash we could palm off onto them for a ridiculous price: tablecloths and napkins embroidered with Napoléon or the Eiffel Tower, cracked bowls the potter couldn't sell, and bags of worm-riddled fruit.

'Impress the Germans?' I said.

'To make them look as if they're co-operating with Vichy. Enough gawping now, Célestine, help me get these boxes unpacked.'

My mother and I set up our stall, laying out her brioches and *pain d'épices*, nut and almond biscuits. We lost the income from my father's carpentry work when the Germans took him to work for the *Reich*, and Maman couldn't make enough from the eggs, goat's cheese and orchard fruit, which we sold fresh and dried or made into jams, liqueurs and tarts. But my mother had her herbal remedies, and her other business — the one she carried out behind the closed doors of L'Auberge des Anges — so we did not go hungry.

'She's still not wearing the star I see,' Maman said, narrowing her eyes at old Madame Abraham, setting up her antiques stall.

'I don't see why she should have to wear a ridiculous yellow star at all.'

'Ridiculous perhaps, Célestine, but they're all supposed to wear them, so people know who they are.'

'Who they are?' I fought to curb the thread of anger her every word provoked in me those days. 'They're just normal people, like the rest of us.'

'Of course they're normal, but it's not me who makes the rules.'

'She's changed her name,' Patrick said, back from the fountain with Olivier. 'She's Marguerite Lemoulin now.'

'Good for her,' Olivier said. 'Can't get much more French than Lemoulin.'

'While I have nothing against a person acquiring a new identity,' Maman said, folding her arms, 'it seems unjust, her having the cash to get false papers while others have to go hungry to afford them. And all because she sells those useless bits and pieces for a small fortune. She probably paid barely a franc for them herself.' She clicked her tongue and moved away to serve an approaching customer.

Patrick and Olivier raised their eyebrows and turned from me.

I caught only a snatch of their mutterings, '… midnight … train … clearing …' but it was enough.

'You could take me with you this time?' I said.

'It's men's work,' Patrick said.

I shifted my gaze to Olivier.

'Sorry,' he said. 'Too dangerous for girls.'

'I'm sure women could do those things as well as men,' I hissed. 'Look what Félicité's doing. If that's not dangerous, I don't know what is.'

'Maybe so,' Patrick said. 'But she's not in the front-line, so to speak. Her stuff is more … more behind the scenes.'

'The Germans might suspect the villagers of Lucie,' Olivier said. 'That's why they set up camp here, but they have no idea what's going on at a convent tucked away in the hills.' He waved an arm towards the Monts du Lyonnais — hills that flanked the village like silent, tireless sentries.

'Anyway,' Patrick said, 'a hot-head like you could never keep her mouth shut.'

'I'd never say a thing that might harm you.'

'Look, Céleste,' Olivier said. 'We just want to keep you out of danger.'

My mother tugged at her apron, which was straight anyway. 'That's enough chatter, you three. There's work to be done.'

I wrapped a strawberry pie for a customer, my hands trembling as a frisson of anguish seized me. Whether Patrick and Olivier wanted me there or not, that coming evening, I would join them.

***

The sun was high over the market square, burning our faces and necks, when I first noticed the three Germans. One was thin, with a malicious cat-eye stare, the second was short and dumpy, his eyes like finger holes in bread dough. The third soldier was taller, with a regal kind of poise and hair the shade of summer wheat.

'Stop your staring, girl.' My mother's crow-like glare cut off my thoughts as smartly as the rose-heads she snapped off. I looked away from the Germans, my cheeks roasting with the blush.

Patrick and I continued serving, while my mother took the money. Maman never let either of us handle the money. She kept it in her apron pockets until we got home, then transferred it to a metal box beneath the floorboards of her herbal room — the same floor under which she concealed her ash-smoked hams, her jars of butter, her pure pork fat, terrines and preserves. She stashed her money and jewellery there too — the jewels I'd never seen her wear.

Minutes later, my gaze crept up again. With the casual stride of someone who has time to waste, the taller German was moving through the crowd towards us. I stiffened, feeling my mother's hand on my arm, her tremor.

He stood before our stall, his eyes directed at me. They were not the milky blue of most Germans I'd seen up close but the strangest violet-blue, like a clot of storm clouds across the hills.

With an elegant finger, he pointed to the mound of cherries I'd plucked yesterday.

'May I?' he said in a feathery voice quite different from the usual harsh sounds of the Germans.

I nodded, and, as he chose the largest, darkest cherry and popped it into his mouth, my mother remained tight-lipped.

'*Délicieuse*,' he said with a smile that lit his face, rosy from the warm air.

'*Ja, ja, délicieuse*,' I said, smirking at his accent, and ignoring my mother's hot and shaky fingers squeezing my arm.

With a brief nod, he turned and made his way back to the other soldiers.

Maman's eyes darkened to the hue of nettles, glowering with the same hatred she usually reserved for the Boche.

'How could you speak to that … that *swine*? Never forget, Célestine, they are the enemy.' She fiddled with stray hair strands, pleating them into the tight chignon that sat low on the back of her head. 'And fraternising with them only invites trouble.'

'You might as well go off and sing *Maréchal nous voilà!* with the rest of those collabos,' Olivier said, tapping a foot up and down.

'I certainly am not fraternising with the enemy,' I said, meeting the three disapproving stares. 'I was simply being polite to a customer. Isn't that good for business?'

The church bell clanged midday, and Maman shook her head as she stalked off to buy a couple of rabbits with a portion of our earnings.

I began packing up the stall, and caught the German looking at me again, his cigarette tip cupped into his hand. As always when I felt out of sorts, I grasped my pendant, twisting it between my thumb and forefinger. As a girl, when the little bone angel had sat against my grandmother's bosom, she told me the sculpture would belong to me one day, or to my sister. But I knew Félicité wouldn't want it, because my sister had vowed to marry God and the only thing she wore around her neck was a crucifix.

Still holding my gaze, the German flicked the cigarette end onto the cobblestones, ground it out with a black heel, and unfastened the jacket of his uniform.

I inhaled sharply, conscious of my scruffy clogs and my dress with its yellow bodice and rust-red skirt, sewn from second-hand fabric.

Maman returned and we finished dismantling the stall, and packed the tarpaulin and trestle onto the trap. Patrick took the bag from Gingembre's nose and guided her between the shafts. He shook the reins over the horse, and as we moved off it struck me that no man had ever looked at me like that before. I couldn't help feeling flattered that someone — even if he was a despised Boche — seemed to admire me.

***

The midnight sky was glittering with stars when I heard the middle stair creak with Patrick's soft footfall. I slid from my bed and watched from the window, as the boys gathered in the U-shaped courtyard below.

I recognised them all, strapping the supplies to their bicycles: Patrick, Olivier, and Gaspard Bénédict — another village boy. André Copeau was there too, the boy who limped from polio, and Ghislaine Dutrottier's brother, Marc.

I didn't doubt Maman knew about the boys' activities in L'Auberge cellar, only pretending to believe they were meeting to play cards; that the shelves of rice and salt lining the cellar walls truly were for the black market. She might be a bitter and unforgiving woman but I knew that such was her hatred for the Germans, she would never betray her son.

Patrick straddled his bicycle, and held a finger to his lips. He beckoned the others to follow, and, their berets pulled low over their ears, they all cycled out beneath the wooden gateway.

I scuttled downstairs, out into the quiet night, and across to the shed. I threw a leg over the rickety bicycle Félicité and I had shared before she left, and cycled away from the farm.

Pools of moonlight bathed fields of shoulder-high wheat, neat vineyards and orchards, the fruit dangling from the branches like Christmas decorations. My heartbeat quickened with every movement, each new shadow that darkened my path. My throat tight, I swallowed hard, pleased I'd remembered to oil the chain.

While I did find it thrilling cycling around at night in Boche-infested country, it was also frightening to be out without an *Ausweis* — the *laissez-passer* which allowed a person to circulate after curfew. I expected a fierce bloom of headlights to blind me any second, the police to demand why I was out cycling at midnight.

I reached the woods and the familiar path, gripping the handlebars as the bicycle bumped and shuddered across the sun-baked ground, speeding by trees that made me think of ranks of soldiers in brown uniform. I did feel safer here, sure the Boche wouldn't be skulking around the woods at night, but a swooping bat startled me so that I shrieked and almost fell off the bike.

I reached the clearing beside the railway tracks — the main line the Germans used to transport munitions and fighting vehicles, and stopped well away from the boys. I concealed the bicycle in the undergrowth, and crept closer to where they were hunched down at the track.

A twig cracked behind me. I spun around, to the luminous amber-green stare of a fox. But the fox too, seemed afraid, and slunk away through the scrub with furtive elegance.

I moved a little further along and crouched behind a rocky cleft, my breath quick and shallow in the cloying air, my eyes and ears alert for the slightest sound or movement.

Patrick, Olivier, André and Gaspard were still down at

the track, while Marc Dutrottier moved off up the line to — I supposed — his lookout post.

An owl hooted into the darkness and I jumped. My quivering fingers grasped my angel pendant, and I willed its strength to my brother, forced to become the man of our house when the Germans took our father for "voluntary" labour service.

Nothing could happen to Patrick and Olivier; to my memories of summers on the Vionne River, of winter snowball fights, of dancing and drinking cider and feasting on stewed meats and pastries at festival time. The little angel seemed to reassure me that even if it meant taking human lives, we were doing the right thing. We had to drive the Boche away.

They were still bent over the railway line, Patrick's ear against the silvery-blue sheen of track. Even as I felt the pulse of my frustration with them, for refusing to let me join in, I was excited to be there, part of the Resistance — that mythical organisation where rumour scrambled after counter-rumour and nobody was certain who was friend and who was foe. It was a word that conjured images of secret meetings, midnight escapades, the thrill of danger.

Patrick raised his head from the track. 'Now!' he cried.

Hands moving like darts, tongues out, sweat glossing their brows, the boys secured the dynamite beneath the rails.

'Time?' Patrick said.

Olivier glanced at his watch. 'Two minutes.'

I could almost hear the seconds tick by, and feel the night air tense with our anxious breaths.

Olivier whistled to Marc, who started jogging back to the others, unravelling the electrical wire as he came.

The train appeared around the twist of valley, belching mushrooms of smoke. Heavy with tanks silhouetted against the mountain range, its rhythmical *dd-dd-dd-dd* seemed more urgent the closer it came.

'Hurry,' Gaspard hissed, and they plunged back into the foliage, hunkering behind a rock.

The helmets of the German soldiers perched atop the train gleamed in the moonlight. I stared at them with hatred, those sinister sentries cradling their guns, their eyes peeling the countryside for danger, and *saboteurs*.

I kneaded my angel talisman harder.

Dd-dd-dd-dd. Faster, it seemed, and deafening, as the train was almost upon us.

'Go!' Olivier shrieked. 'Now! Get down!'

André hit the button and any further sounds were lost as the train exploded in a golden shatter of fireworks. Bursts of sparks fanned into the navy sky, metal shrieking as if it were in agony.

Our hands clamped over our ears, we cowered from shards of flying metal. The Germans were shrieking — one continual, torturous wail — their helmets and uniforms flaming torches as they tried to flee the burning wreckage.

The locomotive screamed like a shot horse and groaned as the whole train lurched sideways, cavorted off the rails and crashed into the ravine on the opposite side of the track.

'Let's move it,' Patrick said.

The moonlight lit their smiling faces as they hurtled back along the woodland path to the bicycles.

I breathed out, long and slow. Another success for *la Résistance*.

3

As the sun reached its blistering peak the following day, we flung our rakes and forks aside and sank down in the shade of the oak tree.

Olivier's Uncle Claude lost his wife to tuberculosis last winter, leaving him with four young children, and since L'Auberge des Anges no longer cultivated crops, Patrick and I and our friends Juliette and Ghislaine had come to help Uncle Claude with his harvest.

'I think we've earned a dip in the river,' I said, looking around the circle of my friends. 'Coming?'

Beneath my shirt, sweat plastered my swimsuit to my skin as we tramped along the ridge towards the river. As children we'd sat here with my father, listening to his tales, and I felt again the pang of his absence.

'You always stop and look at it,' Olivier said as we reached the small stone cross immortalising the two children who'd drowned in the river.

'I can't help it,' I said, one hand shielding my eyes against the sun, the fingers of my other tracing around the heart shape carved into the old stone. 'First the river stole their lives and now sun, ice and frost have robbed them of their names. I feel as if I knew those lost little ancestors.'

'Come on, you two,' Patrick called, 'or there'll be no time to swim.'

We slithered down the grassy slope to where the Vionne River channelled its timeless notch through the Monts du Lyonnais. Frogs croaked incessantly, a bird whistled a merry *chip, chip* and the hot breeze shifted the treetops and puckered the surface of the river.

I swiped a palm across my brow as we threaded between the willows that ribboned the banks, Patrick and Olivier teasing and jostling each other as if they were still young schoolboys sneaking off for a swim.

'Such a magical spot,' Miette said as we reached our special place, flung our clogs aside and stripped down to our swimsuits.

'I don't know about magic,' Patrick said as he and Olivier waded into the shallows. 'More like the only safe place nowadays, away from the eyes of the Boche.'

The Boche.

As the coolness of the river numbed my burning feet, I recalled the pale German from the marketplace. I'd spoken to Germans before, of course, but that had been my first real encounter with the enemy. Like all the villagers, I'd watched them arrive earlier that year to occupy Lucie. We'd all stopped what we were doing. Housewives held mops and dusters in mid-air, the clog-maker's hammer fell silent, the baker stopped kneading his dough and even Père Emmanuel rushed out onto the church steps. It seemed the whole population was standing in shopfronts or leaning over balconies to witness the arrival of the blue-eyed warriors. Officers astride magnificent horses followed the soldiers, motorcycles, and the grey jeeps bearing swastikas. Great armoured tanks pounded the cobblestoned streets and rattled the church windows, small boys brandishing sticks and lengths of wire — anything from which they could make a gun to fire at the enemy.

Despite their professional-soldier expressions, I saw, beneath the Wehrmacht caps, their guarded looks about the place that was to be their home. And from the shadows, old women folded their arms over their aprons and frowned.

'I bet they'll take our best linen,' one said, with a starchy nod.

'My mother would turn in her grave,' said another, 'if she knew the Boche were sleeping on her sheets.'

The invaders had swerved then, to avoid a cluster of girls skipping rope. They tied their horses up to the lime trees beside the War Memorial on the square and the sound of boots, foreign voices and the rattling of spurs filled la place de l'Eglise.

'Come on, Céleste,' Ghislaine called, startling me from my thoughts.

In a few easy strokes I joined the others in the deep pool, a place where the sun's rays stretched right down to the riverbed; where fish darted like fireflies and moss glowed the most startling green.

I leaned back against a boulder alongside Ghislaine and Olivier, and we tilted our faces to the cascading water. Patrick kept diving deep, clutching Miette's ankles. She shrieked each time, but we all laughed. It was no secret my brother had been sweet on Juliette Dubois since they were at nursery school together.

'What's so interesting down there, Patrick?' I said. 'Those creatures from Papa's stories with a hundred eyes, horns and fins?'

'All those stories, just to scare you two off swimming,' Ghislaine said with a laugh.

'Not that his scary tales ever stopped you,' Miette said.

Patrick flung an arc of hair from his face. 'Not us. Félicité maybe.'

'It wasn't fear that stopped Félicité,' I said, the rush of water massaging my harvest-weary shoulders. 'She just found our games pointless. That's what she said, "a frivolous waste of time".'

No, unlike us, our saintly sister never became aware of every ditch of the Vionne, every spot where a whirlpool might snag a person and drag them into the depths. She never learned, like Patrick and I, not to fear *la Vionne Violente*.

***

We headed back to Uncle Claude's farm with the afternoon sun beating down on our backs. We'd almost passed the old witch's hut when I glimpsed a crack of white through the splintered wood.

'There's someone inside.' I clutched Olivier's arm. So well camouflaged amongst ivy, oak leaves and branches, I'd thought no one besides us knew about the hut.

The white of the eye disappeared and Olivier beckoned to Patrick. As they stepped closer, I heard a whimper, and a gasp, from inside.

'Hello?' Patrick called. Even from that distance, I could see the vein in his temple pulsing. 'Anybody in there?'

No answer.

'Who's in here?' Olivier said.

Still no reply. The ancient hinges whined as he pushed the door, and we stood in silent expectation as our eyes adjusted to the weak light. I squinted at the outline of four people huddled in a corner.

'Who are you?' Patrick said.

'What are you doing in here?' Olivier said.

The people remained wordless, and I could almost smell their fear — the terror of hunted prey — and then I saw it in their wide, dark eyes and on their faces, white as milk.

A thin woman, with the same dark beauty as my sister, clutched a small boy in her arms. The man gripped the hand of a girl about eight or nine years old.

'Don't be afraid, we won't hurt you,' Patrick said.

The people still didn't speak; they barely breathed, and the sour air of filth and hunger clung to their soil-streaked clothes.

Olivier nodded. 'Please, you can trust us.'

I edged forward and laid a hand on the woman's arm. 'Don't be frightened.' She flinched, and tightened her hold on the child. 'We wouldn't harm you.'

'My name is Sabine Wolf,' she finally said. She looked up at the man whose round spectacles were foggy with his breath. 'This is my husband, Max and our children, Talia and Jacob.'

I smiled at the children but they remained motionless, saucer-eyed.

'We're from Julien-sur-Vionne,' the woman went on. 'The Gestapo came to our street … rushed into people's homes before they knew what was … we hid … saw them dragging the people — our friends — away. They herded them into trucks, like cattle.' Sabine clutched her little boy even closer to her breast.

'The Germans didn't find us,' her husband said, stroking his ragged beard with quick, rabbity movements. 'But we knew the trucks would be back. It wasn't safe to stay. We had nowhere to go so we ran into the woods.'

'Papa found this hut,' the girl said, still clasping her father's hand.

'What have you been living on?' I said, looking about the dark, dank place. 'There's nowhere to sit, or cook. No place to sleep.'

'Papa caught a rabbit.' Talia looked up at her father. 'And a fat trout in the river. But they tasted awful because Papa says we can't light fires.'

'Quiet, Talia,' her father said, with a prickly glance at his daughter.

Talia was obviously a talkative girl, yet little Jacob remained mute, as if he'd been trained to stay quiet.

'You can't stay here,' I said.

'No you can't,' Miette said. 'They'll find you here, eventually.'

'Nobody can hide from them for long,' Ghislaine said.

'I know a place,' I said, on impulse. 'It's small but you'll be safe, just till we can organise something better.'

'Are you certain, mademoiselle?' Sabine said.

'No, mademoiselle,' her husband said. 'It would only cause trouble for you.'

'Please, call me Céleste. And this is my brother, Patrick, and Olivier, Ghislaine and Miette. And you are no trouble at all. We're very glad to help, but we have to finish today's harvesting, so we'll come later, and take you to our farm.'

'Can I go home and get Cendres, and bring him to the safe place?' Talia said.

'Who's Cendres?' Ghislaine said.

'My cat,' Talia said. 'He's called Cendres because he's all grey and fluffy, like ash.'

'You know we can't go home yet, Talia,' her father said. 'Don't worry about Cendres, he'll catch plenty of mice for his supper.'

'So, we'll see you all later then?' I said.

'Yes, it'll be safer this evening,' Patrick said.

'The Boche probably won't be out and about,' Olivier said, waving an arm towards the Monts du Lyonnais, from where grey-tinged clouds were gathering. 'With this storm brewing, they'll be indoors, scoffing my uncle's best food and getting drunk on his wine.'

The Germans had come to Uncle Claude's farm only yesterday, taking cheese and *pâté*, a side of salted pork, a barrel of oil and several bottles of ill-concealed wine.

They'd not yet visited L'Auberge des Anges to requisition food, animals or anything else they fancied, but our luck wouldn't last. Nobody could escape them, their presence in Lucie like a persistent, sucking leech.

'You know Maman will never allow this,' Patrick said, as we continued on, back to Uncle Claude's.

'So what are we supposed to do?' I said. 'Leave them here for the Boche to catch?'

'We can't let that happen,' Ghislaine said.

'Well, no,' Olivier said, 'but it's dangerous to hide people. We could be …'

'I know it's dangerous,' I said, trying to keep the snap from my voice. 'But now we've found this family I can't turn my back on them.'

'Couldn't they go to Félicité?' Patrick said.

'Perhaps,' I said. 'But I need to speak to her first. For now, we need to get them out of that hut, to a dry place, with proper food.'

'What if somebody finds out?' Miette said. 'You know what the village gossips are like.'

'We'll just make sure they don't,' I said. 'All of us will keep our mouths shout, and Maman, well …' I flicked a willow branch aside. 'Maman wouldn't say anything to the Gestapo or the French police. She'd hardly want to attract any kind of attention to L'Auberge des Anges, would she?'

4

'Did you hear about the Resistance coup last night?' Denise Grosjean said. 'Everybody in Lucie's talking about it.'

'I wouldn't know anything about that,' I said, as Ghislaine, Miette and I continued raking the cut grass into piles, and Uncle Claude's horses kept tramping up and down the field with their slow, measured sway.

Ghislaine gave Denise a sharp look. I knew Ghislaine was aware her brother Marc was part of Patrick's group, but as ever mistrusting of people like Denise Grosjean we kept ignoring her as we flung the pyramids of grass onto the cart until she finally gave an exasperated sigh and shut up.

As well as constantly fluttering her doe-eyes at Olivier, Denise worked at the post office where, it was said, she read everybody's letters. She only came to help with Uncle Claude's harvest in the hope of picking up gossip and, of course, to flirt with Olivier.

By the time the sun slanted low along the bleached grass we were parched again, and slid down against the trunk of an oak tree. Uncle Claude's other workers — the city boys who'd come to Lucie for the harvest work and countryside food — lounged in the shade of the hedge. The two boys who'd taken refuge on Uncle Claude's farm to escape Vichy's compulsory labour service sat with them.

The field ticked with insects, feathery stalks of the still uncut grass haloed in the afternoon sun, and in the distance Mont Blanc shimmered like an ancient volcano. The dogs barked and dashed about with Olivier's cousins — the twins, Justin and Gervais, and Paulette and Anne-Sophie — their grimy cheeks the colour of bruised peaches.

'They remind me of us as kids,' I said, watching the twins scale a tree. I sat cross-legged beside Olivier, and passed him the water pitcher. 'And you and Patrick sniggering at me when I wanted to climb trees too, and saying girls don't do that. You made me so mad.'

'Probably why you turned out the best tree-climber in Lucie,' Ghislaine said.

'Even better than them.' Miette nodded at Patrick and Olivier as she handed around the basket of raspberries and gooseberries.

The boys gave us wry smiles, but said nothing, chewing their hunks of bread and *saucisson*.

'I suppose I'll have to be hiding those two,' Uncle Claude said. My nostrils filled with the sweet aroma of tobacco as the farmer jabbed his pipe at the horses nuzzling across a fence. 'The Boche've demanded everyone take their horses to the Town Hall for more requisitions. I don't know how we're supposed to manage without them, especially at harvest time.'

'Are they paying well?' Olivier asked.

'Not likely, son. The going price for a mare is sixty or seventy thousand francs. They're promising to pay — only promising mind you — half that.'

'Do the Boche expect us to work with our bare hands?' Patrick said.

'Exactly what I told the mayor,' Uncle Claude said. 'And I warned him that if the farmers can't work properly, the whole village will starve to death. They've taken our men,' he went on, waving his pipe towards the boys hiding from the dreaded labour service. 'They took our bread, wheat, flour and potatoes. The petrol and the cars went too. And now the horses! What will they take tomorrow?'

'Bunch of bastards,' Patrick said with a scowl.

'You have to be fair though,' Denise said. 'This *is* war. And remember how worried we were when the Germans arrived? We imagined they'd set about attacking and raping us all, but instead they handed out sandwiches and fruit pies, and real cigarettes. Besides, they're so tall ... so blond and handsome compared with our drunken soldiers who just put down their weapons and surrendered.'

'Surrendered?' Ghislaine said. 'Would you have preferred them to go on until every last one of them was slaughtered or taken prisoner? Is that what you wanted, Denise?'

'Of course not,' Denise said. 'Anyway I'm not worried, Marshal Pétain is a good man. He'll save France.'

'You really believe all those deluded collabos?' Patrick said. 'Who go berserk and jump up in ovation at every word old man Pétain utters; that he's some spiritual being with magical powers?'

'He saved us once before,' Denise said. 'When he saw the Germans off at Verdun. He might be an old grandpa now but surely he can do it again. In any case, Monsieur-unpatriotic-Roussel, we have nowhere else to turn.'

'You're nothing but a Nazi *lèche-cul*,' Patrick went on. 'And like most Nazi arse-lickers you'll realise the truth about Pétain and his government and this occupation soon enough. That's if you've got any kind of brain at all.'

Denise muttered something and skulked off towards the city boys.

Yes, it seemed a nasty stink curled in the nostrils of most people these days — besides ignorant ones like Denise Grosjean — a contempt for our conquerors that had begun the day we heard General de Gaulle's BBC broadcast: *Whatever happens, the flame of French Resistance must not and shall not die.*

Increasing resistance activity had nurtured that scorn, which seemed to have risen to almost fever pitch since the Germans had chosen to occupy Lucie-sur-Vionne, while only patrolling neighbouring areas. "To keep an eye on our suspicious activities," was the whisper that skirted the village. To the casual observer, Lucie-sur-Vionne might seem a sleepy hollow with its shops, gossiping housewives and bustling square, but it seemed the Germans had got word it was a place of secret meetings, of propaganda and smiling deceit.

'Any more letters from your father?' Miette said, as I shared out slices of my mother's walnut cake, made from the flour and sugar she secreted beneath her herbal room floorboards.

'Not a word since his first two letters. It's very worrying.'

Despite the hot breeze gusting down from the hills west of Lucie I shivered, recalling the day Papa announced he was volunteering for work in Germany. He'd told my mother they were promising to pay well, but Maman shook her head as if she didn't believe a word of it.

'I don't understand,' Miette said, smoothing her skirt down over her bare knees. 'Whatever do the Boche want with men like your father?'

'They lost so many of their own in Russia,' Olivier said, 'they're now taking foreigners for the *Reich* war effort.'

'Didn't your father go over on the *Relève* plan?' Ghislaine said.

'Yes, but the one prisoner the Germans release for every three skilled workers sent over, like my father,' Patrick said, 'is always old and incompetent, or sick. The Germans are only glad to be rid of such people. And on top of that, we haven't seen a single franc of his wages.'

'I just hope it's not too awful in the camp,' I said. 'I can't bear thinking of poor Papa breaking his back for the Boche. If only he'd write and let us know he's all right.'

'Maybe they stopped allowing workers to write home?' Miette said.

'Or there's something wrong with the postal service,' Ghislaine said, with a thorny glance at Denise.

'What kind of people don't let workers write home to their families?' I said. 'They even let dangerous prisoners send letters these days.'

'My father would've been taken for *Reich* work too,' Olivier said. 'If my parents hadn't fled across the Channel to Papa's English family.'

'Why didn't you go with them?' Miette said. 'Surely they wanted you to?'

Olivier shrugged. 'Oh yes, my mother pleaded with me to leave, but I told her I had things to do here in Lucie. Besides,' he said, with a wink at Uncle Claude. 'I couldn't leave this old man on his own with such a rowdy tribe of kids.'

I gave Olivier a small smile of admiration, wishing I too could summon the strength to stand up against my own mother. Like the war that raged across Europe, I ached to flee the smaller-scale battle that had entangled my mother and me for as far back as I could remember.

I grabbed the rake again, my yearning to fight with my brother and Olivier, to rid Lucie of our occupiers, mounting with each clump of grass I heaped into the cart.

***

'We should hurry,' I said, as Patrick and I scurried along the ridge, the Wolf family trailing behind us in a thin, straggly line. I kept glancing up at the red-wine sky, the air pressing like dough around me.

'A decent storm might break this drought at least,' Patrick shouted, over the angry wind that had burst from the hills.

The cool gusts were indeed a welcome respite, I only hoped the wind wouldn't mask a whistled warning from Olivier, our lookout posted on the fringe of woods behind L'Auberge.

The wind funnelled along the valley, hurling itself at us in raw bursts, snapping my skirt against my calves. Leaves, torn from branches, littered the ground and the birds seemed frantic, wheeling low in the sky and plummeting into tiny pockets of stagnant air.

Hard splotches of rain began to fall as we caught sight of Olivier, his thumb held high in the "all clear" sign.

'Will we live at this farm all the time now, Papa?' Talia said.

'No, Talia …. just for a while.'

'We'll find fun things for you to do, Talia,' I said. 'You'll see.'

I was relieved there was no sign of Maman, as we passed by her kitchen garden; no snarling face at the window. She must be busy in her bedroom. I would tell her about the Wolfs later. Once we'd settled them into the attic she might be less likely to make a fuss.

'I want to go home, Maman,' Jacob said, his face crumpling. 'I don't want to play hide and seek in the woods anymore.'

'Hush, everything will be all right,' Sabine said, stroking her child's dark curls from his forehead. 'Maman's here.'

The rain began to fall like reams of silver paper, lightning tearing yellow streaks through the sky. The little boy screamed and buried his face in his mother's neck.

'Quickly. Inside, everybody.' Patrick opened the ivy-wreathed gate and we hurried round to the courtyard. The pig gave a welcoming grunt and Gingembre neighed softly from her stable.

Maman still did not appear as we made the Wolf family comfortable in the attic with towels, clean clothes, straw mattresses and blankets. I took up bread and cheese, and a pitcher of milk for the children. Patrick dragged out the box of toy soldiers Papa had carved for him when he was young.

'These are for you, Jacob,' he said, sliding the box in front of the boy.

'I'm sure you'll love playing with them,' I said. 'Like Patrick did when he was your age.'

Jacob peered into the box and picked out a single soldier in a red coat. He barely glanced at the rest of the collection.

'Can you get my father some paints, Céleste?' Talia said. 'And brushes and paper?'

Her father's brow creased. 'Talia!'

'Papa's a great artist,' the girl went on, ignoring her father. 'He uses Gouache. Me too, I like to paint. And Maman's a ballerina. She dances in stage-shows.'

'Please excuse my daughter, Céleste,' Max said. 'She's a little … over-eager. Really, we're all so exhausted from the rough living, we'll be happy just to drop straight to sleep.'

'I'll try my best to find you some art supplies, Talia,' I said, wondering wherever I could get such things. 'Now remember, if you hear me cough twice, from the bottom of the attic ladder, just loosen the panel I showed you, and duck into the alcove.'

'Might it come to that?' Sabine said. 'Surely we're putting you and your family at great peril?'

'Not at all,' I said, with far more confidence than I felt. 'Just a precaution. The police have no reason at all to come up to L'Auberge.'

***

'Where did you two skive off to after the harvest?' Maman said, as I slid the diced courgettes into boiling water. 'And where is your brother? He knows the hen house needs fixing, or foxes will rip those poor beasts to shreds.'

'Still out with Olivier,' I said. 'And we found a family hiding from the Gestapo in the woods,' I went on, as if it was some routine task. 'We brought them here, up to the attic.'

She planted her hands on her aproned hips and glared at me. 'You what? What people? Are you mad, girl? What if those Gestapo thugs come here? You know what happens to people who harbour those types. We'll be lined up against a wall and shot. Shot! Do you understand? Or they'll send us to a slave camp in some German wasteland. And you know nobody comes back from the camps.'

Had she said that to spite me, as if she knew how much I dreamed of my father coming home? Like her barbed eyes could see right into my heart, and the hollow that deepened every day since the Germans had stolen my ally, my friend; the only one apart from Patrick who made life bearable with her.

'How can you say that? He *will* come back.' In that instant, as I grabbed the pot to strain the vegetables, I didn't think it possible to feel more resentment than was wedged in my chest.

In my agitated haste, water splashed and scalded my fingers. I shrieked and dropped the pot, which clattered into the stone sink. I rushed over to the pail of water and sank my hand into it.

Maman didn't ask to see the burnt fingers; she didn't seem to care that I was in pain. She never uttered a word as I told her about the Wolfs' escape and their hideout in the old witch's hut. A fly buzzed around her head but she didn't wave it away; she simply gaped at me with her hateful glare as if she could not believe, or grasp, what I was saying.

'Get that family out of here,' she said, finally swatting at the fly with her tea towel. 'I won't conceal strangers in this house.'

'But they deserve to feel safe.'

'Safe? You must be joking, Célestine. Don't you think I know what goes on in the cellar?' Another sharp flap of the tea towel. 'What your brother, Olivier, and their communist friends get up to? Someone will find out soon enough about their … their activities, and tell the police. No, L'Auberge is not a safe place at all. Besides, why can't your sister take this family?'

'She might. I need to speak to Félicité first, but for now I want them to feel safe and welcome here. Besides, Patrick and his friends are not communists, and nobody will say anything. Most people in Lucie are proud of our resistors. They've had enough of Pétain and Vichy; enough of the Germans. Everyone wants to help get rid of our occupiers.'

Maman shook her head. 'How naïve you are. People — yes

even the friendly villagers — are only interested in protecting themselves. Someone would inform the Germans of their … their *resistance* in a flash, if it suited them.'

I leaned against the table, clamping my scalded fingers in my armpit.

'So what are we supposed to do, Maman? Enemy troops have overtaken our country, and they're not going away. Should we just keep our heads down and accept that we're now powerless, humiliated citizens? Or do we react? *Resist*? Besides, I know you'd never turn in that family upstairs.' I waved an arm in the direction of her bedroom. 'Would you?'

Maman's eyes glittered the brilliant green of unripe grapes. 'You've always been a stubborn little bitch, haven't you?' she said. 'Right from the start.'

She set her mouth in a crabby line as she banged cutlery and crockery onto the blue and white checked tablecloth.

5

The next time I saw the German was on a hot August afternoon. Patrick, Olivier and I had called in to my uncle's clog shop on the village square of Julien-sur-Vionne to give Uncle Félix and Aunt Maude some comforting words about my prisoner-of-war cousins, Paul and Jules.

Sprinkles of blond hair escaping his Wehrmacht cap, the German was lounging against the fountain wall with the same two soldiers who'd been with him that day at the market. As we walked from the shop, his strange, violet eyes met mine.

'We meet again, mam'zelle.' He bowed with a feline kind of grace and offered a pale hand. 'Martin Diehl.' He waved his other arm at the two soldiers. 'Karl Gottlob and Fritz Frankenheimer.'

Karl Gottlob stood stiff and awkward, the cat-eyes as cold as ever. He said something in throaty German I didn't understand.

'*Pon-jour*, mam'zelle, m'sieurs,' the chubby Fritz Frankenheimer said, and a fattened pig flashed through my mind.

'Céleste Roussel,' I said, shaking Martin Diehl's hand. 'And this is my brother Patrick and a friend, Olivier.'

The boys too, shook hands with the three men. Despite their polite nods, I caught the vein ticking in my brother's temple, and Olivier's jittery foot-tapping. So practised they were at hiding their animosity, a bystander might've believed they were truly pleased to make the Germans' acquaintance.

'Come on, we'll miss the movie.' Patrick tugged at my arm, he and Olivier sandwiching me between them as we headed for the queue snaking from *Le Renard Rouge* cinema.

'Why do you insist on speaking to Germans?' Patrick said.

'Like your mother says, don't forget they are the enemy,' Olivier said. 'Besides, you know how careful we have to be.'

'Of course I know not to say a word about anything … to anyone, Boche or not,' I hissed, the heat burning my cheeks as I glimpsed the Germans in the line behind us.

Lucie-sur-Vionne had no cinema, so we'd cycled into Julien-sur-Vionne that steamy afternoon — a rare treat for which Uncle Claude was paying, in return for our harvesting help.

Apart from Lucie's train line, Julien was much the same as our village, with its bustling square, small businesses, closely-built houses and centuries-old church. Its roads wound through orchards, fields and woods and, as Lucie was named for the Roman soldier, Lucius, Julien was named after Julius Caesar because an elderly villager claimed he'd passed by that way.

I sat between Patrick and Olivier in the dark, smoke-stained cinema, aching to look like the actresses in *Hôtel du Nord*: the blonde, sultry Annabelle or the dark, slim Arletty, with her thinly-arched eyebrows. I dreamed of being on the big screen, fans admiring me, and imagined I was in Hollywood, driving up Sunset Boulevard in a limousine, sipping champagne and wearing one of my dozens of elegant dresses.

Between admiring the actresses, I caught Martin Diehl looking at me through the flickering dark. Seated with the group of Germans in one corner, the red glow of his cigarette illuminated his high cheekbones, and I slumped in my seat, hoping he'd not notice my dowdy dress, my bare lips and unpowdered face.

***

The audience filed back onto the square, blinking into the sunlight falling thick and golden on the cobblestones.

'We've got a meeting,' Patrick said, as we retrieved our

bicycles. 'We should be back at L'Auberge in a few hours.'

'I suppose I'm still not allowed to come?'

'I told you,' he said, 'this is not women's business.'

'You're so unfair! Let me tell you that men would never cope with the pain of childbirth that we endure, so the human race can continue. Women would make much tougher soldiers and resistors than all those big-mouthed, honoured war heroes. Besides, you know I'd never say anything to betray you.'

'Not intentionally,' Olivier said. 'But someone might force it out of you … someone you least suspect.'

Patrick and Olivier said nothing more and I knew they wouldn't budge, so I tossed my head, swung a leg over the saddle and pedalled away furiously. I trilled the bell at pedestrians who got in my way, not slowing for anyone as I hurtled across the square, down the main road and veered off onto the path through the woods.

Sweat soon drenched my clothes and I flung the bike against a willow trunk and tramped down to the water's edge. The Vionne blazed with a wealth of sun pennies and a butterfly, fluttering lazily from one rock to another, flitted off as I bent from the gravelly shore and gulped palmfuls of water.

I looked around. Nobody in sight except a few bold birds braving the heat. I tore my dress and underwear off and slid, naked, into the river.

I floated on my back, murmuring with the ecstasy of cool water against hot skin. The current tugged at me like a playful hand, slices of sun casting black shadows into the dark, furtive places on the riverbed.

I flexed my feet, wriggled my toes, and studied my hand, yellowed in that strange underwater light. I laid a palm against my stomach, tracing small circles, and caught my breath as my nipples hardened with the coolness, my small breasts peeking from the surface like milky islands.

When the water crimped my skin like a dried apple, I grabbed a clutch of dangling roots and hauled myself onto the bank.

I brushed stray weeds off, dried myself with my dress, and slipped the damp garment over my head. I shook my hair out, gathered flat pebbles and started skimming them across the water. It was so quiet I could hear the flutter of feathers in nests, the sound of pecking on bark, the fidgeting of insects in the grass.

A pebble skimmed over the water, but not one I'd thrown, and I stopped, my arm held aloft. Another stone flew past, bouncing three times across the water. I heard a rustling noise behind me, too loud for a bird, and spun around to the smiling face of Martin Diehl.

I swallowed my gasp, horrified the German might've glimpsed me naked.

'Did you follow me from Julien?'

'You pedalled away very fast. I thought I would never catch you,' he said. 'Why are you angry?'

'Angry?'

'Your brother and his friend. You looked so fierce at them, and cycling away in a hurry.'

'Oh, that. It wasn't important, just a silly argument.'

He removed his cap and jacket, and as he lit a Gauloise I glimpsed the powerful muscles move in his neck. But I kept my gaze guarded and low, fascinated by his gun peeping from its leather sheath.

'You're a good skimmer, Céleste Roussel.'

'My father taught me. He taught me everything about this river; warned me about the currents and whirlpools, and made me promise never to swim here.'

A long arm reached out, fingertips grazing my wet hair. 'Ah yes, I see you take much notice of him.' I reeled from his touch and he shifted sideways, and sat on a boulder, casually crossing one long leg over the other.

'This is for you.' He pulled a brown paper package from a pocket. 'You might have to come a little closer to reach it though.' He patted a spot beside him.

I couldn't help smiling at his stiff, stilted French, but kept observing him and the package warily. Accepting gifts from the Boche was regarded as collaboration.

'For me?' I edged towards his rock, but kept standing. 'Why?'

'You were admiring them at the market, no? You can open it.'

Despite my misgivings, I tore the paper off and pulled out a packet of nylon stockings.

'Oh they're lovely. I've never had any like this. Thank you, Martin Diehl.'

'There is more where I got these,' he said, as a small bird in a green suit perched on a log, cocking its head as if it too, was admiring the stockings. 'What else do you like? Magazines? Lipstick? Chocolate? Real chocolate, not false, pale chocolate. I can get what you want.'

I laughed a nervy kind of cackle. Why was the German giving me presents? Surely not because of my looks — the unmistakeable stamp of a plain, unworldly farm-girl.

I forced a smile to cover my unease, and mask the prods of doubt at his interest in me; at his curiosity in my spat with Patrick and Olivier, cycling off to their meeting without me.

'Why do you smile, Céleste Roussel?'

'Nothing … your funny accent.'

'Ah, the bad school-boy French. You did not learn German?'

'Your French is very good. But no, sadly, I didn't learn German.'

'Why is this sad? So you cannot listen to our plans at the garrison?'

'What? Listen to what plans?'

'Do not worry, Céleste Roussel, I am only making a joke.'

'Oh. Well, my mother didn't let me stay at school long enough to learn anything much.'

'Your mother is the healer-woman of the village, yes? She believes teaching you the special medicine is more important than school?'

'Not likely. My mother thinks I'm too stupid to learn anything. Anyway, I'm not the least bit interested in all that herbal stuff, and if her remedies are no longer handed down to future generations of L'Auberge, she'll only have herself to blame.'

'Why do you call it L'Auberge des Anges?' Martin said, grinding his cigarette butt beneath a black heel. 'It is not an inn.'

'Not these days. Now it's just a simple farm. We don't even have crops any longer, only the orchard and Maman's kitchen garden and a few animals. My father said it was once the greatest farm in Lucie, but it ran into hard times during the Revolution. The farmer and his wife turned it into an inn — The Inn of Angels.'

We were silent for a moment, listening to the *gaa, gaa* laugh of the green bird until it flew off into the hot twists of light. I fingered the packet of nylons again. Martin Diehl probably got them on the black market, but didn't my mother say the black market was for everyone; that we should all have the right to the same things, and almost everyone was practising it to some extent?

'Well,' I said, imagining Talia's happiness. 'If you really can get more things I'd like some paints … and brushes and paper.'

'So you are not only a champion pebble skimmer, you are an artist too?' His lips curved into a smile, showing impossibly white teeth.

'I dabble in a bit of painting now and then,' I said, with a flippant wave. 'Nothing serious.'

He lit another Gauloise and gathered more pebbles.

'There are rivers where I was a boy,' he said, flicking his stones across the surface. 'We were swimming too, and skimming the stones.' He squinted into the distance, to a point where the Vionne parted around a sandbank, ruffles of current lapping the edges. 'And many orchards and fields, just like your village.' He still clipped his words, but the voice had become faraway, like a

Liza Perrat

melancholic background song.

'You're not a bad skimmer either, Martin Diehl,' I said, throwing my own stones, which bounced further than his did.

'My friends and I would have skimming competitions when we were young,' he went on. 'One of the boys had a beautiful sister. He would steal her underwear, and the one who skimmed his stone the best, got to keep the underwear for a night.' He laughed and shook the blond head, as if recalling the silliness of boyhood games.

'So, did you ever win?'

He frowned. 'Win?'

'The skimming competitions?'

The muscles in his shoulder tightened beneath the starched shirt as he skimmed another stone, further and more smoothly than the last. 'I always won, Céleste Roussel.'

'Oh,' I said, not really sure what to say. 'Well, me too, I like to win.'

He caught me unaware then, as he reached across and took hold of my pendant. I lurched back, imagining the same hand levelling a revolver, a machine-gun or a grenade.

'An unusual pendant.' He stroked the angel between his thumb and forefinger. 'It seems old. A family ... how do you say? Heirloom?'

'I don't think it's worth much,' I said, keeping my gaze away from his peculiar, indigo eyes. 'But yes, a kind of talisman passed from mother to daughter. My grandmother believed the souls of all the women of L'Auberge are trapped inside this old bone.'

'Very fine work,' Martin said. 'What is the bone from?'

'Oh I don't know ... no one really knows. Some say a carpenter carved it for his wife two centuries ago from seal, ox or walrus tusk. Another family legend says it was sculpted long before that, for a famous midwife from the times of the Black Plague. But some think it was even earlier, and is from the bone of a mammoth. Though I can hardly believe that.'

Martin let the pendant go, his fingertips sweeping the damp

hair strands splayed across my shoulders. He bent and kissed me, catching me so off-guard I almost choked.

I jerked away, my eyes darting about the tangle of willows, searching for prying eyes. 'What are you doing? You can't just … just kiss me like that. You're a …'

'A Boche? Germans are the same as all men, Céleste Roussel.'

I swivelled around, ready to stomp off, but he caught my arm.

'Let me go!' I shook off his grip. 'Do you know what happens to girls if they're caught with one of you? They shave our heads and parade us about the village for people to shun, and spit at.'

'I am sorry.' He gave me a small, chivalrous bow. 'Please forgive me.'

'I have to go. If anyone sees me here; catches me with …'

'Will I see you again?'

'You're joking aren't you?' I said, shaking my head in disbelief as I strode off and straddled my bicycle. 'I doubt that very much.'

I rode away without a backward glance.

6

The following morning I whisked through my farm chores, flung my tapestry bag over a shoulder and hurried down the hill to Lucie's railway station.

I stepped off the train three stops up the line in Valeria-sur-Vionne, a village much like Lucie, nestled in a crook of the Monts du Lyonnais.

Quietly pleased to have my sister gone from L'Auberge — less conscious of being the flawed second daughter rather than the long-awaited son; the frail infant who shouldn't have survived — I'd never been to the convent where Félicité was a novice, and a schoolteacher.

I didn't have to walk far before I found the place, a bleak gothic-looking mansion perched atop a hill.

'Sister Marie-Félicité *s'il vous plaît, ma sœur*,' I said to the nun as the heavy door opened with a rasp. 'I know you don't like outsiders coming here, but I'm Céleste Roussel, and I need to see my sister urgently. Just for a few minutes, please.'

The nun remained wordless, but nodded and I followed the quiet sweep of her habit down a corridor of chipped, rust-coloured floor tiles and stained walls on which ancient-looking religious paintings hung. The only light came from small candles set in carved wall sconces, and a musty odour seized my throat.

While I had expected something rustic, I was startled at how rundown the convent was. Paint was peeling off in uneven strips, revealing greenish-stained plaster. Sections had fallen from the ceiling. The wooden floor was damp and when I trod it gave way in places, as if my feet were sinking into sawdust.

My sister glided towards me, the white veil and coif flapping like two doves sewn to the sides of her head.

'Céleste, what —?'

'Sorry to come and bother you here. I have to speak to you about something. It's an emergency. I found a family — '

Félicité took my arm. 'Hush,' she said, leading me into a side room.

Besides a battered desk and two chairs, and a single cross hanging from the wall, the room was bare, and chilly despite the summer heat outside.

'This is where guests are received,' she said, nodding to one of the chairs. 'Now, tell me what's wrong, Céleste.'

'I found a family hiding in the old witch's hut in the woods,' I said, and told her about the Wolfs, and how we'd taken them to L'Auberge attic. 'They're lovely people, but as much as I like having them at the farm, they can't stay up there for long. It's cramped and uncomfortable, and Maman won't let them come downstairs, except at night, to help with housework. I keep telling her — keep reassuring *myself* — they're safe up there, but I'm afraid for them. You know how rumours buzz around the village. And of course our mother is not happy about having them in her home.'

'I'm not surprised she's against concealing people, Céleste. I think she got her hand bitten many years ago, though I never knew the details.'

'Ah yes, Maman's dark secret.'

As a girl, I would ask my older sister why our mother was so hard and unforgiving; why I knew nothing of her thoughts and why I could never look lovingly into her cold, green eyes. Félicité said it was because a terrible thing had happened to her, but when I asked whatever that unbearable secret could be, my sister either didn't know or wouldn't tell me. Eventually I stopped asking.

'I know she'd never turn the family over to the authorities,' I said. 'And risk the police coming up to the farm. But living with her thunderous looks every day, it's so … so tiring.'

My sister fidgeted with the rosary beads dangling from her belt, her usually mellow gaze curdling, as always when Maman's business was mentioned.

'I thought they could come here to the convent? I know you have other people. Others like the Wolfs.'

Félicité sat in the chair opposite me and clasped her large silver cross.

'We only have a few young girls. With false identities, we can pass them off under any name, and in the uniform, the students all look much the same. But an entire family?'

'Couldn't you get false papers for the Wolfs?'

My sister was silent for a moment, fiddling with the cross. 'I'll talk to Mother Superior, but it could take some time to organise. I pray these people can stay safe in the meantime.'

'Thank you, and I'm doing my best to keep them safe for now.' I took a deep breath. 'There's something else I wanted to mention. I met a German from the barracks, an officer I think. He seems to like — to admire — me.' I faltered, aware of the nervous scratch in my voice. 'He gave me a present. Nylons.'

Félicité's eyes widened. 'A gift from a German? You know how danger — '

'Of course I do. And I'm not even sure he does like me. I mean, why would any man? Approving looks were always reserved for you. Men never …'

'Go on, Céleste.'

'I have a niggling suspicion he knows something about Patrick and Olivier's group. I can't help wondering if he's trying to get close to me, to find out information.'

'He might well be doing that, Céleste, it's not unheard of.'

'I know. So I've decided to steer clear of him from now on.'

'Maybe you shouldn't,' Félicité said. 'Keep away from him,

I mean. This officer might be toying with you; using you to glean information, but he's not the only one who can play such games.'

'Games?'

Félicité took my fisted hands in hers. 'Perhaps you shouldn't shun this man. Let him get close, up to a point, of course. And see just how much he knows, if anything.'

I stared at my sister, certain I'd misunderstood what she was suggesting. 'You want me to take up with a *Boche*? Never! Besides, you know what happens to girls —'

'Yes, I know.' My sister's dark eyes moved up the wall behind me, and fixed on the thin crucifix. 'I also know you're smart enough not to get caught. Besides, you've been hankering after joining Patrick and Olivier's group from the start. Just think of this as your personal mission. An important, undercover job.'

'Maman will have a fit. You know how much she despises the Germ —'

'But you won't let Maman find out, will you? Just as nobody, besides Patrick and Olivier of course, can know what you're doing. Not even your closest friends like Ghislaine and Miette.'

I pulled my hands from hers and leaned back in the chair. 'You really think I can do it?'

'I wouldn't have suggested it, Céleste, if I wasn't certain.'

'Well, if it could help the boys' group; keep them out of danger, I suppose I could try.'

'Good,' she said. 'But at the slightest sign of danger you must walk away from this man and never see him again. Don't do anything to compromise yourself, and keep in touch with me by telephone, the one in Au Cochon Tué. And only come to the convent in an emergency. If this German thinks you know about a Resistance group, he might follow you here.'

My sister stood, and I trailed after her, back down the shadowy, cheerless corridor. As we reached the oak door, Félicité kissed me on both cheeks.

'Keep your eyes and ears wide open, Céleste. And take great care.'

7

The heat intensified with every step as I climbed the attic ladder with a bag of sandwiches — the sultry air the attic snared and confined, so that the Wolfs must have felt they were living in an oven.

I heard the soft tap-tap of Sabine's steps across the parquet, and Max humming his usual tune to accompany his wife's dancing. As I stepped up into the attic Sabine stopped mid-step and spun around, an arc of dark hair sweeping her pale face.

'Sorry, I didn't mean to scare you.' I placed the sandwich bag on top of an old trunk. 'Please, don't stop. I love watching you dance.'

Talia started clapping. 'Maman's the best ballerina in the world, isn't she Papa?'

'The best,' Max said, smiling at his daughter and his wife.

Jacob skittered to his mother's side and clung to her legs. As usual, the little boy was clutching the toy soldier with the red coat.

Sabine sank down onto the straw mattress on which the family slept — the only sign of their presence, which we could shove behind the panel if necessary. She hoisted Jacob onto her lap, kissed his forehead, and opened *Les Fables de Jean de la Fontaine*, a favourite childhood book I'd lent her.

'I might have found a better place for you,' I said. 'Somewhere you can walk around, and where Talia and Jacob can play in a garden.'

'Please don't put yourself and your family in any more danger for our sakes,' Max said. 'You've done so much already.'

'It's my pleasure,' I said, ruffling Jacob's hair.

'Aren't we going home soon?' Talia said. 'Your attic is nice, Céleste, but I miss Cendres. And he must be missing me.'

'I'm sure we'll be going home soon, Talia,' her mother said. 'And we can give Céleste and her maman their attic back.'

'Did you get the paints for Papa?' she said.

'Talia!' her father said. 'Céleste can't magically get things like that, especially in wartime.'

'I'm trying,' I said, an image of Martin Diehl rippling through my mind.

'Story, Maman, story.' Jacob jabbed a stumpy finger at the book.

'I'll be back up later,' I said, moving towards the ladder. 'To see if you need anything else.'

***

I'd almost reached the bottom of the ladder when I heard muffled sounds coming from behind my mother's closed bedroom door. I crept across the landing and pressed an eye to the keyhole.

Maman was shaving soapflakes from the block she made with plant oils and caustic soda, into a dish of boiled water. A girl, pale as the sheet on which she lay, stared at the ceiling, her tongue darting over her lips in needle-like movements. I didn't know her, but that wasn't unusual. Most of the girls who came to L'Auberge for Maman's services were strangers, travelling as far as possible from their own village.

My mother followed her usual ritual, filling the tube with water, threading it between the girl's spread legs and pumping the soapy mix into her.

While Dr. Etienne Laforge was Lucie-sur-Vionne's legitimate

medicine man, those who were suspicious of my mother's herbal and floral remedies referred to Marinette Roussel as the village quack — the charlatan. Others, ignoring her curt bedside manner, spoke of her as a healer-woman and swore by her omelette of oats and sawdust, which cured both snakebites and rabid dogs.

My mother was also Lucie's reputed *faiseuse d'anges* — an angel-maker — her methods far superior to those common abortionists whose dirty curtain rails, knitting needles and mustard baths caused feverish sicknesses; deaths even.

'You can get up now,' Maman said as she withdrew the tubing from inside the girl.

I slunk away from the door, down the stairs and outside to the well. I drew water with the hand pump, inhaling the perfume from the knot of rose bushes beside the great brick well.

When I returned with my full bucket, the girl was standing in the kitchen clutching her stomach. Her face was the colour of week-old snow.

She looked away from me, at the wide stone hearth that housed the stove; at Maman's gleaming pots, pans and utensils hanging from racks on the whitewashed walls. Her eyes roved across the ornaments on the mantelpiece as if a pottery dish containing a scattering of dried mugwort, a single cufflink and a broken ornamental comb were the most interesting things in the world.

The girl had the same embarrassed, fearful look as all of them. Poor thing, I itched to say, to get yourself in that bind. But my mother had long ago forbidden me to speak to her customers.

I took onions, carrots and potatoes from the cool room and started chopping them for supper. My knife *chack-chacked* against the chopping board in rhythm with the *tock-tock* of the grandfather clock — the Rubie clock my grandmother had called it, because of its dark red fruitwood stain and because it came from an ancestor named Rubie, a celebrated midwife from the times of Emperor Napoléon.

I could hear Maman fussing about in her herbal room — her sanctuary that was forbidden to us. But my mother's rules had never stopped me as a young girl, and when she was out, or busy in the orchard, I would sneak into the narrow room with its casement windows that let in so much light and poke about at the drying frames netted with gauze, and the hooks above the small fireplace for heat-drying. I loved its smell, like something in the woods hidden under rotting leaves. With tentative fingers I would touch each neatly-labelled bottle, basin and earthenware jar lining the floor-to-ceiling shelves, and feel that chilling, though not unpleasant, sensation amidst the spicy scents. I imagined I was standing in the shadows of all the healer-women who'd inhabited L'Auberge, with their own herbal medicines. The lair of ancient witches.

'Mix this with warm water and drink it,' Maman said, pressing a sachet of dried flowers into the girl's palm. My mother had never taken me with her to gather medicinal stocks, or explained how she used them, but I had picked up a few things over the years, like how she used sage, mugwort or rue to brew angel-tea.

'Go now,' she said to the girl. 'It will all happen in a few hours.'

With another blush the girl glanced at me again. I gave her a brief nod as she scurried along the hallway, and from the window I watched her scuttle across the courtyard like a frightened rabbit.

'You're still doing that?' I said, heating the pot of water on the stove. 'Even after they guillotined the abortionist woman only last month?'

Maman didn't answer as she untied her apron and took a clean one from the hook behind the door.

'And not that I care a flip what Marshal Pétain says,' I went on. 'About there being too few children; that the women of France have neglected their duty by not having enough babies, but you do realise Vichy have strengthened their abortion laws?'

'You know it's simply a question of survival,' Maman said — the same argument she always came back with. 'Even more so since the German pigs took your father.' She glared at me as if it were my fault. 'How else do you suggest I run the farm, buy food for us and the animals? Besides, of course the girls will keep their mouths shut.'

That was true enough. My mother protected her customers' identity while they in turn kept quiet about her violating Marshal Pétain's natal laws, a defiance punishable by death. I also sensed that behind the stony mask she believed, as I did, she was providing an essential service — one she'd learned, like the herbal lore, from her lineage of angel-makers and healer-women.

Patrick kept his nose right out of my mother's illegal business, shrugging it off as women's affairs. But I suspected it was Maman's angel-making that convinced Félicité to take the veil. As if that way she could atone for my mother's sins. Or perhaps it was simply a handy excuse to get away from the farm and banish the ungodly act from her sight.

'What are you gawping at, Célestine?' she said, swiping at wisps of hair.

'Nothing.' I lay the knife on the chopping board and rocked my angel pendant back and forth along its leather thread. 'I want to get my *Baccalauréat* and study at university in Lyon.'

I'd said that to her so many times I'd have thought she'd be fed up, and relent, but still she looked at me as if I'd said I wanted to move to Bordeaux.

'You, study at university?' She dismissed me with a flick of her wrist, her lips curving into a mean little smile. 'Do you think this farm can run on its own? Besides, you're nineteen. If you've got any sense you'll find a good Lucie farmer to marry, have a family and settle down. Children and a family would curb that hot-head temper; would whip the rebel spirit out of you.'

'Live on the farm. Be a wife. Have babies,' I said, sliding the vegetables into the boiling water. 'That's all you think I'm good for.' In my agitation, a clutch of carrots fell to the floor.

'You're just like Marshal Pétain, wanting to keep women in the kitchen with dozens of children hanging off their skirts. It's people like you who keep women inferior to men,' I said, crouching to gather up the vegetables.

My mother almost pushed me aside as she snatched the carrots and started rinsing them. 'I don't know where you've picked up these ideas. Why can't you be like your brother, content to stay put in Lucie?' She slid the washed carrots into the saucepan.

'Of course Patrick doesn't want to get away,' I said. 'He wants nothing beyond being a carpenter in Lucie the rest of his life. Besides, he doesn't have to put up with your spite.'

'Spite? Don't be ridiculous, girl.'

People always remarked that I was like my mother, the only one to inherit the pale, almost transparent skin, the cinnamon-coloured hair and blunt manner. Like her, I was difficult and defiant, but as I grew older I sensed, more and more, those were things Maman could understand. She never knew what to make of the likeable Patrick or the God-fearing Félicité, so she left my siblings alone.

Now, as the war dragged on and my father had volunteered his carpentry skills for the *Reich*, Maman, while bearing her separation like the dutiful Frenchwoman, retreated further and further from us. She simply vented her inexplicable anger on the easiest target — the person she knew like she knew herself.

'The city is not the exciting, adventurous place you imagine,' she said, slapping plates onto the table.

'Well that's something I want to find out for myself, Maman.'

8

I hurried across la place de L'Eglise, my shopping basket swinging from my arm. I waved to Miette's father in his carpentry shopfront, to the greengrocer and to old Monsieur Thimmonier lounging against the door of his wood-carving shop.

I saw they'd pasted more posters on the church wall. One was of a smiling German soldier handing out sandwiches to French children gathered around him. The caption underneath read:

Abandoned citizens, trust in the soldiers of the Third Reich!

Another poster used drawings to illustrate world domination by the English and the tyranny of the Jews, but most of them still began with the word *Verboten.*

Forbidden to be out between nine o'clock in the evening and five o'clock in the morning. Forbidden to keep firearms, forbidden to aid, abet or shelter escaped prisoners, or citizens of countries that are enemies of Germany. Forbidden to listen to the BBC.

Along the bottom of each poster, the warning, in black lettering, was underlined twice: ON PAIN OF DEATH.

I slipped into the butcher's shop, where Ghislaine and her father were serving their last customers.

The butcher gave me his usual friendly nod and I followed Ghislaine from the shop, out the back to where she lived with her father and Marc.

Patrick, Olivier and the other boys were already bunched

around the radio with Miette. Nobody spoke as Marc fiddled with the wireless knobs, an exasperating hum adding to the usual jamming efforts of Vichy and the Germans — piercing sounds like the screeching of crickets.

We listened to the Germans' false information such as claims they'd landed in England, and waited for the BBC's Radio London, operated by General de Gaulle's Free French Forces, to expose the truth — the truth our occupiers tried to conceal.

'Yesterday, September 8, 1943, Italy surrendered and now joins the war on Germany!' the French speaker finally announced. 'General Eisenhower, commander in chief of Allied forces in the Mediterranean, says Italy has signed an unconditional armistice with the Allies; that all Italians who now help eject the German aggressor from Italian soil will have the assistance and support of the United Nations.'

'*Putain!*' Patrick said, jumping to his feet.

Marc punched a fist into the air. 'This calls for celebration.'

'The American armies are pouring across the Atlantic — men, cannon and tanks,' the speaker went on. 'Victory is certain. Absolutely certain.'

We all looked at each other. Living, as we were, in continual fear of arrest for a simple remark, a violation of curfew or a minor black market transaction, such news brightened our spirits and filled our hearts with hope.

"We'll drive the filthy Boche out of our country yet," André said.

'Don't be so sure,' Patrick said. 'The war is far from won, or over.'

Olivier strode across to the window, stretching his legs. 'The war might be looking up for us, but it's looking worse for them.' He nodded down to the square where Madame Abraham was closing her antiques shop. 'They're carting every last one of them off in cattle trains.'

'I've heard they drag people from their homes at any time of day or night,' Ghislaine said.

'And children get home from school to find their parents have disappeared,' Miette said. 'Mothers come back from shopping to sealed homes.'

I thought of the Wolfs and how, despite the occupation, we could roam about in relative freedom, celebrating such small victories, while they were forced to stay hidden in a cramped attic.

'Those poor people,' I said. 'It's so unfair.'

'But Madame Abraham should be safe, now she's Madame Lemoulin,' Miette said.

'Until somebody tells the Boche,' Gaspard said. 'Then they'll ship her off too.'

Ghislaine frowned. 'But where exactly do they take them?'

'To somewhere in Poland,' André said.

'Why would they take them to Poland?' I said.

'To work for the *Reich* in labour camps,' Olivier said. 'Like your father and Gaspard's. The Nazis built thousands of these work camps for their regime.'

'Poland's supposed to be a very Catholic country,' Miette said. 'So they should treat the Jews well there.'

'Oh yes,' Marc said with a twist of his lip. 'Yet isn't France, the eldest daughter of the Church, behaving very badly towards them these days?'

'Whatever rubbish the Germans and Vichy feed us on that thing,' Patrick said, gesturing at the radio. 'I say it's all one big lie.'

***

The setting sun met the Monts du Lyonnais in a blaze of gold, and it seemed the whole of Lucie was out on la place de l'Eglise.

We sat on the terrace of Au Cochon Tué, toasting our victory with Robert Perrault's wine, beer and orangeade.

'They must be pleased victory's in sight,' Miette said, nodding at Yvon and Ginette Monbeau as they came across, the baker in a red shirt and blue trousers, his wife wearing a flashy skirt in stripes of red, white and blue. 'The sooner this war's over, the sooner they get to see their sons again.'

'Robert and Evelyne Perrault too,' Marc said. 'The Boche are holding *three* of their sons prisoner.'

'That's if the bastard Nazis don't kill them all first,' Patrick said.

The old men were playing cards at their usual table, Monsieur Thimmonier's scruffy dog slumped beside his master, his wagging tail painted in slashes of red, white and blue.

Père Emmanuel appeared from Saint Antoine's, dodging the small children charging up and down the church steps mimicking the excitement of the adults.

Olivier's cousins goose-stepped around, Uncle Claude scolding his boys half-heartedly. Since the arrival of the Germans, with boots to touch and marching to imitate, Justin, Gervais and their friends were no longer bored. Finally they had someone who talked to them; people who gave them sweets.

Justin and Gervais' younger sisters, Paulette and Anne-Sophie, were jumping rope with Miette's little sisters, while another group squealed and swung from the old gallows posts.

'Come and celebrate, *Docteur*,' Gaspard called to Dr. Laforge, who was striding from his surgery clutching his black bag. 'Italy's surrendered!'

The doctor lifted his arm in a wave. 'One more home visit and I'll be joining you.'

'You'd think our doc would be the first one celebrating,' André said.

I raised my eyebrows. 'Oh?'

'He despises the Germans more than anyone,' Olivier said. 'Uncle Claude told me his father — old Dr. Pierre Laforge — died a painful death from his Great War injuries. He said the soldiers brutalised his mother too.'

To my usual irritation, Denise Grosjean was batting her

eyelids at every word Olivier uttered.

'Bastard Boche,' Ghislaine said, and swallowed a mouthful of wine.

'Shush.' I nodded at the doctor's brother, Simon Laforge and his wife and children, heading across from the chemist.

'Anyone fancy a game?' Yvon Monbeau said, swinging his bag of *pétanque* balls.

Marc, Gaspard, Ghislaine, Miette and the others wandered off with him to play in the shade of the lime trees, André limping along behind.

'Come on Olivier,' Denise said, tugging at his arm.

He waved her away. 'You go, I'll join you soon.'

Her lips pursed in a pout, Denise stomped off towards the lime trees.

I was so busy smirking at Denise, I didn't notice Martin Diehl at first, and those same two — Karl Gottlob and Fritz Frankenheimer — sitting with the cluster of Germans at a fringe table, their belts strewn across the top.

'Idiot pigs,' Patrick said. 'Sitting here drinking with the rest of us, and no clue we're celebrating their downfall.'

Fritz and Karl ogled me with seedy looks that made me squirm in my seat. Martin smiled as he ground his cigarette end into the cobbles, red sparks striking against the dull stone.

'You're staring at that officer again,' Olivier said.

I jumped, startled at the sting of his words. 'No, I'm not.'

'You'll never get to join our group,' Patrick said, 'if you go around grinning at the Boche. And don't forget, it was his lot who took our father away.'

'It wasn't him personally, Patrick.' I lowered my voice to a murmur. 'Besides, I have a reason to stare at him. I have a job … a mission,' I said, and told them of Félicité's plan.

'What?' Patrick said, his dark eyes wide. 'I can't believe Félicité would suggest that.'

Olivier shook his head. 'Bad idea, too dangerous. You know what happens to girls —'

'I also know how to be discreet,' I said.

'You, discreet?'

'Wait,' Patrick said. 'It might just work, and help us. But for God's sake, be careful. And don't let that thug get *too* close.'

The boys drained their glasses and sauntered over to join the *pétanque* game, Olivier turning back to me, and shaking his head.

I kept my gaze away from the Germans as I sat alone, listening to the card-playing men shouting encouragement as the metal balls rolled through the dust and clanged against each other. His tail flapping like a patriotic flag, Monsieur Thimmonier's dog kept trying to clamp his jaws around one of the balls, the *pétanque* players shooing him away.

I ambled into the empty bar, picked up the telephone and called the convent.

'He's here,' I said, when Félicité came on the line. 'At Au Cochon Tué, with just about everybody in Lucie. I caught him staring at me again.'

'You're certain you want to do this?' I sensed the doubt in my sister's soft voice. 'If you think it's too difficult, too risky, that's all right, I understand.'

'Olivier thinks it's a dangerous charade and I'll never pull it off, but I want the Boche gone as much as everybody else, and this seems the only chance to do my bit.'

'That's good then, Céleste, let me know how it goes.'

I hung up and turned to head for the toilet, but the tall figure of Martin Diehl blocked my path. There was still nobody inside Au Cochon Tué but I felt my tremor as he bent close, fearing he might try to kiss me again, right there, where anybody could walk in and catch me.

'You telephone to a secret admirer?' he said, with a sly, collaborative kind of look.

'No ... no, I haven't got an admirer. I was calling my ... a family member. We don't have a telephone; don't even have electricity, up at L'Auberge.'

He nodded towards the villagers outside, his face so close I felt his breath on my earlobe, his familiar scent of laundered cloth and something like fresh apples flaring my nostrils.

'Such a party, you would think the French had won the war, *n'est-ce pas*? Your brother and his friends are most happy.'

'Everybody is pleased,' I said. 'Not only my brother and his friends.'

'But you do think us Boche are stupid, yes?' he went on. 'We have radios too, Céleste Roussel. Of course we know you are drinking to the surrendering Italians.'

'Well, it is good news for us,' I said, my eyes flickering around the bar again.

'Yes, I can imagine. You French might beat us after all. But enough joking, I wanted to give you this.' He held out a brown paper parcel.

'Are you crazy?' I hissed. 'Anybody could walk in.' With another nervous glance about me, I took the parcel.

'Do not worry so, I am watching the door. I was going to leave your present in the toilet. I am thinking it is a good place to leave notes for each other. That is, if you want … if you would like us to meet again?'

'Meet again? Well … all right, why not? I'd like that, Martin. And yes, leave me a note down behind the cistern. Thank you for the present, it's kind of you.'

I hurried into the cubicle, bolted the door, and eased the paper off. I stared, in awe, at the different-coloured paints and a variety of brushes — round, flat and fan-shaped. There was a roll of paper too — beautiful thick sheets, slightly rough to the touch.

I pushed my unease aside as I thought of Talia and Max's pleasure, and ignored my rising fear of playing that blind man's bluff; that lethal pantomime. The parcel wedged beneath my coat, I almost galloped up the hill to L'Auberge.

9

'I don't know how we're going to survive this year,' Maman said, scrutinising the orchard fruit, split and rotting on the branches, the trunks sitting in puddles of water, their exposed roots decaying.

'What with the summer drought baking the soil rock hard, and this month's storms turning it all into one great mush. Not to mention those extra mouths to feed.' She raised her eyes towards the attic. 'I thought your sister was taking them?'

'It takes time to organise something like that, Maman.'

'Well let's hope it doesn't take much longer,' she said, holding her apron down against the breeze, which caught the scent of lavender, peppermint and thyme that clung perpetually to her. 'Now stop dreaming, Célestine, we have our work cut out gathering what's left of the fruit. Some at least will serve for jam or liqueur.'

'The Wolfs would be more than happy to help,' I said. 'If you'd let them out of the attic in the daytime, instead of only at night to use them as slaves for the heavy housework, and getting Max to fix everything that breaks down.'

Still far from pleased about having them at L'Auberge, I think Maman had resigned herself to their presence because she hadn't ordered me to get "that family" out of her home again. She appeared simply to regard them as a nuisance; extra bodies messing up her tidy home, strangers tarnishing her clean smells of wax and floor polish. And she never looked Max and Sabine in the eye, as they quietly went about their nocturnal tasks.

'I have been thinking about that,' she said. 'It may be our only way of salvaging something from this disaster. And it would be impossible for anyone to come up here to L'Auberge without us seeing them.' She gazed again, at her wasteland of putrid fruit as it plopped to the ground, macerating into a great sugary, insect-riddled soup. 'Besides, it's only right they pay their way. People can't expect free lodgings, no matter who's chasing them.'

'They don't expect anything, Maman. They'd love to help and if you'd bother to get to know them, you'd see how nice they are. Nice, normal people, and the children are so sweet.'

'Nice and normal they may be, but nobody will be sweet, Célestine, if we're caught. You know that, don't you? You know the consequences?'

'We'll keep a special watch out,' I said, hurrying indoors and up the stairs.

'Céleste!' Talia cried, as I climbed the attic ladder. 'Come and look at Papa's paintings.'

She grabbed my hand and pulled me from the last step, up into the attic. 'My father is the best artist, really.'

I kissed Sabine and little Jacob, and Max pivoted around from his chair in front of the window, a brush gripped between his teeth.

'Look,' Talia said, pointing out the window, 'this painting is of that side of the farm and the courtyard.'

'Your papa certainly is a talented artist,' I said, my eye following Max's clump of lavender shrubs down to the bricked well, and its spray of red roses. Heavy brown strokes outlined the wooden gateway of L'Auberge with its Lyonnais-style cornice. He'd sketched the U-shaped courtyard too, the sunlight stippling the timbers of the outhouses and my father's wood-working shed. He'd used the same deep brown for the oak door, and shuttered the windows in a rich green.

'And those are the back steps leading up to the door,' Talia said.

'Oh yes, I can see that.'

'And footprints too.' Talia pointed out the faint depression in the middle of each stone step.

'The steps of every person who's lived at L'Auberge,' I said.

'Even ours,' Talia said. 'But we don't really live here, do we Papa? We're going home soon, aren't we? And Maman's going to set up a gallery for your paintings.'

Max gave her a distracted nod. As always when he was painting, he seemed to vanish into his coloured dabs and smears. Or perhaps it was the fear of his daughter's questions that stopped him meeting her trusting eyes.

I peered over his shoulder at the beginnings of a sketch of the Monts du Lyonnais, and the Vionne River pleating the hills.

I stared at the patches of grey, where the river should be. 'I've never seen a painting made from the start. That's strange, why isn't the river green?'

'Look,' Max said. 'Look at the river.'

Through the window, I caught my mother's glare, her arms planted on her hips. I waved at her and mouthed, 'Coming.'

'Is the river green?' Max said.

'Yes, it's green.'

'Look again, what colours do you really see, Céleste?'

I squinted. 'Oh yes, I can see grey, and brown and yellow and a darkish rust. I've never seen the Vionne that way before.'

'Nothing is how it looks to the naked eye,' Max said. 'You have to concentrate, look closer, to see how things truly are.'

Max gave me a satisfied art-teacher smile, but only his lips moved, the anguish trapped as ever in the dark eyes behind the spectacles. Beneath her joyous facade, Sabine hid her fear well from Talia and Jacob, but I was certain the children had begun to sense their father's desperation.

I thought back to our conversation around the Dutrottier's radio. We were hearing more and more stories of deportations, of families separated, of windowless trains and barbed-wire camps; vague, frightening whispers that raked the air like a foul wind.

'Look, Céleste,' Talia said. 'I did a painting too. It's our house.'

A great sun shone over the home the Wolfs had been forced to flee. Talia's garden was a shower of bright flowers, with enormous birds perched on tree branches. A fluffy grey cat sat at the foot of the trunk, eyeing the birds.

'When the war is over,' I said, 'you'll be able to show me your lovely home, and Cendres.'

Max shot his wife a glance, removed his glasses, and rubbed the lenses with his shirttail. 'Let's pray that day comes soon.'

***

'About time,' my mother said, as we all assembled in the orchard. 'I wondered whatever you were all up to.'

She nodded at Talia and Jacob. 'For a start, this is no place for those children.' She flicked a wrist at the swarm of wasps that had wedged themselves into the crevices in the fruit. 'They'll only get stung and cry. Take them into the kitchen, Célestine. Tell them not to touch anything until I get there, then they can help me store the fruit.'

I was disappointed she still wouldn't address the Wolfs directly, but pleased, and slightly embarrassed, at that first modest attempt at empathy.

Maman distributed thick gloves and the wooden tongs she used for plucking boiled garments from the tub, and we began gathering the half-rotten fruit, flinging it into her large jam-making saucepans.

'I can't be near wasps, Céleste,' Sabine whispered. She let out feeble whimpers, and looked fearfully at my mother, who was waving her tongs about, commanding the operation like a fierce general.

'Do you think the fruit will gather itself?' Maman said who

wasn't afraid of any insect; of anything at all really. She heaved her shoulders. 'Oh, never mind. Go inside and supervise your children until I get there. Then you can help with the jam.'

Sabine's eyes glistened as she scurried away from the humming black mass.

'My wife's allergic to wasp stings,' Max said. 'She loses her breath and gets wheezy.'

'It's all right,' I said, pitying him his frustration — a man powerless to help, or even defend, his wife. 'We'll finish off.'

If my mother had the slightest notion of friendliness or kindness, I might have kept trying to break down those battle lines between us. But it was becoming more and more difficult to tolerate — let alone love — that insensitive, mocking creature.

When we'd gathered the last of the apples and pears we lugged the great saucepans into the kitchen, where Sabine and the children began placing the better fruit in trays.

'Separate each one,' Maman ordered, 'so the rot won't spread.' Her face grim, she set about storing the rest in the cellar for making chutney, jam and pies, and her tart pear liqueur.

The fruit episode over, the Wolfs trundled back up to the attic, and Maman exchanged her stained apron for a clean one. Patrick appeared in the kitchen and began stuffing bread and slices of cured ham into his bag.

'Going out on another coup?' I said, following him outside, and down to the courtyard. 'Where is it tonight?'

'A factory,' my brother said, the vein in his temple flickering as he strapped the bag to the back of his bicycle. 'But I've told you, best stay out of it, then nobody can force information out of you ... especially not that Boche officer.' He dragged his beret over his ears and swung a leg over the bicycle.

'He won't get a thing out of me,' I said, waving as he disappeared down the hill into the twilight. 'Keep safe.'

As night fell, and I snuffed out my bedside candle, I knew I would barely sleep. How much longer would Patrick and Olivier get away with these sabotage attacks? Were the police arresting them that very moment? I kicked the sheet off my clammy body, sick with the thought of the Gestapo marching them away, handcuffed.

I got up and stared from the window at the crowd of stars burning in the navy bowl of sky. The shadow of a clutch of oak leaves mottled the moon, and the silence was absolute, as if all of Lucie had sunk into a mournful kind of sleep.

As the church bell chimed midnight, the moonlight outlined the figure of my brother crossing the courtyard. They were safe. One more storm averted, and one more success for our resistors.

Patrick's step creaked on the middle stair and I lapsed into a restless sleep.

10

'Célestine, Patrick!' Maman's shrill voice cut up the stairs, jolting me from sleep as if she'd shaken me. 'This farm won't run on its own.'

I groaned, stumbled from my bed, and threw the shutters open onto the cold dawn. I breathed in the heavy autumn smell of ripeness and decay — the scent of the Harvest Festival.

The crops harvested in summer and the last pears and apples picked, we looked forward to relaxing and enjoying ourselves at the festival. But with the summer drought, the autumn storms and the miserable harvest — not to mention the occupation — there seemed little to celebrate.

However, it was a week since Patrick and Olivier's Resistance coup at that factory so we all assumed the boys were safe, which was good enough reason to celebrate.

I dashed water over my face, threw on my dress, emptied my night chamber pot and joined Maman and Patrick at the kitchen table.

'Hurry along, Célestine,' my mother said, spreading strawberry jam on her bread — the only fruit in abundance that year, maturing before the drought. 'Have you forgotten the festival?'

'*Oh là là,*' I said. 'As if I'd forget one of the few days of the year when something actually happens around here.'

'You might stop moping about like some underpaid farmhand

then,' Maman said, pouring a dash of her *eau-de-vie* into the ersatz coffee that tasted like dishwater, and which we called *café Pétain*.

'Underpaid? I'm not paid at all. And I don't see why I can't be more than a simple farmhand; do something different like … like Félicité.' I tore off a hunk of bread, slapped on strawberry jam, and crammed it into my mouth.

'Are you mad, girl?' Maman shrieked, rising from the table and carrying her plate to the sink. 'As if they'd let you into a convent.'

'I didn't say I wanted to be a nun. All I want is to finish school and get a proper job, so I can —'

'Don't speak with your mouth full,' she said, rattling cutlery and crockery in the sink. 'You'll get nowhere in life with your head in a book. Hard work and good clean soil under your nails is what pays off.'

My cheeks burned as she crossed to the oven and removed her last cakes and fruit pies, made once again from her stores beneath the herbal room. The Harvest Festival was one of the rare village events in which my mother participated, baking for days and draping mugwort over the door to ward off evil. 'Now go and brush that crow's nest hair,' she said. 'You never know who'll be at the festival.'

'As if it's some cattle show and I'm the prize heifer up for sale!'

'Be careful the Germans don't take you at the next requisition then,' Patrick said with a laugh. 'They only want the best cattle.' He ducked, avoiding my slap, and darted off outside to tend the animals.

'Since the Wolfs are not allowed to enjoy the festival,' I said, loading a tray with portions of tripe gratin, lamb's foot salad, and *clafoutis*, moist with last season's cherries, 'the least I can do is take them up some tasty things.'

Maman fiddled with her chignon. 'It's not my fault those people are being rounded up and shipped off.'

'What exactly, have you got against them?' I said, steadying the tray with both hands.

'I have nothing at all against them, Célestine. The only ones I despise are those pale-faced invaders. And I know we must all do our bit to protect them from such swine, but I'm simply not comfortable hiding that family. Besides, people don't thank you for it. They just scarper off one day and you never hear from them again. Not a word of thanks.'

'But the Wolfs are very grateful.' I handed her the tray as I climbed the attic ladder. 'Don't they show that, with all the chores they do every night?'

'*Humph*, maybe,' she said as she climbed on a chair and passed me up the tray.

She said nothing more, but from her hesitation and the way she stayed perched on the chair, I sensed she'd have liked to go up into the attic and give her harvest food to the Wolfs herself — a kind of peace offering perhaps. But she couldn't, or didn't dare, show the slightest bit of kindness; as if that would be a battle lost in our on-going conflict.

'Your mother is so kind to share her harvest food with us,' Sabine said. She took the tray and Max turned from his window seat, his brush held aloft.

'Yes, please thank her for us, Céleste.'

'Maybe you'll be Harvest Queen this year?' Talia said.

'I doubt that, Talia. Whoever would vote for me?'

'Lots of boys,' she said. 'Because you're lovely.'

I kissed her solemn face. 'And you're such a pretty girl, I bet you'll be Harvest Queen one day.'

***

When the Germans arrived in Lucie seven months ago, they wanted a spacious, centrally-located place with running water to use as their barracks, so they requisitioned the girls' school —

Ecole de Filles Jeanne d'Arc — located between rue Emile Zola and rue Victor Hugo. With its high stone walls, the enclosed playground was handy too, for practising their manoeuvres we were forbidden to observe.

So Ecole de Filles Jeanne d'Arc was closed to the villagers but the boys' school, which the girls had to attend, to the indignation of many mothers, was still running, and we watched all those school children parading around the fountain in their starched clothes decorated with dried flowers, fruit and nuts. They held candles and sang the vile Vichy tune, *Maréchal nous voilà!*

'Still trying to fool the Germans her name is Lemoulin,' my mother said, narrowing her eyes at Rachel Abraham. 'It won't last, they'll catch her out. They'll catch them all out in the end.'

'But what would the *Reich* want with an old woman?' I said. 'She's not much use to them as a worker.'

'No, not much use at all,' Maman said, as we nodded greetings to other villagers passing beneath the vaulted entrance of Saint Antoine's church. 'Unlike your father. Now hurry along, the service is about to start. Even though it is all a lot of rot if you ask me.'

Religion was about the one subject on which my mother and I agreed, and we only attended church at Christmas, Easter and the Harvest Festival. But as much as Mass bored me, once inside Saint Antoine's I was always in awe of the centuries-old granite monument.

We stood in the pews bathed in the autumn sun in soft sections of reds, greens and yellows reflected from the windows. I felt the power of the bronze organ pipes as Père Emmanuel's voice spilled over the altar draped in pretty pinks and golds, and down across the flagstones.

'This year has been difficult for all of us,' the priest said. 'There may be amongst you those who bear resentment against God. That He, supposedly omnipotent, can let such things as this war and the occupation happen. But it is not for us to question God, only to accept with patience, remembering the greater suffering of His Son.' He rapped a fist in the air. 'If you can think of your grief as an extension of that greater grief, then God will surely give you strength. Because our strength and our faith have served us well. Continue as such and we will emerge victorious!'

The bell chimed the end of Mass. 'Now,' he said, his expression softening, 'let us name the Harvest Queen — she who'll wear the crown.'

The congregation traipsed outside as the music started up, and people began shouting out the names of the village girls.

'Juliette Dubois!' Patrick called. Miette giggled and blushed, though I'm sure she wasn't the least bit surprised.

'Agnes Grattaloup!' Marc Dutrottier cried. Everybody laughed, most of all Agnes, who was close on a hundred and had no idea there was a war going on.

I glanced at Denise, her eyes fixed on Olivier as if willing him to call her name.

'Céleste Roussel!' Olivier said.

I thumped his arm. 'One of your silly jokes?'

Denise's mouth folded into a pout as she stalked off, her backside wobbling like jam.

In the end André Copeau's girl, the raven-haired Ghislaine Dutrottier, with eyes her father claimed had caught the sky in them, wore the Harvest Crown. André's lips spread in a great silly grin as we toasted Ghislaine's success.

'Strange, isn't it?' Denise said to me. 'How Ghislaine got those blue eyes when everyone knows that's impossible, with two dark-eyed parents.'

I shrugged. 'Who knows, maybe it can happen?'

'Yes, I suppose anything can happen when odd types mix.' Denise's eyes flickered to the Germans, sitting together at the furthest tables.

My pulse quickened, my eyes darting to the soldiers and back to Denise. She couldn't possibly know about Martin Diehl. Could she? Because if Denise Grosjean found out, the entire village would know. That would be the end of me. And the end of Félicité's plan.

'First dance is mine,' Olivier said, sweeping me from my plate of steaming *boudin* and roasted apple. He whirled me through the crowd, the odour of ginger snaps, buttery crepes and hot *saucisson* in my nostrils, the autumn scent of hewn grass in my hair.

'Did you hear?' Denise said, sidling up to us again, her mouth bursting with sugary crepe. Whatever she had to say, I was sure it was only another ruse to get Olivier's attention.

'People are saying the police know who blew up that factory last week.' She raised her eyebrows at Olivier, as if expecting him to spill the whole story. 'The one the Germans use to make parts for tanks and aeroplanes.'

'Don't believe everything you hear, Denise,' Olivier said.

'Believe me or not,' she went on, 'someone in that group is a traitor.'

'How do you know this?' I said.

'Everybody's talking about it,' Denise said. 'Get the potatoes out of your ears, Céleste. It's only a matter of time before the police arrest the lot of them.'

'Just another gossipy rumour,' Olivier said, with a wave of his hand. He let me go and swirled Denise off into the crowd, who, in her giddy excitement, dropped her crepe.

I dropped into a chair beside Patrick and bit into one of Yvon Monbeau's perfectly risen *soufflés*. 'Do you think it's true?'

'Denise Grosjean talks straight from her fat arse,' Patrick said. 'Everything that comes out is *merde*.'

Despite my brother's casual reassurances, I kept glancing nervously at the boys, but they continued swaggering about, grinning and getting drunker on beer and atmosphere. I did catch a few whispers though, between André, Marc and Gaspard, and Olivier's foot tapping up, down, up, down.

'To *le maréchal!*' Fritz Frankenheimer cried, raising his beer glass.

'To Marshal Pétain!' the other Germans echoed.

Everyone looked around, and it seemed each of us was trying

to mask our reluctance as we raised our glasses with the Germans to old man Pétain.

The chemist's wife, Madame Laforge, lifted her gaze skyward and, behind the Boche's backs, people started sending their usual little signals to each other.

'They think we like them,' Miette's mother confided to mine. 'When all we really like is swindling them. I mean everybody knows the grocer is watering down the milk he sells them, *and* charging a hundred francs for a bottle of Chablis.'

'Olivier's uncle is charging them five francs for a single egg,' Ginette Monbeau said with a laugh. 'Not to mention those pigs Claude slaughters illegally, selling the meat to the Boche at an outrageous price.'

'Well let's hope they'll all soon be at the bottom of the English Channel,' Maman said with a scornful sneer.

Yes, it seemed we'd invented a whole language of gestures and remarks to show we were still free in spirit, whilst under the thumb of the fair-haired occupiers.

I was sure the Germans noticed our sly exchanges but since so few of them understood French, they appeared to interpret them as admiration for their powerful physiques, their confidence, their starched uniforms, and kept smiling politely at us.

I hadn't noticed him approaching, but Martin Diehl's tall frame appeared, looming over me. He offered a creamy hand. I caught Maman's disapproving stare, and hesitated. But all the villagers were dancing with Germans, and the drums and brass instruments that gave the tunes a victorious, heroic tone urged me to dance. After all, it had been forbidden for so long, it would be a shame to waste that rare occasion for which they'd waived the ban, not to mention the opportunity to delve a little deeper into the mind of Martin Diehl.

I flicked Maman a defiant look, tugged my dress down and took his hand. As he pulled me close and we danced to Edith Piaf's rich voice belting out *L'Accordéoniste*, I was sure the officer could feel my heart pummelling against his chest, or at least hear its rapid beats. I wondered if his heart too, was drumming with the first tenuous throbs of our unofficial combat.

I glanced across at Maman again and almost laughed aloud as Karl Gottlob took her hand, muttered something close to her ear and forced her into a jig. They moved together like a single stiff rake, Karl with his mean cat-eyes and Maman obviously struggling not to cringe.

All the Germans joined in, singing the loudest with their throaty accents and with such gusto you'd have thought they truly belonged in Lucie. Fritz Frankenheimer looked like a pig in high heels, dancing with Agnes Grattaloup, who appeared to be enjoying herself without any notion that her partner was a Boche.

Oh yes, to the unknowing eye it must have looked like one great, frolicsome celebration.

'I would have voted you Harvest Queen,' Martin said. 'Especially if you were wearing your nylons.' He lowered his steady gaze to my legs.

I felt the blood rush to my face. 'Don't be silly, as if I could wear them here. Besides, Ghislaine's the prettiest girl in Lucie, she deserves to be Harvest Queen. Anyway, who really cares about a silly crown?'

'I would still have voted for you,' Martin said with a smooth smile. 'And I have another present for you. Do you want us to meet later? Near six o'clock?'

I thought for a minute, trying to master my rearing apprehension.

'I know a good spot,' I said. 'Behind the Community Hall. There's a secluded copse. Just cross over rue Emile Zola and walk up a bit. We won't be seen there.'

My mind suspended in a blur of agitation, I barely recalled the rest of the festivities. I paid no attention to the whisper blowing across the square like a sly breeze; the rumour that a group of Lucie's resistors had blown up a factory and taken German lives.

***

On the sixth chime of the church bell, I slunk away from la place de l'Eglise, alongside the church wall posters of Pétain's fatherly face, a shiver rippling through me as I stepped into the shade of the mustard-coloured lime leaves.

I inhaled the sap-sweet air, the light shining a brilliant red-gold as the sun followed its westward arc towards the hills. I crossed rue Emile Zola and kept walking up to the Community Hall, continually scanning the street for curious eyes.

Once behind the building, I slid into the thicket. Camouflaged in his almond-green uniform, I almost didn't see Martin Diehl leaning against the oak trunk, his long legs entwined at the ankles.

'I am happy you came, Céleste,' he said, as he removed his jacket and spread it on the ground.

Fearful of saying the wrong thing, I kept silent as we sat side by side. Martin dragged a parcel from a pocket, and I tore the paper and pulled out a chocolate bar and a cylinder of lipstick.

'You shouldn't have. You spoil me.'

He took the gold-coloured cylinder. 'Make like this with your lips,' he said, pursing his own, and I struggled to stop my mouth quivering as he painted my lips with the scarlet-coloured gloss.

He leaned back, the blond head cocked as if admiring his art work. 'So now, mam'zelle-I-like-to-win, I put you a challenge. You must eat all of the chocolate without smudging this lipstick.'

'Easy,' I said and began to eat the chocolate carefully, slowly, my lips spread wide. Besides the urge to meet his challenge, I'd not tasted real chocolate for so long and wanted to make it last.

'Stop your tickling,' I said, flicking his hand from my side, trying to mask the unease his touch stirred in me. 'That's cheating.'

I finished the chocolate and licked the silver paper, my mouth still stretched wide, and once it was clean I turned my unsmudged lips to him.

'Look, perfect lipstick. Told you I liked to win.'

'Ah, yes,' he said. 'So you did.'

He caught my hand, forcing me to meet his gaze. 'Did you know your eyes are the same colour as the river? Grey-green, as the Vionne in a storm … river eyes and autumn hair.'

River eyes and autumn hair. It sounded like a famous actress.

'Fiery hair, my mother says,' I said. 'To match a flaming temper. Though she's the one with the real temper.'

'I understand what you say,' Martin said. 'My mother was always preferring my two brothers over me.'

'Mine too,' I said, my lips curving in sympathy for that clever Boche boy who chose his words as precisely as he picked out the largest, ripest cherry from the mound at a market stall. 'Oh I know I'm not beautiful and smart like my sister, or the funny, likeable Patrick. I was the difficult middle one; the disappointment who wasn't a boy to take over Papa's carpentry business. I wasn't even meant to survive birth.'

'This is a strange thing to say, Céleste Roussel.' His eyes didn't shift from my face, as if he was truly interested; as if he sympathised with my childhood — the woeful tale I hoped would encourage him to reveal things about his own past.

'I was born early,' I went on, easing my hand from his. 'I came out blue and they couldn't get me to breathe for ages. That's why my father chose the name Célestine, because it's a fragile mineral, which is sometimes blue. You'd think a mother would want to protect a baby like that, wouldn't you? But to her I was simply the weakling, nuisance girl-child who needed extra looking after.'

'But what a prize jewel Célestine became.'

'Nobody calls me Célestine, except my mother.'

I paused, gathering my thoughts, trying to find that blend of friendliness, shyness and flattery; that mastery of conversation to get him on side.

'I want to get my *Bac*,' I went on. 'You know, the *Baccalauréat*?

Do you have that in Germany? And study at university and get a good job, but my mother wants me to stay in Lucie, on the farm, get married and have a swarm of babies. Just like Marshal Pétain want —'

I clamped a hand across my mouth, as if chiding myself for revealing too much. 'Oh dear, I don't suppose I should be saying that to a ...'

'You can tell me what you want,' Martin said. 'Nothing we say to each other goes further than here. Deal?' He took my hand again and gave it a brief squeeze.

'Deal,' I said. He didn't drop my hand and I resisted a shudder, as his index finger grazed my palm.

'So your brother is taking up the family business?' he said.

'My father was training him to become a carpenter,' I said, my internal antennae twitching at his mention of Patrick. 'That is until Papa left to work for ... for the *Reich*. The clamp tightened around my heart again, at the thought of my dear father working for the enemy.

'Your brother does not appear to do a lot of wood-work,' he said. 'Always in the village, hanging about and chatting with his friend. What is his name, the friend?'

'Olivier.' I saw no harm in saying his name; Martin could easily have discovered everything about Olivier. 'Yes, they've been friends — we all have — since we were kids.'

'They are not interested to work in Germany?' he said.

'No, of course not.' The very idea made me feel ill. 'Anyway, they're not even nineteen yet, not old enough.'

He stood and pulled me to my feet. I thought he was about to try to kiss me again, and I skittered away from his hold.

'I must be going back for supper,' he said, lean fingers flickering across the almond-green trousers as he brushed them down. 'I do not live at the barracks like the soldiers. Officers are billeted. I am at the Delaroche house.'

I nodded. 'I know of the Delaroche house — fancy, a castle almost.'

'Yes, and like the good aristocrat, they eat on time. I must not keep them waiting.'

'You know it's dangerous for us to meet like this,' I said. 'On a normal day when people are bustling about everywhere. I could be severely punished. Shot even. Perhaps we should find a safer place?'

'What of the riverbank, where you were swimming after the cinema?'

'The riverbank?' I said. 'Well yes, I suppose it's the perfect spot. It's too cold to swim now, so nobody will go back till next summer.'

'We could meet there one time a week, on my day off … if that is what you want, Céleste? As we said, we can leave messages in the toilet of the bar, if something happens and we cannot make it.'

I remained silent for a minute, raking together a suitable answer — something that would make me sound eager for secret meetings; nothing that would betray my tightening nerves as I acknowledged we'd rolled the first dice, neither of us knowing whose number would come up.

'All right,' I said. 'Yes, I'd like that.'

Martin smiled. 'Very good. So, *gute Nacht*, Céleste Roussel. *Schlaf gut.*'

'And *gute Nacht* to you too, Martin Diehl.' It felt odd, saying the words in German, but I forced them, endearing myself to the officer and his hateful language.

As he slipped from the thicket, he laughed, perhaps at my accent, or my vulnerability, and how easily he imagined he was going to win the game; as simple as skimming river stones further than the next person.

I stood in the shadows for a moment, capturing the last haughty echoes of his voice.

11

We'd chosen to ignore the gossip flitting around at the Harvest Festival, so when they came to L'Auberge des Anges the following morning it was a jolt that startled me from my dreams like the bang of a single gunshot.

My eyes snapped open. I leapt up and ran to the window. Three black Citroën Tractions screeched into the courtyard. Seven or eight men, perhaps ten, in black uniforms, leapt from the cars and thudded up the steps.

I stumbled into the hallway, and down the stairs, at the same time as Patrick and Maman. Black-gloved hands levelled pistols at our faces and, from a pocket, one of them pulled a bronze badge bearing an eagle and a swastika.

'Gestapo,' he said, through a moustache the colour of old tobacco, and barked a stream of commands at his men. I didn't understand a single word, which only heightened my fear.

My trembling hand clutched Patrick's arm as we shuffled into the kitchen. Maman didn't even blink and I detected only the slightest quiver of her upper lip. I thought of Max and his family, hoping they'd taken refuge in the partition behind the panel. There hadn't even been time to remember the plan, to stand below the pull-down ladder and cough twice.

'What do you want with us?' my mother said without the slightest grace.

'Very sorry to disturb you, madame,' the Gestapo man said.

'But we've received information that a Resistance worker resides here. Patrick Roussel. We'd like to question him over the recent explosion at a factory, in which three German guards perished.'

'I'm Patrick Roussel.' My brother stepped forward, the vein in his temple pulsing like a panicked butterfly. 'Don't harm my mother or sister. They've done nothing wrong.'

'We have no intention of harming your family,' the moustached man said. 'But we have orders to search these premises. The sooner we get it done, the sooner we can leave you in peace. So please, the ladies will wait here in the kitchen and you come with us, boy.'

He took my brother's arm and headed directly for the cellar, as if he instinctively knew where it was, or someone had clearly explained to him the layout of L'Auberge.

Without a word, my mother and I sat opposite each other at the table. The men opened drawers and upturned Maman's sugar, flour and coffee canisters that bore faded harvest scenes from last century. They inspected her gleaming pots and pans hanging from the rack above the cupboards, though what they expected we could conceal in them, I couldn't imagine.

Maman didn't give them a single glance, but stared straight ahead, her spine rigid, her arms folded tightly in her lap. I slid the egg-timer towards me and flipped it upside down.

'… rice, noodles, salt, tins of sardines …' we could hear the Gestapo man saying, from the cellar.

I kept my eyes on the stream of sand trickling slowly, surely, into the lower bulb of the egg-timer, as the Rubie clock *tock-tocked* its rhythmic, melancholy tones.

'Black market … only for the black market,' Patrick was saying, trying to fob him off with the cover story.

'… Resistance group … informed … meetings,' the man went on.

'No, no … black market only,' Patrick insisted.

No doubt the Gestapo officer suspected my brother was lying; that he was attempting to pass himself off as nothing more than a small-time black market dealer, but once the Gestapo discovered the propaganda sheets, the guns and dynamite, he would have certain proof of his suspicions.

'... black market ... serious crime,' the Gestapo man went on. '... imprison you simply for that.'

The men divided up and started invading the rest of L'Auberge, room by room, and I pushed the hourglass aside and gripped the underside of the table.

Three of them entered the herbal room. My mother's eyes tightened to slits, one hand leaping to her chignon. I knew she would be fearful not only for her precious remedies, but for her stocks of food, wine and cash secreted beneath the floorboards.

She needn't have worried because the officers were out of there in less than a minute without touching a single glass jar. Their pale features seemed twisted in suspicion, or was it fear? Their blue eyes skimmed about, as if searching for something invisible to the human eye. Their shoulders quivered, like they were shrugging off a thing that had gripped them in that narrow, secretive den.

We remained silent as they sifted through Maman's drawers and cabinets, disturbing her orderly piles of papers and inspecting each dust-free ornament. They took great care not to damage or break anything as they upturned furniture, their hands running along seams checking for hidden compartments, secret openings.

Minutes passed, the Gestapo's perfect manners and excessive politeness chilling me more than if they'd shouted, thrown things, or pushed us around.

The moustachioed boss returned to the kitchen with Patrick, whose wrists were clamped in handcuffs. I dared only a quick glance at my brother.

Chafed with anguish for the Wolfs, and how petrified they must be crouched behind the attic partition, I felt bewildered more than anything when one of the officers appeared carrying the plastic tubing with its small pump inset. In the shock and confusion of their arrival, I'd completely forgotten Maman's illegal business.

They placed the tubing, coiled in its metal bowl, before her on the table, beside the emptied hourglass.

'Explain, madame, *s'il vous plaît,*' the boss man said. Maman said nothing. She braced her arms across her chest, pursed her lips in a hard line and her eyes widened with the cornered stare of a deer catching the hunter's whiff.

'There's a drop-down ladder here,' another one called from upstairs.

I felt I might faint, as I listened to him climb up to the attic. It was over for the Wolfs; over for all of us. I bit hard on my top lip, my full bladder pressing against my belly. I hadn't had time to use the chamber pot before they forced us out from beneath our eiderdowns.

Please, Jacob, don't cry out, don't make a sound.

Over and over I repeated the words, silently willing the little boy to keep quiet, as the Gestapo soldier rattled about in the attic.

It seemed like an hour, but probably only several minutes had passed when he returned to the kitchen. He muttered something in German, which I gathered meant he hadn't found anything. I glanced at my mother and swallowed my cry of relief.

'You'll have to come with us,' moustache man said, pulling Maman to her feet and snapping handcuffs around her thin wrists.

He nodded at me. '*Bonne journée,* mam'zelle.'

'But why? Where are you taking them?' Tears bleared my vision, and I grabbed Patrick's arm, trying to snag him from the German's grip.

'There are serious accusations against your brother,' he said. 'Not to mention the illegal business Madame Roussel is evidently conducting from her home. Please step aside, mam'zelle, we must leave now.'

I kept hold of Patrick. 'No! Please don't take them. You

can't!'

The German prised my fingers, one by one, from Patrick's arm.

'Look after things, Célestine,' Maman said as the Germans tore her away from me too, and her eyes flickered, for the briefest instant, up to the attic.

I felt the urge to run back to her, to hug her and kiss each incurved cheek. I wanted to tell her I didn't hate her, not at all; that I'd had enough of our eternal battle and only wanted peace. But I couldn't, because we'd never touched or shown emotion. The very idea was bizarre.

From the kitchen window, I watched the shiny boots thunder back down the steps, impatient and heavy, then *click-clicking* across the cobblestones. I grasped my angel pendant, desperate for the comfort of the old bone.

The Gestapo hustled Patrick and Maman into the back seat of one of the cars, slammed the doors and screeched away. As if a harsh hand had shoved me, I reeled back from the window.

I filled a glass with water, my quivering hand spilling most of it over the tiles. As I sank into a chair and gulped the water down, Martin Diehl's face hurtled into my mind. An arrest the very day after I'd spoken to him. Was that too much of a coincidence?

***

After the initial shock ebbed, my first instinct was to jump on a train to Valeria. Félicité would know what to do. I fleetingly thought about going to Uncle Claude's farm, to see if Olivier and the others were safe, but if the Gestapo knew about Patrick there was every chance they knew about the rest of the boys. I ached to see Ghislaine and Miette, but the Gestapo could well be in the village and I had no desire to run into them again. I could have gone to Aunt Maude and Uncle Félix in Julien-sur-Vionne, but with my cousins being held prisoner I was reluctant to heap any extra misery on them. I knew though, whatever I did, however deeply I floundered in that black pit, the farm chores needed to be done first.

I grabbed my coat, stumbled down the steps and went through the motions, my hands working separately from my brain as I filled the buckets with water and brought them inside. It was only as I finished milking the goats, and covered the pail with a muslin cloth, that I remembered the Wolfs.

I shovelled together a breakfast of coffee, milk, bread and apricot jam and hurried up to the attic. The family were still crouched in the partition behind the false panel.

'Don't be afraid,' I said. 'They've gone.'

'They arrested Patrick and your mother, didn't they?' Sabine said. 'How terrible. Where did they take them? Will they be all right? What will you do?'

I patted Sabine's arm, trying to calm her as much as myself. 'I don't know where they've taken them. And I truly have no idea what to do, yet.'

Jacob clung to his mother's skirt with one hand. In the other, he clutched the soldier with the red coat. Max remained silent, as if the terror had stolen his voice.

'Will the Germans come back and find us and take us away?' Talia said, a single tear running down her cheek.

Sabine stroked the hair from her daughter's forehead. 'Don't fret, my girl, Céleste won't let that happen.'

'No, of course I won't,' I said, but in that instant I did not feel capable of helping, or protecting, a single person. I knew though that I had to do something — I could not remain at L'Auberge in that state of bewildered stupor a second longer.

'I need to see my sister,' I said. 'I'll be back as soon as I can.'

Sabine gave me a hasty hug. 'Take great care, Céleste.'

***

The half hour I waited for the train seemed endless and I hopped from one foot to the other, my eyes continually scouring around for the slightest glimpse of a dark Gestapo uniform, or for any other Germans who might be tailing me.

Once with Félicité, in that same sparse and unfriendly visitors' room, my words spewed out in a gibber.

'Slow down, take deep breaths,' my sister urged. She fidgeted with the silver cross that dangled from a black cord around her neck until eventually I got the whole story out.

'I think all of this,' I said, tracing the groove of a deep scratch on the desk top with my fingernail, 'the war, the occupation, has been bearable up to now because we've been taking it one day at a time. Every day people look after their families, their animals, their crops. We live from day to day but nobody seems to plan for tomorrow. All we say is, "Good, another day when nothing really bad has happened".'

I looked up at my sister. 'Well now something really bad has happened, and you know what? I don't have a single plan for tomorrow.'

Félicité sat opposite me, behind the tatty desk.

'Céleste,' she said, cupping a hand over my fisted ones. 'Besides the problem of Maman and Patrick, and most certainly the other boys, the family in L'Auberge attic is in great danger. We'll have to move them immediately, even if their papers are not finalised. Now I'm going to have to trust you with certain information; to depend on you to keep it to yourself.'

'What information? Of course you can trust me.'

Félicité drew her hands from mine. 'I know that, and I'm sure, with this business with the German officer, you're learning to think with your head, not your heart. Now,' she said. 'You should know there are more of Lucie's villagers involved in our brother's group — people the other boys, besides Olivier and Patrick, don't know about for … for safety reasons. They have the contacts, do the organising, rather than go out on missions, like the boys. They might be able to help us with these terrible arrests.'

Even after my sister confided the "trusted information" to me and I began to grasp it all; to understand the people and the stakes involved, I was still stunned.

'I never imagined people like priests and doctors would be involved in such illegal activity,' I said. 'But I suppose it's no more surprising than nuns harbouring children in their convent.'

'We all want to help, Céleste. People from every walk of life are keen to do their bit.'

'I might've guessed,' I said. 'Only the other week I saw Père Emmanuel stand by doing nothing as his Sunday school group giggled at a scarecrow wearing a German helmet. And I suppose they did grow up in Lucie together, he and Dr. Laforge.'

'Childhood bonds certainly are strong,' Félicité said, 'and of course, both of them having the *Ausweis* makes it easier. Doctors and priests are among the few allowed to circulate freely these days.'

I slid my chair back and stood. 'I need to get back to the farm. I don't like leaving the Wolfs alone for too long.'

My sister laid a hand on my arm. 'Before you rush off, any progress with the officer?'

'After the Gestapo left this morning, he was the first person I thought of. I saw him only yesterday, at the Harvest Festival — he had another present for me. But I didn't give him a single scrap of information about Patrick's group, nothing, but —'

'Of course you didn't, Céleste.'

'I don't see how it could've been Martin who told the Gestapo,' I said. 'Really.'

Félicité patted my arm. 'Just a coincidence, I'm certain.'

'But he does play his role to perfection,' I went on. 'His French is good and he's smooth, and at ease with this pleasant, cunning kind of coolness. He's asked a bit about Patrick and Olivier, but nothing direct concerning any sort of activity. I still don't know if he's truly interested in me, or if he's hankering after information.'

'Probably too early to tell,' Félicité said, as she ushered me back into the shadowy hallway. 'Just keep up the good work and take great care.'

She swung open the creaky front door.

'You don't have to worry for me,' I said, kissing my sister's pale cheek. 'I know how to be careful.'

12

When I got back to L'Auberge, a bicycle was leaning crookedly against Papa's woodworking shed, as if flung there in a hurry.

Père Emmanuel strode across the cobbled courtyard, his cassock rippling about him like a single dark wing.

'Your sister called me, Céleste. Are you all right?'

'As all right as I can be, after what's happened.' I picked up the pail of goat's milk and the basket of eggs I'd left at the bottom of the steps in my rush to get to the convent. 'Félicité said you could help us, Father.' I gestured to the priest to follow me inside.

Père Emmanuel began pacing about the kitchen as I set the pails on the tiles and started brewing coffee.

'Sister Marie-Félicité has faith in you,' he said. 'She convinced me you can be trusted.'

'Yes, you can rely on me.' I placed two cups of coffee on the table, his agitated pacing making me more edgy. 'Sit down, please, Father.'

'The Gestapo have arrested the others too — Olivier, Marc Dutrottier and André Copeau,' he said, as he took a sip of the ersatz coffee. 'Incredibly, Gaspard Bénédict escaped. Nobody can understand how the boy managed to get away.'

'Do you know where they are, Father?'

'Your mother is being held in Saint Paul-Saint Joseph prison in Lyon. We don't yet know where they took your brother and the others. Etienne and I are waiting for word from our city contacts.' He swallowed more of the chicory coffee. 'And you do understand this family in your attic is in mortal danger? We're yet to discover who, but someone informed the Gestapo about your brother's group.'

Someone. Martin Diehl?

'The Germans have marked L'Auberge des Anges as a Resistance centre,' the priest went on. 'They didn't find the Wolfs this time, but they may have heard about them hiding here. They will come back, and eventually they'll discover them.'

'What can we do then, Father?'

'As your sister told you, we'll move them to the convent urgently. As you know, there are others like the Wolfs at the Valeria convent, people whom the Reverend Mother has welcomed. The nuns will integrate the little girl into their classes. The father will work as a gardener, while the mother can cook for the students and the nuns. All under assumed identities, of course.'

He drained his coffee. 'We're taking them tonight, in Etienne's car. Let's just pray the Gestapo don't stop him and search the car. Now not a word about this to anyone, Céleste … not even to Miette and Ghislaine. Nobody.'

'I know how to hold my tongue,' I said, breaking off hunks of bread and goat's cheese.

'It's dangerous work,' he said. 'You're young …'

I forced the food down, past the sour liquid rising in my throat, and pushed the bread and cheese across the table to Père Emmanuel. 'I've just turned twenty, Father, quite old enough. I won't let you down. Or my family and friends.'

***

'Everyone in place?' Dr. Laforge said, his thick brows knotting into a single line above his black eyes. In the pale dusk light we all shivered on the cobbles of L'Auberge courtyard: the doctor, the priest, the Wolf family and I. My nostrils flared with the autumn chill that smelled of old capsicums and mown grass and reminded me I'd soon have to put the animals inside for winter. With Maman and Patrick gone, I would have to think of everything.

'Yes, everyone should be in position,' Père Emmanuel said. 'Only Céleste to go. I've posted two lookouts at each junction,' he said. 'At any sign of German vehicles along the route, the lookout will cycle to the next post and pass the message on, and so forth, until it reaches us here.'

For my first Resistance job — besides my secret German officer mission — the doctor had delegated me as lookout at the junction of the Lucie road and the main *départementale*, which he would take to drive the Wolfs to Félicité's convent.

Max Wolf clamped his large hand in his daughter's small one. In the other, he held an old suitcase of my mother's, containing a change of clothes, basic toiletries, a few toys, books and his art supplies: the sum of the family possessions. Bunched up in her coat and trying to hide her fearful eyes, Sabine held Jacob close to her breast, the little boy gripping his soldier with the red coat.

'Ready, Céleste?' Dr. Laforge said. 'You're clear what to do?'

I nodded, rubbing my gloved hands together, my breath forming jets of fog. Despite my fear and anguish for the boys and Maman, I couldn't help feeling the excitement of my first legitimate job.

I kissed each of the Wolf family in turn, blinking away tears. 'I'll miss you all.'

Jacob gave me a small smile and waved with his toy soldier.

'When will we see you again?' Talia said.

'I'll come to your new school as soon as you're settled in and I can get away from the farm.'

Sabine gripped my arm. 'I hope we can repay you one day, for all of this.'

'What you, your friends and family, are still risking to help us,' her husband said, the spectacles fogging with his quick, steamy breaths.

'It's a pleasure, Max,' I said. 'I feel privileged to have met your lovely family.'

'Thank you for the paints and brushes and paper,' Talia said.

Père Emmanuel and Dr. Laforge stared at me, obviously wondering how I'd got hold of such things, and I was glad of the darkness to cover my blush.

'No word from any of the lookouts?' Dr. Laforge said as he bundled the family into his Citroën Traction.

'All clear,' the priest said. 'So far.'

'See you soon,' I called to the Wolf family, hoping my chirpy voice masked my unease.

I pedalled down the hill through the ugly tangle of autumn foliage and the fog that was galloping down from the hills, and as I approached my post, the icy air snipped at my cheeks and my speeding heart.

I had to get it right — to help the Wolfs, and to prove to Père Emmanuel and Dr. Laforge that I was a worthy resistor in whose hands they could entrust lives.

I crouched at my lookout post until the doctor's car drove past. I watched it disappear into the fog, and knew I had played my part. The Wolfs' safety was, from then on, beyond my control, and I cycled back up the hill slowly, towards L'Auberge.

***

In the ghostlike silence of the farm, I knew sleep would be impossible. I could never rest easy until the doctor and the priest came back to tell me they'd hidden the Wolfs safely at the convent.

By the light of my candle I climbed the attic ladder and cleared away all traces of the Wolf family, then I padded downstairs and sat at the kitchen table. Shivering in the sallow candlelight,

I gathered my mother's crocheted blanket tighter around my shoulders.

It seemed the longest night of my life — the torturous waiting, the not knowing. Were Patrick and Olivier cold, and hungry, in whatever prison they were being held? I thought of Maman too, even if she was not the kind of person who would want anyone fretting for her. Marinette Roussel believed she could hold her own in the world; she had no need of others.

I kept leaping from the chair and crossing to the window at the slightest noise — an owl hooting into the blackness, the bray of a donkey across the fields, the hollow bark of a dog.

I eventually heard Dr. Laforge's Traction puttering up the hill, and flew to the door.

'Are they all right?' I said, beckoning them inside. 'Did you get there safely?'

'A German patrol stopped us,' Dr. Laforge said, as they followed me into the kitchen. 'Just before we reached the convent. They wanted to search the car.'

'Oh no! So did they?'

'The doc told them it was urgent,' Père Emmanuel said. 'Said one of the children was seriously ill, and needed a hospital. They let us go.'

I sank into a chair. 'That was lucky.'

'Luck is what it comes down to these days,' the doctor said. 'Anyway, the family should be safe at the convent, for now at least. You've cleared out the attic, Céleste?'

'Of course,' I said, as I crossed to the stove and warmed the pot of onion soup.

'You're not eating with us?' Père Emmanuel said as I placed two bowls of soup on the table.

I shook my head. 'The thought of food makes me feel ill. I can't eat until I know Patrick and Olivier are eating supper too. Maman, even.'

'Unfortunately we can't know that tonight,' the priest said, steam spiralling from the *gruyère* cheese melting into the thick soup. 'But you need to keep strong if you're to help them.'

'You did well tonight, Céleste,' Dr. Laforge said. 'But this is only the beginning; our work is far from done.'

I met the doctor's eyes. 'I'm ready to do whatever it takes … I know I'm capable.'

13

I knew talk of the arrests would start soon and it did — the very next day. Anxious to get to the village to see if Père Emmanuel had any news, I rushed through my jobs. The exhaustion of a sleepless night only made things worse, and my trembling hands slopped water from the pails, spilled goat's milk and scattered the hens' feed erratically.

The morning farm chores done, I jumped on the bicycle, sped down the hill and veered off to Olivier's uncle's farm.

Justin and Gervais were waving small sticks about, charging through the muddle of toys, clothes and dust — the household mess that seemed to overwhelm their widowed father.

'Shoot the Boche!' Justin cried.

'Kill the bastards!' his twin yelled. 'Bang, bang. All dead.'

'Language, Gervais,' Uncle Claude said with a half-hearted waggle of his finger. 'And stop saying "Boche", Justin. We'll all be thrown in prison.'

'The nasty Germans took Olivier,' little Anne-Sophie said.

Claude passed a sun-crimped hand across his face and tapped his pipe against the ashtray. 'I'm out of my mind with worry, Céleste. How would I tell Olivier's parents if anything happened to him? Have you any idea where they're being held?'

'Not yet. But I've been talking to … to some people who might be able to find out where they are, and what's happening with them. I'll come and tell you the minute I know anything.'

The farmer's brow furrowed into deep clefts. 'I don't know how I'm supposed to run this farm without my nephew.' He shook his head. 'Sorry, I forgot you're alone too now, up at L'Auberge. Besides, there's not a lot left to run here, with the Boche requisitioning everything.'

'Don't say "Boche", Papa,' Justin said, still pointing his stick at his father. 'Or we'll all be thrown in prison.'

With a wave to Anne-Sophie and Paulette, I left the farm and pedalled back along the lane, the air hanging low and damp around tree trunks strangled with ivy.

The familiar aromas of la place de l'Eglise — fresh bread from Yvon and Ginette Monbeau's bakery, pungent horse manure and newly-carved wood — comforted my jangled nerves a little. A delivery boy cycled across the square trilling his bell, and through the chemist's window I glimpsed Simon Laforge serving customers. Evelyne Perrault was washing down the Au Cochon Tué terrace, and the usual foursome — the grandfathers of André and Miette, Monsieur Thimmonier and Robert Perrault senior — studied their playing cards, Gauloises clamped between their lips. Catastrophe may have struck my family but village life was carrying on as usual.

The German soldiers were about too, bored as ever, with never much to do throughout their days besides practising manoeuvres. As they marched from shop to shop, their money jingling in their pockets, the villagers continued to snigger and roll their eyes behind their rigid backs. I kept a stealthy eye out for Martin Diehl, but there was no sign of him.

Shopping baskets cradled over their arms, Miette and Ghislaine were standing with Denise Grosjean beside the fountain, beneath the lime trees. The girls hurried over as I leapt off the bicycle.

'*Merde, merde!*' I shrieked, stumbling over a pedal as I propped the bicycle against the church wall.

'*Oh là là,*' Denise chided. 'Clumsy Céleste.'

'Did you hurt yourself?' Miette bent over and inspected

my knee.

'It's only a graze,' I said, rubbing it. 'I can't seem to concentrate, or think properly.'

'I'm not surprised,' Ghislaine said. 'Did you know they took my brother too? And André?'

'I did try to warn you all the Gestapo knew who blew up that factory,' Denise said, her lips flattening into a smug line.

I itched to slap the smile from her face, but I'd known Denise Grosjean long enough not to let her get to me, so I bunched my hand into a fist. 'You don't have to sound so pleased about it.'

'Do you have any idea where they've taken them?' Ghislaine said.

'Not yet, but I hope to know soon.'

'Maman told me they took your mother too?' Miette said, shifting her basket to the other arm.

'Everybody knows what she's been doing for years up at L'Auberge,' Denise went on. 'It's incredible she got away with it this long. I imagine you're out of your mind worrying they'll guillotine her, like that other abortionist woman?'

I inhaled sharply, picturing my mother's head beneath the razor-edged, unflinching blade. 'Let's hope it doesn't come to that,' I said, only too aware it would, most likely, come to that.

'Robert Perrault thinks Gaspard Bénédict is the traitor,' Ghislaine said. 'They're all talking about it at Au Cochon Tué.'

'Apparently the Gestapo were shooting at him as he ran off,' Miette said. 'And everyone knows those monsters never miss their target. Nobody can understand how he escaped.'

'Robert Perrault says it was as if they just let Gaspard run off,' Ghislaine said. 'So that points to him being the traitor.'

'But the Germans took his father with mine,' I said. 'Surely Gaspard would never collaborate with them.'

'Who knows why people do what they do?' Miette said. 'You just don't know who to trust.'

'I'd love to stay gossiping, girls,' Denise said. 'But I'm needed at the post office.'

'I didn't want to say anything in front of her,' Miette said, nodding at Denise as she disappeared into the post office. 'But what of the family from the old witch's hut? The Gestapo didn't find them?'

'No, thank God,' I said. 'Otherwise I wouldn't be here talking about it. But we've moved them out of the attic to a safer place.'

'Where?' Ghislaine said.

I shook my head. 'It's safer if nobody knows.'

'They seem such a lovely family,' Miette said. 'They don't deserve to have to live like that.'

'Nobody should have to live like that,' I said.

'I just wish this war would end,' Miette said, rubbing her arms and stamping her feet against the chill. 'And people like the Wolfs could be free again.'

'And our brothers and fiancés would be released.' Ghislaine threw her arms in the air and strode back towards the butcher's. 'And the Boche would take their ugly arses off back to Germany and leave us in peace.'

Miette's young sisters, Amandine and Séverine, skipped towards us, and I left my friend and headed into Au Cochon Tué. The toilet door bolted, I knelt down and felt behind the cistern, my fingers folding over a scrap of paper.

I wait to see you again. A week seems like eternity. M

The paper shook in my hands as I shredded it, his words ringing so honestly I could almost believe them. I flushed away the scraps, left Au Cochon Tué and crossed over to Saint Antoine's.

Several people were kneeling in the pews, and Père Emmanuel was busy taking confession so I went back out onto the square and across to Dr. Laforge's rooms.

As I passed the butcher's shop, I poked my head around the door, inhaling the tang of fresh blood that always made me shiver. Monsieur Dutrottier looked to be carving up an entire cow.

He glanced up. 'Any news, Céleste?'

I shook my head. 'Nothing yet.'

'I'd like to get my hands on that traitor,' the butcher said, raising his great carving knife above his head.

As he brought his blade down in sharp bursts, slicing through flesh, fat and bone, I hurried away from the shop, and from a high windowsill, a raven flapped into the cold sky from where thin clouds hung like scattered rumours.

***

I nodded to the other people in the waiting room and perched my basket on my lap, like many of the doctor's patients.

'My mother came down with the pneumonia last month,' a fat housewife was saying to a thin one. 'All bunged up she was, with the congestion. We thought it was the end.' She motioned towards the consulting room. 'The good doc came across, took one look at Maman and made an abscess come, right here.' She pointed to a spot below her left breast.

'Oh, why would he do that?' the thin woman said.

'He told us an abscess would divert the poison, and the worse it got, the better Maman would get. We had to phone him every day. Then one evening he came and pierced it. All the pus oozed out, and the infection with it. He saved her life.'

'I don't know what we'd do without him,' the thin woman said.

'And when I think how reluctant people were when he took over his father's practice,' the fat woman said. 'When old doc Pierre finally succumbed to his Great War injuries. Went through years of agony, he did.'

Their incessant chatter was making me more agitated and I resisted tapping my foot.

The thin housewife nodded. 'It's no wonder young Etienne despises the Germans so.'

'Oh, I know. You'd have thought we'd seen the back of those Boche after the last time, but no, here they are again, walking all over us, telling us how to live our lives.'

'Well our doc is a right good catch, if you ask me,' the other one said. 'With those charming looks and bedside manner. So dedicated, working every day, and all those house calls. I don't understand why some woman hasn't nabbed him.'

'Too busy looking after you lot,' an old man said, with a toothless grin.

Dr. Laforge came out of his rooms, his eyes widening for an instant when he saw me. 'Come through, Céleste.'

'But ...' one of the housewives started. 'The Roussel girl came in after us.'

The doctor held a hand up. 'This will only be a brief consultation.'

He closed the door and sat behind his grand mahogany desk. 'I'm sorry,' he said. 'I don't know anything about your brother and the others yet.'

'I wondered if you could drive me to the prison to see my mother.' That inexplicable urge to see Maman startled and vaguely annoyed me.

'As much as I'd like to,' he said, 'it's not a good idea. As you know, I'm not connected with them or with any group. If I'm seen with you at the prison somebody might get suspicious. You can understand I'm no help to them or anyone else if I too am behind bars?'

'I understand,' I said. 'Never mind, I'll take the train into Lyon.'

'It would be safer,' Dr. Laforge said. 'But of course, I'll help any other way I can, Céleste. Now I don't mean to hurt your feelings, but you must know I wasn't keen on including you in our work. You're young —'

I fought to curb the flaring anger. 'As I told Père Emmanuel, I've just turned twenty, Dr. Laforge, a year older than Patrick and all his friends. But nobody questions their ... their *youth*. Is that because they're males? Stronger — more trustworthy somehow — than women?'

'You do have a point,' the doctor said. 'But you've always had a habit of talking before you think. Don't get me wrong, Céleste, you're a good person, with a kind heart. You took the Wolf family in, cared for them. For that I admire you, but you understand we have to be able to count on your discretion. Lives depend on it.'

'Of course I understand, you can count on me.'

The doctor nodded. 'Right, well I don't know if Père Emmanuel told you, but there'll be no more meetings at L'Auberge, for obvious reasons. We're moving everything to Au Cochon Tué. Now, about the boys,' he said, his tone softening. 'I don't mean to frighten you but I don't want you to get your hopes up.'

I frowned. 'What do you mean?'

'The authorities often don't bother to torture resistors for information these days, Céleste, they just …'

The blood thundered through my head and for a moment I couldn't speak.

'I know. You can say it. They just shoot them on the spot.'

Dr. Laforge nodded sharply. 'Even more so nowadays with the militia roaming about.'

'Militia?'

'A French version of the SS,' he said. 'Set up by Vichy — with the Germans' help naturally — to combat democracy, Jewish "leprosy" and especially to fight the Resistance. But they can be far more dangerous than the Gestapo because they speak our language; they know the towns, people and informers. Summary executions and assassinations are their speciality.'

My heart went cold, and lumpy as clay. 'My God, you think they're already dead?'

'I don't know, really I don't, Céleste. What I'm saying is, it could take a long time to check every prison in Lyon. I don't want to alarm you, but it might be easier to check the mortuary first.'

The shock was like icy water hurled in my face and, with shaking fingers, I grappled for my angel pendant, working it between my thumb and forefinger.

'Go to the mortuary? Me? Can a person do that; just walk in and ask if a relative is there?'

'It's not quite so straightforward,' Dr. Laforge said, 'but with some … some simple persuasion, I'm sure you could find out what you need to know.'

'Patrick and Olivier aren't dead,' I said. 'They cannot be dead.'

***

It didn't take the villagers long to find, and punish, the traitor. It happened the following day, in a red-gold dawn, the air clean and crisp and heady as champagne. I thought it ironic such ugliness could take place on one of autumn's loveliest days.

'Where did they do it?' Miette asked Denise, as we stood together in the post-office line.

Denise shrugged as she handed Miette the Dubois family's letters. 'Nobody seems to know where it happened,' she said. 'All I was told is that when Gaspard finally confessed to collaborating with the Boche they whipped him until he swelled to one great purple mass. They say you couldn't recognise him in the end.'

'Do you know who did it?' Miette said.

Denise shook her head, and it seemed nobody knew for certain who'd actually wielded the horsewhip that beat Gaspard Bénédict.

'Is he dead?' I said.

'No, but close to it,' Denise said. 'In a coma, at the hospital. He could end up a *légume*. You know, his brain all gaga.'

She slapped a letter onto the counter. 'Might as well be dead if you ask me.'

14

I felt Maman's absence as an odd quietness, rather than the great void Patrick and Olivier left — the emptiness where their teasing grins, their chatter and their working day smells of earth, horses and hay had been.

The Gestapo had taken them only a few days ago but already L'Auberge felt hollow and abandoned. The rooms seemed bigger, the silence resonating from the stone walls. Someone — perhaps the Germans — had left a window cracked open in Maman's herbal room, and a draught blew dirt and dead leaves across the floorboards.

Apart from the animals I was by myself, and yet I did not feel entirely alone. As I sat at the kitchen table with my bowl of *café Pétain*, I felt a grazing across my nape; something like a hand, and fingers tapping on my shoulder.

I gripped my angel necklace and spun around. Nobody. Nothing. The havoc in my mind was distorting my thoughts. I'd always scoffed at the notion of ghosts, spirits, or whatever my forebears had believed lurked in the crannies of the ancient L'Auberge stones, but I couldn't help feeling a quiet presence hovering in the firelight shadows.

My hands shook as I raised the bowl to my lips. They would surely slice my mother's head off, as they'd done to that other abortionist, Marie-Louise Giraud. And what of Patrick and Olivier? The ersatz coffee tasted sourer than ever.

But Dr. Laforge had told me where to go to learn of the boys' fate, so I grabbed my coat, gloves and my tapestry bag, and hurried outside across the cobbled courtyard.

In the softer light of the mist-clad sky, the farmhouse stones looked a pinkish ochre colour. An unhinged shutter knocked against the wall rhythmically, like a frightened heartbeat, and the iron gate that led around to the back rasped open and shut in the breeze. I saw I'd left a small window open too, airing out the attic after the Wolfs had gone — a staring eye in a stony face, tracking my every step as I set off down the hill for the train station.

***

I got off the train at St. Jean in the Renaissance district of Lyon and walked across the bridge spanning the Saône River. The relentless north wind tugged at the water, pleating the surface into small, spiked crests.

I hadn't been into the city for almost a year, and the Germans' presence came as a shock. With what we grew, sold or bartered in the countryside we hadn't felt the brunt of the food shortages too much, but the housewives of Lyon stood in long lines outside shops. The women all had the same tired, dreary look, waiting with their ration cards for butter, milk and meat that might well have run out by the time they reached the front of the queue.

I scanned the giant wall posters portraying the Germans inviting the French — their *compatriots!* — to work and fight for Hitler, for a better Europe, and against Bolshevism and the common enemy. I rubbed the goosebumps from my arms at the image of a contented woman cradling her child, below the slogan: *Finis les mauvais jours! Papa gagne de l'argent en Allemagne.*

I shook my head in disbelief, the rage rising. We'd had barely a letter, and not a single franc, from Papa. I could not believe his going to work in Germany had signalled the end of our bad days.

A jeep filled with troops in navy coats and wide berets zoomed past. They must be the *miliciens* Dr. Laforge spoke about. I shivered in their noisy wake, and recoiled from a shop sign that was even more aggressive for its bold capitals: NO DOGS OR JEWS ALLOWED.

Once on la place Antonin-Poncet, I followed Dr. Laforge's instructions and took the tramway over Lyon's other river, the Rhône, via the Guillotière bridge.

I got off at Monplaisir station and walked the rest of the way to the mortuary, bent over in my threadbare coat against the icy wind. It seemed I'd been moaning only yesterday about my humdrum farm life, where nothing happened from one day to the next. How quickly I was making up for that, and with a pang I wished to have those uneventful days back.

It wasn't difficult to find the mortuary, in one of the buildings of the Medical Faculty near Grange-Blanche Hospital. I noticed it was also conveniently placed near the dreaded Montluc Prison.

I hesitated in the cool mist before I rang the bell and walked inside.

'Mademoiselle?' a man wearing a worn brown suit and a beret said. 'Can I help you?'

'*Excusez-moi*, monsieur, I'd like to know if you have any bodies that haven't been identified.'

'Plenty of those these days,' the mortuary attendant said. 'Looking for someone in particular?'

'Two men ... well four. All from eighteen to twenty years old. My brother and his friend have dark hair and eyes ... coal-black, actually. And both of them have scars on their knees. They fell out of the same tree.' A short, nervous laugh escaped my lips and I felt the heat of my blush. 'But I suppose you don't want to hear about ... The other two have lighter, sort of mouse-brown hair. Maybe you could let me see the unidentified bodies?'

'Sorry, mademoiselle, that's forbidden without a police officer present.'

I drew the parcel of *pâté* and jam from my bag and placed it on the attendant's desk. 'Please, it's very important. I have to find out if they're … I need to know if they're still alive.'

'Well,' he said, sliding the parcel into the top drawer. 'Perhaps I could make an exception, just this once.'

The attendant led me down a set of stairs, our footsteps resounding eerily into the white silence. My armpits prickled with sweat and my stomach flipped like a crepe on the skillet. I couldn't stop wringing my hands as I pictured the boys lying stiff on a slab, their bodies pocked with bullet holes.

We reached a room where large metal squares lined the walls halfway up to the ceiling. Each one had a handle.

'This is only the first of many with that description,' the attendant said, pulling on a handle, which I saw was the front end of a long box.

I shook, staring at the outline of the body under the cloth; at the point of the nose, where breath should be making the white sheet rise and fall. But in the stillness of death nothing moved. A tag attached to the big toe poked out from the end of the sheet. There was no name, only a number, a date and a time. An anonymous statistic. My legs threatened to fold beneath me and I couldn't stop myself gripping the attendant's arm.

'Ready?' he said, holding the edge of the sheet.

I nodded. He folded the sheet back.

I held my breath as I stared at the pale, navy-tinged face of the corpse, studying each feature in turn — the high smooth forehead, the vacant eyes, the square jawline.

No words came. I shook my head and exhaled a long breath.

He showed me several more bodies of dark-haired young men. Some were whole, others in pieces. One was almost faceless, grinning garishly from a broken jaw; another seemed to roll his dead eyes at me in a macabre welcome.

'No,' I said, shaking my head. 'I don't know any of them, thank God. Oh, thank God.'

'We get fresh ones in every day,' the attendant said. 'But if you come back, remember afternoons are a good time. The police are often here in the mornings. In the afternoons they do the interments; bury them at the Guillotière cemetery. And if you still have your brother and his friends' tobacco cards, I could use their rations.'

I nodded, whispered a hurried thank you and rushed back out onto the street. I couldn't banish the images from my mind — those lifeless bodies of sons, brothers and fathers. I saw the mothers, the sisters, whole families heartbroken. I did not know a single one of them, but I felt bound to them all by some invisible strand, and my grief for those strangers gushed out and drenched me in an icy sweat.

I leaned against the wall, that mortuary stink of death fusing with the autumn scents of decaying vegetation. I lurched forward and threw up.

***

I felt too ill to visit my mother at the Saint Paul-Saint Joseph prison, which was on the other side of the city. Besides I had to get home for the animals, not to mention the curfew. I would go and see Maman the following day.

With feeble steps, I made my way back to St. Jean and caught the Lucie-bound train, crowded as always with city people heading to the countryside to purchase black market food from the farmers.

By the time I climbed the hill to L'Auberge, the despair clenched me as tightly as the hunger and fatigue.

I dragged myself up the steps and peeled off my hat, coat and gloves in the hallway. A familiar musky-lavender smell prickled my nostrils and I looked up sharply.

'Maman?' I took cautious steps towards the kitchen.

My mother stood at the hearth stoking the stove with pieces of wood and charcoal, the usual pale grey apron firmly tied around her waist.

'Where have you been, Célestine?'

'You're back? B-but I don't understand,' I stammered. 'They let you go?'

My mother pressed her lips into the familiar hard line.

'How would I know how they operate?' she said, stirring something in a saucepan. 'So, where have you been?'

'Out,' I said, all my concern for her vanishing in an instant, our familiar battle-lines immediately redrawn. 'Into Lyon.'

My mother nodded towards the attic. 'I see they've gone.'

'It was too dangerous for them to stay here, after the Gestapo visit.'

'And what of your brother?'

I shook my head. 'Nothing yet. But people are trying to find out where they are.'

'What people?'

'Just people.' I was weary of her questions, my gut heaving as I thought of those bodies in the mortuary. I'd been lucky, but next time it could be Patrick and Olivier lying on cold slabs.

'Well let's hope we know soon,' she said. 'Now don't stand there dreaming, put the supper plates out.'

We ate the cabbage and bacon stew in silence. Between mouthfuls, my eyes kept straying across the table to that rigid face. Why had they released her so quickly? No trial, no punishment. Nothing. In these days of blunt and hasty imprisonment, nobody got out that easily.

15

Martin Diehl was late for our first riverbank rendezvous. As I stood in a patch of weak sun, skimming pebbles across the silvery surface of the Vionne, I was convinced he wasn't coming; that he'd tired of trying to get information out of me, if that was his real motive.

But there he was, astride his motorbike, stopping on the crest. With a glance about him, he hid the motorcycle in the bushes and slithered down the slope, a parcel cradled under one arm. As the bed of autumn leaves made *schlus, schlus* noises beneath his feet, my giddiness grew stronger.

The Gestapo's storming of L'Auberge, the mortuary visit and Maman's inexplicable release from prison had left me in a perpetually fretful state, but I continued pitching stones with nonchalant flicks of my wrist.

'I heard of the arrests,' he said. 'Of your brother and his friends. And your mother. I am filled with sorrow for you. Have you any news yet?'

I gathered another handful of pebbles. 'How did you know?'

'Everyone knows,' Martin said, skimming a stone of his own, which skipped further than mine. 'News travels like wind in this village, you must know that.'

'I'm actually sick with worry,' I said, flinging my stones aside. 'I've even been to the mortuary. Nobody seems to be able to tell me where they are, or even if they're still alive.'

I hesitated, gnawing at my top lip. 'I thought maybe … is there anything you could do, to find out about them?'

'Me?' Martin's face creased into a frown. 'I would like to help you, Céleste. Yes, we are on the same side in theory, but really we have nothing to do with the Gestapo.'

'Oh, I'd so hoped …' I stared across the bleak valley, a wad of cloud obscuring the wan sun, brittle leaves trailing to the ground around us. 'I don't know what else to do.'

'I shall try, but I make no promises,' he said, pushing the parcel at me. 'Magazines for you. I know they are not enough to cheer you, but they may give some small comfort.'

I opened the package and started flipping through the magazines. True, they were more interesting than the conservative Catholic Youth magazines — the only ones the Germans permitted us — though I could barely muster any admiration for the beauty of Greta Garbo, Bette Davis or Marlene Dietrich. 'That's nice of you, but you don't have to keep giving me presents.'

'You do not like them?'

'Of course I do, but with Patrick and Olivier gone — dead maybe — all that Hollywood glamour doesn't seem so important.' I snapped the magazine shut. 'I can't think about anything else until I know what's happened to —'

He drew me close, cutting my words off. 'Do not be sad, mademoiselle autumn-hair and river-eyes. I am sure news of them will reach you soon.'

His tender touch, the soft voice oozing sympathy, infused me with a kind of ease and peace. Perhaps an illusion — oh yes, I was aware of that — but even so I was glad of the momentary escape from my bleak thoughts. As a nightingale's rich voice drowned out the slow murmur of the river, and his fingertips grazed my chin, I tilted my head to his and met his parted lips.

Despite the spikes of fear, I let his tongue explore the crevices of my mouth, and when he finally withdrew for breath, he slung an arm across my shoulders, his hand dawdling in the cleft below the bone.

Apart from the ridge of goosebumps scrambling along my arms, it hadn't been so unpleasant, the kiss; something I could surely endure if it meant helping our resistors, but I sidled away, anxious to leave things at that one simple kiss.

Martin pulled a Gauloise pack from the pocket of his greatcoat and offered it to me.

I'd never smoked before but I took one on impulse. He touched his match flame to the tip and as I inhaled, my throat caught fire, and I coughed and spluttered.

'You will get used to it,' he said. 'It is always awful in the beginning.'

'Come on,' I said, anxious to put distance between us. 'It's too cold to stay still. I'll show you where to find mushrooms. My father taught me where to find the best ones. I swear he's got a truffle pig's snout for a nose.

'He'd sniff those mushrooms out,' I went on, as we hurried through the chilly woods. 'Orange girolles that smell like apricots and plums, dark grey *trompette de la mort* with soft, fruity smells, and *cèpes* too. He told me I'd find *cèpes* lurking beneath the chestnut leaves, which are the same dark brown, so they're easy to miss. My father taught me how to brush a horse too, and let me feed carrots to the baby goats, and throw swill into the pig pen.'

'I can hear in your words that you miss him.'

'For weeks after he was sent to Germany,' I said. 'I could still smell him; his yellow scent of sawdust and stale tobacco. But it was gone so soon; every trace of him vanished. Perhaps my mother scrubbed the house clean of him so there'd be no reminders. She never mentions him, just bears their separation bravely, like a true Frenchwoman, and says we're not the only ones — that many families have lost husbands, brothers and sons. "There's no time or energy to waste feeling sorry for ourselves," she says. But she takes out her frustration on me. Oh don't get me wrong, she was like that before Papa left, only she's worse now, and still treats me like some silly child.'

Martin pulled me close again. 'I care about you,' he said, with a small, sad smile.

'I always wondered why my father chose such a sour woman for his wife,' I said, squirming from his hold. 'I asked him once and he said she wasn't really so grim; that you had to know the person inside. My sister told me something awful happened to her when she was young, but we didn't know what. All I know is I have a mother who is as hard as those rocks.' I waved an arm towards the river boulders.

'Not that that stops me fighting back,' I said. 'Or keeps me from trying to find a way to leave L'Auberge.'

'I miss my father too.' Martin started picking at the peeling bark of a tree trunk. 'I do not know if my family is safe, or if our house is blown into pieces. The Allies' bombing offensive was meant to destroy everything, not only our spirit.'

'Don't you write letters?'

'Oh yes we write, but you know what wartime is, letters are getting lost. I have no word from them for three months.'

'I know what you mean. We haven't had a single letter from Papa since July. We're desperately worried why he's stopped writing.'

'It's not that my billet — the Delaroche family — isn't hospitable,' Martin said, 'because they are. The family is polite; they cook and clean for me. But I feel like an intruder. I sense they are thinking: how can he be in our home when his countrymen have taken the head of our house prisoner? Or that I see their house as a hotel, not appreciating the comfortable bed and clean sheets,' he said. 'I do. But I still miss my home, and wish I did not have to stay in theirs.'

'I'm sorry for you too,' I said. 'I hope your family is all right. So why did you go into the army, knowing you'd have to leave your home and family?'

'I think I did not know what it really was — the army, war.' He was silent for a minute, and lifted his strange eyes to a black bird circling above us, its scythe-like beak carving spirals through tufts of fog.

'My father owns a successful bicycle business,' he went on. 'My brothers and I were happy children, sailing boats on the lakes and hunting duck in the pine forests. When the question came up about earning my living, my father suggested the cycle shop. But that sounded so … so, how do you say? Boring. I wanted to see the world, learn how other people live. I imagined the army was such a way.'

'What did your parents think of that?'

'My father was disappointed I would not go into his business but he patted me on the back and wished me luck. My mother shook her head and said I was not born to be a soldier.'

'Your mother was right then?'

He nodded. 'Perhaps. But it is too late for regret.' He eased down onto a silvered log and patted the spot beside him. I sat, placing my basket between us.

'Like all my friends, I went to Hitler Youth camp. We learned things: sport, combat, violence. They taught us the Nazi doctrine,' he said, the chiselled mouth tightening. 'And they taught us how to hate the Jews.'

'Lots of French people dislike them too,' I said. 'I've never understood why.'

'I have seen battle,' Martin went on. 'Horrible death, villages pillaged, men and women tortured and shot in their pyjamas. Now I know people are the same the world over, wherever they come from and whatever their religion. And I see how pointless war is.'

The breeze shifted blond wisps of hair across the sculpted cheeks, settling them on his brow, which was knitted in sadness and a kind of helpless resignation. If that emotion wasn't real, was not pouring straight from a tormented heart, Martin Diehl was the finest actor.

I got up and walked on. 'You know, I always thought war was only hard on the losers,' I said, 'but now I see you victors suffer too.'

'Everybody suffers in battle, Céleste. There is no real victor.' He scuffed his foot through the dead leaves, exposing a cluster of seeds and dried fruit. 'Look, a poor squirrel forgot his supplies.'

'So what *is* the point of this war we're fighting?'

He shrugged. 'Ah, the big question. But no one has a good answer. War is not just the work of politicians and capitalists, the common man is also guilty; man and his urge to murder and destroy. And until that changes wars will go on, and everything man has carefully built and nurtured will be cut down, only to start all over again.'

'Man is crazy,' I said, spotting a patch of wild thyme niched beneath a woody clump, its tiny flowers like purple gems twinkling in the pale grey air.

'My mother will be pleased with this.' I snapped off the thyme and lay it in my basket beside the mushrooms. 'She uses it to make infusions for bad coughs — one of my grandmother's remedies.'

I moved on, clambering over a withered log, and pointed out a patch of late *fraises des bois*. 'Look, strawberries.'

Martin snapped off a clutch of the tiny, dark red fruit.

'Open,' he said, and popped them into my mouth, one after the other, and kissed my lips shut.

'Mmn, delicious,' I said. 'Now come on, let's keep going.'

The sun slipped behind the hills, darkening them to a deep mauve, and I glimpsed the old witch's hut between the tangle of ivy. Fresh thoughts of my father plunged back into my mind; his tales of the Night Washerwoman who'd lived in the hut — the witch who killed her babies and would make any children found wandering in the woods help her wash the bloodied corpses.

I thought back to our childhood games in the hut, with codes, passwords and hidden enemies, and an urgent need for news of Patrick and Olivier seized me.

'I have to get back to the village, Martin.'

'Yes, you must not be caught with the enemy.'

'I don't think of you as my enemy,' I said. 'You're not like the others. Sometimes I can hardly believe you're even a German.'

'Oh but I am as much a Boche as you are a French girl,' he said.

'Be careful saying "Boche",' I said with a smile. 'You can be imprisoned for that.'

'That is not the only thing we could be put in prison for,' he said, his hand lingering on mine. 'But we cannot change what we are, just as we cannot predict who we shall fall in love with. We are a modern-day Romeo and Juliet.'

I frowned. 'Romeo and Juliet?'

'Two people from opposing sides attracted to each other. And how love leaps all barriers.'

Love!

He'd caught me off guard again, and I floundered for a reply.

'Right, so see you in a week then,' I said, trying to dismiss that one unsettling, terrifying word. 'You will try and find out about my brother and the others? Leave me a note in Au Cochon Tué.'

'I will do what I can,' he called, riding off with a wave, clods of damp Vionne earth flying up from beneath the wheels.

The chill slunk beneath the layers of my clothes, the soil he'd kicked up tasting wet and sour in my throat, and snapping me back to the cold reality of the boys' imprisonment. As I scurried through the willows, along the ridge and down to the village, I banished that enemy officer, and his supposed love for me, from the jumble of thoughts swirling in my brain.

***

'I heard your mother's home,' Denise said, from behind her desk. 'That was quick.'

I gave her a non-committal shrug and looked away, out onto la place de l'Eglise.

'Nobody can understand how,' she went on, sorting her

stack of letters. 'No punishment. Nothing. Especially after they guillotined that other *faiseuse d'anges*.'

'Just check the mail, thanks.'

Denise shook her head. 'Sorry, nothing today. Don't give up hope, your father will surely write soon. Any news of Olivier?'

'No.' Not that I'd tell you, I wanted to say, but I merely nodded to the other people waiting and hurried out of the post-office and across to Saint Antoine's.

Apart from Père Emmanuel, lighting the altar candles at the far end of the aisle, the church was empty.

'Céleste,' he said, walking towards me.

From the shadow that darkened his features, I guessed he knew something. It must be bad news.

'You found out something, Father? Where are they? Are they all right?'

The priest took my hand and patted the back of it. 'Go into the confessional.'

I climbed up into the small enclosure and sat on the stool, dribbles of sweat pocking my brow.

'They're alive,' Père Emmanuel said.

I puffed my cheeks out. 'Thank God for that.'

'They're in Montluc Prison, Céleste. You've heard of this place?'

'Oh no! Yes ... yes I've heard of Montluc Prison.' The fear streamed back. We'd all heard the stories of Montluc: prisoners tortured with near drowning in ice-water baths, electric shocks and gruesome beatings.

'They've been sentenced — your brother, Olivier, André and Marc. Please don't mention this to your mother, until we know —'

'Sentenced to what?'

Through the grid, I saw Père Emmanuel glance up at the large painting of Jesus nailed to the cross. He paused before he spoke.

'Death by firing squad.'

16

I tapped on Dr. Laforge's door. 'It's Céleste Roussel,' I said, glancing around at the waiting patients. 'Sorry I'm … I'm very ill. I need to see the doctor immediately.'

'Take a seat, Céleste,' he called. 'I'll be out shortly.'

Out shortly? What is he thinking? There's no time to sit, or wait.

It seemed hours before the door opened, the patient left and Dr. Laforge beckoned me inside.

'They're in Montluc Prison, and … and they're going to be shot,' I said. 'They're all in together, cell D60 whatever that means. Père Emmanuel said to come and see you; that you could help. You said you would … said you'd help.'

Dr. Laforge nodded. 'Yes, I know about Montluc, and of course I'll help. But first, stop pacing and sit down, you're no good to anyone in this state.'

I edged onto the corner of the chair, crossing and recrossing my ankles.

'We have to think how best we can help them,' he said. 'But before we do anything I'm prescribing you a daily glass of red wine and a dose of cod-liver oil to fortify and calm you.'

'I don't care about cod-liver oil. Anyway, my mother already makes me take it. Please, what can we do?'

The doctor's eyebrows merged into one. 'I do have an idea. But I'm not certain you could —'

'I can do it. Please, I'll do anything to help them.' I lurched forward, almost sliding from the chair in my eagerness. 'What's the idea?'

'People rarely escape Montluc,' the doctor said. 'Only one prisoner — General Devigny — has ever broken out. That Klaus Barbie monster tortured him for weeks and when he got nothing out of him, he told the General he'd be shot within days. I suppose that was motivation enough. But nobody else has managed it, and escape carries the utmost risk. They shoot fleeing prisoners on the spot.'

'They're going to shoot them anyway,' I said. 'But I've heard of sending big groups of resistors into prisons to break people out. Can't we do that?'

'We don't have the strength of numbers to carry off such a raid, Céleste. And even if we did, the Germans would charge in from the adjoining fortress and from the Part-Dieu barracks before we ever found cell D60.'

'So?' I clenched and unclenched my hands.

'There's far more chance of escape from the Antiquaille hospital,' Dr. Laforge went on.

'Antiqu —?'

'The hospital where they send sick prisoners and where we have contacts, nurses who work with us.'

He opened a drawer and held up a glass bottle. 'These pills will make the boys feverish. And when they're ill, the guards will hopefully move them to the prisoners' section of the Antiquaille hospital. We'll have far more chance of breaking them out from there, rather than Montluc.'

'You want to make them ill? But what if ... if they die?'

'Don't worry,' the doctor said. 'It's my job to know the exact dose needed to make them just a little off-colour. Now your job, Céleste, is to ensure they swallow the pills and act much sicker than they truly are.'

'I can do it. But how?'

Dr. Laforge leaned back in his chair and clasped his hands in his lap. 'I have a plan.'

***

I held a match to my bedside candle then sewed the pills into each of the boys' shirt collars as per the doctor's instructions. I wrote a note in the tiniest writing possible, folded the paper and sewed it into one of the wrist cuffs. I knew they wouldn't know to look there, but Dr. Laforge said people often sent messages that way, something the boys would learn from other prisoners.

Once I'd prepared the clean clothes — underwear, socks, a shirt each and a towel — I dozed on and off, thinking about going to Montluc Prison, the fear welling in every nook of my mind. At five o'clock I flung the covers off, scrambled into my dress and rushed to my chores.

There was no sign of my mother when I carried a pail of water, and another of goat's milk, into the kitchen. The Rubie clock chimed seven and I could hardly believe she'd still be in bed. I set the buckets down on the tiles, kneaded my icy hands together and trundled back upstairs for the prison clothes.

At the top of the stairs, I heard muffled voices coming from my mother's room. Whoever would be with Maman in her bedroom at that hour?

I crept to her door, pressed an eye against the keyhole and caught sight of a bare leg. I almost fell backwards in disbelief.

I focused on the frightened face of the girl lying on the bed, and Maman's taut bun, as she bent over, threading the tubing between the girl's spread legs and pumping soapy water inside her.

Once the shock of what she was doing — still doing — subsided, I noticed something else: a bar of soap, sitting next to the bowl of water. Real soap. Two other bars sat on the dresser.

My mother made our soap from plant oils or animal fat

and caustic soda. Everybody did, since there was so little of the proper stuff around. But there were three bars of real soap — something you could only get on the black market, if you had the money, which my mother didn't. I knew of only one other way to get items such as soap, lipstick and chocolate.

I crept back downstairs and sank into a kitchen chair, a quiet tremble humming through me. I lifted a bowl of leftover *café Pétain* to my lips, barely aware it was cold and stale. The Rubie clock *tock-tocked* away the seconds.

Footsteps on the stairs jolted me from my reverie. I bolted upright. There was no time to worry about my mother's insane behaviour. I forced a gulp of cod-liver oil down and slathered *rillettes de porc* onto a slab of bread.

I finished wrapping the boys' clothes in a brown paper parcel just as my mother and her young customer came down to the kitchen. I shoved the parcel out of sight, onto a chair, beneath the waxed tablecloth.

Without the slightest acknowledgement of me, Maman disappeared into her herbal room. The girl raised her eyes to me in a flushed glance. I threw her a quick — hopefully comforting — smile.

'Go now,' Maman said, pressing the sachet of herbs into her palm. 'Expect it to happen in a few hours.'

'How can you still be doing that?' I said, as the girl skittered from the kitchen and out the door. 'You must truly be mad. Oh I do realise you're providing an essential service; a *vital* one, but still … the risk. You got away with it once, though I still don't know why they released you so easily, but surely not a second time?'

My mother avoided my stare, untying her apron and lifting it over her head with unusual slowness. 'Don't concern yourself about the prison affair, Célestine, that's my business. Supporting this family is the burden on my shoulders, not yours.' She took a clean apron from the hook behind the door. 'Besides, with your father gone, and now Patrick, I don't see that I have a choice.'

She eyed the parcel, peeking from beneath the blue and white checked cloth. 'What's in the package?'

I said nothing but my mind whirled like the Vionne in a storm. Nobody was ever released from prison so easily, unless they had the Germans on side. I could never imagine my mother with one of them — with *any* man. But how else had she got out?

There was the real soap too, but if I challenged my mother about bars of soap she'd know I spied on her. Though I suspected she knew I'd been watching her angel-making for years.

'Célestine! What is in that parcel?'

'Clothes for the boys. I'm taking them to Montluc Prison.'

'*Montluc*? Is that where they are? How do you know?'

'Someone, whose information can be trusted, told me. But please don't concern yourself with this prison affair, Maman. It's my business.'

'I believe my son *is* my business.'

She lowered her stare to my legs. 'And where did those nylons come from?'

'Again, my business, Maman.'

I did not look at her as I shoved the parcel into my tapestry bag, took my coat and hurried out the door.

17

The train clattered into Lyon, and I got off at St. Jean station, took the Charité-Monplaisir tramway once again, and stepped down on grande rue de la Guillotière. I continued on foot, clutching my coat lapels, my skirt whipping my calves as I crunched through brittle autumn leaves.

I was shivering when I finally reached Montluc Prison and joined the long queue at the gates.

'Two lines,' the guard repeated every few minutes. 'Visitors in one, those with packages in the other.'

I kept smoothing down my coat and hitching the bag back onto my shoulder. I'd tried for the sophisticated look, with Martin's lipstick and nylons. My dress of the mismatched bodice and skirt was concealed beneath my coat but I feared I still had the air of an awkward country girl.

It seemed they'd only have to glance at me to know about hidden notes and pills. I imagined everyone was staring at me as if the word "resistor" was carved across my forehead.

I was barely able to contain my impatience. The tram had been crowded, people jostling me, and my parcel had come loose. I pictured myself handing it over to the guard and the clothes spilling out, the pills bursting from the shirt collars and rolling across the ground. I tightened my grip on the bag and tried to concentrate on something else; on the game with Martin Diehl. The more I saw him, the less convinced I'd become that he was trying to use me for information. He seemed so caring and trustworthy, his declaration of love blurted deep from the heart.

The women in the queue all seemed perfectly at home standing in lines outside a prison, laughing and chatting amongst themselves as if gathered around the village fountain.

'That one loves chocolate cake,' a girl in a pillbox hat said, nodding to the guard at the front of the line. 'Though getting cake of any sort nowadays is like striking gold.'

'Make sure you take a silk scarf when you see the judge,' another said. 'For his wife. Otherwise your husband won't have a hope of getting out.'

'Silk?' her companion said, with a laugh. 'You'd have to shoot a parachutist down to get silk these days. But I've heard there are more and more of them, dropping supplies all over the countryside in the dead of night.'

The first woman nodded. 'They bring proper coffee. Chocolate too and real tobacco, not that awful stuff made from dandelion leaves.'

It seemed those women knew everything about the occupation, the judges, lawyers and prison life. They were obviously experts in effective ways of handling the different guards too, and the tricks used to communicate with prisoners. My note and pills would barely raise an eyebrow.

By the time I reached the front of the line, my feet ached with the cold. 'I've come to collect the dirty clothes from cell D60,' I said to the guard.

'Who exactly in cell D60, mademoiselle?' the guard said, frowning as he consulted his long list. 'There are four prisoners in D60.'

'I have clean clothes for all of them. One of the prisoners is my brother.'

I licked my scarlet lips, giving him what I hoped was a charming smile, and reached into my bag for the smaller parcel containing my mother's *pâté*.

'Please would you be kind enough to make sure they get the clean clothes?' I said, handing him the *pâté*.

'Wait there,' the guard said, snatching the clothes and *pâté* without another glance at me. He turned back to the line and barked, 'Next!' to the woman behind me.

After about twenty minutes the guard bellowed, 'Dirty clothes from D60!'

I stepped forward and he threw a bundle at me.

I walked off into the fog clutching the filthy garments — proof the boys were alive, at least. Dead men's clothes don't get washed.

***

I stayed on the train as it passed Lucie, and got off three stops later, in Valeria. I hiked up the hill to the convent and as if she'd been expecting me, Félicité opened the door.

'Patrick and Olivier are in prison, but they're alive,' I murmured, though even whispers sounded loud in that cavernous corridor. 'There's good news about Maman too.'

'Come to my room, Céleste. You'll tell me everything there. The visitors' room is occupied right now.' She led me up a wide staircase, a hint of stocking showing beneath her hem as she gathered her skirts. We reached another narrow corridor and I followed my sister to the end.

As Félicité bent to open her door, I glanced out the window. In the ordered garden below, a man was bent over, weeding a pumpkin patch.

'That's Max! How are they?'

My sister hustled me into her room. 'Their new name is Favier,' she said. 'They've only kept their first names.'

'Favier … that's very French. How are the children? Can I see them?'

'Best not to disturb Talia's class,' she said. 'We shouldn't attract attention to any one child in particular. I think Talia is happy, even though she understands a lot of what's going on. But little Jacob is so young. We had to make a game of it, teaching him his new name. Fortunately he's not old enough for school and can stay by his mother's side in the kitchen most of the day. You know how attached he is to his maman.'

My sister poured two glasses of water from a pitcher on the otherwise bare dresser and came to sit beside me on the bed. I told her about Maman's sudden, inexplicable release from prison, but avoided mentioning my suspicion of how that might have come about. Nor did I say the angel-making was carrying on as usual.

'All the boys are in Montluc Prison, and —'

'Montluc!' She laid a hand on my arm, and with the other grasped her silver cross. 'And what? Tell me, Céleste.'

'They've been sentenced to …'

My sister remained silent, but the skin about the edges of her coif flushed scarlet.

'Sentenced to what?' she finally said. 'Death?'

I nodded. 'But Dr. Laforge has a plan to break them out. I've just come from the prison.' I explained about the pills and the note. 'I have to wait a few days before I go back. You know, give them time to get sick enough to be transferred to the hospital. That's if they do find the note and the pills.'

'Be very careful at Montluc, Céleste. I know this work appeals to your sense of excitement and adventure, but it's a dangerous place. If they have the slightest suspicion you're trying something they'll imprison you too. Or simply shoot you.'

'You don't have to worry about me.' I fought to mask the agitation I felt when my sister lectured me. 'I'm not a child.'

'I'll pray for you anyway.'

'So, if I can't see the children,' I said, 'maybe I could see Max and Sabine?'

'I might be able to arrange a quick visit. Wait here.'

In a starchy bustle Félicité slipped out, and I peered about her room — the place my elusive sister slept, prayed and dressed to hide her curvy body and her long dark braids beneath the grim habit.

I don't know what I'd imagined, but I'd never pictured the narrow bed, the scuffed dressing table and wardrobe, and the single decoration — a plain wooden cross above the bedhead — the things for which my sister had given up everything. A life she'd relinquished for God.

Next to that barest and saddest of rooms, the centuries-old L'Auberge des Anges seemed a place of great homeliness and timeless comfort.

I plied the angel pendant between my thumb and forefinger. The worn piece of bone warmed me in that dim starkness, and I understood religion was not, as I'd presumed, simply a convenient escape route for Félicité. As I took my strength from the angel talisman, my sister took hers from God.

Félicité came back into the room, the rosary beads dangling from her belt *clack-clacking* softly as she sat on the bed.

'We'll see them in the kitchen shortly. It will seem more natural, in Sabine's working place.'

'You don't ever regret it?' I said, my gaze moving around the room again. 'The convent, this religious life?'

'I didn't choose it, Céleste. God chose me.'

'I wish something would choose me, and I could get away from Maman too.'

'Don't think like that. Imagine Papa's relief, knowing you're keeping the farm going without him and Patrick,' Félicité said with her soft smile. 'He'd be proud of you. I'm proud of you. One day you'll get your chance to do what you want.'

'We'll see if that ever happens,' I said. 'But I always imagined a boy might come along and change your mind, and you wouldn't want to be a nun anymore.'

'It's true,' she said with a sigh. 'The thought did come over me at times, but not now.'

'When?'

'Oh, I don't know. When I was younger … on sad days. So, tell me how things are going with the German officer?'

'Well, no more questions about the boys, so I'm fairly certain he doesn't know anything about their activities, or that he's trying to get information from me. It seems he likes me a lot in fact … that's what he says.'

'That's reassuring,' Félicité said. 'If you believe he knows nothing about the boys. You've done your job well. So, there's perhaps no point in seeing him any longer?' She took my arm. 'Come on, let's go and see our friends.'

We stepped back into the corridor and I felt the unease stirring inside me, the same indefinable feeling I'd had since our riverbank meeting, which had my mind flailing about in confusion. There was, naturally, the fear I'd be caught with a Boche; the risk of playing with a lethal toy. There was the danger of being caught at our cat and mouse game too. But alongside all these things I felt a kind of gentleness and longing; a desire to lose myself in him and to forget the conflicts of my humdrum farm life with Maman.

I was so consumed with thoughts of the flaxen-haired German, I didn't notice Félicité beckoning me to the window.

'Look, there's Talia.'

From the group of girls standing in a courtyard below, I picked out Talia's dark frizz. In her pleated navy skirt and sweater, with its celluloid collar attached by buttons, she looked just like all the other girls. I went to crack the window open, to call out to my little friend, but resisted the urge.

'Thankfully,' Félicité said, 'in these times of scarcity, kind mothers leave their children's outgrown uniforms at the school.'

We watched the girls divide into parallel rows, holding their arms straight out until they touched their neighbour's fingertips. They began their exercise session, soles squeaking on the paving stones with every jump, young bodies bending and straightening. The seats of knickers appeared and disappeared to the rhythm of the clapper, until the nun in charge blew her whistle and the girls fell into a double line and hurried back inside the building.

'She does look happy,' I said. 'I'm so glad.'

'She's doing well in class too,' Félicité said as I followed her down the stairs and along another sombre hallway. 'Such a bright girl, and she's painting more and more, like her father.'

The vast, shadowy kitchen stank of cabbage and rancid grease. We stood in the doorway, reluctant to disturb Sabine, dancing across the tiles. Young Jacob sat on the floor, his little head nodding up and down in rhythm to each of his mother's steps, one hand clutching the toy soldier in the red coat.

'Céleste!' Sabine wiped her hands down her apron, rushed across and threw her arms around me. 'We've missed you. How is your brother, and Olivier? And your maman? Are they all safe?'

'Maman's been released,' I said. 'The boys are still in prison, but they're alive. How are you all?'

'Your sister has the kindest soul.' Sabine's laid a hand on Félicité's forearm. 'I'm becoming quite the chef. Your mother would be proud of me.'

'I doubt Maman is ever proud of *anyone*,' I said with a snort.

Max sloped into the kitchen in a pair of blue overalls, which on such a studious man looked like some comical party costume. He gave us a hesitant smile and slumped into a chair at the table in the centre of the room.

'Papa,' Jacob said, clambering onto his lap.

Sabine placed a bowl of *café Pétain* before Max. 'And I think my husband's acquiring green fingers,' she said, squeezing his shoulder.

'What about your paintings?' I said. 'I'd love to see them.'

Max removed the rimless spectacles and wiped the lenses with his handkerchief. 'Perhaps next time, Céleste. They're not that good, really.'

Sabine gave her husband's cheek a peck. 'Don't be humble, you're a master.'

'Oh I know he is,' I said. 'And soon, after this war is over, everyone else will know it too, when they admire them in the gallery.'

'Who can assure us this war will be over soon?' Max said. 'And that nothing will have happened to us, or our helpers?' He gulped down his ersatz coffee, lifted Jacob from his lap and handed the child to his wife. 'No one! Now, I'd best get back to the garden ... can't be absent too long. Thank you for coming to see us, Céleste.'

'And I should prepare the beans and artichokes for supper,' Sabine said.

I hugged them both and kissed Jacob on the forehead.

'Give Talia a hug from me. I'll see her next time.'

'Take care, Céleste,' Sabine said.

'Thank goodness Max has his painting,' I said as my sister closed the door behind us.

'I think it's become more a crutch to him than the hobby it once was,' Félicité said. 'But he paints with such a reckless kind of frenzy these days that I'm not certain it gives him much pleasure at all. It's simply a way to escape what's going on around him and what might happen to them. As you probably noticed, he barely talks anymore. Not even to Talia.'

'I can't imagine how awful it is,' I said. 'And I know Sabine's cheerful face is nothing but a mask for the children but at least it's more comfortable here, and safer, than our attic.'

'More comfortable perhaps, Céleste, but terrifying all the same. Gestapo men were here only the day before yesterday looking for a child — a little girl of five whose parents had been deported. They couldn't account for the daughter and somebody had informed them we were hiding her here. Thankfully she had false papers and they failed to identify her.'

'But what harm could a five-year old do? And what would they've done with her?'

'What they do with them all, Céleste — send her to one of their special camps.'

'We're hearing so many rumours,' I said, 'but what really

happens in the camps?'

Félicité's eyes met mine and I noticed something odd about my sister's face — a darkness that was not hers; a shadow across the features that had always given the impression everything would be all right.

'Nobody knows for certain,' she said. 'But I'm sure we have only God to thank that our friends have not yet been sent away.'

18

On that Saturday market day, the mist obscured the Monts du Lyonnais and clung low and tight about the bare lime trees. With the shop doors closed against the cold, there were none of the usual smiling faces of Lucie's artisans, and a joyless chill hung over la place de l'Eglise. It seemed more forlorn without the chatter and laughter of Patrick, Olivier, Marc and André, lounging around the fountain. It even seemed odd without the freckle-faced Gaspard Bénédict. I longed for the day to be over; for tomorrow to come, when I could return to Montluc Prison.

'It seems we're not the only ones with so little to sell,' Maman said nodding at the other stall holders hunched beneath their tarpaulins, wearing their desperation like brands on their thready woollen coats. 'Since the German swine are requisitioning more and more food. Not to mention the disastrous harvest. The farmers are the only happy ones these days,' she went on, straightening her apron. 'People like Olivier's uncle, demanding ridiculous prices from the Germans instead of saving stocks for their own kind. I believe Ghislaine's father's playing the same game, flogging his meat on the black market.'

'Well they obviously don't have a choice,' I said. 'You do keep reminding me these are hard times, and we're all just trying to get by.'

'Still, it's not right,' Maman said, her face turning sour as she watched Rachel Abraham setting up her stall. 'Unlike us, no drought, storm or German requisition seems to affect *her*.'

'Why do you hate her? Madame Abraham is such a sweet old woman.'

'Wherever did you get that notion, Célestine? I don't despise her at all. Sweet she may be, but it just doesn't seem right, all of us suffering with the weather … this *occupation*, while she goes on making a tidy living as usual.'

'Madame Lemoulin sells antiques,' I said, unpacking the winter stocks Maman had taken to selling: her terrines, *pâtés* and *saucisson,* all made from last winter's pig. 'Of course the weather doesn't bother her.'

Maman mumbled something incomprehensible and turned to greet our first customer.

I made myself busy, serving several people, but at the first chance of a break, I sidled off to Au Cochon Tué.

The stale odour of wine and tobacco assaulted my nostrils as I entered the empty bar, which would only fill with noisy banter and cigarette smoke when the market was over.

As I reached the alcove behind the bar area, Denise Grosjean scuttled from the toilet and almost barged straight into me.

'Oh, Céleste, what are you doing here?'

'Er … what do you think?' I stared at Denise's tomato-red cheeks, and at Fritz Frankenheimer, strutting out behind her.

'Good, well have a n-nice time,' Denise stammered, swiping at clumps of hair that had fallen across her face. Fritz scuttled after her, his huge thighs and fat bottom threatening to split his breeches.

They left the bar separately and the simplest dimwit could've guessed why the German's face had the satisfied, defiant look of a fat cat purring by a stove. I shook my head, shocked at the flagrant risk Denise was obviously taking. At least I kept my "fraternising" humble and hidden.

I bolted the door, reached behind the cistern, the skip in my heartbeat surprising me as my fingers closed around the scrap of paper.

Four more days until I see you. It will seem like four years. M.

I felt a quick pulse of something I could not define and I was aware of a strange feeling growing within me; an intense mixture of fright and tenderness, something like stroking a wild animal. I flushed the bits of paper away and struggled to compose my face as I weaved my way back through people and animals.

As I approached our stall, I saw Karl Gottlob standing, with majestic ease, before my mother, as if the power of all Germany reflected on him.

I edged closer. Maman was jabbing her finger at Karl and shaking her head as if chiding him. That wouldn't surprise me, Maman giving the enemy a good telling-off as if she, rather than Karl Gottlob, were the occupier. But I couldn't catch a word, so brief was their conversation.

As I took my place beside her, Karl gave me one of his ogling looks, as if the cat-eyes were stripping my clothes from me. He marched off, empty-handed.

'I can't imagine what he'd want to buy from us,' I said, as Karl disappeared into the crowd, 'when they get all they need from stripping every home and farm in Lucie. Whatever did he want?'

'None of your concern, Célestine. Merely a … he simply wanted advice about a medical problem.'

Maman fussed about transferring our takings to her money tin, and since people were staring at us, I sensed it wasn't the moment to press her for details.

Besides, since her release from prison and Patrick's arrest, my mother had grown ever more peculiar. Always gruff and unrelenting, she'd become so distanced from me — from everyone — as if she no longer inhabited the same world. She barely spoke, going about her daily tasks with ordered efficiency until the twilight stopped her and she sank into her Napoléon III armchair and assaulted her knitting, her brow creased low over the savagely clicking needles.

The only conversations she had were with the trickle of people who climbed the hill to L'Auberge for castor oil to purge their systems, or cod-liver oil to encourage their children's growth. They came with their respiratory troubles, for her *ventouses* and leech treatments, and for the poultices she made from flax and mustard seeds. They bought bottles of her famous *eau-de-vie*, the miracle remedy she made from leftover fruit, which she claimed banished every last germ. A splash in the morning coffee for the elderly, she advised them. A drop in the ear for infections, and a dash in the children's morning milk.

The girls kept coming too. Not only young girls, but married women — mothers who, with the rising ravages of war, could barely feed their children, let alone a newcomer. There were others also, whose husbands were prisoners or voluntary workers in German camps, who didn't want to have to explain a fair-haired toddler when their spouse finally trundled home. I overheard their hushed excuses, their whispered justifications, as they made the sign of the cross and spread their trembling legs.

But still, after her arrest, and more so with the guillotining of the *faiseuse d'anges* Marie-Louise Giraud, it was hard to comprehend why Maman kept taking such a risk. Surely she could find another, legal, way to earn a living?

'Célestine!' she snapped. 'Stop your dreaming.'

I jumped to attention.

***

The bells of Saint Antoine chimed midday and as the stallholders began packing their goods back into boxes, I glimpsed Fritz Frankenheimer and Karl Gottlob marching into Monsieur Dutrottier's butcher shop. My eyes flickered across the square but there was no sign of Martin with them.

I hurried to the butcher's shop. Did Karl and Fritz know

something about Marc and the others? Or — God forbid — had someone informed them we listened to the BBC on the Dutrottier's radio?

I peeked around the doorway. The Germans were saluting Ghislaine's father with their exaggerated, almost insolent politeness. They spoke in low tones. I caught Ghislaine's eye. She gave her head a quick shake and I moved away, back out onto the square.

I kept one eye on the Dutrottier shop as I helped Maman pack up our stall. Minutes passed, and Karl and Fritz stomped from the shop. There was no sign of the radio, or of a handcuffed butcher.

'Back in a minute,' I said, hurrying away to the shop before Maman could argue.

Ghislaine was standing behind the counter counting the takings. I caught a glimpse of her father out the back, scrubbing his giant cleaver.

'Did they come about Marc?' I said.

'No, I think that's strictly Gestapo business. Someone informed those two my father is trading his meat on the black market; that he sells it at a great profit to rich city people.'

'But the Germans get enough to eat,' I said. 'Why would they want your father's meat?'

'Oh they don't want to *eat* it,' Ghislaine said. 'They want to flog it to the rich city people themselves. They'll denounce him to the authorities if he doesn't sell the lot to them from now on.' The blue eyes narrowed. 'Trading with the Lyon people was the only way poor Papa could make ends meet these days.'

'I suppose it could've been anyone,' I said. 'Informing on him. My mother keeps telling me we can't trust anyone; that people are only interested in protecting themselves and would tell the Germans anything, if it suited them.'

'Yes,' Ghislaine said. 'Times are harsh and people are doing what they have to, to get by, even if it means tattling on their friends and neighbours. I've also heard people are accepting presents from the Boche, in return for information … things about people; about our resistors. Personally, I'd rather die of starvation or cold before I accepted a single thing from any of those creepy soldiers.'

I had never given Martin the slightest speck of information, but I couldn't stem my guilty flush, or the fear that rose inside me.

'You never know what odd things people will do,' I said. 'Especially in a war … or occupation.'

'Besides,' Ghislaine went on, 'the Germans are a bunch of bores. What *could* a girl see in them? Oh yes, in the beginning we all thought of them as handsome Nordic super-warriors but now we've realised they're just a bunch of dreary, heel-clicking morons who go around snapping "Heil Hitler".'

'Oh yes,' I said, trying to keep the quiver from my voice. 'Just a bunch of old bores.' I glanced back at our stall. My mother was frowning at me, one arm held high in a beckoning gesture.

'I have to go, Ghislaine. The general is ordering me back to my post.'

As I passed Madame Abraham's stall, I almost tripped over my feet. Karl and Fritz were looming over the old woman.

'*Ihre Papiere*, madame,' Karl said, standing stiffly beside Fritz, who was fingering the antiques, turning them over and sniffing each one.

My breath snagged in my throat as Madame Abraham pulled her papers from her handbag — the papers that identified her as Madame Marguerite Lemoulin, childless widow of pure French origin.

'Stop your gawping, Célestine,' my mother called. 'It's time to go.'

I sidled back to our stall, one eye still on the Germans and Madame Abraham.

'Anyway,' Maman went on, as we packed our boxes into the trap. 'What was all that about, the flitting around and secretive muttering?'

'Nothing. It's just I … I can't keep still, or stop worrying about Patrick and the others.'

As we climbed into the trap and she gathered Gingembre's reins, I almost blurted out the firing squad sentence. Did I really want to share that burden with my mother, or was I simply yearning to provoke some sort of emotion from that seemingly soulless woman? But my promise to Père Emmanuel — not to worry her, perhaps unnecessarily — stilled my tongue.

We rode away, and I twisted back to the two Germans, still hovering about Madame Abraham, Fritz inspecting every one of the antiques, Karl frowning over her papers. Why were they taking so long?

As Gingembre clomped up the hill, I feared next time I came down to the village Madame Abraham-Lemoulin would be gone.

19

When I arrived at the Montluc Prison gates I saw some of the same women from my first visit. They must have recognised me too, as a few smiled and nodded.

'Why are you standing in the line for packages?' a woman in a tight beige skirt and matching pillbox hat asked. 'Aren't you allowed to visit your man?'

'You should go to court and insist on your rights,' another woman said.

'I'm not married to any of the prisoners, but one of them is my brother, the others are close friends.'

'Don't worry, someday all this will change,' the beige-skirted woman went on. 'The Boche swine and that Vichy mob won't always be in charge.'

'D60!' the duty guard shouted. I came forward and handed him the parcel of clean clothes and a few slices of *saucisson* from Maman's dwindling supplies. He threw me the bunch of dirty clothes.

'But …' I frowned as I started shovelling the smelly garments into my tapestry bag. 'There are only two shirts, two sets of underwear. Four socks. Where's the rest?'

The guard shrugged. 'Next!' he shouted, not giving me another look.

'There are only clothes from two men here,' I insisted.

'How should I know, girly? Move right along, others are waiting.'

I ran my quivering fingers over the collars and cuffs, and when they slid over the pills and the note, it felt as if my heart dropped to my feet.

'Where are the rest of the clothes?' I asked again.

'Look, mademoiselle, information is only given to family.'

'I *am* family. I'm one of the prisoner's sisters. Please, I have to know.'

I pulled the wrapped slices of chocolate cake from my bag — the cake made from real eggs and Maman's secret stock of chocolate — and pushed them at him.

The guard snatched the cake, let out a bored sigh and said, 'They already shot two of them, that's why ... firing squad.'

'Sh-shot?' The shock numbed me so, my words stuttered out. 'But w-why?'

'Because they were criminals. Terrorists who deserved nothing better.' He spat a gob of green-stained spit onto the pavement. 'Next!'

I lifted a grimy garment to my nose, trying to identify Patrick and Olivier's special earthy, horse scent. I smelt only crusty blood and filth, and a bitter, vinegary taste surged from my gut, up into my throat.

'Which two were shot?'

'That I can't say, girly. But what I can say is the other two are scheduled for the next line-up.'

I couldn't help myself, and grabbed the lapels of the guard's jacket.

'W-when? Tell me,' I hissed. 'I'll get you anything you want. More chocolate cake, butter, tobacco, whatever you need. Just tell me when it's going to happen.' I wanted to shake the guard long and hard, and slap his ugly face.

He shook me off with an annoyed frown, dusting down his jacket as if brushing off vermin.

'I couldn't tell you that either, girly.'

***

'Your stop, *n'est-ce pas?*' the ticket officer said. '*Hé*, you dreaming, mademoiselle?'

I hitched the bag onto my shoulder and scurried off the train. I didn't recall walking away from the prison, getting on the tram or the train trip back to Lucie. I felt like some ghostly thing gliding through the dead leaves, as if my feet were hovering above the damp ground. I had no sensation of cold or warm, or if a wind blew, or rain fell. I couldn't think or cry. I felt dead.

I headed towards la place de l'Eglise and the sound of the church bell droning into the pearly mist made me think of Père Emmanuel. He'd know what to do, or Dr. Laforge. They'd know how to find out who'd been shot, and surely they'd have a plan to try and save the others. I started running.

In my agitated haste I ran straight into Miette's mother and her two younger sisters, coming around the church corner.

'Sorry. Oh, sorry,' I said, trying to catch my breath. 'Did I hurt any of you?'

'We're all fine, Céleste,' Madame Dubois said. 'What's wrong? Is it the boys? Has something happened to them in that dreaded Montluc place?'

I shook my head, not surprised Miette's mother knew the boys were in Montluc. News moved faster than a bullet in Lucie.

'No … no, I don't know. I'm just so worried about them. Sorry, I wasn't looking where I was going.'

'We're all sick with worry for those poor boys,' she said, clicking her tongue.

'I have to go,' I said, hurrying off with a hasty wave.

I paused at the steps of Saint Antoine's, tucking my hair back under my hat. Someone was shaking my arm.

'Are you all right, Céleste? Is it your brother?' I swivelled about to Madame Abraham-Lemoulin, her blinking eyes like two brown pips from a last season's apple.

'Yes, I'm all right thank you. I've just had a bit of a shock but really don't worry about me.'

'You should go home and have a lie down,' she said. 'Ask your maman for one of her magic potions. That'll fix those chattering teeth.'

I nodded. 'Yes, thank you. I'll do that.'

'Take care, my dear,' Madame Abraham said, shuffling off towards the bakery, her shopping basket over her arm. 'We must all take great care these days.'

I started to climb the steps, a strange murmur humming in my brain. I twisted back around.

'Wait,' I called.

Madame Abraham turned back. 'What is it?'

I wanted to tell her how glad I was Karl and Fritz believed she was Marguerite Lemoulin; how pleased I was to see her still in Lucie. But I simply dropped my arm. 'It's nice to see you,' I said. 'Good day to you, Madame Lemoulin.'

'*Bonne journée* to you too, Céleste.' She smiled and waved a gnarly hand.

At least I'd learned one happy thing on that terrible day.

***

I slipped into the confessional, glanced up at the crucifix and spoke into the grid. 'Forgive me, Father for I have sinned.'

'What is it, Céleste?' Père Emmanuel said, his voice hushed.

'Two of the boys are dead. Shot. The guard wouldn't tell me which two. The others are scheduled to be shot sometime soon, I don't know exactly when. I can't bear it, Father, I have to know. We have to get them out of there!'

'I'll inform Dr. Laforge and the others, Céleste. We'll make a new plan.'

'When? When can we make a plan? There's no time to waste. We have to act now!'

'We'll meet tonight,' the priest said. 'In the cellar of Au

Cochon Tué. Use the back entrance. Behind the portrait of Marshal Pétain there's a false panel, which will give way if you push on it. That will get you down to the cellar without having to pass through the bar itself.'

***

I raised the lid on the kitchen stove. Maman had already laid the fire so I held a lighted match to the crumpled papers and interlaced twigs, and fanned the rising flame with the bellows. I placed a few pieces of coal on top and when the fire was hot, I poured boiling water into the tin washtub and threw in the prison clothing.

Whose clothes was I washing? Did they belong to Patrick, Olivier, André or Marc? The boys' destiny seemed as fragile as those houses of cards the old men of Au Cochon Tué fashioned — one small, clumsy gesture and the whole pyramid would collapse.

Stained with dried blood, streaked with dirt and crawling with lice, the garments gave off a foul stench. My stomach lurched but I had to ease my frantic mind; there was nothing more I could do to find out about the boys. So I scoured away at the stubborn stains, swiping at my cheeks where tears and sweat mingled and dribbled into the pot.

I didn't look up when my mother came into the kitchen, which I supposed was enough to tell her something was terribly wrong.

'What's happened to them, Célestine?'

My arm ached but I persisted working at a brown stain.

Maman came and hovered beside me and started fidgeting with her chignon, patting it and smoothing her hair behind her ears. Her herbally smell made me nauseous and I sidestepped away from her.

'I have a right to know what's happened to my son.'

I spun around to face her. 'They shot two of them. I don't know which ones.'

I caught my mother's strangled breath, and her eyes took on a glaze of panic as a fresh stream of tears gathered behind my eyes.

'God, let it not be Patrick and Olivier,' I said, scowling hard to calm the flow of tears. 'It's not that I want the others dead, but please, not them.' I kept plunging the garments into the steaming water — lift, plunge, lift, plunge. 'And now I have to wash these filthy clothes and go back there and try and get them out.' I couldn't stop rambling, telling her far more than I wanted.

'Get them out, you?' She let out a humourless shriek, which set my spine prickling, as if a legion of spiders were marching down my back. 'However do you propose to do such a thing?'

'You don't need to know how … only that I'm doing my best.'

Maman narrowed her mouth into its habitual, dour line. 'Sit, Célestine, I'll finish the clothes.'

I sank into a chair, turned the hourglass upside down and fixed my eyes on the trickling sand.

'Good God, armies of lice.' My mother's mouth twisted in disgust as a trail of black insects scrambled from the scalding water. 'I'll have to get them with the hot iron.'

'I'd say lice are the least of their problems, Maman.'

'If we don't want that vermin infesting our entire home, I'll have to get rid of them,' she said, as she wrung the clothes out and hung them on the line over the stove.

I kept my eyes on the moving sand. Maman removed the washing apron, clamped on a clean one and busied herself at the stove. Steam soon curled from the pan, reaching like urgent fingers for the ceiling beams.

She ladled out two bowls of carrot and chicory soup and pushed the bottle of cod-liver oil and a beaker of red wine in front of me.

'Eat. Drink,' she said, taking her place opposite me. 'We need to keep your strength up if you're to save anyone from the firing squad.'

I looked up sharply. Was that a streak of warmth; a glimmer of some primitive, long-forgotten love in a corner of her thorny green eye?

20

The same evening, under cover of autumn's early gloaming, I hurried along the alleyway behind Au Cochon Tué and slipped into a small back room via the rear doorway. I felt around the wall behind the portrait of Marshal Pétain until the false panel gave way, and squeezed through the opening into a broom cupboard. I pushed the cleaning things aside and opened another door, which gave onto a stone staircase.

Au Cochon Tué had been Lucie's bar for as long as anyone could remember, handed down through generations of Robert Perrault's family. Papa would tell me stories about his own father taking him there when he was a boy after a hard day working the wood, to gather with the other men for card games.

Besides drinking, the villagers sang and danced to piano tunes, while others tried their hand at any musical instrument someone happened to bring along. That was before the war though, when singing and dancing were allowed. But during the occupation, the Germans came to Au Cochon Tué to guzzle our wine and beer and, it was said, to entertain their city whores.

The chill settled beneath my skin as I hurried down the uneven steps. The dun candlelight outlined several figures seated on upturned crates. All around them, on makeshift shelves lining the walls, sat piles of newssheets, guns, flashlights, rope, and things that might be grenades.

I stared at my friends Ghislaine and Miette. 'What —?'

'Dr. Laforge believes my German language skills might be useful,' Miette said.

'And Papa said I could help find out about my brother and André,' Ghislaine said.

I sensed my friends were as anxious about the boys as I, so I simply nodded and sat on the empty crate beside Dr. Laforge.

'Père Emmanuel has told us everything,' the doctor said. 'We've devised another strategy.'

I stayed perched on the edge of the crate, kneading the cold from my hands, crossing and recrossing my legs. I looked around at them all, sitting there with Miette and Ghislaine: the priest and the doctor, Simon Laforge the pharmacist, Robert Perrault, Monsieur Dubois — Miette's father — and Ghislaine's father, Monsieur Dutrottier. The men fiddled with their berets, which they held between their knees.

I looked at Dr. Laforge. 'So, what are we going to do?'

'You're to return to Montluc with more clothes, Céleste.'

'Take in more clothes?' I said with a frown. 'What good —?'

'Not only clothes,' he said. 'More pills. This time we're going to make them sick with typhus. The Germans are terrified of contagious infections and will want those boys out of Montluc and into the hospital quicker than they can fire cannon.'

'It's true,' Simon Laforge said. 'The Boche do fear infectious diseases. We were inundated at the chemist when they ordered us to vaccinate all our children.'

'Besides the few who said they'd rather have a handful of sick kids,' Dr. Laforge said. 'Hoping that might scare the Fritz away.'

'But it didn't,' Monsieur Dutrottier said. 'The Germans are still here.'

'Won't they just shoot the boys as soon as they get ill?' Monsieur Dubois said. 'Why bother to send them to hospital if they're due to be executed?'

Dr. Laforge shook his head. 'If they were going to execute all of them, they'd have done so by now. They must believe the ones still alive are withholding vital Resistance information. They'll want to keep them that way to force it out of them.'

'How will you get this typhus thing?' Robert Perrault asked.

'A colleague at the *Institut Pasteur* laboratory in Lyon has a cultured specimen,' Dr. Laforge said. He leaned forward, pulling a cellophane package of *La Marquise de Sévigné* sour balls from his pocket. 'It's a form of typhus I've injected into these boiled sweets.'

'The sweets are wrapped in transparent paper,' Père Emmanuel explained, 'so the guards won't suspect they contain a message, or anything else.'

'What if your typhus makes them really sick and they die?' Ghislaine said.

'I won't let them die,' the doctor said. 'I am aware of the right dosage just to make them feverish and ill.'

'We'll have to trust the good doctor, Ghislaine,' her father said. 'Besides, as he says, what other choice have we?'

***

Dr. Laforge thought it an extra safety measure if we all attend the Au Cochon Tué *soirée*, in case the Germans spotted any of us in the back alley. The meeting over, we left separately, via the same passage through the broom cupboard.

In twos and threes, we doubled back along the alleyway and entered the bar via the front door. Beneath the copper ceiling lamp — polished by so many generations of Perraults that its original pink glow had become the pale yellow of a crescent moon — the *soirée* was in full swing. The room was awash with smoke and the smelly, greenstick odour of tobacco laced with dandelion leaves.

Maman had always forbidden me to go anywhere near the bar after dark, but she'd made no move to stop me that evening. I think she sensed it was her only chance of learning the fate of her son.

'What about curfew?' I said. 'Why do the Germans let people stay out?'

'And what of the dancing ban?' Miette said.

'My father says the Boche ignore curfew and the ban on dancing when it suits them,' Ghislaine said.

She nodded towards the group of Germans who'd sauntered in with an entourage of rouge-cheeked women — city women, I supposed. They sat down in a fug of smoke, clanging heavy guns and helmets onto the table, which crashed against their belt buckles. They were soon swilling beer and wine, and singing loudly with the joyous racket of proud people, drunk with their power over us.

Trink'mal noch ein Tröpfchen!

Ach! Susanna ...

They draped their arms casually over the shoulders of the rouge-cheeked women, who wore fur stoles and sipped drinks from cocktail glasses — the types my mother called "fallen women".

'And of course,' Ghislaine said raising her eyebrows at the whores, '*they* are allowed out after curfew every night.'

I recognised Fritz Frankenheimer and Karl Gottlob and craned my neck, looking around for Martin. Yet even if he was there, I knew I couldn't approach him, or breathe a single word in his ear.

I hadn't seen him in the village for four days and I'd begun to feel his absence as a physical ache; the same dense pang that made it hard to breathe when I thought of Patrick and Olivier.

Etienne and Simon Laforge, Bernard Dutrottier and Monsieur Dubois joined several men at a table. They were soon laughing and chatting with the other revellers as if they'd come to Au Cochon Tué for nothing more than an evening of merriment and relaxation.

'Isn't it funny to think of those Germans up here,' Miette said. 'Completely ignorant of our plans downstairs?'

'What better cover than right out in the open?' Ghislaine said.

'The stupid Nazis wouldn't think to check under their noses. And my father told me there's more going on at Au Cochon Tué the Boche don't know about,' she went on. 'He says Robert Perrault's head of a trafficking ring bringing Burgundy wine down here. Robert buys it for ten francs a bottle and sells it to the Boche for fifty-five.'

'Good for him,' I said. 'If the Germans are willing to pay ridiculous prices, all the better for us.'

We sipped our wine and stood around the piano, on which Père Emmanuel belted out Jean Lenoir's *Parlez-moi d'amour*. It seemed odd, hearing music. I heard it so rarely — the organ at Mass, trumpets and drums on Bastille Day and the Great War commemoration. Amidst the festivity of piano music, dancing couples and happy voices, I tried to forget the plight of Patrick, Olivier, Marc and André, if only for a few moments. But despite the flush of wine, it kept clamping me like the sharp cogs of a giant wheel.

Ghislaine leaned in, speaking close to our ears. 'I saw that Nazi in the post office,' she said, nodding at the Germans. 'You know, the fat one who's always with the skinny one? Anyway the fat one — I don't know his name — gave Denise a parcel.'

'Fritz Frankenheimer,' I blurted out.

'How do you know?' Miette said.

'Oh, I just heard it somewhere,' I said, my shrug casual.

'But taking parcels is Denise's job,' Miette said.

'She didn't put the package in the bin with the others,' Ghislaine said. 'I'm sure I saw her slide it into her own basket.'

'A present from this Fritz, you think?' Miette said. 'Come to think of it, I'm sure I have seen Denise wearing real nylons. And lipstick.'

I bristled again.

'Well someone told the Germans about my father selling his meat on the black market,' Ghislaine said nodding at Karl and Fritz. 'We're barely getting by now he has to sell it all to them.'

'Yes, it might be Denise,' I said, and told them about seeing her and Fritz, coming from the bar's toilet.

'And remember Uncle Claude's hay harvest?' Ghislaine said. 'Denise knew about those boys hiding on his farm to escape labour service, and then the police arrested them.'

'None of us would've denounced them,' Miette said.

'Everybody knows that girl is desperate for a man,' Ghislaine said, 'but surely she wouldn't stoop so low as to give away our secrets to the Boche?'

'And that might explain what happened to my neighbour, Madame Abraham,' Miette said, with a glance about us. 'Just this morning those same two — the fat one and the thin one — knocked on her door.'

'They didn't find out her real name, did they?' I said. 'And arrest her?'

'Well, they do know she's not Marguerite Lemoulin,' Miette said. 'But they didn't take her away. When they left, I went over. The poor woman was shaking so much she could barely speak. She said someone told the Boche about her false papers.'

'So why didn't they arrest her?' I said.

'It seems those two have taken a liking to her fine collection of antiques,' she said. 'The pieces her dead husband spent his lifetime collecting. They left with a stack of valuable items — loaded them into a wheelbarrow and just wheeled them away.'

'But they could've done that anyway,' Ghislaine said. 'And still arrested her.'

'Yes, that's what they do,' I said. 'Take what they want then round the people up.'

Miette shook her head. 'Madame Abraham told me as long as she keeps supplying the Boche with valuable items regularly, they'll say nothing about the false papers. They said they'd be back every week for new things.'

'Blackmail,' Ghislaine said, shaking her head. 'Just like Papa.'

'My mother says it's happening to other villagers too,' Miette went on. 'Someone told them the grocer's been cheating them on weights and prices. He's to pay them for their silence. She also said Monsieur Thimmonier was heard making "anti-German" remarks in church. Under the threat of arrest, they've ordered him to carve fancy wooden boxes for them to send back to Germany as presents. And my father said someone told them Raymond Bollet and René Tallon were hiding guns in their hay lofts.'

'Bastard pigs,' I said. 'Everybody knows we cheat the Boche; that people keep their guns instead of handing them in at the Town Hall.'

'All I can say,' Miette said. 'If it is Denise, she's taking a big risk for a few silly presents from an ogre like that Fritz. And if the villagers find out she's seeing a Nazi, they'll shave her head, or do what they did to Gaspard Bénédict.'

I felt my face blanch with fear and wanted to rush from the bar to hide my guilt. But I could hardly do that, so I lifted my wine glass and lowered my eyes.

I was on my third glass of wine when the motorcycle pulled up outside. I watched through the window as two people got off. The woman was still squealing in delight from the night ride, her straw-blonde hair curved into one of those low movie-star rolls. Her eyebrows were plucked into thin arches, her lips a glistening cherry butterfly of lipstick, as she gazed up into the man's eyes. The indigo eyes of a heavenly dawn.

21

They strutted inside, the woman wobbling on her heels and hanging off Martin's arm, laughing at something he said. I was too stunned to speak; too shocked to think. She shrugged out of her coat, which Martin took, and I saw she was wearing a sheer red dress and nylon stockings with a seam running up the back. They were the perfect match, both tall, slim and fine-boned, except the whore's face was covered in paint, making her look like some garish puppet, and the blonde hair was obviously dyed.

Something nasty unwound from deep in my gut; a horrible thing like a cobra uncoiling itself. It spiralled into my throat, cut off my breath, and made my head spin with the lack of air.

I gripped the side of the piano with one hand, the other clutching my glass. I didn't understand, couldn't grasp the strength of it; of how Martin Diehl had warped my feelings. And, in that instant, I hated myself. I swallowed the rest of the wine in a single gulp.

Martin hadn't seen me. Of course he'd never expect the frumpy Céleste Roussel to be at an Au Cochon Tué *soirée*. I watched from the corner of my eye as they joined the table of Germans. The bone-haired whore sat down and I caught a glimpse of her stocking top and the garter of black lace that held it.

I tried to look casual, to keep singing along with Ghislaine and Miette but my voice faltered and inside me burned a red-black rage. The bitch was still grinning, showing off her straight white teeth, one long-fingered hand draped around a wine glass. I wanted to kill her. And him.

Martin stood, took the woman by the hand and started to dance with her. He held her close, their lips almost touching. With a trembling hand, I poured more wine from the pitcher, slopping it across the table. I was vaguely aware of Ghislaine and Miette hovering about me, and of Père Emmanuel thumping out another tune on the piano.

Martin and the whore waltzed closer to the piano. He glanced up over her creamy shoulder and saw me. His eyes widened for an instant, his lips moving in a quick, hesitant twitch. Then he turned away.

I clung to the piano to stop myself marching up and slapping both Martin and his whore across the face. I wanted to scream at him, 'How could you do that to me? How could you?' I wanted to spit in the violet-blue eyes. But I couldn't let anyone notice my incomprehensible fury; the hurt that was splitting me in two, so I breathed deeply, trying to calm my speeding heart.

Martin and the whore sat back at the table where the city women were still throwing their coiffed heads back and screeching like peacocks at every word the Germans spoke.

Sweat peppered my forehead and my belly heaved. I knew I'd throw up if I didn't get out of the smoke-filled, airless room.

I left the girls around the piano and weaved through the suffocating crowd, bracing my stomach. I flung the door open and stumbled outside. I started to run, but as I reached the alleyway at the back of the bar, I bent over and vomited into a pot of dead geraniums.

I straightened, leaned against the wall and took in great gulps of air. The cold stung my cheeks and revived me a little and I lurched on, anxious to be far away from Au Cochon Tué.

The shadowy figures of a couple approached. I ducked into the alley, and made out a ribbon in flowing hair, a gleaming boot and a belt buckle. I heard the rustling of her skirts, and the man's laughter.

'How do you say that in French?' he said.

'*Je t'aime.*'

'Oh yes, *je t'aime*. How pretty.'

I started off again but a movement in the darkness stopped me. A straggly tomcat was sidling up the alley, his back arched. He raised his head and meowed a long, harsh cry. I let out a breath of relief and walked away from the cat.

Two more figures approached the alley, staggering drunkenly through the fog. Fritz Frankenheimer and Karl Gottlob. I ducked back again, cowering against the damp wall. Perhaps they'd simply pass by without noticing me.

I held my breath, which only made my head spin more.

Karl muttered something to Fritz in German and, to my horror, turned into the alley. I backed up a few paces, further into the darkness, and flattened myself against the wall. Close by, the tomcat let out a frustrated little cry of desire. I jumped, my hand flying over my heart.

Karl staggered towards me, and stopped so close I could hear his ragged breath. He farted twice, undid his trousers and pissed a long, hard flow up against the wall. The sickness rose again, and I couldn't stop myself gagging and retching.

'Who's there?' Karl said the whites of his eyes flashing as he shook off the last few drops and did up his trousers.

Certain he'd see me any second, I took my chance, shoved past him and shot from the shadows.

'*Ach, ach,*' Karl slurred, grabbing my sleeve. 'If it isn't Céleste, the farm-girl. She seems ill doesn't she, Fritz?' He looked me up and down, through the tight slits of his feline eyes. 'Poor child. Too much wine, *chérie*?

'Leave me alone,' I said. 'I'm fine.'

'You don't look fine from here,' Karl's voice grated out. 'Besides, what sort of a man would leave you here, a sick girl alone in the cold and dark?'

Fritz was nodding and grinning. 'Anyone could come along and take advantage.'

I tried to twist from Karl's grip.

'Try and run, or utter the slightest sound,' Karl hissed, 'and I'll put a shot into your dizzy head.' He pulled out his weapon and levelled it at my temple.

I cowered, one arm covering my head, the other grappling for my angel necklace. My fingers wrapped around the old bone and like a cornered animal I stayed still, mewling small, pathetic whimpers.

The blood thumped in my head, so hard I imagined my skull might explode. I was too numb to speak, watching in terror as Karl unbuttoned his trousers with one hand, the other holding the gun steady.

'Me first if you don't mind, Fritz,' he said, still in the guttural French. He pushed me to the ground and pressed his hard frame on top of me. 'Sloppy cunts are such a turn-off.'

I felt the cold barrel pressed against my head. I thought I would die with the fright. I wished he'd shoot me right then. In that instant I envied the dead.

'My pleasure,' Fritz said, his chubby cheeks stretched in a grin. 'Besides, half the fun will be watching the show.'

Karl yanked my skirt above my waist and jerked my legs wide apart. I didn't dare move or scream for help. I felt his hardness pushing against me. I clamped my buttocks tight, trying to close my legs.

Oh God no. No!

'Bit of a fighter isn't she, Fritz?' Karl said with a cackle, and I smelt his foul beer-stained breath against my cheek, and heard the clatter of his gun as it fell to the cobblestones beside us.

Another sound rapped out from the darkness. I didn't understand the German words, but I'd have recognised the voice anywhere.

Brandishing his gun in one hand, Martin yanked Karl off me with the other. He snapped more words at them, nodding at me, as he grabbed Karl's pistol from where it had fallen. He dragged him upright and pointed both guns at the two sub-officers.

Of course I still couldn't understand, but I could imagine what Martin's steely words signified.

Karl and Fritz held up their hands in a gesture of surrender, muttered something and backed away. Hanging onto each other, they lurched off into the darkness.

I was still unable to move from where I lay on the cold, damp cobbles.

'Did they hurt you?' Martin wrapped his arms around me and lifted me upright. 'Are you all right?'

'I'm fine, just a bit shaken.'

He lit two cigarettes and handed me one. My hand trembling, I took a deep drag and coughed into the fog.

'Thank you,' I said.

'I will not let anyone hurt you, Céleste. Ever.' He started smoothing my tangled hair with his long fingers.

I remembered then, and shoved him away. 'Where is she, your city whore?' I spat the words out and shifted further back. 'How could you do that? I thought it was me you loved. That's what you said.'

Martin stepped towards me. 'She is nothing. Just a stupid whore to make me look like a normal German officer. So nobody suspects us.'

'Well Karl and Fritz probably know about us now,' I said, flinging the cigarette onto the cobblestones and stamping on it.

'They know nothing,' Martin said. 'And they are drunk. They will not remember a thing tomorrow.'

I fell silent for a few seconds.

'Why should I believe you, Martin? And how did you know what was happening out here?'

'You looked ill and I saw you run outside. I came after you, to see if you were all right.'

'Where is she now, your whore?' I said, stamping off across the square.

'I do not know, or care. Come back to me, Céleste.' He caught me and took my arm with one slim hand — the hands I realised, despite my firmest will, I'd so desired. Yet all I felt was overwhelming disgust with him. And with myself.

He drew me closer, the cold buckle of his uniform pressing into the cleft below my breasts.

'Don't you dare touch me after that ... that *woman*. Just get away from me, and leave me alone.'

I moved off again, the clomp of his boots hard on the cobbles behind me.

'Please, let me walk you home, Céleste. We can talk ... discuss this, away from here, where people may see us.'

I ignored him and kept walking, and as I climbed the hill towards L'Auberge, he drew alongside me, and took my arm again.

'Stop. Talk to me,' he said. In the stream of moonlight, the elegant features seemed distorted with hurt and anguish.

I clamped my arms across my chest. 'You know, Martin, at first I suspected you'd only taken up with me in the hope of getting some sort of information —'

'Information?' he frowned. 'What information?'

'Oh I don't know ... about Resistance activities in Lucie, which I haven't a clue about.'

'You suspected me of using you?' The brow pleated in a deeper frown.

'Yes, at first. But I cast those suspicions aside, and I did come to trust you. I couldn't think of you as my enemy, as one of the foreign invaders we despise so. But now ....' I shook my head. 'I wonder if I didn't get it all wrong — all terribly wrong from the beginning. I can't believe I was that stupid, to imagine it was real.'

'Please, Céleste, you are being silly.'

'Don't "please Céleste" me! Anyway, why should I waste time caring about you? I've got more important things to worry about. My brother and Olivier might be dead.'

'What? How do you know? I mean, you are sure?'

'No, I'm not sure,' I said, and told him what the Montluc Prison guard said.

'*Mein Gott!* I am so sorry for you. Perhaps I can help?'

'Help? Why now, Martin, when you didn't help me before?'

'I had no chance before, but I might be able to organise a meeting for you with SS Obersturmführer Barbie. You could perhaps plead their cause. Though what cause, I do not know. Besides, I imagine you must want to find out which two are still living?'

'I hope to know that soon.' I hugged my arms around myself against the chill, my mind racing with Dr. Laforge's plan — our only chance to save whoever was still alive.

We walked on, and reached L'Auberge des Anges, stopping beneath the sign dangling above the wooden gateway.

'Will I see you in three days then ... at our usual place?' he said, hunkering into his greatcoat and sliding the black-gloved hands into his pockets.

'I don't know, Martin. After this I really don't know what to think.'

'I will count every minute, my love, and hope you will come.'

He strode away, the blond wisps around his cap gleaming gold in the moonlight. I kept staring down the hill long after he was gone, trying to push aside my self-loathing for letting things get so out of hand. They'd all been right to be wary of me; Céleste Roussel was not up to any sort of Resistance mission.

I knew I should heed Félicité's warning and stop everything right then. I should take a knife and gouge Martin Diehl out of my head and my heart. But it seemed he had bewitched my every thought and move, and as much as that enraged me it only made me want him more.

My clogs slid across the dew-damp cobblestones, and I imagined my sister's disappointment — no, her horror — if she discovered I'd not only lost the game, but that I'd crossed into no-man's land and fallen into the gulf of enemy love.

I trudged up the steps, the sobs swelling in my throat.

22

I stood once again in the snap of cold at the gates of Montluc Prison. After Martin's betrayal at Au Cochon Tué, Karl and Fritz's attack, and my anguish over the boys, my night had alternated between miserable sleeplessness and confused nightmares.

Beneath the eiderdown I wrestled with my agitated mind; fought my self-loathing at allowing Martin Diehl to steal my reluctant heart. I watched the moonlight shadows of semi-bare trees shifting across the wall like grotesque creatures. But beyond the hurt and anger, I was still lucid enough to realise that a co-operative German officer might be useful to the boys.

Downstairs, Maman paced the kitchen tiles, and several times I'd had the urge to pad downstairs and join her. Perhaps we could have united our concern, somehow making it more bearable, or at least given each other moral support. But the fear that we might be forced to talk for once, to lay bare our private thoughts to each other, stopped me. The very idea was bizarre.

I was so lost in my ruminating I'd have missed my turn if the woman behind hadn't nudged me.

'Get a move on, mademoiselle,' the guard said, as I handed him the parcel of clean clothes, which also contained Dr. Laforge's bag of boiled sweets. 'You're not the only one here.'

I stood back and waited for another half hour until the guard shouted, 'D60! Dirty clothes for cell D60.'

'That's for me.' I stepped forward and the guard threw me the usual bundle of stinking garments.

'And this is for you.' I slid him the tobacco rations donated by Dr. Laforge, his brother and Père Emmanuel.

'I must know,' I went on. 'Which of the prisoners in D60 are still alive?'

'I told you, girly,' he said, pocketing the tobacco. 'I don't know … don't much care either.'

'Please.' I slid him a wad of francs I'd taken from Maman's stash beneath the herbal room floorboards.

The guard slipped the money into his pocket and looked at his board, frowning as he moved his pen up and down the list. 'Let's see then. D60 was it?'

'Yes. D60.'

'Hmm,' the guard murmured. I itched to punch him in the face and snatch the board from him.

'Copeau and Dutrottier were shot.'

I reeled backwards, stumbled and fell against the line of waiting women.

'There, there, poor thing,' a woman said, holding me up. 'The shock's the worst. Is there someone who can see you home?'

I gaped at the woman, not seeing her; barely hearing her words. 'No, thank you … I'll be all right.'

I clutched my bag to my chest and hurried away from the prison, my footsteps weaving across the pavement, my mind a swarm of confusion.

As I stepped onto the Lucie-bound train, the terrible reality of it all swelled inside me. I felt it burst like a pus-laden sore. André and Marc, gone. Poor Ghislaine. Her poor father. I saw how closely they touched, grief and relief, and how fragile the line between them was. Flimsy as a skein of Maman's sewing yarn.

***

The early autumn dusk had fallen by the time I got back to Lucie, and walked across to Saint Antoine's to give Père Emmanuel the terrible news. Afterwards I used the telephone in Au Cochon Tué to call the convent. There was only a straggle of people in the bar, but still I kept my voice low.

'Patrick and Olivier are still alive,' I hissed, when Félicité came on the line.

'And you?' she said. 'You're all right?'

'I'm fine. Still working on things … on the German. I'll let you know.'

'Bless you,' she said.

I hung up, feeling the sting of guilt; the betrayal of my sister, of our cause, which clung to my shoulders like a putrid cloak. I should walk away from Martin, and never see him again. It sounded so simple. Why, then, was it beyond me?

I plodded back up to L'Auberge, perched on the hill like a giant brooding mare, and headed for the slant of light coming from the stable door. Maman was brushing Gingembre; long, repetitive strokes across the glossy chestnut coat, her knuckles white around the brush. The horse let out a soft neigh, and from the way my mother glanced up sharply I knew she'd been waiting for me.

'Patrick and Olivier are still alive,' I said.

The horse-brush clattered to the ground and her shoulders slackened.

'Thank God. And the others?'

I shook my head.

'And Madame Dutrottier dead only a year,' she said, with a final pat on Gingembre's flank. 'The poor wretch of a man.'

'Père Emmanuel has gone to see Monsieur Dutrottier and Ghislaine,' I said as we crossed the cobblestones and climbed the steps.

'Your friend too, must be stricken,' she said, hovering about me as I removed my coat and hat and snagged them on the rack in the hallway.

I sank into a chair at the kitchen table and started fidgeting with the egg timer. 'Ghislaine's lost more than a brother, André Copeau was her fiancé.'

My mother removed her apron, took a fresh one from behind the door and started rattling about at the stove.

'But your brother and Olivier are still prisoners?' she said, plunging a clutch of leeks into boiling water. 'Still going to be shot?'

'I hope to get them out before that, Maman.'

'I suppose you still won't tell me how you propose to do that?' She wiped the back of her hand across her steamy brow. 'Still refuse to tell me these secretive plans?'

'I can't discuss it with anyone. You'll just have to trust me for once.'

Neither of us said a word for a time, Maman fussing about cooking and setting the table as I stared up at the great exposed beams striping the ceiling; staring but seeing nothing except flashes of Patrick and Olivier's tortured faces, the grisly bodies of Marc and André. And Martin Diehl who, it seemed, had won our game with a single, triumphant hand of cards.

'Well it seems I have no choice,' Maman said, her wooden spoon thudding onto each plate as she dished out our meal. 'But to trust you.'

As we ate wordlessly by the muted candlelight, I thought of Patrick and Olivier again, and how precarious life had become. They might be alive now, tonight, but would they avoid the firing squad for another two days? Would they even be transferred to the Antiquaille hospital, and would Dr. Laforge's breakout strategy succeed?

23

In the fog-swamped dawn, I fed the animals, milked the goats and collected eggs as if I were a machine. All I could think of was returning to Montluc as soon as possible.

I'd spent the last two days in a fresh spiral of worry, peaks of hope plummeting to depths of despair and back again.

I almost forgot I was to see Martin again that day. As I carried the pail of water inside, his betrayal at Au Cochon Tué and the raw, horrifying shock of my feelings for him reared in my mind again. How had it all gone so wildly wrong?

I set the bucket on Maman's sleek kitchen tiles and vowed I would not go to our afternoon riverbank rendezvous. I would never see him again. Then I remembered the meeting Martin might have arranged with Obersturmführer Barbie.

'Go,' my mother said, her palm grazing my forearm. 'Quickly. And see what's happening with your brother and Olivier.' The touch of her hand on my arm felt strange; an odd prickling that snaked up to my shoulder, and around my neck. 'But be careful for God's sake, Célestine. I have enough to worry about without you getting yourself arrested too.'

I was part way down the hill, headed for Lucie's train station when the dark-clad figure of Père Emmanuel appeared.

'We have a reprieve,' he said, leaping from his bicycle. 'Our contacts at the Antiquaille sent Etienne a message. Patrick and Olivier have been transferred to the hospital.'

'Thank God,' I said, a seed of new hope sprouting. 'Shouldn't we go to the hospital now, Father, and try to get them out?'

'We must be patient, Céleste, if the breakout plan is to succeed. You'll go to the Antiquaille tomorrow with Etienne, to get acquainted with the place and our contacts.'

***

Later in the afternoon, as I wove through the screen of willows, I saw Martin was already at the riverbank. He looked smaller somehow, sitting on the big rock, huddled beneath his greatcoat in the cool, unlovely tangle of autumn. One long arm jerked out as he threw a stone across the smooth water. It dropped straight down without the slightest skim.

He swivelled around, stood, and smoothed down his coat with his palms. 'I was afraid you would not come.'

'I still don't know whether I should have.' I ignored his gloved hand on my elbow, gathered a few pebbles and skimmed them deftly across the water in quick succession.

'*Mein Gott!* Céleste, you have to believe me. The whore was only for appearances. Surely you can understand I was trying to protect us both? Anyway, what of your brother and his friends?'

'Patrick and Olivier are still alive. Thank you for asking.'

I looked away, towards the Monts du Lyonnais, the peaks invisible beneath the mist. I shivered as a rat scurried along the riverbank, its tail curling around a silvered log as it disappeared into the dead foliage.

'Say something, Céleste. Tell me you understand.'

'I don't know what to say. Why should I believe you? And what about my meeting at the Gestapo headquarters?'

'I am working on this,' he said. 'But it is no simple matter to arrange a meeting with SS Obersturmführer Barbie. Besides, what would you say to him? They have been arrested as resistors.

I am truly sorry but you have no cause to plead, Céleste.'

'I'd think of something. But I bet you haven't even tried to organise the meeting.'

He planted his hands on my shoulders and pivoted me around to face him. 'Look at me. I *am* trying. I care about you. Would I have saved you from Karl and Fritz if I didn't?'

I shrugged, still avoiding his eyes. 'Maybe, maybe not.'

'How can you doubt my feelings? How can you question what we have?'

I crossed my arms, my words puffing out in foggy snaps of air. 'What if you saw me with another man? How would you feel?'

'Come and sit with me,' he said. 'Please.' We shuffled across to a rock and I sat beside him.

'Have you heard of those cyclones that rage in the South Seas of the Pacific Ocean?'

'What have cyclones got to do with anything?' I snapped.

'These cyclones form a kind of circle,' he went on. 'The edges are made of wind and rain, but the centre remains so still even the smallest bird caught in the middle of terrible destruction is not one bit harmed.'

'So? I still don't —'

'When we are together,' he said, clasping my hands between his. 'I feel we are those birds, safe together in the middle. And when this cyclone has blown itself out, we can truly be like that. Not just in these snatched riverbank meetings, but all the time. We can be like any other couple.'

He draped an arm across my shoulder and drew me close. As much as I tried to ignore it, his familiar warmth spread through me. Perhaps I had overreacted, and the whore was only for appearances.

'When we are apart,' he went on. 'When I am filled with loneliness and desperate to see you, to feel you, I wish we could run away together.'

'Run away? Where?'

He shrugged. 'Anywhere that is far from this awful madness of war; from this Europe dripping with blood. A place where nobody would judge us for being on opposite sides. Somewhere our love would be as natural as a blooming rose.'

'You should've been a poet,' I said, unable to resist a smile. 'Instead of a soldier.'

'I have told you the army was a mistake. I would much prefer if we could all live together peacefully, instead of destroying each other.'

'That sounds odd, coming from an officer. So why are you here then, occupying Lucie?'

'You would not know this, Céleste, but long postings to occupied France are for those the Wehrmacht believe are better suited to non-combat activities — reluctant warriors. And if the truth be known, I am grateful to be here, rather than risking my life on that ghastly, blood-stained Eastern Front.'

'I'm glad you were sent here,' I said, leaning into him, breathing in his special smell. Unable to resist his potent magnetism — no longer fighting it — I closed my eyes and imagined us together every minute of the day, every second of the night, a long way from my mother and the farm. Far from this terrible war, this crazy world. After all, there was really nothing binding me to Lucie, or even France. We could go anywhere. The thought both pleased and terrified me.

'I could study at university,' I said, feeling the hardness of his gun barrel beneath the coat. 'Get a good job. Something better than a farmhand.'

'What?' he said. I heard the flick of a match and smelt the smoke.

'In the faraway place, where we'd go. I'd study at university. I don't know what. Something ... I'd think of something.'

Martin laughed and I felt the hiccup of his chest against my head. 'Ah yes. Yes, of course. We could do whatever we wanted in the faraway place. Though I cannot imagine what you would find more interesting than caring for our children ... and our home.'

My eyes snapped open. 'Children? Our home? You really mean that?'

'I am quite serious. But I fear we must wait until the war is over. I desperately want the insanity to end, and I want us to survive it. That's what is important, to survive, one day at a time.'

'All right,' I said, keeping hold of him, afraid that if I let go that solid yet so fragile thing I had with Martin would have vanished into the mist. 'We'll find the faraway place when the war's over. You'll look after our children, won't you, while I'm studying to get a good job? You know, more and more women are becoming educated these days. We want to be independent and not have to rely on our husbands for income.'

'We shall see,' he said with a small laugh. 'We will work it out when the time comes.'

'I'm sorry for not believing you about the whore.' I gazed about me, at the leafless willows, silent without their birdsong. 'I'm just mad with worry for my brother and Olivier. I'm not myself.'

'I understand. It must fill you with pain, not knowing.'

I patted the outline of his weapon. 'Can I hold it? I've never held a gun before.'

Martin ground his cigarette into the damp earth and unholstered his gun. He took my hand and placed it on the brown handle. 'It is a Luger,' he said, wrapping his hand around mine.

A thrill rippled through me as I levelled the heavy pistol. 'Is it loaded?' I squinted down the barrel, feeling, in that moment, all-powerful.

'As if I would let you loose with a loaded gun, my fiery *Spatz*.' He patted his leather holster. 'The bullets are safe, in here.'

I frowned. '*Spatz?*'

'Sparrow.'

I turned the gun over. 'How do you load it?'

'You put a magazine in the end, see here.' He indicated the

butt. 'And push until it clicks into place.'

'Then it's ready to shoot?'

'Not ready,' he said. 'You have to pull these two knobs backwards, until you see this.' He pointed to the word *geladen*. 'It means "loaded".'

'Can I have a go at firing it?'

'Not a chance,' Martin said. 'It is a deadly weapon; you have to know how to use it properly.'

'You're such a spoilsport, Martin Diehl.' I smiled, one eye still cocked over the sights. 'Oh don't worry, I wouldn't shoot *you*. I'll simply shoot every other German around. Then the war would have to be over, wouldn't it?

'Sometimes I think you would take us all on single-handed, my little *Vulkan*.' He smiled, taking the gun from me.

He sheathed the weapon and as he wrapped his arms around me, I wondered what his legs looked like beneath the starched trousers; what his hands would feel like on my bare back. He kissed me, and I tried to push my dread for Patrick and Olivier to the back of my mind, if only for that divine moment. I let my eyes close, blotting out the drab countryside and the Vionne slithering along the valley like a drugged snake.

A delicious thrill rippled through me as his fingers crept beneath the layers of my clothes. His hand moved across my breast, caressing, kneading, a warm prickle scurrying up my legs to the peak of my thighs.

My head felt light, giddy almost, and I sensed that was the moment I'd been waiting for — waiting, it seemed, since the first time I'd seen him at the market. Anything was possible. Anything at all.

I quickly snapped off the prods of guilt that stabbed at me. Details such as enemy countries and different uniforms suddenly seemed so unimportant.

Martin dragged me across to an oak tree, and pinned me against the trunk.

'We should use this,' he said, fumbling in his pocket and

pulling out a small sachet. 'We do not want a nasty accident.'

I shivered with the cold, with the feverish longing, as he lifted my dress and pushed himself between my thighs that I curled about his waist.

***

The wind flared, snapping at my bare legs but I wanted to stay like that, our flesh pressed together, feeling his heat; the kind of warmth I'd never felt before. I might have had doubts before, but I was certain Martin Diehl had seized a part of me that no one had ever reached, except in my dreams. He'd taken hold of me and turned me inside out.

I knew it was madness, what I'd done, but I had not the slightest regret. I felt only a quiet contentment, as if I'd shed my childhood like a well-worn dress to languish in the sophisticated garments of a woman. I wanted to yell it to the world but I could not even whisper it to a soul.

Martin eased himself away from me and started buttoning his clothes. 'Get dressed, Céleste, you will catch cold.'

'Yes, I suppose.' Even my own voice sounded like a stranger's, deeper and more vibrant.

'I am due some leave,' he said, threading his arms back into the greatcoat. 'I will go home. I must see if my family is all right.'

I stopped still, the chill reaching my bones. 'Yes, of course I understand you are worried. But how long will you be gone?'

'Not long. I shall be back before you know it.' He pulled a small photograph from his top pocket. 'Maybe you would like to keep this while I'm away?'

I took the photo and studied Martin's face — the snip of pale hair falling across the high forehead, the small pointed nose, the square jaw. All in perfect symmetry.

'Maybe I can give you something to remind you of me?' I said. 'I don't have any photos though.'

Martin's fingers folded around my necklace. 'I am certain this little angel is your most valuable possession?'

'Oh yes, it is. But I could never part with it, even though I think I only started wearing it to spite my mother. She couldn't bear the sight of it for some reason, and always looked at it suspiciously, like it was a bad luck charm.' I shook my head. 'As if a bit of old bone could harm you. But my grandmother always told me to take great care of it so I can pass it onto my own daughter.'

'And won't that child be my daughter too?' Martin said, his thumb and index finger rubbing the old bone. 'I understand though, if you do not trust me to take care of it.'

'I do trust you. It's just … I suppose you're right, the angel will belong to you too, in a way, when we have a family together.'

I unclasped the pendant from around my neck and held it in my palm, as if waiting for the little sculpture to send me a sign that it was all right to give it to Martin. I kissed the angel and slid it into his hand.

'I will take great care of it, Céleste.'

'I know you will. I just need to think of a reason for not wearing it … I always wear it, people will notice.' I linked my arm through his as we hurried away from the river's rising chill.

'How will you let me know when you're back?' I said. 'And what about my Gestapo meeting with this Barbie person?'

'I will write you a note explaining everything,' he said. 'In the usual place in the bar. Perhaps when I return you can show me some of your paintings?'

'Paintings?' I frowned. 'Oh yes! My paintings. But really, they're not very good. Terrible actually.' I almost laughed aloud — I wouldn't know one end of a paintbrush from the other.

At the top of the riverbank slope, where Martin had hidden his motorcycle, I unhooked my arm from his.

'See you next time, my love,' he called as he straddled the motorcycle.

I lifted my arm in a wave, inhaling a last whiff of his scent of starchy cloth and fresh apples, and watched him ride away, his hair blown back, his lean figure disappearing into the fog-warped valley.

Once he was gone, I swelled with a sense of loss. It hadn't been enough. I wanted more; wanted it never to end.

Love.

The word chimed like a child's lullaby. So this was real love. It had never felt like that before, not in the fierce loyalty for my father, brother and sister, not in the resentful affection for my mother, nor in the fondness for friends like Olivier, Ghislaine and Miette.

I felt the ache of loneliness — an empty place from where I'd mislaid some vital part of me, and wondered how I could have doubted Martin; how I could have contemplated never seeing him again.

I finally knew what love meant — understanding, caring for someone, sharing their joy and sorrow. I wanted more of it, and I bit my lip in desperation. I reasoned that whether or not you were married, losing your virtue didn't really matter as long as the person understood you — that someone you didn't have to share with anyone else.

I headed back to L'Auberge, feeling as if I'd stepped outside my normal little world into some far more exotic place. I felt I was astride a gleaming mare, riding high on the warm throb of that new love; the Céleste who loved the enemy and would be severely punished, perhaps killed, if caught. And I felt it clanging against another, cooler beat — the Céleste who was an active Resistance fighter — and it gripped me with alternating spasms of cold, lightness and fear.

***

Maman pointed her fork at me. 'Where have you been all afternoon?'

Her voice startled me from my fearful thoughts of the boys;

my tremulous thoughts of Martin Diehl.

'Just around … around the village. Nowhere.' I stabbed the fork into my *paupiette.*

'Do you take me for a fool, Célestine?' she said, the green eyes sharp and bright. 'How long did you think you could keep it from me? How long, in a place like this?'

'Keep what from you?'

'I know you sneak off to see him, your German officer. Down at the riverbank, I imagine. I saw the way you looked at him at the Harvest Festival. I can even *smell* him on you, girl.' She shuddered. 'Oh don't give me that look of yours.'

She swiped her chunk of bread across the plate in short, sharp bursts, removing every trace of gravy. 'You do know what happens to girls accused of horizontal collaboration — those *filles à Boche*?'

'I am not collaborating. I've never given him a scrap of information, ever!'

'They arrest them,' she went on, as if I hadn't spoken. 'Shave their heads and parade them to crowds who maul them.' She slid her chair back and stood over me, her arms folded across her apron. 'And don't think your German is any different.'

'He's not my Germ —'

'They're all the same. All brutes, every one of them. War, yes, we all know war is terrible. But occupation is worse. Far worse, because people get used to each other; they become friends. Much more than friends! They tell themselves the others are just like them, but they are most definitely not. We're two irreconcilable species; enemies forever. And you're a fool if you think otherwise. A silly fool of a girl.'

My mother shook her head, one side of her mouth hitching up in scorn. 'You always were such a naïve, exasperating child.'

I wanted to shout back at her and say Martin Diehl was different; that he did care about me, unlike my own mother. I wanted to tell her he loved me for myself, and had never tried to use me to discover any sort of information. And in the same breath I wanted to demand she tell me why they let her out of prison with not the slightest punishment, and why she insisted on continuing the abortions in the face of such danger. And why she had a liberal supply of real soap.

But her words, her battle-decisive accusations — the realisation that my dark secret was out — shocked me into silence. So I simply planted my elbows on the table, which she despised, and shook my head.

'Whatever happened to make you like this, Maman?'

'And tell me, Célestine, whatever did I do to deserve a daughter like you?'

The Rubie clock *tock-tocked* into the silence that followed.

Gabrielle Fontaine
Winter 1943 – 1944

24

It was still early, stripes of sunlight struggling to reach the narrow entrance of Dr. Laforge's sister's flat.

'This is, Jacqueline,' Dr. Laforge said, as his sister came to greet us. 'She teaches history at a local high school.'

'*Bonjour,* Gabrielle.' It sounded strange hearing my new name for the first time.

Jacqueline Laforge ground out her cigarette and gave my hand a brief, serious shake. She looked around thirty, ten years or so younger than her brother, and had the same heavy black eyebrows. Like the doctor's, her features were handsome, and she seemed a bit man-like with the peaked cap perched on her cropped hair and a shirt tucked into slim-waisted trousers.

Jacqueline handed me a bag. 'Here's what you'll need for your hospital mission, Gabrielle.'

My mission.

I might have swelled with my own importance if I hadn't been so impatient to see Patrick and Olivier and move along with the rescue operation.

I peered into the bag at the nurse's gown. 'Should I put this on now?'

'Not here,' Dr. Laforge said. 'You'll dress at the hospital, in the toilet. Now I'll go through the instructions with you again.'

Jacqueline led us into a cramped living room with peeling floral wallpaper and served her brother and me *café Pétain*. She poured herself a half-tumbler of red wine and waved me towards the faded sofa.

'Right,' Dr. Laforge said, taking a sip of coffee. 'The most plausible way to get them out is for some German police — fake of course — to come and demand they be taken for interrogation. But for that we need the right kind of transport, which we should have in a few days.'

'A few days?' I slumped into the sofa. 'What if they've been sent back to Montluc before then? Aren't we getting them out today?'

'Patience, Gabrielle. Our contacts at the hospital will ensure they look sick enough to remain there several more days. So today,' the doctor went on, 'you'll locate the prison section at the hospital and sketch a map, showing access to where the detainees are. Our contacts with the cars will study this map. Oh, and don't forget to be friendly with the guard outside the prisoners' room.' He swallowed another mouthful of ersatz coffee. 'Now, you've learned your new identity by heart?'

I patted my canvas bag containing the false papers. 'I know Gabrielle better than I know myself.'

'Because that's the most difficult job of all,' Jacqueline said, the eyebrows knotting like her brother's. 'The art of taking on a new identity, of assuming it so completely that every trace of your old personality is lost. You might think it's easy, Gabrielle, rather fun even, like dressing up or playing charades, but it's extremely difficult. It must be full of imperfections, because if you answer questions too quickly, too glibly, it will sound suspicious.'

'The Gestapo are shrewd, trained interrogators,' the doctor said. 'And should never be underrated. It will be mentally exhausting, living these lies day in, day out.'

'And if you get caught,' Jacqueline said. 'We can't do much to save you.'

I nodded. I didn't need to ask from what they couldn't save me.

Dr. Laforge stood and shook down his trouser legs. 'I'll be off then. You remember where to meet?'

I nodded again. 'I'll leave in five minutes, as you said.'

'*Merde*, Etienne,' Jacqueline said — the "good luck" wish.

Her brother left the flat and I swallowed the dregs of my coffee. 'Thank you for your help, Jacqueline.'

'We have to help each other,' she said, with a brief clasp of my hand. 'Until we've sent those pigs squealing back to Germany. Or got rid of them all.'

Got rid of them all.

It struck me then, and I wondered why I hadn't thought of that before. If France did win the war, they'd surely imprison Martin, or send him back to Germany. Perhaps even shoot him. The only way we could stay together was if Germany were victorious, which I certainly did not want. But I couldn't dwell on those unsettling things, I needed to concentrate on my mission.

I left the flat, reminding myself not to hurry. I breathed evenly to calm my jangling nerves as I jumped onto the trolleybus, and made the slow ascent of Fourvière hill to the Antiquaille hospital.

***

Gabrielle Fontaine's bag slung over one arm, I marched into the hospital as if I was perfectly at home. Amidst the efficient bustle of people coming and going, nobody took the slightest notice of me, and I did feel less exposed.

I found the toilet, where I emptied my pressing bladder and slipped on the white gown. I took a deep breath and walked out, making my way towards one of the general medical wards.

'*Bonjour*,' a passing nurse said, showing no sign of surprise.

'*Bonjour*,' I replied with a casual smile.

I spotted Dr. Laforge standing at the foot of one of the twenty beds of the medical ward. I strolled over and stood beside him.

'*Bonjour*, madame,' I said in my brightest voice to the elderly patient. She didn't answer. Except for the shallow rise and fall of the sheet, she looked dead.

We conferred in low tones, flicking through her medical chart, the doctor pointing out where and how everything was noted: temperature curve, date of admission, diagnosis, frequency and name of medications.

'*Au revoir*, madame,' I said, as Dr. Laforge and I moved on to another patient.

I left the ward two minutes after the doctor and headed down to the ground floor, where he'd told me they housed the sick prisoners.

I walked the length of the corridor, feeling so close to Olivier and Patrick that I could almost smell their working-day scents, and my heart beat hard.

I strode past the guard, who was slumped on a chair mid-way down the corridor. '*Bonjour*, monsieur,' I said with a pleasant nod.

He nodded back. 'Mademoiselle.'

Good, no accent. Far easier to strike up an acquaintance with a Frenchman than a German. I almost laughed aloud, at the irony.

Neither the guard nor the busy nurses paid me any attention. In these needy times for working hands, there were so many extra nurses about that nobody questioned a new face.

I could easily have poked my head around each doorway and located the boys. But I resisted the urge and limited myself, as instructed, to a single stroll up and down the corridor, eyeing the entry and exit.

***

At lunchtime I left the hospital and strolled into the city, to meet "Pierre", my male nurse contact.

Lyon was one drab bulk of greys and browns. Hunched over

in their coats, the people had a thin, haggard look about them as they hurried along the street, weaving between trolleybuses, trams, Wehrmacht vehicles and bicycles. The swastika flag flapped arrogantly from windows and everyone seemed defeated by the weather, the war and the occupation that seemed to be going on forever.

There was a comforting feeling of security amongst the crowd, with my simple excuse of being just another worker on her lunch break, yet a persistent discomfort shadowed me. Jacqueline had warned me it was easy to be followed without detecting it and, amongst many people and temptations, to forget the safety rules. She'd said that was how so many agents were caught in the big cities.

The queues outside the shops seemed longer and bleaker than the first time I'd seen them on my way to the mortuary. Clutching their precious ration coupons, the people seemed to sag like their shabby clothes and worn shoes, desperation pocking their faces.

As I stopped to cross a street, a long list of names pasted on the wall caught my eye and I almost cried out: fifteen Frenchmen and patriots who had, that very day, been shot as *terroristes* for acts of sabotage against railway lines and other structures.

I pulled my coat around me against the chill as I scanned the names of the martyrs who'd died to help rid our country of the occupier. I knew none of them but at the same time, I felt I knew them all. My heart heavy for those brave people, I crossed the street, aware that each step I took was a little more dangerous than the last.

I found the café indicated by Dr. Laforge, the sign in the window spiking another chill in me: NO DOGS. NO JEWS.

I sat at a window table and picked up a menu.

'I'll have the *coq au vin* please,' I said to the waiter. Too nervous to swallow much at breakfast, my stomach was growling.

'Sorry, mademoiselle. We have no *coq au vin*.'

I nodded to a table of Germans in the corner. 'But over there

... I can see it.'

The waiter's expressionless face didn't change. 'We have no *coq au vin*.'

I sighed and shook my head. 'The lamb then.'

'No lamb either,' he said. 'Only asparagus soup.'

'Right. I'll have the soup.' I felt the knot in my stomach tightening; the ache to eat something that didn't taste like watery cabbage.

My soup arrived as a young man in a beret strolled in and sat at the table next to mine.

He draped his coat over the back of the chair, ordered the soup and pulled out a cigarette. '*Excusez-moi*, mademoiselle,' he said. 'Can I trouble you for a light?'

'Certainly.' I pulled the box from my bag and struck a match.

Pierre bent close to me and lit his cigarette. 'Room 6,' he mumbled.

'Are they all right?'

'We're dragging it out as long as we can. You've got two days at the most.'

Pierre waved the cigarette at me as he sat back down. 'Thank you, mademoiselle.'

I nodded, and glanced over at the table of Germans in the corner. So busy enjoying their *coq au vin*, swilling it down with wine, they hadn't raised a single blond eyebrow at us.

As I finished the soup, with bread that tasted as if it was made from birdseed, I hated them even more. All of them besides one, whose precious photo I'd had to leave back at L'Auberge.

The Germans patted their stomachs and got up, retrieving their caps and overcoats. Most of them left the bar, with their cackling, throaty laughs. The two who remained started moving amongst the lunch patrons, demanding their papers.

'*Ihre Papiere bitte*,' one of them said, his pale bulk towering over me.

The hand holding my spoon began shaking, soup dribbling

across the table.

I fumbled in my bag for my identity papers and handed them to the officer. How sickening it was to have to submit to inspection by those people when all I wanted was to get on with my job.

'Name?'

'Gabrielle Fontaine.'

'Occupation?'

'Nurse.'

'Date of birth?'

'October 20, 1920.' The first part was true, at least. My false papers made me three years older. Dr. Laforge reasoned that twenty-three seemed more likely for a trained nurse.

It had been easy enough to tell my cover story convincingly but seeing the details of my masquerade set out coldly and officially in the hands of a German gave me a shock. My photograph and the fine purple etchings of my fingerprints stared at me from the printed card as if it all said, "One Big Lie".

'Why are you shaking so, mam'zelle?' he said, with a malicious grin. 'What have you got to be nervous about?'

'I'm not nervous. It's nothing. It's just …. I'm late. I need to get back to the hospital. There are patients who need me.'

'You'd better get a move on then,' he said with a sneer, handing me back my papers.

I resisted the urge to spit in his face, paid my bill and walked out of the café.

***

I spent the afternoon alone at the hospital. Dr. Laforge said it would look suspicious if we were seen together too often. There were far more visitors to the hospital in the afternoon, and fewer medical teams, and I understood why the doctor believed it would be safer to carry out the escape operation in the afternoon.

At 3.50 pm I went to the ground floor, recalling my instructions.

Shift change at four pm. Nobody there for a few minutes while they smoke a cigarette together before the new guard takes up his post. Check exactly how long post remains unmanned.

I nodded at the same guard as the morning, seated close to room 6.

'How's this assignment?' I said, in a friendly voice. 'Not too boring?'

He gave me a rueful grin. 'Could be worse.'

The man seemed pleasant enough; the type who probably had a wife and children waiting for him at home, and it was hard to accept I might have to kill him. I wasn't convinced I could murder anyone at all.

I entered room 6. Eight beds.

When I saw Patrick and Olivier's battered bodies; their skin blistered with grime, I clamped a hand over my mouth and stopped myself from rushing to them. Their blackened eyes and the smears of dried blood trailing from their noses — swollen to twice-normal size — told a tale of torture. Teeth were missing from mouths that resembled open wounds. I wanted to bundle them up right then and take them home. They managed thin, bewildered smiles as I approached.

I took Patrick's temperature, the perfect excuse to lean close to him.

'Ate th-the sw-weets,' my brother stammered. I reached for his hand, hiding it from the other patients. Though the rest of the sick prisoners, too weak from similar beatings, didn't look the least bit interested.

I squeezed Patrick's hand; it was hot and clammy. Good, the typhus was still keeping him feverish. 'We're getting you out,' I whispered. 'The day after tomorrow hopefully.'

I moved across to Olivier. 'It will be as if they're taking you both off for a Gestapo interrogation. Play your part, but don't overdo it.'

Olivier clutched my hand, a faint light shining from his dark eyes, beyond the patchwork of bruises.

I left the room, my steps brisk to mask my shaking limbs.

The guard checked his watch and nodded at me as he got up and moved off down the corridor. '*Au revoir*, mademoiselle.'

'See you tomorrow,' I called in the chirpy voice.

I entered the next room, busied myself taking more temperatures, and counting the minutes before the next duty guard took up his post.

A far-off church bell chimed four o'clock. Five minutes. That's all we'd have to get them out.

25

Dusk had already darkened the city by the time Dr.
Laforge and I left Jacqueline's flat after our debriefing.
We almost bumped into a young woman cradling a
baby, as she came in the front door.

'How's young Samuel doing, Ellie?' the doctor said, patting
the baby on the head.

'He's over his cold,' the woman said. 'Thanks to your treatment,
doctor, which I insist on paying you for, as soon as —'

Dr. Laforge waved an arm. 'Don't worry about that.' He
dropped his voice. 'I'm more concerned about you and the child,
here in Lyon. Have you thought about what I said; about new
papers?'

'Thank you, doctor,' Ellie said. 'But Samuel and I are leaving
the city shortly. I'm taking him to the countryside.'

'Well, just let Jacqueline know,' he said, 'if you change your
mind.'

She nodded and started climbing the stairs. Baby Samuel
wriggled a fist from his wrap and it bounced up and down in
the air like a little drummer's baton, in perfect rhythm to his
mother's steps.

'Can you drop me off at the convent please?' I said as we
drove off in Dr. Laforge's Traction. 'I need to let my sister know
the boys are still all right. I'll make certain nobody hears us
talking.'

Forty minutes later we pulled up at the foot of the slope from which the convent towered like a decrepit haunted mansion.

'It'll soon be gone curfew time,' he said. 'You'd best stay the night at the convent. I'll pick you up in the morning for our next shift at the Antiquaille.'

I stepped out of the car. 'Okay. Goodnight then, doctor.'

'You did well today, Gabrielle.'

'Thank you. As I told you, I'll do whatever it takes.' I waved goodbye and walked the rest of the way.

The same nun from my first visit opened the door. Without waiting for me to say anything, she ushered me inside, and it struck me that all the nuns were likely aware of the convent's illicit business of concealing people.

'Sister Marie-Félicité is in the kitchen,' she said, a hand on her beads to still them. 'I'll take you straight to her.'

I followed the rustle of her skirts down the dank hallway, past the piled-up shoe cubbies where the children stored polish, rags and brushes.

The same pale light bathed the kitchen, drenched in the stink of old cabbage and cooking fat. My sister was sitting at the table with two other nuns, sewing by candlelight. She looked up at me and lay her darning on the waxed red cloth.

She rose in a swish of black and white, and kissed me on both cheeks. 'Sit, Céleste. You look exhausted. I'll fix you something to eat and drink.'

'We'll leave you to talk with your sister,' one of the other nuns said. They both gathered up their embroidery and left the room, their coifs glinting in the candlelight.

I sank into a chair as Félicité crossed to the stove, and stood over one of the copper-handled cauldrons, her rosary beads *clack-clacking* softly as she stirred something that smelled of fish.

In hushed tones I told her about my day at the hospital.

'Nothing can go wrong,' I said, wringing my hands. 'It's our — the boys' — only chance.'

She fingered her silver cross. 'Patrick and Olivier will be all right,' she said. 'I feel it. They'll survive this war.'

I grappled about my neck, but there was only a great gap where the pendant usually sat — a space that seemed to penetrate the layers of my skin and, in that instant, I regretted leaving it with Martin.

'You're not wearing your angel?' she said, placing a plate of fish stew before me.

'I left it with … I left it at L'Auberge.' I hoped my sister didn't detect the timorous crackle in my voice; my guilt at failing my mission with the German officer.

Love for Martin Diehl had come upon me as swiftly, and unexpectedly, as a March snowstorm. My feelings defined, my doubts flushed away, I found it hard to picture myself before, in a time we'd not been in love. I wanted to tell my sister how sweet it was; to explain those moments of petrified joy when I was with him and the aching desperation when we were separated. Not to mention the relief that dreamy love gave me from my hostile days with Maman. I wanted to tell her how, finally, I felt like a human being, in control of my own life.

If only I could share my dark secret — that whole world beyond the one in which I fought to rid France of that same, hated man.

'I'm not to wear anything conspicuous; nothing to identify me as Céleste Roussel. You're to call me Gabrielle now.'

Marie-Félicité nodded. 'Very prudent.'

'How are the … the Faviers? Can I see them?'

She shook her head. 'They went to their room straight after dinner. It's like that most evenings.'

'They're all right, aren't they?'

'Bless them,' Félicité said, the beads slipping mechanically through her fingers. 'Sabine still puts on her cheery face, and dances to entertain everyone. She was obviously quite the ballerina before all this. But Max is fed up. His paintings tell the story — wild splashes of colour that don't make a lot of sense.

He's more and more fearful for his family and, of course, for us. I can tell Sabine is concerned about … about his mental state.'

'Poor man.'

'But the children are well,' she said. 'They both send you lots of kisses.'

'I'd love to see them,' I said, aligning my knife and fork on my empty plate. 'Just for a minute.'

'Jacob sleeps with his parents in their room,' she said. 'I don't like disturbing them in the evenings, but Talia sleeps in the dormitory with the other girls.' She got up. 'She might be asleep already but come on, let's see.'

I followed my sister upstairs to one of the girls' dormitories. The silence made the room seem larger, and the scant light from the single bulb left pockets of shadow over the straight rows of beds, separated by small tables. Behind the windows, between which hung a wooden crucifix, the little girls' breath floated through the air in frail gusts of vapour.

I gazed down at the sleeping Talia, her hair splayed across the pillow like the wingspan of a blackbird.

'Keep safe, my Talia,' I said, giving her a quick kiss on the forehead.

Talia screwed up her nose and turned over, but didn't wake.

'Let us all keep safe,' Félicité said, as we tiptoed from the dormitory.

26

I returned to the hospital the following morning.

'*Bonjour*, monsieur,' I said to the same guard sitting outside room 6. 'Cold out today, isn't it?'

'Touch of snow in the air, mademoiselle,' he said, patting his hip. 'So the old joints tell me.'

I saw Patrick and Olivier once more, both still feverish and horribly ill looking.

'This afternoon,' I murmured, as I took their temperatures. They answered with feeble nods, and closed their swollen eyes.

The morning crawled by. I busied myself pacing corridors and wards, glancing at patients' charts from time to time, not daring to go near the boys again. I rehearsed my part, over and over.

Afternoon finally came, and my pulse quickened when I saw one of the two stolen Wehrmacht cars enter the courtyard — a black Traction of the type the French and German police used, complete with fake license plates and German stickers on the windscreen. I recognised Pierre, my male nurse contact from the café, as the driver.

The other stolen car, an ambulance van, drove into the courtyard behind the Traction. Pierre and the three other "Gestapo" agents leapt from the two vehicles and marched into the building.

I could hardly believe it was really happening, and was

thankful there wasn't a second to dwell on what we were doing; the danger we were courting. I hurried back along the corridor to the prisoners' section.

'Must be nearly home time for you?' I said to the guard. 'I bet you'll be glad to be out of that chair?'

He checked his watch. 'Another minute and I'll be a free man, mademoiselle.' He sighed and tapped his fingertips against the barrel of his gun.

I thought of two others who, with luck, would also soon be free men.

A minute passed. The guard checked his watch again, got up and moved off down the corridor, his boots squeaking on the waxed floor.

The guard had not quite reached the exit when the fake Gestapo agents appeared in the corridor.

God help us, the rescuers had arrived a few vital seconds too soon.

The guard stopped. 'Can I help you?' he said to the "Gestapo" agents.

'The presence of two prisoners is required immediately at Montluc Prison,' one of them demanded in a German accent.

'You'll need permission from the hospital director to take any of the patients away,' the guard said.

The "Gestapo" men remained motionless, as if they didn't know what to say or do next.

'You can't just march in and take them like that,' the guard went on.

'We have orders from SS Obersturmführer Barbie,' the agent with the German accent said. 'To take two prisoners from room 6 for interrogation.'

'I told you, the hospital director must give his authorisation,' the guard repeated. 'You can't —'

Before he could finish speaking one of the "Gestapo" struck him across the head with his gun. The man crumpled to the floor.

I felt a queasy jab of pity for him, thankful to see his chest was still rising and falling.

But there wasn't a second to worry about an unconscious guard, as the agents pushed past me into room 6 and began sliding Patrick and Olivier onto the stretchers.

I stayed in the corridor keeping watch, my legs quivering so much I thought they'd give out on me. People would surely come running any second. The guard still lay on the floor, unmoving.

The agents moved out of room 6 with Patrick and Olivier on the stretchers and started hurrying back along the corridor. I ripped my hospital gown off, stuffed it into my bag and tore after them.

The agents were almost out of the entrance when the hospital director appeared, flanked by two new guards. Other staff members were also gathering around.

'*Arrêtez-vous!*' the director shouted. 'Where are you taking those prisoners?' His eyes flickered to the guard sprawled across the floor.

The new guards gripped me by the arms and sandwiched me between them. 'What's going on here, mademoiselle?'

I couldn't speak, or move. All I could do was shake my head. I couldn't stop shaking it. I could hear the director in room 6 on the telephone, signalling the breakout.

The guards kept a firm grip on me. 'Well, mademoiselle?' It felt as if my heart had stopped beating, but I remained wordless as the German-accented "Gestapo" man, with one of the others, reappeared in front of us.

A coldness froze me as, with steady hands, they raised their guns and shot both the guards in the face.

Their grips on me slackened. I shook their clinging fingers off and raced after the two fake agents, out of the building. Behind me, the shouts of the hospital director beat against my eardrums.

The ambulance van containing Patrick, Olivier, Pierre and another "agent" had already sped off. I dived into the Traction with the other two "Gestapo", the driver hurtling off before we'd shut the doors.

I barely breathed, gripping the door-handle as the car screeched out of the courtyard and onto the street. As we careened away from the hospital, I let my breath out, but my heart still banged so hard against my chest it hurt.

'Hold tight,' the driver said, as I heard the roar behind us. 'Motorcycle on our tail.'

27

The police motorcycle caught up with us in less than a minute. I kept my head bent low, not daring to glance through the rear window.

Our driver sped up as we left the narrow streets of the old district of Lyon and reached the wider road that headed westward. The motorcycle clung to our tail.

'Oh God, oh God,' I kept saying in a panicked kind of whimper.

The two "Gestapo" agents didn't say a word but the driver's knuckles blanched as he gripped the steering wheel.

I stole a quick glance behind. The motorcycle was pulling out into the middle of the road to overtake us. So close it was, I could see the determination in the rider's eyes. He drew level with us, then his eyes widened for less than a second as an oncoming van slammed head-on into the motorcycle.

I shrieked, the blood pulsing hard in my head, as our vehicle swerved to avoid the van. I snatched only a glimpse of the horrific smash littering the road behind.

'That got rid of him, at least,' the German-accented agent said with a smirk.

As we continued west, towards the Monts du Lyonnais, passing through familiar villages, I took in great gulps of air. I was still unable to utter a single word. We were soon driving through the autumn golds and crimsons of the foothills, violet fringes of heather lapping the slopes. We passed the Julien-sur-Vionne turn-off, then the road that led to Lucie, and when we'd climbed the hill to the village of Saint Martin-en-Haut, the driver veered off onto a dirt track.

'You know why this is a good place to hide people?' the driver said to me.

I shook my head. 'No idea.'

'Because the Boche absolutely hate driving up hills. They avoid coming here at all costs. Stupid pigs.'

The men laughed as the Traction bumped along the rutted track and I thought of how Marie-Félicité's convent, too, stood on a hill.

We stopped in front of a small, tumbledown farm at the end of the stony, isolated track. I recognised Dr. Laforge's car parked beside a chestnut tree. The ambulance van was there too, Pierre and the other fake agents unloading the stretchers and carrying Patrick and Olivier inside.

I leapt from the Traction as Père Emmanuel, Dr. Laforge and Jacqueline appeared from the cottage with a man and a woman. From the man's blue overalls, and the woman's apron, it was obvious they were the farmer and his wife.

'Well done, Gabrielle,' Dr. Laforge said. 'Good work, everybody.'

'This is my brother, Georges,' Père Emmanuel said, introducing the farmer. 'And his wife, Perrine.'

'Come in, quickly,' Perrine said, taking my arm and ushering me up the crumbling porch steps. 'You look fagged out. What a time you must've had.'

'I'm all right, thank you,' I said. 'I'd just like to see the boys … to take care of them.'

I followed the woman into a dim hallway, leaving the others murmuring outside with the agents.

Perrine lit a candle and I saw we were in the kitchen, the stove set into a blackened hearth, the pots and skillets dangling from racks above the low cupboards, much like Maman's at

L'Auberge.

'They're in the living room,' Perrine said as she added a shovelful of charcoal to the stove and placed a wide cauldron on top. 'Why don't you go through and bring me their clothes? I'll put them in to soak while you tend their wounds.' She started filling the cauldron with water.

My brother's smile revealed a mouthful of broken teeth as he turned his face to Olivier. 'Can you believe it … what my sister just did?'

'Best resistor around these parts,' Olivier said.

'Oh I know that.' My casual shrug masked the surge of pride I felt as I began cleansing their wounds. 'And you're to call me Gabrielle Fontaine now.'

Olivier smiled. 'Gabrielle. It suits you … very heroine-ish.'

I could tell the boys were trying not to wince or cry out as I peeled away their grimy, bloodstained garments and for the next few minutes I filled them in on the news. I told them about Maman and her release from prison. Reluctant to worry them more than necessary, I didn't voice my suspicions as to why she was released so easily, and how she was carrying on the angel-making as usual, with real soap. I could hardly believe it myself. The very thought of my mother with a German was vulgar.

'The Boche took Maman's pig and some hens,' I said. 'So there'll be no pork next year. And someone from Lucie is giving the Germans information about the villagers, who they then blackmail. Ghislaine, Miette and I have our suspicions, but no proof … yet.'

'So much for patriotism,' Patrick said. 'While we're risking our lives, all some people think about is what they can get out of this occupation; taking their cut from those Nazi bastards.'

Nazi bastards.

It struck me then, was Martin a Nazi? I'd never thought about it. I only knew that, kneeling beside my heroes, Patrick and Olivier, I wanted to beat Martin's image from my mind; to snap the threads of those two conflicting strands that stretched my nerves so tightly I feared something inside me would snap. How could I truly dedicate myself to our Resistance while Martin Diehl was hanging off every one of my thoughts? How could I be certain never to reveal the tiniest morsel of confidential information — unconsciously perhaps — in a moment of unthinking desire?

The talk of collaboration reminded me of Gaspard Bénédict but when I told Patrick and Olivier about his beating and how he lay, brain-dead, in his mother's back room, they barely flinched.

'Traitors get what they deserve,' Patrick said, his words a bitter whisper.

'Many of the prisoners talked,' Olivier said. 'Couldn't cope with the torture, and told the barbarians what they wanted. But we never did.'

'Because we knew they'd shoot us whether we spoke or not,' Patrick said.

My brother and Olivier may not have revealed their secrets to the Gestapo, but as I continued dabbing their wounds with warm water, I sensed those brutes had broken something inside them. They'd stolen their youth; their *joie de vivre*.

'How's Ghislaine ... and her father?' Olivier said.

'Not good,' I said. 'Père Emmanuel says Bernard Dutrottier's a broken man. He doesn't speak anymore. And he's had to close the shop. Two of the Boche found out he was selling his meat on the black market, so now he has to sell it all to them. There's none left over for the villagers, or for his family.'

'Bastard pigs,' Olivier said with a groan as he shifted to his other side. I tried not to flinch at the whip marks criss-crossing his back.

'And the family?' he said. 'They're in a safe place?'

'As safe as possible.'

'Nowhere is safe these days,' Patrick said.

'There's more and more talk of this Allied invasion coming to save us,' Olivier said.

'Well I wish they'd hurry,' I said as I continued cleaning

the wounds. 'Now don't speak too much. Save your energy to recover.'

'Yeah, so we can go back out and shoot their ugly Boche arses,' Patrick said.

'Go back out?' I said. 'You're surely not …?'

'You know we can't return to Lucie,' Patrick said. 'Or L'Auberge. Besides do you want to live the rest of your life under the rule of those pigs?'

'Of course I don't, Patrick. That's what I was trying to tell you both from the beginning. I need to fight too.'

'I thought your job was finding out if the Boche officer knows about us?'

'He doesn't know a thing,' I said, swivelling about to hide my flushed cheeks. 'I'm sure of that.'

'We're joining the Maquis,' Olivier said. 'Père Emmanuel's brother — Georges' group. We'll be staying on here in Saint Martin-en-Haut.'

'The Maquis,' I said. 'Yes, I've heard about them.'

'At first,' Olivier said, 'they were just men running off into the hills to avoid compulsory labour serv —'

'Unlike our father,' Patrick said, with a bitter twist of his lip.

'But now they're highly-organised Resistance groups,' Olivier went on.

'That's dangerous work.' I dabbed their wounds with antiseptic. 'Living out in the hills … the cold, the threat of informants. Not to mention the Nazi reprisals — punishing the villagers — for Maquis sabotages.'

'Georges and Perrine will watch out for us,' Olivier said. 'Three of their five boys are prisoners-of-war; they're dedicated to helping the Maquisards.'

'They seem lovely,' I said. 'I didn't know Père Emmanuel had a brother. It's strange to imagine him with a real family, you know …'

'You understand we won't be able to have any contact with you, Maman or anyone else,' Patrick said.

'No contact at all?'

'We'll send messages when we can,' Olivier said, pressing a palm to my arm. 'Through our contacts. You understand why we have to keep fighting?'

'Yes … yes I do, but it seems I've only just got you both back. Back from the dead!'

The SS might have beaten the boyish, carefree joy from Patrick and Olivier, but something entirely different had awoken from the darkness of those savage beatings — a passionate, almost feral urge to fight for us; to risk their lives for what they believed in. It was a strength I realised, that Martin Diehl no longer possessed — a quality he'd perhaps never had, even before he became disillusioned with the war. For a fleeting instant the German officer struck me as a weakling who lacked the fierce dedication of Patrick and Olivier.

I swatted those unsettling thoughts aside as Perrine appeared with bowls of vegetable soup. She handed one to me, knelt beside my brother and began spoon-feeding him.

'Be a good boy now,' I said, holding the spoon to Olivier's swollen lips. 'Drink up your soup.'

'*Oui*, Maman Gabrielle,' he said with a small grin, and swallowed the warm liquid.

Sitting by Olivier's side, gripped with the same kind of maternal protection I felt for Talia and Jacob Wolf, I sensed the change that had come over us both. The gleeful children who'd jibed, teased and swum together were gone. Age, war and the occupation had transformed us, and I knew things could never be the same.

***

I left Patrick and Olivier sleeping and took the soup bowls back to the kitchen. Our "Gestapo" agents finished their coffee and, with nods all round, they got up and drove away into the bruised dusk light. Apart from Pierre, I hadn't learned their names, and suspected I never would.

'Coffee, Gabrielle?' Perrine said. She pushed aside the already long scarf she was knitting and crossed to the stove.

I sat at the table with the others. 'Who were they, the fake agents?'

'Members of our group,' Jacqueline said, lighting a Gauloise. 'The one with the German accent is from Luxembourg. He ran away from forced German military service; deserted the beloved Führer. As you can imagine, he's quite useful to us.'

'And the one who looks like Pierre,' Dr. Laforge said. 'Is codenamed Antoine. He and Pierre are law students at the Université Lyon 2. They work there as cleaners in return for free lectures.'

'The Boche killed three of Pierre's brothers and two of Antoine's,' Jacqueline said, cigarette smoke streaming from her nostrils.

'We need to let my mother and my sister know the boys are safe,' I said to Dr. Laforge.

'Père Emmanuel and I are going back to Lucie now,' the doctor said. 'I'll call in at L'Auberge … on the pretext of a medical visit.'

'I'll telephone your sister,' Père Emmanuel said. 'Best you stay away from L'Auberge for a while. The police will be like ants, crawling all over the farm looking for Patrick and Olivier. And while they can't connect the girl who lives there to Gabrielle Fontaine, it's better to be safe.'

Dr. Laforge and Père Emmanuel drove off too, and Georges plugged the cork into his wine bottle.

'*Bonne nuit*, ladies.' The old farmer lifted his arm in a wave and turned to climb the stairs. 'Sleep in peace.'

I was weary beyond exhaustion but knew I was too charged up to sleep, so I left Jacqueline in the kitchen with Perrine, and the scarves and socks she was knitting for her prisoner-of-war sons.

I slipped outside and stood on the porch, my arms clamped

across my chest against the cold. I couldn't help feeling a surge of pride. The boys were safe. Despite the Martin Diehl dilemma, I'd proved myself a worthy Resistance fighter. Nobody could treat me as silly, rash or hot-tempered.

The door creaked open and Jacqueline came to stand beside me. She pulled her pack of Gauloise from her pocket, lit two cigarettes and handed one to me. She took a few deep drags and laid a large masculine hand on my shoulder.

'What would you think about coming to stay at my flat in Lyon?' she said. 'To continue working with our group?'

I couldn't resist a smile. 'I'd like that very much, Jacqueline.'

'Right,' she said, in her no-nonsense tone, 'it's settled then. You should get some sleep now. It's been a long day.' She patted my shoulder, the manly hand lingering, then slipping away.

'I'll be in soon,' I said, breathing in the sweet night air. 'It's just so peaceful out here, after … after today.'

Jacqueline nodded and flicked her cigarette butt into the frosty darkness. It fizzed on the damp ground and she disappeared inside. I stared out into the quiet night, and up at the amber cloud obscuring the moon. The sky was clearer, away from the city, the stars blinking at me like the eyes of a thousand, protective gods. The scent of cow dung, rotting leaves and moist earth filled my nostrils. Familiar, safe smells.

I hooked my arms around myself, hugging my elbows, and thought of L'Auberge. I'd been bursting to get away, but once gone, those comforting scents seemed to call me home. Nobody could connect Céleste Roussel to an Antiquaille nurse who'd helped break out two prisoners, but Père Emmanuel was right and I should stay away for a time. Besides, Martin being away on leave certainly doused any urge to rush back to Lucie.

A lick of wind shifted the cloud from the moon, and the ivory face peered down at me from the blackness. The soft light streaming onto my face, I felt the anguish of the past weeks seeping from me.

I had no idea what would happen to Patrick and Olivier —

and to me — from then on. And what of my future with Martin? That too, was foggy. But after such a harrowing day, all I could think of was the bliss of sleeping in peace for the first time in weeks.

***

Jacqueline and I stayed with Georges and Perrine four more days, nursing the boys back to health. Besides the farmer and his wife, we didn't see another soul. On the fifth day, when Dr. Laforge came to take us back to Lyon, Patrick and Olivier were up and walking, their wounds healing, all traces of the typhus infection gone.

I walked down the porch steps, and across the grass that was knee-deep in a milky mist, to meet him.

'All is well at L'Auberge,' he said. 'As Père Emmanuel predicted, the Gestapo went there, searching for your brother and Olivier.'

I imagined Maman, pottering along with her business as usual, certain she wouldn't get away with it a second time.

'I managed to see your mother before they got there,' Dr. Laforge said, as if reading my thoughts. 'She was prepared for their arrival.'

'And my sister knows the boys are safe?'

The doctor nodded.

'Thank you,' I said. 'Thank you for everything. Félicité must've been frantic with worry. But I'd still like to see her. And the Faviers.'

'Once the Gestapo discover Patrick Roussel has a sister at the convent, they'll be all over Valeria, looking for him and Olivier.'

'So I shouldn't go to the convent?'

'You certainly shouldn't go as Sister Marie-Félicité's sibling, or anywhere else as Céleste Roussel right now, for that matter.'

'Couldn't I be at the convent as Gabrielle Fontaine?' I said. 'Vaccinating the students or something? You know how much the Germans fear contagious diseases, ordering all the children to be vaccinated, and I'd really like to see my sister.'

'Yes, that sounds like the perfect alibi,' he said with a nod. 'Put your hospital uniform back on. You'll be at the convent as Nurse Gabrielle Fontaine, immunising the students against diphtheria. I'll come back for you after I've dropped Jacqueline at the flat.'

Georges and Perrine came outside with Patrick and Olivier to see us off. My throat clenched at the thought of leaving that haven.

'You've been so kind and generous,' I said to the farmer and his wife. 'Thank you.'

'Our pleasure, mademoiselle,' Georges said. 'We'll do whatever it takes to drive the enemy out and bring our sons home, where they belong.'

Perrine kissed me on each cheek. 'Keep safe, Gabrielle.'

I turned to my brother and Olivier. 'I can't believe I won't see you for so long. Promise you'll take care.'

'You too, Agent Fontaine,' Patrick said, and I saw the vein ticking in his temple as he kissed both my cheeks.

'See you soon, Gabrielle,' Olivier said. 'As soon as we've beaten the lederhosen off those Boche.' He placed a palm on either side of my face and kissed me on the mouth.

I was startled but didn't pull away. And I didn't want him to stop.

28

I sat in the convent kitchen, jiggling Jacob up and down on my lap. He pumped his little hands together in glee as his mother glided, swan-like, across the tiled floor. Félicité and another sister sat beside us humming a tune, while a third sister strummed a battered guitar. We were so enchanted with Sabine's graceful dancing that we barely noticed the car doors slamming outside.

Before we had a chance to react, to move or run anywhere, the great oak door flew open and the hallway was rattling with the noise of boots and snappy French voices.

The humming stopped. The nun flung the illicit guitar behind a wide cauldron. Sabine stood still, her eyes growing wide. 'What shall we do?'

Félicité patted her arm. 'Madame Favier's papers are in order. You have nothing to fear.'

Sabine shrugged my sister's arm off, pulled Jacob from my lap and ran out the back door towards the garden. Félicité and I did not budge from our chairs, and I noticed my sister's hands turn white, as she gripped the table edge.

Four militiamen, revolvers in hand, burst into the kitchen. 'Where is the Mother Superior? We'd like a word with her.'

'Please, take a seat,' Félicité said. 'I will bring our Reverend Mother to you.'

Still cradling their guns, the militiamen all rose and dipped their heads as the Reverend Mother Madeleine-Louise swept into the kitchen.

'How may I help you, sirs?' the Reverend Mother said.

'We've been informed that a relative of one of your sisters — Sister Marie-Félicité — has recently escaped custody, Reverend Mother,' the militiaman said. 'We simply wondered if the man and his accomplice might have taken refuge here.'

The other three stood, legs apart, their eyes darting about as if they might glimpse the fugitives dashing off into dark corners.

'We also have reason to believe,' the boss militiaman said, 'you're hiding Yids here.'

'I would never permit such a thing, sir,' the Reverend Mother said. 'We're all good citizens here and respect the laws of Marshal Pétain. But if you wish to search the school, one of my teachers will be happy to escort you.' She nodded at my sister.

Félicité stepped forward. 'Certainly, and I am Sister Marie-Félicité. Come with me, sirs,' she said, one arm outstretched, inviting them to follow.

From beneath his wide beret, the one who seemed to be in charge frowned as I rose from my chair. 'What's this nurse doing here?'

'Nurse Gabrielle Fontaine, sir,' I said, automatically handing him my papers. 'Here to vaccinate the students against diphtheria.'

'So what are you doing in the kitchen, mademoiselle, instead of jabbing needles into children?'

'I was just saying hello to the nuns,' I said, 'before I start work.'

I was getting so good at lying, my voice betrayed not the slightest quiver.

'The girls' health is our concern,' the Reverend Mother said as the man examined my identity papers. 'We want them to grow into healthy young women; strong childbearing women. Just as our Vichy government desires.'

'All seems to be in order, mademoiselle,' he said, handing my papers back. He waved his gun at Félicité. 'Now, let's visit your pupils. You three,' he barked to the others, 'check the grounds, the dormitories, the cupboards. No stone left unturned.'

He followed Félicité along the hallway, his boots clomping on the worn parquet. I scuttled along behind, at a distance.

My sister knocked on the first classroom door and opened it.

'Please.' She gestured the militiaman into the room, but remained in the doorway, more like a queen than a nun, in her long gown and the coif that concealed every last dark hair strand. My sister certainly did not resemble any kind of Resistance fighter.

I stayed behind Félicité, peering around her, through the open doorway. I couldn't let Talia see me and risk her calling me "Céleste".

The girls looked up, startled. The nun, who had been writing on the blackboard, stiffened, holding the chalk in mid-air as all the students rose to their feet.

'Sit down, girls,' the militiaman said in a friendly tone. 'Don't let me disturb you,' he said to the nun. 'I only want to know if any of your pupils are better at Yiddish than French.'

From where I was standing in the corridor, I couldn't see the whole classroom but I could picture Talia's pale, frightened face.

The girls stared wide-eyed at the man's revolver as he toyed with it casually, the stamp of his boots on the floorboards falling silent as he stopped at each new desk. Nobody uttered a sound as he flipped the books open to the first page with the butt of his gun, and checked the name.

After several minutes of tense silence, he tucked his revolver into his belt, clicked his heels, turned and marched from the room.

I breathed easily, certain I saw my sister's shoulders slump in relief.

Once Félicité had escorted the man back down the hallway

and out the front door, I allowed myself a relieved smile. The Wolfs — the Faviers — were safe.

I stood beside Félicité, watching through a crack in the curtains as the militiaman strode back towards the waiting cars. He'd almost reached the convent entrance when two of his men appeared from the direction of the chapel.

'You might want to see this, sir,' one of them cried.

My eyes darted to my sister, whose hands flew to her rosary beads. A shadow distorted her serene features as we watched the two men drag a load of guns, grenades and clandestine newspapers from the chapel.

The one in charge hurried back to us and flung the door open again. Mother Superior came from the kitchen into the hallway.

'So, this is your idea of abiding by the laws of Marshal Pétain, Reverend Mother?' he said, jabbing his gun at the illegal items. 'Though I suppose you're all in on the nasty little secret.' His pitiless eyes roved around the circle of frightened nuns who'd gathered in the hallway. 'Hiding clandestine articles, weapons and ammunition?'

'Nobody else knows anything about those things,' Félicité said, stepping forward. 'It's entirely my doing.'

My head started to spin and I felt giddy; confused. How could she take all the blame when the other nuns, as well as the Mother Superior, must surely be aware of the cache in the chapel? Félicité would never have acted alone, putting the lives of others in danger.

For several, terrifying moments, the militiaman said nothing, his eyes straying across the wide-eyed faces of the nuns.

'You'll both come with us,' he said, taking Félicité and the Reverend Mother by the arm.

I wanted to scream out, to tell him to let her go; that my sister was a good, godly person and didn't deserve that. But she threw me a guarded look and I stopped myself rushing to her side. The two men hustled Félicité and the Reverend Mother outside.

The last militiaman appeared around a corner of the building, gripping Max by the shoulder. Sabine, with little Jacob in her arms, skittered along behind them.

The blood cut through my veins, cold and sharp as ice chips. I wasn't the least bit religious, but I feared only some divine miracle could save the Wolfs.

'Tells me his name is Favier, sir. Says they're pure French. Him and his wife and kid.'

'And?' the one in charge said, looking Max and Sabine up and down as if appraising cattle at a fair.

Jacob started to cry and buried his face in his mother's neck.

'But when I asked the good Monsieur Favier to unbutton his trousers, I saw different - saw they were about as pure French as the great Führer himself!'

Sabine threw him a look crusted with more hatred than I could ever have imagined in such a sweet person. Max hung his head and said nothing, his breath fogging the spectacles.

'The gardener and the cook, eh?' The boss militiaman said, still clutching Félicité. 'I suppose this is your doing too?'

'Monsieur and Madame Favier have done nothing wrong,' she said. 'Please leave them. Just take me, sir.'

'But we have orders to round them all up,' he said. 'All those wearing the yellow star and all those who *should* be.' His mouth twisted in a nasty smirk at Max and Sabine.

As they started shoving Max, Sabine, Jacob, my sister and the Mother Superior towards the cars, Talia rushed from the building.

Oh God no. No!

I felt my insides shear apart with the pain.

'Maman! Papa! Where are you taking them?'

'Ha, another one.' He gripped Talia's arm. 'Any more, sister?'

Félicité shook her head.

'Where are you taking us?' Talia shouted. 'Leave us alone, we haven't done anything wrong!'

'Hush, *chérie*,' her mother said. 'Just do what they say, everything will be all right.'

Max gave his wife a miserable, defeated stare.

'No, I don't want to leave,' Talia went on. 'I can't miss school; I'll get behind in my lessons.'

'You won't need your lessons where you're going, miss,' the man said with a grotesque grin. 'Come along now, stop making trouble.'

Talia threw the nuns a last wild look, as they stood motionless on the cobblestones, mumbling Hail Marys into their beads.

Stilled with the shock, the disbelief, I watched the militia bundle them all into the two cars and slam the doors.

As they drove away, the fog thickened, dropping over the convent; closing in like a stage curtain on the final act.

***

I had no idea how long I stayed in the courtyard. I didn't know where else to go, or what to do.

By the time I forced myself to move, all the nuns had disappeared. The fog, thick and clingy as wax, magnified the sound of my wooden shoes on the uneven cobbles, and against the milky sky the skeletal tree branches looked even more bedraggled.

Some unexplained force propelled me towards the chapel. Perhaps, instinctively, I thought it was a place I might feel my sister's presence.

Once inside, I inhaled the smells of stale incense and candle wax. With its high ceiling and damp stone walls, the chapel was even colder than the rest of the building.

I shivered, hesitating before the altar, regretting for the first time in my life I didn't believe in any of it; that in my desperate hour, I had nowhere to turn. I knelt hastily and crossed myself as I'd seen Félicité — Sister Marie-Félicité — do, so many times. As if, in that brief foreign gesture, she would still be with me.

It wasn't my sister's fault our parents loved her more than

me; that she wasn't born a sickly blue infant. I might be proud of my recent Resistance success, but I would never have the good, selfless blood that flowed through Félicité's veins.

The pain of her absence tore into me like a winter gale, and I shuddered at the sight of Jesus on the cross, the plain cloth knotted about his loins; the bare legs, one straight, the other bent, and the nail piercing the pink feet. I felt for my pendant, missing it more than ever.

From the great abyss of grief, I recognised that as the unexplained — perhaps imaginary — powers of the talisman gave me comfort and strength, my sister gained the same force from the effigy of Christ. Even as the blood, dripping dark from the nailed feet, simply made my stomach churn, I felt great respect for my sister's beliefs.

I slumped into one of the pews, wondering how I could help Félicité and the Wolfs, wherever they'd taken them. But I knew that alone I was powerless.

I rubbed my frozen arms as I hurried back to the main building and out to the small room Max and Sabine had shared with Jacob. I packed up the brushes and paints and rolled Max's paintings into a thick scroll. They would be safe at L'Auberge behind the false panel in the attic.

I picked up the phone and called Jacqueline's flat, then I sat, quite still, in the dim kitchen and waited for Dr. Laforge to return.

29

Rattling with the cold, still numb with the shock, I climbed into Dr. Laforge's car.

'Sorry to keep you waiting,' he said. 'I've been trying to find out where they took them.'

'Did you find out anything?'

The doctor's eyebrows tightened into the single thick line. 'Unfortunately, they took the Wolf family straight to the train station. They've been sent to Drancy.'

'Drancy?'

'It's a suburb of Paris. A holding centre for prisoners, Jews, resistors — anyone the Germans consider a "terrorist" — before deporting them to the camps.'

'Could I go to this Drancy place?' I said. 'Maybe try to see … to help them, somehow?'

'I know you mean well, Céleste, but I'm sorry, you'd never be allowed to see them.'

'But surely, just a quick visit. I mean, we did break Patrick and Olivier out …'

Dr. Laforge shook his head. 'Not a chance. And you going off on some wild goose chase to Drancy would simply be a waste of time and our precious funds.'

'You're right, I suppose. But I'd use my own money.' I fell silent for a minute, thoughts streaming through my mind. 'And Félicité? You haven't said anything about her?'

'Apparently they took your sister and the Reverend Mother straight to the Gestapo headquarters in Avenue Berthelot.'

I gripped the door handle. 'Oh God, no!'

'With that cache of arms in the chapel, they're convinced the nuns are withholding Resistance information, or hiding terrorists, namely your brother and Olivier. The Gestapo are questioning them right now. Then they'll transfer them to Montluc Prison, for daily interrogation. I'm so sorry.'

My hand flew across my heart. 'The same torture that almost killed my brother and Olivier.' As Dr. Laforge took a wide corner, my head started to spin. I teetered on the brink of throwing up, and swallowed hard. 'What can we do?'

The doctor shook his head. 'Not much, I'm afraid. I do have one idea though.'

'What?'

'Jacqueline told me you've accepted her offer to live at her flat and continue our work,' he said. 'What would you think about a position with the Red Cross as a nurse in the Montluc Infirmary?'

'Me, a nurse?'

'As you know from the Antiquaille, people are desperate for any willing hands in times of war,' he said. 'The Red Cross is a respected organisation, even with the Germans, and we have people who could get you a position there; give you the necessary training. It would be a good cover to pass on Jacqueline's messages to our contacts,' he said. 'And it may be your only chance of seeing your sister.'

'When do I start?'

'Tonight,' he said, turning off the main road towards fog-shrouded Lucie-sur-Vionne. 'I just need to pay a few house calls to some sick patients. I'll be about an hour. Then we'll go back to the city.' He pulled up on la place de l'Eglise, quiet and deserted in the misty twilight.

'And I've informed Père Emmanuel about the arrests. He's gone to let Claude know his nephew is safe, then he'll head up to the farm to tell your mother about your sister. And to let her know you won't be home for some time. Remember, you mustn't go anywhere near L'Auberge just yet, Céleste.'

'I remember,' I said as I got out of the car. 'Anyway, I need to see Ghislaine.'

***

As I crossed the square to Ghislaine's home, I took a detour via Au Cochon Tué bar. No note from Martin. He mustn't have been able to organise the meeting with Obersturmführer Barbie before he left for Germany. Not that I needed it anymore, I'd just hankered after his words, to touch the paper he'd held. More than ever, I chafed for his warm love.

Once in Lyon, when it was safe to return to L'Auberge, I would slip home from time to time and check if Martin was back. I couldn't imagine what reason I would give him about living in the city, but I would think of something.

I read the sign in the window of Monsieur Dutrottier's butcher shop: Closed Until Further Notice, and felt the anger boil up inside me.

When Ghislaine opened the door, neither of us said a word. What was there to say for the death of a brother, and a fiancé? I circled her in my arms and felt her heaving shoulders against mine; her quiet sobs.

'I'm so sorry,' I said, tears blistering my own eyes. 'I don't know what to say ... how to help.'

'Just you being here helps,' Ghislaine said. 'Besides, they did warn us it was treacherous work. Now we know just how treacherous.'

I followed her through to the kitchen, from where I glimpsed her father in the living room. His back turned to me, Monsieur Dutrottier was seated in a rocking chair, his shoulders bent over, a blanket spread across his legs. He looked like an old demented person, staring out the window at nothing. He didn't turn, or say anything as I sat with Ghislaine at the kitchen table.

'Poor man,' I said. 'Shouldn't I go to him? Say something?'

Ghislaine shook her head. 'It would only remind him Marc is dead, while your brother is alive.'

'You're probably right.'

'But I'm so glad you saved them, Céleste. Père Emmanuel told me. You're very brave.'

'I only did what anyone would have. You'd have done the same,' I said, and told her about the terrible arrests of my sister and the Wolfs.

'Dr. Laforge says it's a waste of time to rush off to this Drancy place, but I feel so useless staying here, not doing a single thing to try and help them.'

I laid my hand on Ghislaine's forearm. 'But that's not the only reason I came. I wanted to say sorry for … for what happened to André and Marc, and I wanted to tell you something; something I can't say to anyone else, but I've always trusted you with all — well most — of my secrets.'

'Tell me what, Céleste?'

'I'm leaving Lucie, to go and work with the Resistance in Lyon. Properly I mean, not our half-baked village efforts. Dr. Laforge is arranging everything.'

'I understand,' she said, her eyes glistening. 'I'd have done anything to save Marc and André. And of course, I won't breathe a word.'

'I know you won't.'

'My father's shop's closed now,' Ghislaine said. 'I no longer have work here in Lucie, or anything much to do. And as you can see,' she said, with a bitter nod towards the living room. 'My father's a sick man. He still won't speak; doesn't even recognise me sometimes. My aunt — his sister — is coming from Auvergne tomorrow, to take care of him.'

She gestured at the chair creaking rhythmically into the tragedy-tinged silence. 'I can't bear to sit here and watch him slide towards the grave a little more each day. I have to do something.'

Her hands bunched into fists, Ghislaine pressed them into her belly, kneading and twisting as if trying to unravel a hard knot.

'Before you came — just now — I didn't know what,' she went on, the blue eyes filling with a rage I'd never seen before. 'But now I do. I'm coming with you to Lyon.'

30

'You'll be just fine in a few days,' I said to the prisoner, his face twisting in pain as I gently scraped off the dead skin.

I was thankful I was wearing a mask to hide my grimace and my gagging at the foul rust-coloured discharge from the prisoner's wound. The first three toes of one foot were black, edged in a mustardy-yellow from which dead skin sloughed off, while the fourth toe was a swollen, navy hue and I knew it too would soon blacken and die. After only one day as a nurse at the Montluc Prison Infirmary, I recognised the terrible sight and smell of gangrene.

Jacqueline Laforge had quickly found false papers for Ghislaine, codename Lucie, which I was certain neither of us would forget. Another Red Cross Resistance nurse from the Montluc Infirmary trained us in a day, our willing hands only too welcome in such desperate times.

'Thank you, dear,' the man said with a weak smile. 'You're a great comfort to us, you good Red Cross people.'

I dressed his foot as best I could with our scant supplies but I knew that type of infection was beyond any treatment a novice nurse could provide. He would soon lapse into shock and coma. The wretched man would be dead within days. The SS only insisted we keep him alive as they were convinced he was concealing vital information.

I left the desperately-ill man to rest and moved across to Ghislaine, who was dabbing antiseptic onto the facial wounds of another prisoner.

'That should feel better,' she said with a comforting pat on his arm.

The man grabbed Ghislaine's hand and held onto it. While the prisoners' stomachs craved food, their bodies craved the touch of friendly human hands.

'Thank you, mademoiselle,' he said, finally releasing her hand. He shuffled out of the Infirmary, where a guard was waiting to return him to his cell.

'Everything all right?' I whispered to Ghislaine, with a glance at the armed sentry, visible through the open doorway.

'It's so frustrating, isn't it?' Ghislaine murmured, resting the back of her hand against her brow. 'When all we can do is offer a bit of antiseptic and a few soothing words, knowing our work will be undone as soon as those SS bullies torture them again.'

'The doc warned us it wouldn't be easy.'

Ghislaine's hands shook as she wrung them. 'Yes I know, but I still don't see how you'll manage to get to the women's section,' she said with another nervous glance at the guard. 'You know he won't leave his post for a second, or ever let us out of here.'

'I'll find a way.'

'Duties will be carried out in silence!' the sentry shouted as our next patient shuffled in, a scarlet trickle from a gash staining one cheek.

'Lie down, we'll take care of you,' I said, and began to bathe the fresh wound.

'Bless you,' he said, as I slid our copy of the underground newspaper — *Combat* — within his view.

I kept one eye on the guard as the prisoner quickly scanned the newspaper, containing mainly articles criticising the actions of the Vichy government, Nazism and collaboration.

'Thank you, mademoiselle,' he said, shuffling off to return to his cell, where he would pass on the precious information he'd gleaned about what was truly happening in the war.

Ghislaine and I worked together to plaster a man's arm, which the SS had twisted and broken.

'Sorry, it's a bit messy,' I said, the mixture slopping over the floor and our white aprons. 'It's our first plaster.'

'I'm sure you'll do a great job,' the prisoner said, his eyes scanning the articles of another underground paper — *Libération* — I'd slid beneath his gaze. His arm in an untidy sling, also our first, he thanked us and left as the bell sounded midday.

Lunch break, and my only chance to catch a glimpse of Félicité; perhaps a hurried word.

***

As Ghislaine — Lucie — and I stood in the dining area ladling out soup to long lines of haggard prisoners, I scanned the room for my sister.

'Thank you, dear,' one man said with a small smile. 'This German soup isn't too bad. Shame the Boche are so stupid, spoiling it with all that cumin. At least it's better than their other one, though.' His mouth twisted in a grimace. 'Tastes like bitter almonds.'

'Nothing like the good Red Cross evening soup, eh?' the next prisoner said, with a weary wink. 'At least you get something in the water — a potato, a carrot, maybe a leek.'

'Prisoners will cease to speak!' the guard snapped, standing stiffly beside the queue. 'Or you'll be back in the cells with nothing at all in your miserable bellies.'

My eyes kept skittering across the desperate faces. None of them was Félicité.

'She must be here somewhere.'

'We'll keep looking,' Ghislaine muttered, as we continued spooning out the stipulated half-litre of soup into bowls marked with *Secours National* and *La Croix-Rouge*.

'Just the sight of that insignia alone is a comfort,' another prisoner said to us as he moved off.

By the end of lunchtime I was certain my sister had not been in the eating area.

'Maybe they're keeping her locked up like they do some of the prisoners?' Ghislaine said. 'Giving her soup in her cell?'

I shuddered at the image of Félicité beaten and lying on some cockroach-infested straw mattress.

***

'I don't know about you, but I'm exhausted,' Ghislaine said, as we left the sour stench of Montluc Prison after our first gruelling day. There had been no news, or sight, of Félicité.

'Not too tired to come to the station with me, I hope? I want to see if I can get a ticket to Drancy. I can't bear the idea of not doing a single thing to try and help the Wolfs. Of course, I wouldn't think of using our funds though, I've got enough of my own money.'

'Isn't it dangerous to go near the holding camps?' Ghislaine said, as we squeezed onto the crowded trolleybus. 'They might throw you in there too. But I suppose if you insist, we could go and see.'

Amidst the crowd at the Perrache railway station, I glimpsed flashes of the Germans' almond-green uniforms amidst the drab garments of the Lyonnais people.

'Let's find the ticket-office,' I shouted over the screech of axles and the hiss of steam. I took her arm and we fought our way through the cursing, crushing throng.

'You must be joking, mademoiselle?' the man said, when I asked for a ticket that would get me to the Drancy holding camp. 'Why ever would you want to go there?

'My friends are being held in the camp,' I said. 'I must try and see them.'

The ticket man shook his head. 'They don't let visitors in,' he said. 'Ever. You'd be wasting your time and money, mademoiselle.'

Ghislaine touched my elbow. 'It would be silly to go chasing off to Drancy for nothing. Let's go home.'

'All I want is to try and help them,' I said, clutching Ghislaine's arm as we made our way out of the ticket-office. 'I didn't get to see my sister and it seems I won't get to see the Wolfs either.'

As we started walking away from the station, a jumble of suitcases and bundles on a siding caught my eye.

'What are all those things?' I looked about us. 'Nobody seems to be guarding them, or the least bit worried about them sitting out there in the open.'

'I'm amazed someone hasn't already made off with them,' Ghislaine said as we took tentative steps towards the pile.

Many of the suitcases gaped open, the contents spilled out onto the tracks in a muddle of dirty clothes, single shoes, books, a child's doll — its china face cracked and grit-stained. The bags and items littered the ground over a wide area, surely many more things than from one single trainload of people. Much of it was sodden and flattened, as if it had been sitting there for days.

'Who do all these things belong to?' Ghislaine said.

I shook my head as we kept walking amongst the mess, trying not to step on anything. 'I have no idea, but I can't imagine any little girl abandoning her doll.'

In the lamplight, a flash of something bright caught my eye. I looked closer, bent down and plucked it from the debris. It was a little wooden soldier, with a red coat. The face of the toy was crushed, almost split in two, as if a careless heel had trampled on it.

It was a little newer-looking, and larger than the soldier Papa had carved for Patrick, but my fingers tightened around the figure as I lifted it to my chest. With my other hand, I groped about for my angel pendant. There was nothing, only a great, gaping emptiness where it normally sat. But, as if it were still around my neck, the leather cord seemed to tighten, so much that I felt it was strangling me.

I gulped in breaths of air, one hand grappling with that invisible choker, the other still clutching the soldier with the red coat.

My tears came, dripping silently onto the pile of abandoned belongings, and the first snow fell, light and soft as a ballerina's step.

31

The frigid north wind tugged at my flimsy coat as we headed back to Jacqueline's flat in the old district, the grief, the bitter disappointment, tearing at my heart.

A group of German soldiers swaggered along the pavement towards us, laughing loudly.

'*Pon-soir*, mam'zelles,' one of them said with a lecherous grin. 'Care to share a drink with us? Warm yourselves on such a cold evening?'

'No, thank you,' I said.

'It seems those pigs have truly made themselves at home here,' Ghislaine said, as they sauntered away.

'Be careful,' I hissed. 'They'll hear you.'

'The Boche control everything now,' Ghislaine said later, as we got off the trolleybus and continued the rest of the way on foot. 'Traffic, food, newspapers, movies, the French police. I just wonder what will be left of our city once the war is over. '

'At least we have the Red Cross *laissez-passer*,' I said. 'They can't stop us going out at night, when we have to.'

'I'll do whatever it takes to get rid of those murderers,' she said, and even in the dim streetlight I could see the determination in her eyes glinting a steely blue.

'Don't forget what Dr. Laforge says,' I said. 'The Germans can afford to pay informers well. Trust nobody. Say nothing.'

As we climbed the steps to Jacqueline's flat, I saw the same woman, clutching her infant son. The girl's eyes grew wide and she held the boy closer.

'What a sweet baby,' Ghislaine said. 'A boy or a girl?'

'H-his name's S-samuel,' Ellie stammered.

'The doctor's our friend, Ellie,' I said. 'I heard you tell him you were leaving Lyon, going to a safe place?'

'It's dangerous for you here,' Ghislaine said. 'They're rounding up more and more of your people.'

'I'm taking Samuel to the countryside as soon as I … when I can get the money for our train tickets,' Ellie said. 'But thank you for your concern.'

'Take care, Ellie,' I said as she scuttled off up the stairs.

'Poor girl,' Ghislaine said. 'How humiliating to have to wear a stupid star, and to live in terror of their roundups. Nazi Bastards.'

'But the doctor is right,' I said. 'She should leave now; it's only a matter of time before they catch up with her.'

I thought of Max and Sabine, Talia and Jacob in Drancy, or perhaps already in Poland or Germany. I hated thinking of them in some harsh labour camp, working through the frozen German winter. I hoped they would give them enough to eat at least, and clothes to keep them warm.

***

Ghislaine looked as startled as I was, to see Miette Dubois at Jacqueline's flat.

'What are you doing here?' Ghislaine said. 'Has something happened in Lucie?'

'My father told me where you'd both gone,' Miette said, with her usual bright smile. 'I convinced him, and Dr. Laforge, that my German language skills could be useful here in the city. His sister got me papers; I'll be working as a courier.'

'Of course,' Ghislaine said with a smirk, as we hooked our

coats on the rack. 'The Boche would never suspect such a sweet, innocent face.'

'How was it at the prison?' Miette said. 'I suppose you'd have said if …'

I shook my head. 'Nothing. No sign of my sister.'

She laid a hand over mine. 'I hope you get to see her soon.'

In the cramped living room where Ghislaine and I — and now Miette, I supposed — shared the sofa bed, we peeled our white caps off, our aprons and blue blouses.

'I love your new look,' Miette said, admiring our other "uniform" — trousers and a shirt like Jacqueline's, with a forage cap for outdoors.

'Jacqueline believes if we dress like men,' I said, 'it will give women the power to live like them; to gain the same respect as men.'

'She says we need to be free of men,' Ghislaine said, tucking her shirt into her trousers. 'And that we should liberate ourselves from the bonds of this country's old-fashioned Catholic government.'

Miette laughed. 'It reminds me of you as a kid, Cél — Gabrielle, climbing trees and playing cowboys and Indians with Olivier and your brother. Just like another boy.'

Olivier's cheeky grin flashed into my head, and I felt his lips pressed against mine. How impressed he'd be, to see me like that. Patrick too. Maybe even Maman would finally be proud of me.

'Yes, it was fun,' I said with a nostalgic smile. 'But I'm not that kid anymore.'

No, I was Gabrielle Fontaine now, free of the restraints and flaws that had tied Céleste Roussel to her monotonous, uneventful existence. Yet a part of me still pined for the old life.

'I know it's too soon for any word from the boys,' I said, as we squeezed around Jacqueline's table. 'They've only been gone a few days, but I can't stop thinking about them.'

'Try not to worry too much,' Miette said, patting my arm. 'I'm sure they'll be careful.'

'Eat quickly, girls,' Jacqueline said in her no-nonsense manner, swallowing mouthfuls of red wine between picking the stones out of the bowl of lentils. 'Pierre and Antoine will be over shortly to pick up the news-sheets for tomorrow's distribution. You'll take some too,' she said, pointing her fork at Miette, 'and I'll take the rest to my school. The more people we get word out to, the better.'

'Thank you for preparing a nice dinner, Jacqueline,' Miette said, passing me the Jerusalem artichokes and rutabagas. 'And for having all of us here, crowding out your flat.'

'Dinner was pretty awful,' Jacqueline said with a snort. 'It all tastes the same — of the grease we're forced to cook with, instead of real butter.' She pushed her plate aside, lit a Gauloise and flanked one leg across the other. I couldn't help smiling at her man-like gestures.

'At least we have food,' Miette said.

After our pumpkin compote and custard dessert, Ghislaine and I washed up while Jacqueline and Miette set up the printing press.

Jacqueline lifted the piano lid and sat on the stool. She started playing as Miette fed paper into the press, Ghislaine turned the handle and I collected up the single sheets, silently reading the printed words:

Each sabotaged piece, every working minute lost, saves a human life. A fault in the machine — a tool, an unscrewed nut, a pinhole in a food tin — hastens the German defeat.

'Sorry, no more paper,' Miette said, as Pierre's coded knock tapped on the door.

'I don't know how much longer we're going to be able to keep this up,' Jacqueline said, closing the piano lid. 'With supplies so severely rationed now. I suppose we'll have to pay some exorbitant price for newsprint on the black market. Or steal it.'

Pierre and Antoine nodded at us wordlessly as they each began wrapping half the pile of pamphlets around their calves.

'Do you want coffee?' Jacqueline said.

Pierre shook his head of straggly hair as he pulled his socks back up over the papers. 'I timed the German patrol. We've only got five minutes before they're back in this street.'

'Be safe,' we all whispered, our words escaping in puffs of vapour as the boys slipped away into the icy night.

We were about to collapse onto the sofa bed when we heard another knock — Dr. Laforge's distinctive six-knock code.

The doctor strode in, rubbing his gloved hands together. He looked straight at me. 'I'm sorry to bring bad news, but your sister has been deported.'

'Deported?' Queasy waves fluttered deep in my belly. I gripped Ghislaine's arm. 'Where?

'She left last night,' he said, as Miette came and held my other arm. 'On a train bound for a place called Ravensbrück. I believe they've sent Madame Wolf and her children there too. I have no information about the father though.'

'Ravensbrück?' I said. 'Where's that?'

'It's in Germany,' Miette said.

'Yes,' Dr. Laforge said. 'A *Reich* prison. I'm so sorry.'

'If it's just a prison,' I went on, still confused, 'why didn't they simply leave Félicité at Montluc? Why bother sending her all the way to Germany? I don't understand.'

32

Ghislaine and I exchanged nervous glances as Pierre set the thick leather-bound book on Jacqueline's kitchen table. He took a ruler and carefully cut out a square chunk of most of the pages.

'You look tired,' I said to Antoine. He didn't look especially tired, I just wanted to talk — anything to calm my jangling nerves. Miette, who I could always count on for a comforting chat, was away on an overnight courier job.

Antoine said nothing, his eyes fixed on the book as Pierre placed the bottom half of a small box into the cut-out square, into which he laid three sticks of dynamite. With steady, practised fingers, he connected the wires to the battery and set the clock.

By day, Ghislaine and I continued our nursing work at Montluc Prison which, with the endless raids and massive arrests of Resistance members, was bursting with prisoners. So far, our night-time work had involved letting down Nazi truck tyres and pasting news-sheets to the walls of telephone boxes, public urinals and *métro* tunnels, printed with such slogans as: *vive le Général de Gaulle* and *nous sommes pour le Général de Gaulle*. But tonight they'd assigned us our first real job, and I sensed Ghislaine was as nervous as I was.

Pierre closed the book. 'All clear with the address, your instructions?'

'We're ready,' I said, carefully placing the book in my classy leather bag.

'*Merde* then, girls,' Pierre said, and we left Jacqueline's flat, the wintry December air freezing on our cheeks.

Snow fell lightly, mixing with city grit, as our high heels slipped about on the cobblestones. A few people hurried by, men in overcoats, women in coats with the wool hoods pulled up, all anxious to be home before curfew. We walked in silence, passing people huddled in doorways, shivering.

It was a week since Dr. Laforge told us they'd sent Marie-Félicité to Ravensbrück, but I still hadn't found out anything about the place. Nobody seemed to have heard of it. The thought then struck me — surely Martin would know about it. I'd been back to Lucie only once, when Dr. Laforge gave me the all clear, but there was no message in Au Cochon Tué. I was certain Martin would be back any day though. As we hurried on through the old district of Lyon, I felt a pulse of warmth, and hope, at the thought of seeing him again.

With people home for curfew, the cold streets had fallen quiet, the snarls of two fighting cats the only sounds piercing the darkness.

We rounded a corner, almost colliding with a group of officers in black uniform. My eyes leapt to their symbol gleaming in the lamplight — a sideways Z with a vertical line through the middle: the wolf's hook, or Wolfsangel. Despite the Renaissance buildings around us clinging to their timeless French aristocratic air, that sinister insignia of the *Reich*'s SS only shouted the message louder: our city was truly under the enemy's heel.

The SS men passed us with curt, polite nods and we veered off down another dimly lit street. We'd only walked a few steps when Ghislaine stopped in the angle of an iron staircase zigzagging down a sooty wall. She pointed down into the shadows.

'What's that?'

I took her arm. 'It looks like people, lying on the ground.'

Our steps hesitant, we walked over.

'Oh God!' I gripped Ghislaine's arm tighter.

We stood motionless, staring in horror at the two corpses, and the surprised looks on their faces, flung back in the agony of death. Blood had leaked from the gaping slashes across their throats, staining the surrounding snow patches the colour of rust.

There was no martyr's halo glowing about their blood-matted hair, no medals pinned to their still chests, only the rats that had come to gnaw at their bodies, cast aside like rubbish.

'These two,' Ghislaine said, hacking her words into the freezing air, 'are why we're doing this tonight. And for all the others those monsters have murdered.'

A church bell chimed eight-thirty. 'Come on,' I said, 'there's nothing we can do for them now and if we don't hurry, we could end up with our throats slashed too.'

We finally reached rue de la Charité. Distracted as I was, searching for the street number, I didn't notice the two French police officers come upon us.

'And where might two lovely ladies be going on such a vile night?' one of them said, running his eyes over our made-up faces, our fur-lined coats, the nylons and high heels.

'We're invited to a book launch,' I said, as we handed them our papers, along with our Red Cross *laissez-passer*.

I tried to keep still, acutely aware of the explosive secreted in my bag, the precious seconds ticking away. I was sure they could hear the slow, dull thud of my rebel heart.

'Mmn, Red Cross nurses,' he said. 'Take care out at night on your own,' the first one said, his smile showing bad teeth. 'It's dangerous for young ladies on these streets.'

'*Oui*, monsieur,' we both said with winning smiles as they walked off.

A little further along, I pointed across the street to the bookshop. 'There it is, Librairie Voltaire.'

Ghislaine and I retreated into the shadows of a bombed building, which had a good view of Librairie Voltaire. As Jacqueline had predicted, the shop was brimming with Germans, for the launch of some book one of them had written — spouting a fountain of hateful Nazi propaganda, no doubt.

We watched the crowd of Germans, their uniforms a sickly green in the amber light, and the city women hanging off their arms, decked out in their tight-fitting suits, platform shoes and coquettish hats perched on wavy hair rolls. Elegant hands clutching fake crocodile purses, slender fingers wrapped around glasses filled with champagne, they grinned and laughed at everything the Germans said.

'How can they do that?' Ghislaine hissed. 'Sleep with the enemy?'

'Stupid whores,' I said, thankful of the darkness to mask my burning cheeks.

'You wouldn't catch me with one of those filthy Boche for all the money in Munich.'

'God, me neither,' I said. 'Anyway, we don't care about them. I should go now. Ready?'

Ghislaine nodded, her eyes peeled for patrolling police as I crossed the street, my stride jaunty in my society clothes.

I waited for a group of guests to enter the bookshop and tagged along with them. Once inside, I mingled and smiled at people, and eyed the table displaying a collection of books. Soft music played and I moved between the people to the table, on which the German's new book sat.

As other people were doing, I picked up different books — *Devant L'Opinion, Philippe Pétain, Les Décombres* — flicking through each one. I glanced at my watch. Five minutes.

When I was certain nobody was watching, I pulled the leather-bound volume from my bag, slid it beneath the book I was holding and placed them, one on top of the other, on the table.

I didn't realise I'd been holding my breath until, as I turned to walk out of the shop, it gushed from me.

I'd almost made it to the door when a German officer stopped me.

'*Bonsoir*, mam'zelle. May I see your invitation?'

I groped in my bag, my hands starting to shake as I caught a glimpse of my watch. Three minutes.

'Oh dear,' I said with a coy smile. 'I must have left it at home.'

'Sorry, mam'zelle, invitation only.'

'Oh well,' I said, my voice level, flippant even. 'I'll just have to go back and get it.'

'You do that,' he said with a leer. 'And hurry back, I'll be waiting for you.'

I hurried out of the bookshop, almost stumbling on the high heels to get away, across the street.

Once back in the shadows of the bombed building, I grabbed Ghislaine's arm. 'They wanted to see my invitation.'

'*Merde!* We didn't plan on that. But did you get the book on the table?'

'Of course I did. Now let's get out of here.'

A minute later, as we turned off rue de la Charité, a great boom and the sound of smashing glass broke the quiet of the night. The sound of sirens soon followed and, in the streetlight, I saw Ghislaine's blue eyes glazed with excitement, and venom.

As we hurried back to the old district of Lyon, I understood that look on Ghislaine's face. I saw how the occupation had changed us; how the Resistance had brought together people from every level of society and turned us all — from the aristocrat to the simple farm-girl — into counterfeiters, thieves and murderers.

It was a strange thing to realise how effortlessly I had become Gabrielle Fontaine the killer, helping rid my country of its enemy. It felt almost as if some human part of me had disappeared; vanished into the winter air that stiffened my face. Once the war was over, would I still be the same cool killer — a girl I barely knew, but one of whom I felt proud?

***

Jacqueline opened the door to our coded knocks. 'Come in and get warm,' she said, giving us one of her rare smiles.

'Great job, girls,' Dr. Laforge said, already seated at Jacqueline's table, a whole salami, three different goat's cheeses and a bottle of Juliénas wine in front of him.

'What a feast,' Ghislaine said, slotting between Miette and me.

'Though naturally,' Dr. Laforge said, filling our glasses with wine, 'there will be reprisals. And tonight's success doesn't mean we can forget those less fortunate — those arrested, tortured and gunned down.'

'But all that,' Ghislaine said, 'and those hideous cattle trains, where they don't even allow the people to take their suitcases, only makes me more determined.'

Dr. Laforge swallowed a mouthful of the heavenly wine. 'Don't let your emotions cloud your judgement, Lucie.'

'Still no news of your sister?' Miette said.

I shook my head. 'Not a word. And I still don't know a thing about Ravensbrück.'

'We never seem to get news of *any* deportees,' Ghislaine said. 'People like Gabrielle's sister, and her father.'

'They took Papa for labour service back in February,' I said. 'And we've not heard a word since July. Six months ago!'

'It does seem strange that not one person we know of,' Miette said, 'has received a single one of those pre-printed postcards listing every possible situation: so and so is in good health/ slightly/seriously ill/wounded/deceased.'

'Apparently a few messages have reached families of Resistance members,' Dr. Laforge said. 'But it's true, the Jews do seem to be shrouded in the strangest silence. We know the police are relentlessly tracking down the last ones in the city.' He waved an arm upstairs, in the direction of Ellie Kohen's flat.

'Why doesn't she just leave, right now?' Miette said.

'I got the feeling she doesn't have the money for the tickets,' I said.

'Why didn't you say so?' Dr. Laforge said. He slapped his napkin onto the table, got up and strode out of the flat.

'You'd think we'd have heard something on the BBC at least,' Ghislaine said, as I listened to the thud of the doctor's feet climbing the stairs to Ellie's flat. 'Surely some information would be filtered out of the camps? I mean, a few people have escaped.'

'Perhaps the BBC doesn't have any information,' Jacqueline said, draining her wine glass. 'Or maybe those high up in the network have reasons to hide or conceal certain things. This is war and nobody can be trusted.'

'I'm afraid only God alone really knows what goes on in the camps, Miette said.

'I've never heard of jailers inhuman enough to forbid the sending and receiving of mail,' I said.

'And why hasn't the Red Cross intervened?' Ghislaine said. 'Surely they would?'

'Speaking about the Red Cross —' Dr. Laforge said, as he came back inside.

'Did you see Ellie?' Jacqueline said.

The doctor shook his head. 'Nobody home.'

'Maybe she's already left the city?' I said. 'Or … Oh, it's so unjust. Poor Ellie, and that sweet baby boy.'

The doctor cleared his throat and looked at Ghislaine and me. 'As I was about to say, you two have been at Montluc for some time now. It's not safe to stay in a job for too long. If people see the same faces for any length of time they get suspicious; start asking questions and delving deeper into backgrounds … especially after tonight.'

'But we feel useful there,' I said.

'You would also be useful working at Perrache train station,' the doctor said. 'Supplying the needy passengers with food. And, of course, distributing news-sheets and delivering messages.'

'That's a good idea!' I said, excited, for a fleeting instant, at the notion of prisoners arriving home for Christmas by train.

But even as I blurted the words out, I acknowledged they were simply the naïve dreams of desperation.

Dr. Laforge glanced sharply at his sister. Jacqueline puffed away on her Gauloise, refusing to meet my eyes.

'I don't want to dampen your spirits,' the doctor said. 'But I doubt any of your family will be home for the festive season.'

'Oh I know. I know,' I said with a flick of my hand, tears smarting my eyes. 'I just hoped … I was only dreaming.'

33

Early on Christmas Eve afternoon, Ghislaine, Miette and I pushed our way onto the train crammed with people not only in the compartments, but also in the corridors and between cars. Even in the toilets.

Hordes of them were traipsing out to the countryside, even more so at Christmas time, to buy black market food from the farmers; commodities that were so scant in Lyon.

We sat on our bags in the corridor as the train rattled out of town, towards Lucie. I was glad I was small, as I observed the man scrunched up beside me, his tall frame bent almost in half, someone else's head resting on his feet.

Exhausted from the past arduous days at Montluc Infirmary, and the nightmare images of Patrick, Olivier, Félicité and the Wolfs that visited my restless nights on Jacqueline's sofa bed, I closed my eyes and laid my head against the grimy wall. I'd barely had a moment to think of seeing Martin again, and I patted the spot where the angel necklace usually lay and let him meander about my mind. What would I say to him?

I missed you. No, too ordinary.

I love you. Pfft, that's what everyone says. I would more likely ask him about Ravensbrück, and what the hell went on there.

Remorse surged through me again. I should not be dreaming of Martin; I should be thinking of the Wolf family and my sister, and Patrick and Olivier freezing on some isolated mountainside, living in constant fear of Boche bullets.

It seemed that when my mind lingered on Martin, the guilt wracked me, but if I pushed him aside and let my loved ones take over, those same barbs of self-reproach still stung me, as if I didn't love Martin Diehl completely, utterly. Like two distinct parts of my brain were constantly in motion, continually colliding. And it made me giddy.

My eyes flicked open when a passenger stepped on my coat as he clambered over me.

He held up a hand. '*Pardon*, mademoiselle.'

I waved away his apology, and looked at the people around me. By Ghislaine's side, a child slept, stretched over his mother's lap, his head lolling from side to side with the movement of the train. A man stared at me with a wide, absent look. I gave him a quick nod, and he nodded back. In the dim light, they all had the look of cadavers, as they kept a wary eye on their luggage.

I closed my eyes again, trying to snatch a few minutes of sleep, but the noise of the train's whistle at every stop was unbearable, the rattling, squeaking coach grating on my nerves. At each track joint, the *clack-clack* of the wheels let out a bang. I was hungry, stiff and beyond fatigue, but sleep still eluded me.

The trip became more unbearable when the police started examining everyone's papers. I could hear them in the corridor, just beyond our carriage. 'Papers, please. Papers, please.'

Eyes opened. People shifted position and I could almost smell the collective fear rising from the suffocating air.

The man who'd nodded earlier leaned across to the woman beside Ghislaine who was holding the child. He tapped her on the shoulder.

'Madame, please can I hold the child?'

Everyone looked at the woman, who hesitated for a moment, then handed the sleeping child over to the man. Nobody said a word.

'My boy's only just dropped off to sleep,' the man said, as the police asked for his papers. 'Maybe you could finish checking this carriage while I wake him gently, then I can get my papers out to show you.'

The two policemen loomed over him, saying nothing. In the end one of them said, 'All right,' and they moved on, clambering over the bags and people sitting on the floor.

They eventually reached the end of the carriage, finished checking the papers and turned back to the man holding the child. He still hadn't woken the small boy, but was waving his wallet at them at arm's length.

The policemen hesitated at the coupling between the cars. The first one mumbled something to the other, who shrugged his shoulders. They both walked on to the next carriage.

In our crowded compartment, shoulders relaxed and a few quick smiles passed between strangers.

'God bless you, madame,' the man said, handing the woman back her child. They would probably never speak again; would never exchange names or know a thing about each other but that small human gesture marked the greatest sense of closeness. Another tiny victory in our collective fight against the hated occupier.

The train reached Lucie-sur-Vionne and I stepped out into an almost arctic cold with Ghislaine and Miette.

The Monts du Lyonnais, the fields and trees, had vanished beneath the slate grey sky, and the countryside had become an endless white mass, save for a few crows wheeling above us.

As we walked towards la place de l'Eglise a slant of sun eased through the cloud cover, painting the cobblestones in a yellow hue. Beside the church, the thin trunks of the lime trees stood tall — spectral sentinels guarding the Great War monument and its withered wreaths.

I caught the scent of wood smoke and heard the boom of the hunters' guns followed by the short, expectant barking of hounds which broke the frigid silence descending from the hills.

Village housewives hurried about, clutching shopping baskets and whatever version of bread Yvon Monbeau had managed to conjure up. Hunched against the cold, they gripped coat fronts and the mittened hands of their children as they scuttled to the warmth of their homes.

From his woodcarving shop, old Monsieur Thimmonier lifted his arm in a wave.

'Merry Christmas!' we called in unison.

'Be a darn sight merrier if those Boche were gone,' he said, flinging an arm at the group of soldiers marching towards their barracks in Ecole de Filles Jeanne d'Arc. I spotted Karl Gottlob and Fritz Frankenheimer amongst them, but not Martin, and acknowledged I'd come to yearn for the briefest furtive glimpse of him between our meetings.

They'd all left on leave at the same time so I was certain he too, would be back in Lucie. I skipped a few trepid steps at the thought of seeing him again.

'Merry Christmas to you all,' Simon Laforge said, as he strode out of the chemist. 'Looks like we'll have a lot of snow this year,' he said with a glance at the sky.

'As every year,' Ghislaine said, with a smile.

Amandine and Séverine rushed from Monsieur Dubois' carpenter shop to greet their older sister. 'Did you bring us presents?' Amandine said, throwing her arms around Miette.

Little Séverine frowned. 'She doesn't bring the presents, silly, that's *Père Noël*'s job.'

We all smiled, but I wondered if Father Christmas would have much at all for the children of France that year.

'Girls!' Miette's mother called. 'Come back inside, you'll catch your deaths without your coats.'

'Have a nice Christmas,' I said to Miette.

'See you the day after tomorrow.' Miette kissed our cheeks and disappeared inside with her family.

It seemed nothing had changed in Lucie. Everyone was waiting — waiting for the rations to be lifted, for the Germans to leave, for the prisoners to come home, and for the war to end.

Although I had almost lost hope of hearing from Papa and

Félicité, Ghislaine and I called into the post office.

'Well, well, I wondered where you two and Juliette Dubois had disappeared.' Denise said, eyeing us as if we were errant children. 'And before you ask, there's no mail for either of you,' she added with a smug look.

'We're doing nursing work for the Red Cross,' I said.

The post office was no longer heated and Denise sat with a camel-hair coat wrapped around her ample body.

'*Oh là, là* fancy coat,' Ghislaine said. 'Incredible what clothes' coupons can buy, isn't it, Céleste?'

Denise sniffed and looked down her nose at us. 'It was a present from a … from a friend.'

'The friend who wears a green uniform?' Ghislaine said.

Denise clutched the coat lapels as if we were about to leap over the desk and tear it from her. 'It's none of your business who my friends are.'

'We should go,' I said, anxious as always when conversation lurked near the subject of German soldiers.

'Well, Merry Christmas, Denise,' Ghislaine said, with a cheeky wink. 'Or should that be *Fröhe Weihnachten*?'

Denise glared at us and turned to her next customer.

'I hope your father's feeling better,' I said as Ghislaine and I stood before the still-closed butcher's shop.

'I don't think my father will ever feel better,' she said. 'Anyway, you have a nice Christmas.'

My friend disappeared inside and I hurried across to Au Cochon Tué, and into the toilet. I almost bounced with the thrill, as I retrieved the paper stuffed behind the cistern.

Meet me Christmas Eve afternoon if you can.

***

I took the muddied track through the great flattened landscape to Uncle Claude's farm. Trees dotted the fields like snowmen, the

leafless limbs sagging at odd angles under their snowy weights.
Sheets of ice plastered the fields and I recalled when Patrick,
Olivier and I would break off pieces of ice and marvel, with a
child's wonder, at the fossilised blades of brown grass.

The sweet aroma of Uncle Claude's pipe hit me as he opened
the door, and the shouts and squeals of Justin, Gervais, Paulette
and Anne-Sophie, as they bounded about the household
clutter.

Uncle Claude immediately frowned, his face creasing like a
sun-dried apricot.

I laid a hand on his arm. 'Don't worry, Olivier is safe, and
well.'

The farmer's wide shoulders relaxed. 'Thank God. I'll send
word to his parents. They worry so, being far away across the
channel.'

He stepped aside and gestured me in. 'Are you coming inside?
The kids would love to see you.'

From the scoops of laughter and the rough-and-tumble
din, it seemed Olivier's cousins were having a good enough
time without seeing me. Besides, I was anxious to get to the
riverbank.

'I can't stay today,' I said. 'I just wanted to let you know they'd
sent a message; that they're safe and in good health. They're
sorry they can't be home for Christmas. Maybe next year.'

Uncle Claude nodded. 'Let's hope this war is over by then.
I don't know what'll become of us if it goes on much longer.
I've had the Boche here only today, the two who always march
around together — skinny mean-looking one, and the fat one.
Seems somebody told them about me slaughtering a couple of
pigs and flogging the meat on the black market.' He sighed. 'But
what choice do we farmers have? My equipment is wearing out
and I can only replace it with expensive black market parts. I can
only get fodder too on the black market, and you can imagine
the prices! It's no wonder I have to engage in a touch of illegal
activity myself.' He puffed on his pipe. 'Anyway, they say they'll

denounce me to the authorities if I don't sell my meat to them, so *they* can make the profit. And I'm not the only one, Céleste,' he said, jabbing the pipe at me. 'It seems someone here in Lucie is informing on many villagers. They've got a profitable business going, getting information then blackmailing the people for money, or goods, to send home to their families. Why only the other day they raided the Au Cochon Tué cellar.'

'They didn't find our —?'

He shook his head. 'The pigs were so happy when they found Robert's illegal wine, they never bothered looking for another secret partition in his cellar.'

'Thank God, but poor Monsieur Perrault, what happened to him?'

'Oh not gaol, or a fine, or anything like that,' Claude said. 'No, like myself, and our dear butcher, Robert's got to sell all the wine to those two thugs now. It's *them* who'll be making the forty-franc resale profit.'

Uncle Claude waved the pipe about. 'If I get my hands on the filthy collabo who's feeding them information I'll thread him through my wheat-cutter.'

***

The wind was about the woods, savage spots of sleet stabbing my face. I paused at the cross with its little heart engraved into the stone, commemorating the children who'd drowned in the Vionne. I felt the familiar jabs of grief for those lost children.

What if they'd not drowned, those young ancestors of mine, and had lived long enough to have children of their own? Everything would be different. I, Céleste Roussel, might not be here today. It struck me then how filled with our own importance we all were; as if we really mattered, when our fragile lives — our lifelines — hinged on nothing more than the whim of a river current.

I slithered down the slippery verge and followed the track through the willow trees. Swathed in scraps of ice, the water struggled across the boulders. I never ventured to the river in winter and it seemed odd without the noise of crickets and honeybees, not even the snap of crows' wings or the rustle of foraging squirrels.

Martin wasn't at our special place, but I was early. It was too cold to sit on our rock, so I paced about, stamping my feet to keep the blood flowing.

A robin redbreast settled on a branch and began preening itself. I closed my eyes and made the traditional wish for the first sighting of a winter robin. Seconds later the bird spread its wings and flew away — a drop of blood on cotton wool. I hoped wherever he went he'd keep my wish close to his scarlet breast.

I kept glancing at the bare willows, rubbing the cold from my arms. I spun around at a rustling sound. Only a rabbit, hopping into a clearing. It must've caught my scent, as it cocked its ears and bobbed away.

I waited at least half an hour, the cold numbing me so I could barely move my limbs. Martin wasn't coming. I wouldn't see him today; wouldn't get my angel necklace back. Nor would I find out anything about Ravensbrück. Perhaps he'd got a girl back home and had forgotten about me, and was never coming back. I might have known meeting someone so right for me was only a dream; that such luck only belonged to other people.

My feet heavy as lead, I turned to start back along the path. A figure in a greatcoat blocked my way.

'Martin! You scared me.' A hand flew over my heart. 'I thought you weren't coming.'

'Sorry, I could not come sooner.'

He drew me close and, giddy with anticipation, my hungry lips found his. As he kissed me another face flashed into my mind — the image of a fearless Maquisard freezing out in the Monts du Lyonnais hills, fighting for our cause. But as Martin's heat unfurled inside me, I knew my destiny was still with him.

Nothing had changed that.

'How was your leave?' I said. 'And your family?'

'Well my home has not been bombed,' he said. 'Like so many others. But the whole of Germany is a grim wasteland.' He shook his head. 'Such a different Berlin from the one I remember with wide, clean avenues and ordered buildings. The people are hungry too. No better off than you French, in fact.'

Martin removed a glove and dug into his pocket. 'Oh, I almost forgot.' He took my hand and placed the angel necklace in my palm. 'I replaced the old leather with a chain.'

'You what? But why?'

'It was worn almost right through,' he said, 'and would have snapped any minute. That's why I wanted you to leave it with me, so I could surprise you with a new chain.'

I let the fine chain slide between my fingers, which shook a little. 'It's real gold?'

'Of course,' Martin said. 'Only the best for my girl.'

'What did you do with the leather thread? Surely it could've been fixed?'

Martin shrugged. 'Oh I don't know, probably threw it away. But what is wrong, you prefer silver to gold, perhaps?'

'It's … it's different,' I said, already missing the soft smell of the leather that had lain against the breasts of so many before me. I turned around. 'Can you fasten the clasp?'

'I have been back in Lucie a few days now,' he said, swivelling me back to face him. 'But I did not see you around the village.'

'I'm living in Lyon now,' I said. 'Working as a Red Cross nurse at Montluc Prison. You were gone and I couldn't just sit around doing nothing. I need to feel useful. And I've decided I'd like to become a proper nurse. You know, study and get my certificate, like we spoke about before.'

'Ah, I understand.' Martin gave me a knowing look. 'Montluc Prison. That must mean your brother and his friend are still alive? I am happy for you, but I am sorry I could not arrange a meeting with SS Obersturmführer Barbie.'

'I don't think any meeting with your Obersturmführer Barbie would've helped. As you said, they were arrested as terrorists. I have no good reason to plead their cause. I can only hope the war will end soon and they'll be released.'

What a convincing liar my Resistance training had made me, yet I did feel a shard of guilt about deceiving Martin; the sting of remorse for all the half-truths I would have to continue feeding him. It would be a relief, the day it was all history, and I could tell him everything.

'You are cold.' He unbuttoned his greatcoat, wrapped it around my shoulders and hugged me close. I was glad of the warmth but felt odd enveloped in a German coat — like a reluctant collaborator.

'What a pity we do not have a warm place to be alone,' he said. 'Perhaps I could come into Lyon? We could take a hotel room?'

I thought of Martin with me in the city and how tricky it would be not only to see him, but also to carry out my missions. It was far safer to keep him out here in Lucie, away from all that. But the thought of having him alone, in a warm hotel room, too tempting. Like a scene from a Hollywood romance movie.

'That would be lovely, Martin.'

'What is wrong, Céleste? You seem … I don't know, distant.'

'I'm worried to death,' I said. 'My sister was arrested for … for something or other. She's been deported to Germany, to a camp at some place called Ravensbrück. Do you know it?'

Martin took a sharp breath, bent over and scraped up a few pebbles. 'Ravensbrück — bridge of ravens,' he said, skimming the stones, one after the other, across the silvery-grey surface of the water.

I brushed the pebbles from his hand, and they scattered on the ground. 'Let's not play skimming games anymore, Martin. Tell me about Ravensbrück.'

'It is about eighty kilometres from Berlin. The camp was built on the edge of a lake, a nice —'

'I don't care about lakes and bridges! Surely you know something about the actual camp?'

'Well, there are about twelve thousand women being held there.' The athletic shoulders tightened.

'You're still not telling me everything, Martin.'

'Apparently,' he began again, 'this is one of many labour camps for terrorists, resistors, anybody who is working against the Führer. I do not know what happens to French prisoners like your sister, and I do not have a scrap of proof, but in keeping with Hitler's Aryan ideology, they are supposedly exterminating Jews in these sorts of camps.'

He held a hand up. 'Not that I agree, or even begin to understand this insane idea of the Führer's. I mean, how can you hate someone you do not personally know, or claim to know them when they are based only on poisonous propaganda? Man, whatever his appearance, his religion, is the same the world over.'

I was barely listening to Martin, so consumed I was with the searing pain that flared deep inside me, like a great wound exploding. Perhaps how a gunshot would feel. I couldn't speak. I even stopped shivering, and as I recalled a little soldier in a red coat, I felt something inside me wither and die.

34

In the thin light of the early dusk marching down from the Monts du Lyonnais, I hurried back to L'Auberge des Anges. Maman would be wondering where I was, and my heart beat fast with the cold, and with Martin's words about Ravensbrück.

I thought of the Wolfs and how Max would have loved to paint that — snow dripping like tears from the boughs of trees, the silver earth stiff with frost. While I couldn't bear to think of them, images of the family kept burning into my mind — desperate, helpless Max, the graceful dark beauty of Sabine, the innocence of Talia and Jacob. *Exterminated.* What a terrifying word. No, Martin must have got it wrong. It was simply more evil propaganda spread by the Germans to keep their heels firmly stamped upon us. The Wolfs hadn't committed any crime; they'd never harmed a soul, and whatever did they do with the other prisoners like Félicité?

The courtyard of L'Auberge was silent, the roses beside the well shrivelled and brittle, like dismal ghosts of a bygone happier time. I glanced up to the light slanting from the kitchen window and glimpsed my mother's face, though she gave no sign or welcoming gesture.

I saw she'd put the hens and the goats inside for winter, and I thought of the hard work raking out their straw beds in the cold and darkness of the short days to come. But however much I tried to think of something else — anything — the word

Ravensbrück kept hammering at my brain.

As I climbed the steps, I unfastened the angel pendant and slid it into my pocket. I didn't need Maman asking questions about a new gold chain. I'd already thought of the perfect hiding place, next to Max's paintings — the only other precious things in my possession.

The farmhouse was quiet apart from the softly-purring stove, its heat filling the kitchen along with the sweet smell of roasting chestnuts. I caught a snatch of conversation coming from Maman's herbal room.

I peeked around the doorway. Miette's mother, one of the few people my mother could call a friend, was perched on a stool, my mother bent over her hand.

'What's happened?'

'Nothing too serious, Céleste,' Madame Dubois said. 'A slight Christmas dinner cooking accident. But at least it gave me the excuse to come up to L'Auberge and wish your maman a Merry Christmas, seeing as she's on her own … Anyway, she's not now, you're here.'

Maman frowned. 'Not such a slight accident,' she said, applying her poultice to the burn.

'But as you can see, your mother insisted on fussing over me as usual,' Madame Dubois said. 'I don't know what she puts in these remedies, though they seem to do the trick.'

'Just a simple mixture of cloves, cinnamon and nutmeg,' my mother said. 'Soaked in a cloth in white wine. Right,' she said, as she finished bandaging the injured hand. 'Don't disturb the dressing and come back and see me in two days.'

With a grateful smile, Miette's mother kissed us both and left the farm, hurrying back to her family gathering.

'That's nice of Miette's maman,' I said. 'Coming up to see her friend, alone on Christmas Eve. I doubt the injury really needed your care?'

'Of course it required treatment,' Maman snapped, but the usual venom was missing from her voice. 'Now I realise there are only two of us this year,' she went on, a hand flying to her chignon. 'Dr. Laforge told me your brother is safe, but wouldn't be joining us. He also told me about … about where they've sent your sister. But Christmas is Christmas, so I've set our places in the living room.'

'The table looks lovely,' I said. We rarely ate anywhere besides the kitchen, so it was obvious she'd made a special effort. I sank into the sofa, eased my shoes off and snuggled my cold feet into my slippers. I bent close to the fireplace, spreading my palms near the crackling flames and remembering Christmases that seemed so distant they might have existed only in my imagination. I saw the three of us sitting with our father around the hearth, the fire blazing with as much wood as we wanted, our bellies bursting with seasoned turkey, cardoons, roasted chestnuts and my mother's macaroons. Wood grains clinging like gold to the hair of his forearms, Papa would wave his glass of vervain liqueur at the andirons supporting the logs in the fireplace and remind us how they came from our ancestors, from the times of Louis XVI. He'd squeeze between us, on that same sofa with its tired floral pattern, and speak of the legends of Lucie — tales of noble lords with servants and gilt carriages, and the story of the peasant farmers who turned our farm into L'Auberge des Anges. The Inn of Angels.

Patrick especially loved to hear about the witches burned at the stake, or drowned in the Vionne River. He grinned when Papa told us how the birds would peck at rotting corpses left dangling from Lucie's gallows. Félicité would shudder and turn away and grasp her crucifix.

Once she'd washed up, every last plate sparkling, the bench tops gleaming and the tiles waxed, Maman would join us. She rarely spoke or joined in our conversation; she simply sank into her special Napoléon armchair and attacked her sewing as if it was something she hated.

All those things I'd so longed to escape for the excitement of the city. But amidst the loss and destruction I was seeing every day, I basked in the comfort of that homely place. It seemed empty with only Maman and me, but at the same time I sensed L'Auberge was crowded; filled with all the people who'd ever lived there. Perhaps they were the spirits my sister spoke of — those angels of the inn.

My hands warm, I slumped back into the sofa, and looked about me at the paintings I'd grown up with; the faded watercolours from which Maman meticulously flicked off the first tendrils of spider web: the grape and wheat harvest, a jade ribbon of the Vionne cleaving the valley, and the village of Lucie-sur-Vionne enclosed in its *vingtain* — fourteenth century stone fortification built to keep out the conquering, plundering hordes of a different war. Perhaps Max's paintings, more life-giving than those faded old scenes, would one day decorate our walls.

'Sit at the table, Célestine, you must be hungry with all this … this Red Cross work.'

'I've decided I'd like to study nursing,' I said. 'Properly I mean. Once the war is over.'

'Oh,' she said. 'Well I imagine your father will find the fees somehow … if he ever comes home.'

'He *will* come back, Maman. But really, you don't mind me leaving the farm?'

'I suppose you must follow whatever you believe is your path,' she said, setting a plate of brioche toasts laden with smoky *foie gras,* on the table.

My mother poured two glasses of wine that glowed amber in the light of the oil lamp.

'Mmn, delicious,' I said, swallowing a mouthful of the silky wine.

'I still manage to hide some things from the Boche,' Maman said, eyeing the bottle. 'Even if they have taken almost every precious thing from me.'

'I think I'd make a good nurse — a proper, trained one,' I said, savouring each delicious forkful of the *foie gras.* 'Since I've been away I've realised women's eyes are opening, Maman. Modern women want to be independent; we want the same respect as men, and the only way we'll get that is by getting educated, so we can free ourselves from their money chains.'

Maman pushed invisible hair strands back into her bun. 'I can't imagine whoever gave you such ideas,' she said. 'Obviously those types who smoke and drink like men and wear men's clothes.' She cast a disapproving stare over my trousers and shirt.

'What's wrong with wanting independence, a life I choose?' I said. 'I can do it. I know now I'm not totally useless. I have skills, training.'

'I never said you were useless, Célestine.'

'Not outright.' The wine must have loosened my tongue, or perhaps I'd reached the stage where I was simply no longer frightened of my mother. 'But you've always seemed to despise me.'

My mother banged the tripe gratin and cabbage parcels stuffed with chestnuts onto the table. 'Who said I despise you?'

'Nobody.' I swallowed more wine. 'It's just, I don't know, you've always been so much harder on me than the others. Félicité said it was because something happened to you. Something terrible.'

'Don't bring your sister into this, especially at a time like Christmas when she's in some godforsaken place they call Ravensbrück.'

Ravensbrück.

It clanged in my mind like a funeral bell, but I said nothing about what supposedly went on there. I couldn't believe it myself. Or maybe I was simply afraid that voicing that word — exterminated — might make it true.

We ate in silence and I thought of those who were most likely having only thin, watery soup for Christmas dinner.

'What happened?' I said. 'I think I'm old enough now, for you to tell me.'

'When? What are you talking about, Célestine?'

'When you were young,' I said. 'What made you like … like

you are? Why can't you tell me?'

My mother started fidgeting with her apron. 'Some things are better left unsaid.'

'Why? What things? And why should I have to suffer because of those things? I have a right to know.'

Her eyes hardened, her lips settling into that dogged line. She placed her knife and fork together on her empty plate, nudging them into neat alignment. 'Nobody has the right to intrude into the mind of another person.'

I clattered my cutlery onto the plate. 'Not even your own daughter?'

'Nobody.' Her chair scraped on the tiles, as she got up to clear the table.

35

'*Préparez-vous, préparez du ravitaillement pour tous. Un train va passer!*' cried the Stationmaster of Perrache, one of Lyon's two main train stations.

On Dr. Laforge's advice to change jobs, Ghislaine and I had been working for several weeks at the Perrache Welcome Centre, set up by the Red Cross to provision starving train passengers.

'Remember your instructions, girls,' the Stationmaster went on. 'Don't appear to be hiding anything. And only large, easily identifiable gestures so as not to attract the Germans' suspicion.'

We were stationed at the Red Cross headquarters on la place Antonin-Poncet, to be ready for the call at any time, day or night, or the passengers would miss out on food and water and any medical help they might require.

The incoming trains were loaded with returning, wounded or escaped prisoners, while those departing transported people from the prisons like Montluc. Other trains were simply passing through, taking unfortunate deportees to compulsory labour camps in Germany, and yet more — their wagons normally reserved for cattle — carted haggard throngs of people to unknown destinations.

So far, there had been no sighting of my father or my sister.

It was close to midday but the station was dark, the bleak January cold hacking through the air like a scythe. Snow fell onto the railway tracks, and its weight had snapped and dragged to the ground some of the telegraph wires. The snow fell on the almond-green uniforms of the German soldiers guarding the entrance to their barracks too, and on the red flags with their swastikas that they'd draped over our monuments. The black mourning veils of widows also gathered snowflakes, all of it casting a mournful pallor which made everything feel much colder and more inhospitable.

Ghislaine and I stamped our frozen feet as the train approached in a stream of cold wind.

'Ugly pigs,' Ghislaine hissed, nodding towards the stern, heavily-armed SS watchmen perched on the carriage roofs and hanging from the wagon steps.

The train squealed to a halt and several German women searched all the Red Cross workers for hidden messages.

We moved from carriage to carriage, distributing water from buckets, hot soup in aluminium plates and dressings and bandages for the more seriously wounded. We dared not utter a word; speaking to passengers was forbidden, the sub-officer and two armed soldiers watching our every move.

'No speaking. Hurry up!' they kept saying in bad French, as we made our way through the throng of thin, exhausted humanity.

In one carriage, an old man was wearing only underpants. His chest seemed to have caved in on his protruding ribs, his lined jowls hanging from his face like hollow bags. His arms and legs were bound to the seat. I had to stop myself crying out.

'I'm a priest,' the man whispered. 'Look how they treat me.'

I opened my mouth to reply, but his watery eyes widened. 'Say nothing, they might do the same to you.'

I turned to one of the German soldiers. 'How do you suppose this man can eat, tied up like that?'

The soldier shrugged.

'Please, just release him long enough for his soup,' I said. 'He's an exhausted old man; he's hardly going to run off.'

The soldier shrugged again but he did untie the bindings, and the priest rewarded me with a warm smile as I handed him his bowl of soup.

Once the passengers finished their food, the Germans examined the aluminium plates to make sure nobody had engraved a message on the bottom, and the women searched us once again.

When the whole operation was over, a whistle blew, steam choked the misty air and the train slid away.

'*Au revoir, au revoir,*' we chimed, as we always did, because, what else was there to say? And when the train disappeared, we hid our teary eyes from the Germans.

***

Ghislaine and I chatted with the other girls as we walked away from the platform, relieved to be free of the tension whenever a train came through. As usual, war and the occupation were the main topics.

'People are saying that when the Germans retreat,' a girl called Margot said, 'they'll take all of us with them.'

'Surely the Boche wouldn't have enough trains for all those people,' Ghislaine said.

'Trains?' Margot said, wide-eyed. 'They won't bother with trains. We'll all have to walk!'

'I find that hard to believe,' another girl said. 'Why would they take all the civilians with them?'

'The Germans' excuse is,' Margot said. 'If we go under, we drag everyone else down with us.'

'But you don't know anything for sure, Margot,' Ghislaine said. 'You're just guessing.'

'Ah, it's always the same,' Margot went on. 'Everyone ignores danger until it's staring them in the face.'

'Shush,' I said, nodding up ahead, to where a squad of German soldiers was lining up on the roadbed alongside a cattle train. A column of people straggled along behind them. They clutched suitcases in one hand and bewildered-looking children in the other.

On pain of instant death, civilians were never allowed near these sorts of trains. Red Cross workers were prohibited from approaching them and the passengers were never permitted water, soup or medical treatment.

'*Schnell, schnell!*' the soldiers barked as the men, women and children of all ages started to climb up into the train, dragging their cases behind them.

'*Schnell, schnell!*'

'Look,' I hissed to Ghislaine. 'Isn't that Ellie Kohen — Jacqueline's upstairs neighbour?' I nodded at a young woman holding her baby in one arm and a suitcase in the other. 'And little Samuel?'

We strayed a few steps closer.

'Yes, it's her,' Ghislaine said. 'But I thought — assumed — our doc was going to give her the train fare to get out of Lyon?'

'She wasn't home, remember?' I said. 'He probably didn't find time to go back. You know how busy he is.'

We walked slowly, watching Ellie climb aboard. The first step was high above the rocky roadbed. She placed her suitcase on the step and held onto the door handle with one hand, but she couldn't seem to hoist herself up.

'Oh no, poor Ellie.' On impulse, I moved forward to go and help her.

Ghislaine gripped my arm. 'Don't.'

Ellie still couldn't manage to board the train. The sergeant major came marching over, yelled something at her in German and gave her a hard kick in the bottom. Wide-eyed, Ellie lost her balance. She shrieked a scream that marbled my blood, and I watched in horror as her swaddled baby fell to the ground and lay there in a wailing heap.

'Oh my God, the monsters!' Ghislaine said.

'Poor Ellie,' I said. 'I hope Samuel is all right.'

But we didn't find out if Ellie's baby was badly hurt, as the sergeant-major grabbed the screaming bundle, threw it into the train after its mother and rammed the door home.

In that instant, struggling to control the hot and cold waves of sweat swamping me, I knew what hate was. Real hate.

The whistle blew. As the train rumbled off, obscured by grey smoke, we heard the desperate shouts from those inside — names, addresses, messages called out to us. But in the din of voices and the departing train, we couldn't make out a single thing.

'They'll pay for this,' I said, breathing deeply to stop myself throwing up. 'Some day they'll pay.'

36

The March sun warming our cheeks, Ghislaine and I walked from Perrache station, alongside the Saône River, towards the centre of Lyon.

We crossed la place Bellecour, site of Pierre and Antoine's recent bomb attack that had destroyed the business premises of a known Nazi collaborator. Someone had painted *vive de Gaulle* across the equestrian statue of Louis XIV in the middle of the square.

The weather had changed over the last week. The pink snow clouds had slunk away to the west, the first rays of spring sun piercing the cool air, and the last snow had merged with the first flowers — an uncertain sort of inter-season. In grim, war-ravaged Lyon however, everything was still one drab, brownish mass. The ground was grey and hard as iron, and there was none of the brightness of new spring growth. Even the birds seemed to have abandoned the occupied city.

We stopped on rue de la Barre, checking the restaurant across the road. There was no "Daily Specials" sign on the pavement; it was safe to enter Franck-the-forger's shop.

'See you in five minutes,' I said, leaving Ghislaine to wait outside for her contact, to deliver Jacqueline's latest message. 'Remember, we're meeting Miette for a drink afterwards.'

'I can't wait to see her again,' Ghislaine said. 'I miss not having her with us at the flat.'

With her angelic face, and her German language skills, Miette had infiltrated the circle of economic intelligence, working as an interpreter for the Boche as her cover. Wherever the Germans were, in all the fancy bars and hotels, Miette would be present — a fly on the wall — listening, gathering information. Since it was likely she'd be followed home one day, Jacqueline had moved Miette from her flat.

I walked into the shop and greeted the forger with a loud, '*Salut*, Franck. Nice day, isn't it?' and continued through to the back room, where Franck was scrutinising a batch of papers.

'Ah, Gabrielle, there you are,' he said, holding up the papers. 'I've got everything ready for you.'

It was not advised amongst group members, but Franck and I had become friends over the past few months, and I sensed he was not his usual cheery self.

'Is everything all right, Franck?'

'My brother's been arrested,' he said, rubbing at his brow. 'The militia tracked him down, along with three other resistors on their way back from monitoring operations among the Maquis. Apparently some are badly wounded, maybe even dead. That's all I know.'

The Maquis. I burned with anguish, at the mention of them.

I laid a hand on Franck's arm. 'I'm so sorry, I know how you must feel.'

'Things like that are happening more and more,' he said, 'which only soothes my conscience about all this.' He waved an arm around the cramped but tidy space filled with the usual drawers of engraving tools and paraphernalia. What the authorities didn't know was that those same drawers also contained a collection of models of official identity cards, passes and permits, certificates, Town Hall and rubber stamps from the local police. From these originals, with the patience and accuracy of an expert engraver, Franck would make fake documents that, everyone agreed, looked perfectly legitimate.

Franck knew all the towns in which the records office had

been destroyed during the war, and had built up a genuine file of people who'd gone abroad or were prisoners of war. He'd also found some accomplices inside the administrative bureaucracy and was able to tell us places we could raid for blank identity cards, even German passes.

'You're doing a great job,' I said, slipping the papers into my bag.

'As long as it pays off one day, Gabrielle.'

It was then I heard the chilling sound of a series of gunshots from outside, and people screaming. I started to rush from the back room.

'Wait,' Franck said, snagging my arm. 'It might be dangerous.'

Bent over so we couldn't be seen from the window, Franck and I crept into the front of the shop and crouched down behind the counter. I peeked over the top, out onto the street.

'What's happening?' he hissed. 'Can you see anything?'

'Militia. Four of them. And three people on the ground. My hand flew to my mouth as I recognised Ghislaine's coat. 'Oh God! My friend, they've shot my friend!' I stood up.

'No, wait till the militia go,' Franck said, yanking me back down.

We must have waited only minutes, but it seemed like hours. As soon as the militia jeep roared off I dashed outside, Franck close behind me.

People had started milling around the three bodies.

'Those two … robbing the jeweller over there …'

'… girl … trying … stop militia shooting those lads.'

'… should've kept … mouth shut.'

'… the price … pay … protect others. Poor, brave girl.'

'Militia monsters … not even staying to see what they'd done.'

The force of the bullets had thrown the two boys, no older than Patrick and Olivier, flat on their backs, a single dark hole puncturing each forehead. Their faces wore stunned expressions, as if in surprise of death. Or perhaps surprised they'd been caught with their jewellery shop booty, which seemed to have vanished along with the militiamen who'd gunned them down.

Ghislaine was sprawled sideways, her legs bent up as they'd buckled when she fell. Blood leaked from an unseen wound, staining the pavement around her a dirty crimson.

I bent over Ghislaine. With my practised — though shaky — nurse's fingers, I found a feeble pulse.

'She's alive!' I moved her slightly, trying to locate the bullet wound. I tore my coat off and clamped it against the hole in her left side. 'Keep pressing on the wound, Franck and don't let go.'

I hurtled back inside and called Dr. Laforge, who said he'd meet me at the hospital. 'Ensure everything is … all is in order, Gabrielle. And be brave.'

I checked Ghislaine's pockets for incriminating messages, and took over from Franck. Blood still seeped from the wound. Ghislaine's face was white as milk. She opened her eyes to slits.

'Wh-what happened?'

'You were being brave,' I said, 'trying to save two boys from the militia's bullets. They shot you too but don't worry, I'm taking care of you. The ambulance is on its way.'

Her eyes closed again. A new spurt of blood gushed over my hand. She was losing too much.

'Stay with me,' I said. I gripped her hand and squeezed it. 'Don't you dare leave me, Ghislaine.'

***

Miette, Dr. Laforge, Jacqueline and I stayed by Ghislaine's bedside through the night. Pierre and Antoine came too for a time, as "cousins" of the patient.

'I'll go and see her father tomorrow,' Dr. Laforge said. 'The man is in no state to hear about this now, let alone make a trip into the city. The bullet wound itself,' he went on, pacing up and down alongside the bed, 'is not that serious, but she's lost a lot of blood. And with all the war wounded, there aren't nearly enough donors.'

Miette and I exchanged desperate glances and I vowed I would go and donate my blood the next day.

'She's young and strong,' Jacqueline said. 'She'll pull through.'

'She has to,' I said.

We took turns sleeping in the one visitor's chair. Around two o'clock a church bell woke me. Miette was shaking my arm, and I bolted upright. 'What is it? Is she all right?'

'I don't know,' she said. 'She seems worse.'

I rushed to the bedside. Miette told me Dr. Laforge had returned to Lucie on an urgent call and Jacqueline had left to grab a few hours' sleep at the flat.

Ghislaine's breaths were shallow and weak. A grey mask had dropped over her face — the veil I'd seen on the faces of so many Montluc prisoners; a gauzy screen I knew no medical treatment could lift.

'Get the nurse, please, Miette. Hurry!'

Miette returned with the nurse after several minutes.

'She looks worse,' I said. 'Can't you do anything?'

The nurse shook her head. 'I'm so sorry, we've done all we can for her.' She left the room with a sympathetic look.

Miette and I stood on either side of the bed. We didn't speak, each of us holding one of Ghislaine's hands, our watchful eyes filling with sadness and despair.

For a long time there was no sound in the room, except our friend's spasms of breath, as she slowly lost her grip on life.

'She's cold,' I said, tucking the blanket more closely around her.

Ghislaine's lips turned the hue of faded hydrangeas, and we dabbed the sweat from her damp face.

Several hours later the scarlet band of dawn pierced the sky, as if smearing blood across the night darkness. Ghislaine raised her head slightly. She turned and gazed outside to the coming sun and gave us a small smile. Perhaps it was our countryside love of a heavenly dawn, in which we'd always sensed hope, that renewed my energy. I felt, with that new day, she would be all right.

She fumbled for my hand, which I put in hers. 'Please … take care … my father.' Because they were so simple, her choked words seemed sadder.

'Yes, yes, of course,' I said, the burning tears blinding me. 'But you're going to get better. You must fight this and come back to us.'

Our friend slumped back on the pillows, her dark hair fanned like an Egyptian queen's. She never spoke another word.

Miette and I held onto Ghislaine until the end, so tightly that when finally she was gone, we couldn't pull our hands away, and we remained standing on either side of her, clasping her cooling fingers.

The sadness, the numbness, paralysed me. I couldn't cry. I was somewhere beyond all pain and grief. I kept hold of my friend's hand. Perhaps that way I imagined she wouldn't truly be gone from us.

37

Our grief warped the silence as Dr. Laforge drove Miette and me back to Lucie for Ghislaine's funeral. No words, no feelings seemed adequate for the void in which I felt suspended.

'We all knew it was dangerous,' Miette finally said, shaking her head. 'We knew, we knew! But I never thought ... never imagined ...'

She dabbed her swollen eyes, and I took her hand and we kept them clamped together for the rest of the journey.

'I told Bernard Dutrottier his daughter died a heroine,' the doctor said. 'Fighting for our country.'

'I bet that was comforting,' I said, feeling the first spark of rage ignite from the pit of my sorrow.

'I'm not sure the poor man quite understood what I was saying,' Dr. Laforge said as he parked the Traction on la place de l'Eglise. 'Right, I'll see you at the church tomorrow, girls,' he said. 'Be strong.' He grabbed his black bag, got out of the car and headed across the square to his rooms.

'I'm going to call in on Ghislaine's father,' I said to Miette. 'Before I go up to L'Auberge. Not that I can give him much comfort, but he might appreciate a friendly face. Or perhaps I shouldn't go ... maybe I'll remind him too much of her?'

'Yes, you should go,' Miette said. 'I could come with you?'

I shook my head. 'Both of us might seem like too much of

a crowd … or something. You go to your family, I'll see you tomorrow.'

The shop was unlocked, but that didn't surprise me. Nobody bolted doors in Lucie. The shelves were empty — such a pity to see no enticing displays of joints, cutlets, tongue, pigs' feet or sausages, though I still caught the familiar edges of the bloody, butcher's tang.

I knocked on the flat door. No answer. Not a sound from inside. Where was the sister from Auvergne who was meant to be caring for him? Maybe she'd popped out on an errand.

I entered the silent home. 'Monsieur Dutrottier?' Still no answer. 'Anybody there?' I called again, as I passed through the kitchen.

The door of the living room, where I expected to find Ghislaine's father in his rocker, was closed. I pushed it open.

My first instinct was to pick up the armchair that was lying sideways on the worn parquet floor, but my next step stopped me. It made my head spin, and my heart start beating out of control. My horrified gaze travelled from the two dangling legs up to the swollen, purple face and the neck about which the cord was pulled, taut.

'Oh God!' I ran from the flat, stifling my screams, and the swell of bile rising in my throat. I dashed across the square and banged on Dr. Laforge's door.

***

My mother and I joined the solemn procession winding from Saint Antoine's church and out along the road to the cemetery. The whole of Lucie had come to the funeral of Ghislaine and her father and, united in our grief, it seemed we moved as one single mourning body.

Just as the winter winds came from nowhere, snapping off tree branches and whipping rooftops in their blind rage, so the gales had disappeared, carrying off the last of the snow on the Monts du Lyonnais. As we struggled up the hill like a defeated battalion, the sun broke through the grey, its wan light haloing the foothills.

As chief pallbearer, Père Emmanuel led the way. Dr. Laforge and his brother Simon, Miette's father, Uncle Claude, Yvon Monbeau, Robert Perrault and Monsieur Thimmonier also bore the weight of the coffins on their shoulders.

Nobody spoke much. People clung to their loved ones and pressed handkerchiefs to their eyes, the priest's words from the service still clear in our minds.

'Courageous girl … sacrificed herself trying to save others …'

'… our loved and respected butcher. A man the war broke …'

I caught the whispers of several people who were nodding at Rachel Abraham.

'… refuses to wear a star.'

'… Germans … Madame Lemoulin.'

I was glad to see the gentle old woman was still safely with us, whatever name she was forced to go by. I nodded a greeting as she gave me a small wave.

'I still can't believe we'll never see Ghislaine again,' Miette said, walking beside my mother and me.

'It won't be the same here, without her,' I said. 'I really thought we'd be all right … that we'd survive this thing.'

'But Ghislaine didn't,' Madame Dubois said, with a glance at my mother. 'And I'll wager Marinette wishes, as much as I do, that you two would give it all up and come back to Lucie.'

'Well someone has to try and get rid of the despicable swine,' my mother said. 'We can't just let them stay here, trampling all over us for the rest of our sorry lives.'

If I hadn't been so filled with sadness, my mother's uncharacteristic words might have made me smile.

'We're very careful, Madame Dubois,' I said.

'So, I imagine, was Ghislaine.' Miette's mother was still shaking her head.

The line of mourners passed through the wrought iron gates that stood wide open as if the graveyard were expecting us. Our solemn faces matched the sober rows of tombs, some of them well tended by loving families at the *fête des morts* each All Saints Day. Weeds and wisps of dead grass littered other, more ancient graves, the neglected headstones leaning towards the ground as if they too, longed to lie down like the dead.

Despite the crowd, it remained quiet. I looked around me, at all those silent notches in the earth, at the jam jars filled with flowers, and the framed photographs.

Obviously bored, Olivier's cousins Justin and Gervais broke from the group and started scampering along the rows of graves and upsetting the jars, the flowers spilling out in their rowdy wake.

Their sisters, Paulette and Anne-Sophie, began gathering the flowers and bunching them into little posies with the help of Miette's two sisters.

'Boys!' Uncle Claude hissed. 'Stop that, right now.'

People were staring at the children and whispering amongst themselves.

'Amandine, Séverine,' Miette's mother called. 'Put those flowers back in the jars and come here.'

The children eventually settled, several people coughed and sniffed, and it was quiet again.

As the silent arc of mourners lined up around the thin brown lip of the Dutrottier family tomb, Père Emmanuel began speaking again. The men removed their berets and held them with both hands across their fronts. No one looked anyone else in the face. We all stared blankly into the hole in the earth, as if it might hold the answer as to how a lovely girl could die such a tragic death. As the clouds obscured the sun again, painting the graveyard a mournful grey, I gripped my bone angel between my thumb and forefinger, glad I'd taken it from the attic for the small comfort it gave me on that terrible day.

'What are *they* doing here?' my mother said, a corner of her mouth hitching up in scorn as she nodded at the group of uniformed men marching through the cemetery gates — Germans, from the garrison. Grouped so close, it seemed they were joined by the perfect seams of their uniforms.

'The nerve of those Fritz,' Uncle Claude said with a scowl, and people started shaking their heads.

I picked out Karl's lean figure and the fat Fritz Frankenheimer. I stiffened when I saw Martin's blond head.

His eyes flicked towards me, and away just as quickly.

I ignored my mother's grim-lipped stare.

'Merely come to give our condolences,' one of the officers called. 'To pay our respects.' The Germans all held up a saluting hand.

'How dare they?' Yvon Monbeau said, as the villagers fixed dark, guarded stares on the occupiers. 'Isn't it enough they imprison our sons for years on end? Now they think they can barge in on private funerals.'

'Hush, dear,' Ginette said, laying a hand on her husband's arm. 'Whatever you say, it'll do no good.'

'I'm amazed nobody's found out about her sleeping with that fat Boche yet,' Miette said, as I caught Denise Grosjean sending Fritz Frankenheimer a sly wink.

'Yes, incredible, isn't it.' I felt the blush darken my face, and cleared my throat. 'Just incredible.'

As the pallbearers looped straps beneath the two coffins to lower them, I glanced at Martin again. His gaze was directed straight ahead, but I could tell he was looking at me from the corner of his eye.

He lifted a hand to his nose and rubbed the top of it. I caught a flash of white paper. He lowered his hand back into his pocket.

I felt my mother's hand on my elbow; a brief squeeze and she let her arm drop. Was it a sympathetic gesture for the loss of a lifelong friend, or had she too, glimpsed Martin's message?

Sweat slated my brow as I stared into the hole, teetering on my trembling legs, afraid I might slide into that vast, dark tomb with Ghislaine.

A chill skittered down my arms as they replaced the great concrete slab over the opening. The dull thud echoed across the graveyard as we laid Ghislaine and her father to eternal rest alongside Marc, brother and son, and their mother and wife. An entire family gone forever.

I shifted uneasily, not daring to glance in Martin's direction.

After that there was nothing else to do, so we all turned from the grave and started walking away. The first rain of spring began to fall from the bleak sky; it came heavy and urgent and I pictured it carving its way through the layers of soil down to the mysterious dark heart of the earth.

38

10 am. Hôtel des Traboules.

I read Martin's message over and over. It was more than a month since I'd picked up his note in Au Cochon Tué after Ghislaine's funeral, and I had to be certain that, in my anticipation, I hadn't mistaken the time or place.

If I was to waltz into a city hotel as a woman the staff wouldn't suspect, or question, I needed to look the society woman. So, to meet Martin, I'd raided Jacqueline's mission supplies and taken the same clothes I'd worn to blow up Librairie Voltaire.

Miette and I had been back in Lyon for over three weeks but the tragedy of Ghislaine's death, and our misery, still hung over us like a storm-stained cloud. Interspersed with Resistance missions, I continued my Red Cross work at Perrache station, flitting from one to the other so as not to leave myself a moment to dwell on her absence.

We continued holding our meetings in Jacqueline's flat, speaking in muted tones — rendezvous, times, places, codenames — the fear of arrest, torture and death a constant, volatile ticking in our minds. Jacqueline kept playing the piano, effectively masking the noise of our clandestine printer.

From across the street I watched Martin enter the hotel, and wrapped the chic coat more tightly around me. Though it was quite warm, April was an unpredictable month when sunny days raised hopes until grey clouded the skies again.

I swept into the hotel five minutes later. With a self-assured smile at the receptionist, I slid into the lift and got off on the second floor. I hurried along the hallway to room twenty-four and tapped on the door.

'Yes?' Martin's voice called.

His lean figure reclined on the bed, one elbow propping himself up, the other stretched in a welcoming gesture. I dumped my coat and bag on the chair.

'*Oh là là*, as you French say. Fancy clothes.'

'I wanted to look nice for you, for a change,' I said, falling into his arms.

We kissed, our tongues searching, our fingers frenzied, grappling with each other's clothes. Embraced in Martin's sturdy protection, my grief and despair boiled away for a few heavenly moments.

It was only afterwards as we lay quiet and sated, our limbs interlaced, that those familiar, frantic twitches of guilt seized me like a bat flapping about in a hot attic. How could I stay in a hotel room doing this when my father and my sister were imprisoned in some far-off work camp? If they could see me lying naked with a German officer — Miette, Jacqueline, Dr. Laforge, Patrick and Olivier; Olivier who'd been there my whole life, someone I knew better than I knew myself.

After all, who was Martin Diehl, really? All I knew of him, besides that he was a poet and not a soldier, were our snatched moments of pleasure — the heat of two bodies thrown together to shunt the cold, which had invaded us both in one way or another.

I checked my watch. 'I'll have to go soon.'

'More Red Cross work?' A fingertip trailed up my arm and caressed the crook of my elbow.

'I'm working at the Perrache Welcome Centre now,' I said. 'If it wasn't for us, the hungry passengers wouldn't get a thing to eat or drink. And I want to do something useful for our effort. I know you don't care much about the war anymore, but surely you can understand that?'

'Oh I do understand,' he said. 'But where did you say you were living? Do not look so worried, I would not think of going there. I'd just like to know where you are, so I can picture you when we are apart.'

'I told you, Martin. I'm staying at a friend's flat. You don't know her.'

'At least it's a "her". I wonder, sometimes, if there is not somebody else.'

'Don't be silly, nobody could replace Martin Diehl.' I smiled, unlacing my limbs from his. 'But your jealousy does flatter me.'

'Something is wrong; something has changed. You are not the usual Céleste.'

'Would you be your usual self if your father and sister were being held in some camp where you claim people are being exterminated? And I still miss Ghislaine terribly. I'd known her since —'

'I am most sorry for your family,' he cut in. 'And your friend.'

'And her poor father,' I went on. 'He'd lost his entire family. No wonder he couldn't bear to live any longer. Your lot took every last thing from him!' I felt, suddenly, ridiculously self-conscious of my nakedness. I lurched from the bed and scrabbled about for my clothes.

'"Your lot?"' His eyes widened, the hurt look crumpling his features.

'I'm sorry,' I said. 'I shouldn't have said that. I'm just … angry. So mad at this unfair world. I know you aren't my enemy; you aren't one of those heartless barbarians.'

'We should not have secrets from each other,' Martin said. 'That is no way to start a life together. A marriage.'

I felt a panicky fluttering inside my chest, unsure if it was excitement at the prospect or terror it might actually happen. 'Aren't we a bit young to think of marriage, Martin? Isn't there so much else to do before?'

'I thought that is what you wanted?' he said, as I drew away from him and started dressing. 'Besides, what else is there?'

'Lots of things … study, get a good job, travel the world. I've always wanted to go to Hollywood, haven't you? And see all those Sunset Boulevard stars. Now I really must go, they're expecting me at the station.' I shrugged into my coat.

He stood, still naked. I didn't trust myself to leave that model of human perfection, so I averted my eyes.

'I am staying in Lyon for a few days, Céleste.'

My eyes snapped back to him. 'Staying in Lyon?'

'I have some more leave. I hoped we might see more of each other if I stayed in the city. Perhaps you could come back this evening, after your work? I would get something nice for our supper. We could have our first whole night together.'

'I'd love to,' I said, shifting towards the door. 'But I never know how long I'll be caught up with the trains. I'll see how the afternoon goes.'

I gave him a peck on the cheek and hurried out. I hesitated in the hotel lobby, checking left, right and behind, and stepped back outside into my real world.

As I moved off down the street, preparing my mind for my afternoon mission, a gust of wind hit me. It came from nowhere, and caught me by surprise. The gale tugged at me as I grappled with the coat buttons to fasten them. It jerked at my limbs, my face, and my hair, as if trying to tear out the jumbled puzzle of half-truths and outright lies that cluttered my mind, and organise them into some sort of ordered, coherent structure.

***

There was no time to return to the flat before my afternoon mission, so I ate a hurried lunch of the usual tasteless soup, and dashed off to meet Pierre at the pre-arranged spot.

Arm in arm, with the casual closeness of young lovers, Pierre and I made our way across the city to Parc de la Tête D'or — Lyon's grandest park.

We strolled past the usual long, hungry-looking queue stretching along the pavement from a grocery shop, slipping our leaflets into their shopping baskets — news-sheets informing them that our food shortages were not caused, as the Germans would have us believe, by the British blockade, but the consequence of their systematic plundering of our reserves.

'Do you have a K8, madame?' one woman said. K8s were ration coupons entitling the three youth categories — J1, 2 and 3 — to 140 grams of processed meat.

'No, but I have two KCs,' she replied, which were for pregnant women and hard labourers. 'But what labour isn't hard these days?' she went on. 'When we're forced to eat rutabagas instead of potatoes, and when you have to sleep with the fishmonger to get even a carp's head?'

'It's shameful, shameful,' said another. 'When we have to pay twenty-seven francs for a paltry nub of butter and that you can only get on the black market.'

'Oh yes, it's fine for people with money, but for the rest of us …'

Pierre and I entered the park via the enormous gilded wrought iron gate, the scent of fairy floss and crepes filling my nostrils, the clear laughter of children tinkling on the spring air.

We bent our heads close, smiling at something the other had said, squirrels darting across our paths and up tree trunks as we headed past the deer park towards the puppet theatre. After all what could be more innocent than a young couple enjoying the puppet show in a public park?

I kept running over Jacqueline's instructions in my mind: identify the contact — Jeanine — who would hand me a batch of Michelin maps with notes on reception centres for those evading compulsory labour service. Pierre and I would then make a roundabout circuit along the park's maze of alleyways and transfer the maps to Antoine, waiting for us beside the pier of the lake. Antoine was then to cycle up north somewhere, to hand the maps over to the next contact.

At the puppet theatre we purchased a bag of caramelised peanuts and sat at the end of a row, leaving one vacant seat next to me, on which I placed my bag. We didn't glance across at the group of Germans lounging in the back row smoking and laughing their throaty cackles. And we ignored the militia, cradling their guns and eyeing the crowd suspiciously.

The contact was late. I kept nudging Pierre, who stole peeks at his watch. Our instructions were clear — wait five minutes at the rendezvous, then leave. Come back the following day. If the contact still doesn't turn up, they've probably been arrested.

Four minutes and fifty seconds. We were about to leave when I glimpsed the corner of a pink handkerchief poking from a woman's jacket pocket.

'Is this seat free?' she asked me.

I nodded, making no sign of recognition, and shifted my bag onto my lap.

The woman placed her bag on her lap as Guignol, the main puppet show character whose courage and generosity always triumphed over evil, bounced onto the scene.

The audience laughed and clapped as Gnafron, the wine-loving cobbler, started beating the ugly Gendarme Flagéolot over the head. I thought of those Vichy-collaborating gendarmes, certain the irony of that innocent scenario wasn't lost on the other spectators either.

My eyes still on the stage, I took the maps from beneath Jeanine's bag and slid them into the bag of caramelised nuts, which Pierre and I continued to share.

The audience applauded long and hard as Guignol, his wife Madelon, and the other puppets took a bow. Everybody started getting up and leaving their seats. Without a backward glance, Jeanine vanished into the crowd. That part, at least, had been easy.

The afternoon sun warming our cheeks, Pierre and I strolled

away from the puppet theatre, and on past the zoo, amidst the chatting, smiling public of Lyon. Antoine was due in five minutes.

Gently swaying rowboats, filled with couples, or families, spotted the lake. Birds sang from the treetops and small dogs barked, held tightly on leads close to their owner's heels. Everybody seemed in good spirits, out enjoying a sunny spring day.

'Back in a minute, Pierre.' I gestured towards the toilet block and left Pierre negotiating a price with the boat rental man.

As I entered the public toilets, I glimpsed Antoine's raggedy dark hair as he approached, but took not the slightest notice of him.

Minutes later, as I went to walk out of the building, a metallic glint in the sun's reflection stopped me. I caught the flash of dark uniform and the gleam of black boots. Militia. I shrank back out of sight.

I caught my breath and peered around the entrance. Their guns drawn, four militiamen had surrounded Pierre and Antoine. I clamped a hand over my mouth to stop myself crying out.

I grasped at the tangle of threads; at each possible, different strand, trying to understand how it had gone wrong; how the militia had known. Had they seen me with Pierre? Why then, hadn't they arrested me too? Or perhaps they'd only caught the boys at handover, when Antoine picked up the bag of nuts? I was certain nobody had noticed or suspected Pierre and me when I took the maps from the contact, but perhaps Jeanine was the informer. In such a perilous game, no one could be certain of trustworthy players.

I peered around the doorway again. One of the militiamen was waving the Michelin maps and shouting something at Pierre and Antoine. The others clamped handcuffs about the boys' wrists and shoved them forwards, the guns trained on their backs. I didn't dare glance at my friends as the militia led them away.

I stumbled across to the sink and splashed cold water on my face. Thankfully I was alone and I leaned against the wall, breathing hard to settle my sprinting heart and order my thoughts.

With damp and quivering hands, I tucked my shirt back into my trousers and turned to walk out. A tall figure, shadowing the doorway, barred my way.

'Martin!' The blood ran cool in my veins. 'W-what are you doing here?'

'I have a few days leave, remember? How did you enjoy the puppet show?'

'Pupp … what?'

'You and your boyfriend, did you enjoy the Guignol show? All of us sitting in the back row found it hilarious.' The soft features of his face hardened like setting concrete, and there was no trace of the usual smile that kinked the corners of his mouth.

'He's not my boyfriend … I can explain.' But I couldn't explain anything and I stood there, unable to utter another word. I stared at Martin, thoughts ricocheting about my brain. Had he tailed me from the hotel and informed the militia? Had Pierre and Antoine been arrested because of *him*? No, no, then I too, would have been arrested. So many questions and doubts. I couldn't focus on any one of them, and I felt dizzy, as if I might pass out. I realised that fainting was, perhaps, my only escape.

'There is nothing to explain, Céleste. I know he is not your lover. But do not worry, your act was convincing. Nobody would guess, besides me. The only person who knows your every gesture; every angle of your body language. Intimately.'

'You followed me from the hotel, didn't you, Martin?

'I knew something was wrong; you were different. I had to find out what.'

'We can't talk here,' I said, trying to put him off, to give myself time to think about what I could say.

He raised a long arm and rested it against the doorway above my head, effectively blocking my passage. Not that I was going to make a run for it, I knew that was pointless.

'But we have nothing to talk about, my sweet Céleste.' He bent down, leaning close to me, his lips almost but not quite touching mine. 'Now I know what your Red Cross work is really about.'

I remained speechless as, without another look at me, Martin turned and walked off with his long powerful strides.

***

Hurtling back to Jacqueline's flat in a panic would only draw attention to me, so I forced myself down to a brisk walk back to the old district. I took a roundabout route to ensure Martin — or anybody else — wouldn't follow me.

I couldn't stop shaking, and throwing furtive glances over each shoulder. It was certain Martin knew I was working for the Resistance, but what did he feel about that? With the shock of the arrests, and Martin surprising me, I hadn't been able to gauge his reaction. Could I trust him to keep my work to himself, or would his patriotic duty overrule his heart and make him turn me in? But even if Martin Diehl did keep his mouth shut, Pierre and Antoine's arrest had certainly compromised our operation, and perhaps all our lives.

My heart rapped in time with my three-knock door code, and when Jacqueline opened it, I fell inside, my words rushing out in a gibberish stream.

'… militia … Pi-Pierre and Antoine … arrested …'

Jacqueline took my arm and almost pushed me into the sofa.

'Sit, Gabrielle.' She lit two cigarettes and handed me one. 'Calm down and tell me the whole story.'

My knees knocked together as Jacqueline set a cup of *café Pétain* before me, my trembling hand spilling rivulets of coffee down my front as I told her about the failed mission.

I did not mention Martin, who only knew me as Céleste Roussel, unaware that Gabrielle Fontaine even existed. Even if he did turn in Céleste Roussel from Lucie-sur-Vionne, they could not connect her with Gabrielle, residing at Jacqueline Laforge's flat. The very best I could do — my only option if I wanted to cling onto the barest fibre of pride — was flee Jacqueline's flat as quickly as possible, and avoid endangering the others. I would have to return to L'Auberge and take all the flak myself.

Without a word, Jacqueline ground out her cigarette, picked up the phone and called her brother.

***

Dr. Laforge arrived with the news that the authorities were holding Pierre and Antoine in Saint Paul prison. I remained silent, trying not to think of our friends being tortured, perhaps even shot.

'I know you're certain you weren't followed home,' the doctor said. 'But we'll disband operations here. Jacqueline will start organising a new place immediately.'

'The militia must not have seen or known about you, Gabrielle,' Jacqueline said. 'Otherwise they'd have arrested you too, but it would be safer if you disappeared for a while. Gabrielle Fontaine will go back to Lucie-sur-Vionne and assume her true identity,' she said. 'For the moment.'

'Of course,' I said, thankful she had come to the same conclusion as me, albeit for a different reason. 'I understand, but I feel terrible about Pierre and Antoine. Maybe I should've done something differently?'

'It wasn't your fault,' the doctor said. 'Sadly, arrests like this are becoming more and more frequent.'

'And sometimes we never even discover who the informer is,' Jacqueline said. 'I'm thankful you were able to warn us, so we can take precautions.'

I stuffed my few clothes into my bag and left Jacqueline's flat with the doctor. My head hanging low, I felt closed up, tighter than a drum, trying to battle the war that raged between my heart and my head.

39

After several weeks as Céleste Roussel, away from the thrill and tension of city life, I felt bored, defeated and discouraged. I yearned for a friend, someone to rake over my fears about Martin's knowledge, and what part he might have played in Pierre and Antoine's arrest. I needed to talk to someone about how the whole thing with Martin might have been one great mistake from the beginning. But there was no one. I was totally alone.

When Maman asked me to cycle to the bakery or run an errand in the village, where I might run into Martin, I invented some excuse about feeling tired or ill. At least I knew he would never venture up here to the farm to ask where I was.

But it seemed Martin had kept his mouth shut, because the Gestapo did not barge into L'Auberge to arrest me, or to interrogate my mother as to my whereabouts.

My mother hadn't questioned my return and I didn't offer any explanation. On the evening of Pierre and Antoine's arrest when I arrived back at the farm, she simply ordered me to sit at the kitchen table, placed a plate of lentils before me, with a few anchovies from her secret stocks, and muttered something about being glad I was safe.

I milked the goats, fed the few hens left after the German roundups, collected their eggs, carted water up to the kitchen, and lead Gingembre out into her pasture — all those chores that passed the time but did nothing to ease my anguished mind.

I longed for Dr. Laforge to come to L'Auberge and take me back to Lyon, but the only people who came were sick villagers, for Maman's cures, or girls for her services. My fascination with the angel-making process had waned to a kind of resigned acceptance though, and I no longer crept upstairs to stare through the keyhole.

***

One morning early in May, I was pacing the kitchen with my usual frustration, watching through the window as Maman turned the soil of her kitchen garden and spread manure around the bases of the fruit trees. The early breeze had strengthened to a gusty wind, whipping the grey-streaked hair across her pleated brow.

I could have gone out and helped her but I was far too agitated to be around my mother. On impulse I climbed the ladder to the attic, crossed the dusty space and slipped into the alcove where the Wolf family had hidden the morning of the Gestapo arrest.

I took the small wooden box from the place I'd stashed Max's paintings and the toy soldier with its red coat, opened it and picked up the photo. With a fingertip, I traced across the high brow, down the slant of a chiselled cheek and around the curve of his lips. As I stared into his eyes, pale on the photograph but violet-blue in my mind's eye, I thought I'd go mad if I didn't see him soon; if I couldn't know what was happening between us.

I replaced the box, took the roll of Max's artwork and sat cross-legged on the floor. I unravelled the paintings, anchoring the stubborn corners with volumes of some rodent-gnawed book.

In the pale light slanting from the dormer windows, I studied Max's image of L'Auberge, and its Lyonnais-style wooden gateway. My eye followed the slope leading down to Lucie — the village that had stood unchanged for centuries, even under the stamp of the German enemy.

At the foot of the slope behind the farmhouse, the silvery spine of river wove through an early pink mist. The sun slanted gold across the water and, beyond the Vionne, the Monts du Lyonnais rose in a moss-green backdrop.

The next painting — a view from the opposite window — portrayed Mont Blanc and its eternal crown of snow away in the distance, fringing the once great silk city of Lyon.

I flattened out several more sheets, in stronger, bolder colours: scarlet cherries, milky winter snow, and brilliant yellow, crimson and orange autumn leaves.

There was one of Sabine in a ballerina's pose. She wore a tutu and ballet shoes, her hair a dark smooth spiral atop her head. Her creamy face, tilted upwards, looked even paler against the black background. The light from the window bathing her face looked so warm it seemed the sun was truly shining on her. In the attic silence, I saw her dancing again. I heard Max humming the tunes and the children's proud applause.

The rest of the paintings were later scenes, from the Wolfs' time at the convent. The difference was astounding. The long, fluid strokes of when they'd first come to L'Auberge were replaced with savage dabs and slashes.

I remembered Félicité saying how, towards the end, they'd barely been able to coax Max away from his art to eat. He'd said there was no time to waste on eating and drinking.

His final works echoed the torment that had consumed him; the mania forced upon him: terrified children, gleaming Citroëns and black-uniformed men rounding up groups of bedraggled people.

Outside, great white mushrooms of cloud obscured the sun. The sky was darkening to the hue of an old bruise and throwing the attic into a mustard-coloured shadow.

The first gusts of wind rattled the open window, and a chill scurried up my arms as I stared at Max's final, unfinished painting

— a truck loaded with a blur of bewildered faces. I rubbed my arms, almost smelling those fumes that would have lingered on the road after the truck screeched away.

It was as if those bursts of wind were carrying the stink of it all to me; the stench of the whole awful mess, and it snagged in my throat as I battled to hold the paper down flat. The gusts snarled in through the window, stubbornly curling the edges of the painting as if trying to hide the images from me; to mask what I suddenly knew in the miserable but proper light of responsibility, was most important.

As I rolled the artwork back up, careful to replace the sheet of cooking paper between each painting, I knew I couldn't skulk away at L'Auberge a moment longer, avoiding Martin; skirting the painful issue.

I hurried down the steps, leapt on the bicycle and sped down to the village.

***

It was a normal day in Lucie. Despite the wind, housewives stood chatting around the fountain, the artisans were hard at work and the old men played cards in their usual spot at Au Cochon Tué.

Martin was not amongst the Germans on the square. Sunlight pierced the cloud cover, glinting off the silver stripes on their uniforms and metal belt buckles, and the energetic, joyful air they gave la place de l'Eglise seemed horribly ironic.

Some of the older women — mothers of prisoners, or war widows — had as usual drawn their curtains so they wouldn't have to look at the Germans, but the young children still crowded around them, fascinated by the uniforms and horses. Justin and Gervais and Paulette and Anne-Sophie pawed at the soldiers' jackets with grubby little fingers. The Germans smiled, and when they started filling their hands with sweets, it seemed every child in Lucie gathered around them.

Liza Perrat

'Girls!' Miette's mother called, from the doorway of the carpenter's shop. 'Come back inside, now.' Busy cramming sweets into their mouths, Amandine and Séverine seemed not to hear her.

'Time for lunch, children,' Simon Laforge's wife called to her three little ones. The chemist's children too, ignored their mother.

I parked the bicycle and walked towards the bar. One of the Germans was standing at the card players' table, asking for a light.

Miette's grandfather handed him a box of matches and the German saluted, turned and walked away. The old man rolled his eyes, which brought muted laughter from the others.

'Just how long are they going to stay?' Monsieur Thimmonier muttered, around the Gauloise clamped between his lips.

'Seems like they've been here forever,' Miette's grandfather said.

'They might be gone sooner than we think,' Robert Perrault senior said. 'I've heard things are going well on the Russian front.'

'Let's just hope they'll be on their way soon,' André Copeau's grandfather said.

With a wave to Robert and Evelyne Perrault, I disappeared into the toilet and locked the door. I bent down. No message from Martin. I scrawled a hasty note:

Meet me tomorrow, usual time, if you can.

305

40

'I 'm off out to gather the spring growth,' Maman said the following afternoon. She took her basket from its hook on the kitchen wall and fixed the grey-green eyes on me as if she'd guessed where I was going. 'Why don't you come with me, Célestine?'

My mother had never asked me to accompany her when she gathered the herbs and flowers that she dried and stored in her special room. I should have been delighted after all those years but I knew she'd be gone for hours, losing herself in the woods and the valleys of the Monts du Lyonnais.

'I … normally I'd have liked to,' I said. 'But I have other plans. I'll come next time.'

My mother gave her chignon a pat and walked out, her basket swinging from her arm. From the kitchen window, I watched her cross the courtyard, thinking how strange it was to see her opening herself to me. Perhaps though, it was simply that even the coldest, most distant person needs some sort of company in the end, and I was her only choice. I watched her step through the gateway and disappear into the back garden towards the woodland path.

I filled the tin tub with hot water, and stripped my clothes off — the trousers and blouse I wore, like Jacqueline — and slid into the water. I scrubbed my skin until it tingled.

I'd been in my bath only minutes when I heard the rap at

the door. I climbed out, hoping it was Dr. Laforge, or Père Emmanuel. The knock came again, more impatient.

I snagged my father's old coat from the hook in the hallway. Traces of his yellow smell of sawdust still clung to it, and I draped it around my wet body and hurried down the hallway.

'Who's there?'

'Requisition, madame.'

On no, not them again. I couldn't imagine what more the Germans could possibly want from us. Like every other farm around, they'd almost stripped L'Auberge. I opened the door a crack and stared into the smug faces of Karl Gottlob and Fritz Frankenheimer.

Fear jolted through me. I went to shut the door but Karl jammed a shiny black boot in the doorway.

'Ah,' he said. 'We were expecting the abortionist. We were wondering where you'd got to, Céleste, weren't we Fritz?'

'We have almost nothing left on the farm,' I said. 'You'll have to try elsewhere.'

'But I see you have some goats, hens and a horse,' Karl went on. 'They'll do us fine.'

'Open up,' Fritz said. 'We've come on official business, nothing more.'

I had no choice, they'd only report me for being insubordinate so I opened the door wider.

'Don't take our animals,' I said, clutching Papa's coat tightly around me with one hand, the other fumbling for my pendant. 'They're all we have left.'

'But we soldiers are hungry,' Karl said. 'How are we to fight a war on empty stomachs?'

'That horse looks nice and juicy,' Fritz said. 'Tender flesh.' He rubbed circles over his great paunch.

'Gingembre? You want to *eat* Gingembre? No!' My fingers tightened around the bone angel. 'Our stomachs aren't full either, but I'd starve before I ate my horse.'

'Now, now, Céleste, don't get nasty,' Fritz said, pushing the door open wider. 'It's not our fault you French bungled up and lost the war.'

'You haven't won,' I said. 'The Allies are coming.'

'The Allies are coming, the Allies are coming,' Karl sneered. 'What a tiresome joke that's become.' He pushed past me into the hallway. 'Now, what did Fritz say, Céleste? Don't get nasty. We don't like nasty girls.'

I stared at them, not knowing what else to say, as their sinister leers ran from my head to my toes.

Fritz stepped towards me and my heartbeat quickened. The milky grey-blue eyes stared into mine, his onion and cabbage breath rank on my cheek. He unsheathed his Luger, and, with the butt, traced a line down one side of my face. I shuddered, my eyes darting to the kitchen; at the beam of sunlight splicing through the window. Karl stood before me too, his legs spread, one hand fingering his own gun. There was nowhere to run.

I trembled all over. 'T-take the goats, the hens, Gi-Gingembre. Whatever you want but please, leave me alone.'

'Aw look, Karl,' Fritz said, a crabby hand clawing at my coat front. 'Little Céleste is scared. What a pity big strong Martin isn't here to save her this time.'

Karl's lips curved in a mean smile, his cat-eyes almost luminous.

'No, please no!' I tried to back away again. I knew I was begging and I hated myself for that. I jumped with fright as the fabric of my father's coat sheared apart in Fritz's hands.

He grabbed my angel necklace, ripped it from my neck and flung it aside. I heard it clatter on the tiles and I felt not only naked, but totally disarmed.

Fritz clutched one of my bare breasts and squeezed it hard. His doughy cheeks flushed red, he flung me backwards onto the floor. Bent over me, he jerked my legs apart.

Karl laughed his hideous, throaty cackle, and when I saw the bulge in his trousers, I gagged on the rising vomit.

'No, no!' I pleaded again. 'Please, no!'

'Shut up, bitch,' Karl said.

Sweat pouring from his face — the matte pink shade of a slaughtered pig — Fritz fumbled with his trousers and, with a single stab, thrust into me. I gasped with the pain, so fierce it ripped through my entire body. I tried to clamp my buttocks together to close my legs, but it was useless. I was trapped, as helpless as a mouse in a crow's beak.

'No, stop, you're hurting me!'

Karl laughed again. Fritz said nothing as he tore my flesh apart, hammering into my body — a solid, unrelenting pounding that seemed to reach right to my womb with every stroke.

I closed my eyes and sucked my breath in, trying to tear myself from his clutch. My thighs ached more and more with each fresh stab, and pinned beneath Fritz's huge hands, I felt my wrists would snap.

My body tightened into spasms as he battered me harder and harder. Droplets of his sweat, mixed with drools of saliva, moistened my breasts.

I fought to the edge of surrender; tried to scream. Fritz's breath came hot and fast, the exhaled air rancid as sour milk. He grabbed my hair, wrenching my head backwards, forcing my eyes to meet his, glowering with furious triumph. He gave a single grunt and slumped, sweat-slick and heavy, on me.

He pushed himself off me, took a corner of my father's discarded coat and wiped the sticky sheen from his rust-coloured fuzz.

When Karl Gottlob had taken his turn, they left me there, splayed on the uneven terracotta tiles like a wounded animal, shot purely for sport.

They swaggered away from L'Auberge without a backward glance.

I didn't know how long I stayed there, too numb to move, but eventually I rolled onto my front and raised myself onto all fours. I crawled across to where my pendant lay, and clasped it in my bloodless fist, my tears leaking onto Maman's waxed tiles.

41

When my mother returned from her gathering, I was crouched back in the washing tub.

'What in God's name has happened?' she said. 'The hens, the goats and Gingembre are gone.'

'B-boche.' My voice was no more than a husky whisper.

She dipped a hand into the tub. 'This water's stone cold. And you're all a shiver, Célestine. Look at your arms, they're raked raw.'

She didn't say anything more as she hooked her arms beneath mine and half-carried, half-dragged me into the living room and lay me gently on the sofa.

'Vile pigs,' she said, the rage in her eyes matching the venom in her voice. She covered me with the crocheted blanket that always sat across her Napoléon III armchair and dabbed disinfectant on the bloody grazes streaking my arms.

She tucked my arms back under the blanket and as she bent to pull it up under my chin, I caught her homely scent of musky lavender, peppermint and wild thyme.

'Stay put, Célestine, I'll be back with tea.'

'What is it?' I said, as she lifted my head and held the steaming cup to my lips.

'Camomile, an age-old herb. Used for virtually everything that is wrong with you.'

'Even this?' I said, sipping the warm infusion.

'It will help for now,' she said with a sigh, 'but later, when you're feeling strong enough, you'll need to come upstairs to my bedroom.'

'Your bedroom? God no, not that.'

'Preventive treatment,' she said, as she placed the teacup on the table and held a beaker to my lips. I tasted the bite of cognac.

'Better to be on the safe side,' she said. 'Besides, it will give you a good clean out; help rid you of the demon filth of those monsters.'

'I'll never be rid of their filth.' A single tear ran down my cheek, which I swiped away.

My mother's lips narrowed into the firm line. 'Don't let them destroy you,' she said. 'You must not let them destroy you, like they destroyed ...'

'Like they destroyed what?'

Maman had lowered her eyes, and held her fisted hands in her lap.

'Like me?' I said. 'You were going to say, "Like they destroyed me"?'

She refused to meet my questioning eyes.

'Is that what happened to you?' I said. 'The terrible, secret thing?'

She didn't move, her gaze still fixed beyond, on the peaks of the Monts du Lyonnais, a nauseous olive green in the afternoon sun, and when she finally spoke, it seemed she was reaching far into her past, seeing and feeling it all again.

'It was 1914,' she said with a sigh, as if emerging from the trenches; as if she'd run out of fight, and was ready to relinquish everything to the adversary. 'The Great War had just begun. There was a young man, a boy really, though he seemed like a man to a naïve sixteen year old.' She took a breath. 'Axel, his name was, and after he fought in the bloody battle of the Marne he could no longer bear the war. He deserted from the German army ... ran away and, somehow, ended up at L'Auberge. I found him hiding in the barn, exhausted, starving and wounded.'

'Weren't you scared? I said. 'To find a German soldier here?'

'Of course I was, but when he spoke of the terrible bloodshed, violence and savagery he'd witnessed, I was no longer afraid. I felt sorry for him, pity. So I hid him in the old witch's hut in the woods.'

'You know about the hut?'

'You've grown; matured so this past year,' she said, with a small, sad smile, 'but sometimes I find you still such a child. Generations before you knew of that hut.'

'Right,' I said. 'So what about Axel?'

'I took care of him,' she said. 'Used the skills my mother taught me to tend his wounds. I fed him and kept him warm.'

'And you fell in love,' I said.

She nodded. 'I did. And I thought he did too.'

'But he didn't?'

'One morning, when he was fit and strong again, he attacked me, brutally, without warning. I didn't see it coming. Just like those German pigs did to you. Then he disappeared. Scarpered off and I never saw him again.' She fell silent for a minute.

'That's the thanks I got for hiding him; for risking my life — my family's safety — to take care of someone. And look at the price I paid — what it made me! — for falling in love with the wrong person. I've never been able to ... to shake it off, it seems. The bitterness, the resentment.'

I wasn't conscious of it, but my hand had crept from beneath the blanket and I laid it over hers, which was still locked into a fist.

'Not even when you married Papa?' She didn't pull her hand away.

'Your father has been a good husband, Célestine. He deserved better than me. There could never be any real romance. No passion. I think he only married me because he thought I'd make an efficient wife.'

'Why didn't you tell me this before?' I said.

'When I said anything — a single word — against your German officer, it only drove you deeper into his arms, Célestine. Didn't it? Isn't that why it all started in the first place, simply to defy me?' I thought I saw a glint of madness in the grey flecks of her green eyes. 'I could never accept you and him.'

'I didn't feel anything for him in the beginning, but he seemed to admire me,' I said and I told her, then, of Félicité's plan.

'Your *sister* suggested such a thing? I can hardly believe that of Félicité.'

'Well she did, and I failed my mission. But now I know it can't go on. There are other things … far more important things I must concentrate on. But all the same, Martin *is* good to me, and kind. He's not like other Ger —'

'They're all the same,' she snapped, pulling her hand away and fidgeting with her chignon. 'The devil's blood flows in every one of their veins. Just don't let them crush the life from you too.' She gathered up the teacup and the cognac beaker and turned to go back to the kitchen. 'Now you'd better come upstairs. Best to get it over and done with.'

Over and done with. I feared, as with Maman, that thing would never be over and done with.

***

'Go to your room and rest now,' Maman said, coiling her tubing into the empty bowl on the stand next to her bed. My insides full of soapy water, my body still stiff and raw, I could barely move.

'If you hate the Germans so much,' I said, nodding at the bar of soap she was storing in its special box. 'How come you've got proper soap, when nobody else has any? We don't have money to buy things like that on the black market so you must be getting it from the Boche. And why do they let you keep up this business when they obviously know about it?'

My mother sat on the bed beside my outstretched legs.

'After Axel's betrayal, I thought I was rid of the Germans, rid of them forever. But no, back they came into my life, and this time they took your father to work for them — to work for them! I understood immediately, that if they weren't to break me again, I had to beat them at their own game.'

'Their own game?'

'All I do is feed them harmless information,' she said, 'in return for things I need, like soap, and to keep my business going.'

I shook my head as if I hadn't heard properly, searching her unflinching eyes.

'It was *you*? You told the Boche about Madame Abraham's false papers? And that Monsieur Thimmonier made anti-German remarks, and Raymond Bollet and René Tallon were hiding guns? It was you who sent them to raid Robert Perrault's wine cellar?'

I took a breath, couldn't stop myself shaking. 'You told them about Uncle Claude hiding horses and slaughtering his pigs to sell the meat? I can't believe you'd do such a thing to our friends; to Olivier's uncle.'

She started pulling at her apron, straightening it. 'As I've told you countless times, it's a matter of survival, Célestine. Those nasty little extortionists — Gottlob and Frankenheimer — simply use the information to claim objects or money from these people for themselves, and to send back home. Don't think they're any better off in Germany than us. They have nothing there either.' She sniffed. 'Besides, whatever I say, no real harm comes to those people.'

'No harm!' You can't truly believe that? You denounce friends, people we know. And what about Ghislaine's father?'

'It was a tragedy the poor man took his life,' she said. 'But I was not responsible.'

'Maybe not directly,' I said, 'but he'd lost his wife, the war took his son, his daughter. Having to close his shop — because of what you said — was the last straw.'

Maman kept on as if I hadn't spoken. 'Madame Abraham's antique shop is still open. She's still here in Lucie, not in some camp —'

'They steal her best antiques!' I said. 'They go back every week, demanding more and more. Miette told me the poor woman lives in terror, fearful she won't be able to satisfy their weekly orders.'

'Giving up useless knick-knacks is far preferable to being deported, Célestine. Haven't you heard what they're doing to her kind in those camps? *Death* camps, that's what they are.'

I caught my breath, thinking of the Wolfs. 'Yes, I've heard but nobody's certain. We have no proof.'

She tugged at her apron again. 'Times are hard, Célestine, which makes people hard. We live in a dark era, where stocks of compassion have run out and there is no more generosity. Each for himself or for the few people he cares about. We're all wearing masks; all engaged in bluff and counter-bluff.' She pushed at invisible meshes of hair. 'You are well aware I despise the Germans, and now you have my reasons for this hatred, but I absolutely need their cooperation if we are to get through this occupation; if we, and L'Auberge, are to survive the war.'

'I see,' I said. 'That also explains why they released you from prison so quickly, with no punishment, and why they didn't send you to the guillotine like Marie-Louise Giraud.'

'What would have happened to you, and this farm, if they'd sliced my head off?'

'Oh I don't know, Maman, I really don't. I pushed her aside, stumbled from her bedroom and across the landing. 'I'd like to be alone now,' I said, and shut my bedroom door.

***

I lay on the bed for the rest of the afternoon watching the sky darken over the hills. Dusk eventually washed the light from the fields and covered the woods in a sinister navy shade.

I'd missed my meeting with Martin, but I couldn't bear to see anyone, especially a man.

My mother, informing on the people of Lucie. It made me angry; a rage that confused and exhausted me, though part of me could understand. Survival. Playing the game. Things with which I could identify.

I closed my eyes and saw the frightening woman of my childhood, hidden behind her laundered grey aprons, her dusting cloths, and her old-time remedies — a woman who lived by hard work and a spotless home. Only forty-six years old, but a stolen girlhood and many seasons of harsh farm labour had stooped her shoulders and creped the skin around her eyes. Her face had shrunk like an old apple, and the hair she stretched into the taut bun was more grey than chestnut.

I saw her scouring away at us children with pumice crystals and camphor, applying the same fierce energy as she did to cleaning the farmhouse, so I'd felt like just another thing that had to be scrubbed. I understood, then, just what stubborn grime she'd been trying to shift.

In an ideal world I was certain my mother would never collaborate with the enemy but, as she said, ours was no ideal existence. Like fish trapped in a net, all we could do was writhe about and hope to wriggle through the mortal threads.

I tried to think of other things, anything to blot out the horrifying images; the pain of Karl and Fritz stealing their terrible pleasure. But sleep defied me as my fury grew, ebbing low at first, then swelling like a great wave until it consumed my mind and obliterated every other thought.

My eyes snapped open. I grabbed my pendant from the bedside table and clutched the broken chain. How dare they rip it from me, and fling it aside like some insignificant object; as if they were discarding every spirit L'Auberge des Anges had known.

My knuckles turned white, gripping the broken chain. I knew

I did not want to become the same cold and bitter mother I'd had to endure. So I too, would have to play the game. Karl Gottlob and Fritz Frankenheimer had to pay. An eye for an eye.

As I drifted into a fitful sleep, an idea began to leach into my mind. But for something so diabolical, I would need time, and precise planning.

42

In the weeks following the attack I stayed close to the farmhouse. Martin would be wondering what had happened to me, but I still didn't feel up to facing him. I couldn't bear the thought of seeing anyone until I'd punished Karl Gottlob and Fritz Frankenheimer; until I could I free my tortured mind.

My mother made little conversation. I think she sensed the rage smouldering inside me but knew I would no longer discuss what had happened. Perhaps she imagined I was still angry with her too, but Maman's collaboration with the Germans had paled almost to insignificance, against the vengeful thoughts that clotted my mind.

She nourished me as best she could from our dwindling supplies, and coddled me with potions from her herbal room stocks: peppermint tea to unravel the knots in my stomach, St John's Wort for emotional shock, and Vervain infusions to combat nerves and sleeplessness.

One morning she pushed my hair aside to fasten the angel necklace around my neck. 'I had the chain fixed,' she said.

'I thought you hated this pendant … that you couldn't bear to touch it?'

'My own mother gave it to me,' she said. 'The very day Axel …'

Her fingers, grappling with the clasp, prickled my nape. 'I thought of it as bad luck; some cursed bit of old bone. Which is ridiculous, I do see that now, but …'

'I'd probably have thought the same,' I said.

'I'm pleased you wear it though, Célestine; that you've been able to feel the courage and strength it's given to generations of L'Auberge women … something I could never give you.' She patted the chain against the back of my neck. 'There, good as new.'

'Can anyone be as good as new after …? But yes, I'll be all right. Soon, I'll be all right.'

'I know,' she said. 'You're strong; determined enough to be right again. And then, so will I.'

I almost smiled at the irony; the absurdity that for my mother to free herself from the binds of her mental prison, it seemed her own daughter had had to suffer the same violence.

I moved across to the small mirror of the Rubie clock and stared at the reflection of the angel pendant. Martin's gold chain was pretty to look at, sitting against my pale throat, but still I couldn't help seeing it as some sort of foreign object; an alien intruder.

'But I did believe,' she went on, 'that the leather was as much a part of this heirloom as the angel carving itself. It doesn't seem quite the same, without it.'

I imagined the fingers of all those women who'd touched the worn leather thread; those to whom it had given comfort before me, and recalled how Martin Diehl — the German — had discarded it like something meaningless. He may have simply wanted to please me with the sparkling gold chain, but that only showed how he didn't really know me; how he never could have known me.

'No, Maman,' I said. 'No, it's not quite the same.'

A rap on the door startled me, and my mother went to answer it.

Dr. Laforge strode into the kitchen, and Maman crossed to the stove and started brewing coffee.

'Ah, Céleste. I haven't seen you around the village for a while.

I wondered if …' He nodded at my mother. 'If you and Marinette were all right?'

The doctor raised the single eyebrow at me. My eyes flickered to Maman, her back still turned to us.

'My daughter's been ill with … with some kind of affliction,' Maman said, setting three cups of coffee on the table.

'I'm sorry to hear that.' He swallowed a mouthful of the barley mixture. 'Are you certain I can't do anything to help? Perhaps she needs some … some particular medication or treatment?'

'I had everything she needed here at L'Auberge thank you, doctor,' Maman said.

'Right, well yes, I'm certain you have everything she needs, Marinette.'

'I'm fully recovered now,' I said.

Dr. Laforge swallowed the dregs of his cup and stood. 'Thanks for the coffee but I must rush off. As always, plenty of ailing people to call on.'

'I'll see you out,' I said, scurrying down the hallway after his brisk strides.

'I'd like to go back to Lyon,' I said, as I opened the door for him. 'But I can't, just yet.'

'Nothing you need to tell me about, Céleste?'

I shook my head. 'No, no … nothing to do with our work.'

'Right, well come down to my rooms when you're ready.'

I watched him hurry down the steps, two at a time, and across the courtyard.

Soon I would be ready. Yes, very soon.

***

By late May I felt strong enough to return to the village; to face people again. I propped the bicycle against the fountain wall and crossed over to Au Cochon Tué, keeping a stealthy eye out for Martin.

I called cheery greetings to Robert and Evelyne Perrault and the card-playing men, as I hurried through the bar and into the toilet.

I bolted the door and bent down, my fingers curling around the slip of paper.

Sorry you didn't come. I waited all afternoon. Please come next week.

I tore the paper up and flushed the scraps away. Next week, and the one after, had come and gone but I scribbled a message, asking Martin to meet on our usual day — two days' time.

I walked back across la place de l'Eglise and onto rue Emile Zola, and stood across the road from Ecole de Filles Jeanne d'Arc. From my years as a schoolgirl, I knew every nook of the place but still I needed to go over it all one final time.

I could hear the Germans carrying out their manoeuvres — the rhythmical *tap-tap* of boots on pavement, the bark of an order, the clatter of weapons. Nobody was supposed to watch them goose-stepping about in their high black boots, but I sidled up to the wall surrounding the school and put an eye to a gap in the stones.

The soldiers stood, their heads held high, before the officer on horseback in command, as the music began, soft, like something was holding it back. As it sprung into magnificent, solemn notes, the soldiers began moving their lips in song.

I glimpsed Karl and Fritz amongst them, and the anger snapped at me again. Their uniforms looked brutally smart, their rigid bodies confident — an arrogance I would take the greatest pleasure in shattering.

Amongst the many skills I'd acquired from the Resistance, I'd learned patience and discipline. I couldn't bear to wait much longer but I wasn't about to let any hasty moves destroy my plan.

'*Achtung!*' the commandant barked, and I jumped back a step.

The soldiers started whistling as they finished grooming their horses. They left them to munch on the green shoots of the trees and marched off towards their canteen.

When I saw Martin and the other officers leave the barracks for lunch in their billets' homes, I drew away from the gap and looked around me again. Still nobody in sight. I hurried around the corner, into the alley with its small copse onto which the Community Hall backed — the place I'd been alone with Martin, at the Harvest Festival. The perfect place to conceal myself.

I strolled back down rue Emile Zola towards the square, alongside gardens bordering the road where men in shirtsleeves and corduroy trousers tilled, sowed and watered.

'*Bonjour, bonjour*,' I called to each of them as I passed by their homes.

They all tipped their straw hats and smiled back at me.

I didn't know why I climbed the steps of Saint Antoine's. Perhaps I thought the church would, somehow, give me some kind of benediction for what I was about to do. Or I simply hungered for the friendly voice of Père Emmanuel.

'Forgive me, Father, for I have sinned,' I said, as I sat in the confessional.

'It's nice to see you, Céleste,' Père Emmanuel said. 'The doctor told me you've been ill.'

'Nothing serious, Father. I'm well now, thank you. Ready to continue our battle.'

'I'm glad to hear that. Still no word of your father or your sister? Or the others?'

'Not a word, Father. I'm beginning to wonder if we'll ever hear from them again. And I'm so afraid for Patrick and Olivier. We both know the Maquisards' success — their survival — depends on the food and silence of people like your brother, Georges. But with all the reprisals — German *and* French — the locals are becoming too afraid to help them. Did you hear, just the other day the militia shot fifty-five civilians in cold blood?'

'I certainly am aware that punishing civilians for acts of Maquis sabotage is becoming more and more savage,' the priest said, 'but we can't let that threat put us off. Besides, Georges and Perrine won't let them down. Keep faith, Céleste. And keep fighting. I feel the end is near. Everyone's talking about the Allied invasion, discussing it, making bets and … and hoping.'

'Yes, thank you, Father, I know we must keep hoping, and fighting.'

I walked out of Saint Antoine's and back across la place de l'Eglise. I rocked my angel pendant back and forth along the gold chain, and ran the plan through my mind again.

I could not detect a single flaw.

43

Two days later I threaded through the Vionne River willows. Martin was waiting for me beside our rounded stone, skimming pebbles across the water. His lean frame swivelled around as I approached, his smile spreading.

'I thought you were never coming back, Céleste?'

'Sorry, I wasn't well, but I'm fine now.'

'I imagined you had stayed in Lyon, to continue your … your work?'

'Ah yes, that.' I took a few steps to the gravelly shore, gathered a handful of pebbles and turned my back to him.

'You understand why I couldn't tell you?' I started skimming the stones, one after the other.

'I do. I even understand why you became a resistor. I did suspect it. In fact, I would not have expected anything less of my fiery little *Spatz*.'

I heard him lighting two cigarettes, but didn't look around as he handed me one. 'In case you are wondering, Céleste, it was not me who informed those militia who arrested your friends. I was as surprised as you to see them.'

I took short, sharp puffs on the cigarette, between sliding the pebbles across the water.

'I did nothing to compromise you,' he went on. 'I would never do that, even if it does mean I would be court-martialled and shot, if they found me out.'

I turned to face him and clamped my arms across my chest. 'So why did you walk off at the park, without a word? I didn't know what to think.'

Martin took a long drag before he spoke.

'I was angry, disappointed … let down because you could not trust me; because you kept lying. I was convinced we could be honest with each other.'

'I couldn't tell you, Martin. You're a German officer for God sake! I couldn't know your reaction. I could've been putting not only my life in danger, but all those I was working with. Don't you see that?'

He edged towards me. 'Even so, you should have trusted me.'

He slid one hand around the nape of my neck and went to kiss me. I jerked away awkwardly, sat on the rock, and scrabbled about for more pebbles.

'What is wrong, Céleste? Put down those stones, please. Is it not time we stopped playing games?'

'Yes it is, Martin.' I flung the pebbles aside and rubbed my palms together; kept rubbing long after the grit was gone. 'I can't … I won't be coming to the riverbank to meet you anymore.'

'Won't be coming … what do you mean?' His mouth folded in a child-like pout.

'Some of my friends, and half my family, are in camps in Germany, Martin. Another is living each day in great danger.' I took a shaky breath. 'I worry about them constantly, but there's nothing — *nothing* — to do for them. All I can do is dedicate myself to our fight to rid France of the occupier — you — as quickly as possible. Because only then can they be free.'

'Your love has soured.'

'No … no it hasn't, but don't you see that being with you, a German, goes against what's so crucial to me right now?'

Martin sighed and looked away, at the Vionne running fast and proud after the spring rains. He pulled out his cigarette packet and offered it to me again. I shook my head and he lit a single one. For several moments he didn't speak, puffing on the Gauloise and staring at the river.

'You remember we spoke about running away together, Céleste? To the faraway place?'

'Yes, but things are different, everything has chang —'

'Let's do it,' he said. 'Go to Switzerland. Now, today. You know I am a soldier fighting against his will; a hater of militarism who sees not the slightest romance in war, only butchery and inhuman degradation. While I have you, there is a reason to keep going, to stay here day after day, just trying to survive until it's over. But now, if you are not …'

He shook his head as he dropped the half-smoked cigarette and ground the butt under his heel. 'All that Nazi propaganda they stuffed into our heads. I see how cruel and barbaric it all is, and how the Führer is a diabolical monster who should be destroyed. I no longer desire to serve in his army.'

He took my hands and clamped them, prayer-position, between his. 'We could be married in Switzerland, start a family. We will go to Germany when the war is over.'

'Desert the army and elope to Switzerland? Are you insane, Martin? We'd be court-martialled and shot. Both of us.'

'We would be cautious, like we have always been; careful not to get caught.'

I shook my head. 'I know you despise the war … that you're a peaceful person, but I can't believe what you're saying; what you're asking me.' I pulled my hands from his. 'Besides, we don't have money, or a place to stay. It's madness!'

'We would work it out,' he said.

'Anyway, I don't want to live in Germany. I could never leave L'Auberge. Not for good. Yes, I can go away to study, get a profession, but I'd always come home. The farm has been in my family for centuries — for hundreds of years! It's a part of me, just like this angel is a part of me.' I fingered the old bone between my thumb and forefinger. 'As the leather thread was part of me.'

'Where is the girl who could not wait to get away from the farm?' he said, with more than a hint of bitterness.

'I don't know … perhaps that girl has changed. Really, Martin, it has to be like this. I need to focus on the people I love who are imprisoned; dedicate myself to helping them.'

'It seems you have made up your mind.'

'I hope you understand, and respect, my decision. That you won't …'

'Won't what?' Martin's eyes filled with hurt, and a shadow of anger. 'You think I would turn you in to the authorities?' He shook his head. '*Mein Gott*, Céleste, what do you take me for? Besides, if I was going to do such a thing, I would have done it weeks ago.'

'Well no, I don't honestly think that, but I can't … couldn't help worrying.'

'Can we at least write to each other?' he said.

'Of course, if you want.'

'We might be together again one day,' he said. 'When it is all over?'

'I'd like that,' I said. 'Really, I would. Just not now.'

We fell silent, listening to the *ack-ack* of a bird and the quiet burble of the Vionne. My thoughts drifted to my brother and Olivier, living rough and dodging German gunfire high on the cold, isolated hillsides of the Monts du Lyonnais. True, devoted warriors. How different they were to this soldier with his starched, unstained uniform and his romantic poems; the officer who didn't care if his country won or lost the war.

'I must get going, Martin.'

'I would like to see you,' he said. 'One last time.'

'No, I don't —'

'Just once more, Céleste. There is something I want to give you. I will leave you a note, as usual, in Au Cochon Tué.'

'All right, if you insist.'

He opened his mouth and let out a brief, hesitant sound, as if he was about to say something else, but I turned away, cutting him off.

Convinced I'd done the right thing — the only thing — I hurried back along the woodland path, a small distant murmur telling me that Martin Diehl and I had come to the end of our game. I was not deluded enough to imagine we'd be dealt another hand of cards, once the war was over, and for that, I felt only a heavy sadness.

His strange dawn-coloured eyes seemed to peer at me amongst the net of willows and, beyond them, I saw an endless stream of never, stretching as far as the Vionne. Martin and I would never grow old together; never spend another night together. Never would I feel his arms about me again, or smell his delicious scent as I slid my fingers through his golden hair. We would never walk the wide avenues of Berlin hand in hand, or picnic beside those rivers of his childhood. We would never have that daughter, to whom I would bequeath the angel necklace.

I gripped the pendant, rubbed it, and pressed it to my trembling lips.

44

Dawn crawled into a clear morning, bringing with it a trace of breeze. I tackled my jobs, listening to the church bell chime out the hours, waiting for eleven-thirty. Half an hour to get down to the village and across to Ecole de Filles Jeanne d'Arc.

As if on a usual shopping trip, I took my basket and cycled down the hill, across rue du Docteur Pierre Laforge. The grass sparkled, the damp paths overgrown with daisies and cornflowers, the perfume of the lilacs flaring my nostrils as I cycled by.

A group of mothers came towards me, pushing prams and holding the hands of young children they'd collected for lunch from the nursery school.

'*Bonjour, bonjour,*' I called to them all, smiling as if I hadn't a care in the world.

'Ah, there you are, Céleste,' Miette's mother said. Five-year old Séverine was with her, and Anne-Sophie, Olivier's youngest cousin. 'Marinette told me you've been ill, I hope you're better now?'

'I'm quite well, thank you, Madame Dubois.'

'So you'll be returning to the city soon, to your Red Cross work with Miette?'

'Tomorrow,' I said. 'If all goes to plan.'

'Just take care, won't you?' she said. 'After what happened to poor Ghislaine, I live in constant anguish for you and Miette.'

'I will, I promise.' I started pedalling away. *'Bon appétit.'*

'Bon appétit, Céleste,' Séverine and Anne-Sophie called with smiles and waves.

I leaned my bicycle against the church wall beneath the hateful posters of Pétain and waved at Evelyne and Robert Perrault, busy wiping down tables on the terrace of Au Cochon Tué.

'Looks like we're in for a hot summer this year, eh, Céleste?' Monsieur Thimmonier called from his shop front. He sat on a low stool, carving what looked like a little wooden box. No doubt another for the Germans to send home. 'Let's hope those Boche have gone by then, so we can enjoy it.'

'Yes, let's hope,' I said, trying to banish the rancid thoughts of my mother's collaboration. I had a far more important mission to concentrate on.

Denise Grosjean sauntered from the post-office, plump as ever. No doubt the Fritz pig was giving her black market food, as well as camel-hair coats. Just make the most of it, Denise, your sneaky gifts won't last much longer.

'So, what are you up to on such a nice day?' Denise said.

'Not much. The usual. Farm chores, bit of shopping, you know.'

'I imagined you'd be back in the city,' she said. 'Busy with that important work of yours?'

Anxious to get away, I ignored Denise's taunts, gave her a shrug and walked around into the alleyway at the back of Au Cochon Tué. The doorknob refused to budge.

'Merde, merde and *merde!'* I should have known Robert Perrault would keep the rear access to his cellar bolted. I glanced at my watch. Time was running short. I cursed my stupidity at overlooking the one vital thing upon which my entire plan hinged.

I hurried back around to the square and entered the bar via the front entrance, my eyes scanning the room for

Monsieur Perrault.

'Céleste!' I spun around to the cheerful face of his wife. 'I heard you've been ill?'

'I'm fine now thank you,' I said, trying to keep the snap from my voice. 'But I need to see your husband.'

'Whatever do you want with Robert?'

'I ...' My mind raced. 'My mother wanted me to tell him his gout remedy is ready.'

'Well, I'll tell him,' Evelyne said, looking around the bar. 'He can't be far away.'

I jumped from one foot to the other. Another minute and it would be too late; I'd have to call the whole thing off. I couldn't bear to wait yet another day.

'Look, there's your husband,' I said, hurrying away before she could stop me.

'I think I left my wallet in the cellar. I need the key,' I said to Robert, amazed at the lies I could sprout without a qualm.

'I won't be long,' I said, taking the small key he plucked from a hook beneath the counter.

I almost ran down the uneven steps to the secret back section of the cellar, shivering with the damp chill of the stones, my eyes continually flitting to my watch.

I took what I needed from the shelves lining the walls, placing the items carefully in my shopping basket.

One hand holding the basket steady, I returned the key to Monsieur Perrault and forced myself to a nonchalant stroll across la place de l'Eglise.

The bell of Saint Antoine's chimed midday. Martin would be gone from the barracks, back to the Delaroche home for lunch. He might not be mine any longer, but I certainly did not want to harm him.

The last villagers were crossing the square on their way home as I walked to the opposite side of rue Emile Zola and up to Ecole de Filles Jeanne d'Arc. I strode along with a casual manner until the last person disappeared. Not a soul in sight, I turned the corner into the alley onto which the Community Hall backed.

My eyes flitted about. Still nobody. I could stop it all. I could turn around and trudge back up to L'Auberge and forget everything. But I knew I would not forget it; could never rid my stained mind and body of those two monsters unless they paid for their crime.

I was well aware that reckless act of mine could invite German punishment but I took comfort in the thought that, up till then, the only actual retribution the villagers of Lucie had suffered was punishment dealt by our own hand — the punishment inflicted on Gaspard Bénédict when he betrayed his own people.

I reached into my basket and took, with care, the first hand grenade. I recalled how Pierre and Antoine had taught Ghislaine and me, a lifetime ago it seemed, how to launch one. By the end, when Ghislaine died, we'd been proud of our lethal proficiency.

My hand steady, I grasped the safety pin with my left index finger, and pulled and twisted, to remove it. I took a breath and, with a smooth, overarm action, flung the grenade over the wall in the direction of the barracks' canteen. I watched it sail through the air for a second then repeated the same, practised manoeuvre with a second, and a third, grenade.

I darted into the copse as the first explosion echoed against my eardrums. Even as the screams and shouts from the school drilled into my brain, I felt strangely calm, concealed behind the oak trunk.

Mud-brown palls of smoke began to mushroom over the stone wall, followed shortly by flames — small and silent at first, then lengthening into crackling orange fingers.

I hunched behind the tree, not moving, barely breathing, as the fire took hold, quickly raging. I still made no move as I heard the first villagers come running towards the burning school, and caught snatches of their shaky conversations.

'… blown up … school destroyed …'

'… Boche … dead …'

'… see anyone?'

'Nobody.'

'... who?'

The voices were all French. Not a single harsh, guttural sound.

I stayed behind the tree until I heard the army of villagers gathering around the corner, about the school entrance.

I slid from the copse and hurried down the road and around the corner into rue Emile Zola. My face set in the same grim consternation as theirs, I tagged onto the end of the line; simply another concerned villager passing buckets of water along the human chain.

The fire was not the inferno I'd first imagined, and hoped, for. After only half an hour, the villagers had it in hand. I slunk away from the core of the crowd, and back across rue Emile Zola; away from the heat of the flames and the dark clot of smoke that was sending people into spluttering fits.

By the time I reached la place de l'Eglise, my heartbeat and breathing were steady and calm. It was over. I'd done it. The festering wound salved, I could begin to knit back together the edges.

I headed for my bicycle, still standing against the church wall. I'd almost reached it, ready to throw a leg across the saddle, when I saw them huffing and puffing across the square towards their destroyed barracks. Karl Gottlob and Fritz Frankenheimer.

***

I didn't know whether to walk normally or run for my life. On instinct, I ducked low, behind the fountain wall. I peered over the ledge. They were gone from the square. I left the bicycle where it was and scurried across to Dr. Laforge's rooms. I pushed the door open and almost collided with the doctor, clutching his black bag.

'Céleste, what is it? I'm on my way up to the school. There's been an expl —'

'It was me.'

'You?' He hustled me into his consulting room and shut the door.

'Sit.' He nodded at the chair and perched on the edge of his mahogany desk. 'Take deep breaths and calm down.'

A babble of words streamed out as I told the doctor about Karl and Fritz's visit to L'Auberge, and what they'd done to me.

'They had to pay,' I said. 'Or I knew I'd never be the same again.' I flung my hands in the air. 'But they didn't. I just saw them both, alive and well.'

He listened in silence, the one eyebrow raised. When I'd finished he let out a heavy sigh.

'It's one thing to fight for our cause, Céleste, to help rid our country of the occupiers, but it's an entirely different thing to take the law into your own hands and set off on a cold-blooded murdering spree.'

'What about what they did to me? They can't be allowed to get away with it. I had to do it. Don't you see?'

'I do understand,' he said. 'But this sort of wild, solo action was what I feared about you, Céleste, right from the beginning — hot-tempered and irrational thinking. Over the last months you've proved yourself a dedicated, trustworthy group member, and I believed you'd changed. But after this ...' he flung an arm in the direction of the school. 'I can't help thinking I was wrong. You should have come to me. Besides, as you say, those two — Gottlob and Frankenheimer — are not dead, so you might still be bitter and angry the rest of your life.'

'But this was different.' Tears smarted my eyes, the heat burning my cheeks. 'Nothing to do with our work. I had to make them pay. I'm sorry, but I was so ... so filled with rage.'

Dr. Laforge shook his head. 'I do sympathise with you, Céleste but that ... that unfortunate incident at L'Auberge will have to be dealt with in another way.'

'What way?'

'I don't know yet,' he said. 'But the pressing concern is whether or not Karl Gottlob and Fritz Frankenheimer put two and two together and realised you attempted to kill them. But even if they haven't, you know there will be reprisals.'

'But the Germans have never actually punished the people of Lucie,' I said. 'Up till —'

'We can't know when, or in what form,' the doctor went on, 'but I can't see the Germans letting such an act of sabotage go unpunished.'

He stepped down from the desk. 'I must get up to the school. You'd best stay here in the flat out of sight for now. And your mother will have to leave L'Auberge.'

'Won't that make her, or me, look guilty?'

'Not necessarily,' he said. 'She could be leaving the farm for any number of reasons. Hasn't she got family in Julien-sur-Vionne?'

'Yes, her sister lives there — Aunt Maude, with my Uncle Félix. But she'll hate to leave the farm.'

'Maybe so, but it's unavoidable. Right, I'll check they don't need me at the school, then I'll head up to L'Auberge and take your mother across to Julien.'

'Can't you just take me straight back to Lyon? I really want to go ba —'

'I'm sure you do,' the doctor said. 'But your actions today demonstrate you're not thinking rationally; unable to work in a team. I think you've forgotten what our hero, Jean Moulin said about efficient combat with unified groups.'

'Will you ever let me go back to Lyon?'

'Perhaps,' he said, opening the door. 'But right now you're in no mind to be a capable Resistance fighter.'

45

I paced the small living area. I sat on the edge of the sofa and gnawed my top lip. I paced again.

I'd failed not only myself, but our entire cause. Dr. Laforge was angry and disappointed, and he had every right to be. And for what? Karl and Fritz had escaped my revenge and I felt none of the elation or satisfaction for which I'd yearned.

A few hours later the doctor's footsteps thudded back up the stairs. He hung his hat and coat on a hook and flung his keys on the mantelpiece.

'Your mother is with your aunt and uncle in Julien. She sends her wishes, and hopes you're all right.'

'Did you say why she had to leave the farm?'

'I didn't have to. As soon as she heard there'd been an attack on the German barracks, she seemed to guess who was responsible.'

How absurd, that the only person who might understand why I'd blown up the primary school was my merciless mother.

'Thankfully,' the doctor went on, 'nobody perished in the explosion. A few soldiers received superficial burns, but it was the building that suffered all the damage.'

'I suppose I do feel better,' I said, 'knowing I didn't actually kill anybody.'

'Perhaps the reprisals won't be as savage, since nobody died,' Dr. Laforge said, setting out a late lunch of boiled eggs and grainy bread. 'There's also something I'm afraid you'll find difficult to hear.'

'What?'

'Since the Germans no longer have the school to live in, they've requisitioned L'Auberge. They're moving in as we speak.'

'Taken over L'Auberge? But how, why? How dare they? Besides, there are barely any supplies or animals left.' Even as I spoke, I remembered there was my mother's food stocks though, her cash and jewellery, beneath the herbal room floorboards. There were precious paintings and a toy soldier in the attic, along with a photo of a German officer, secreted away in a wooden box.

As we ate in silence, I imagined the hateful Boche moving into L'Auberge. They'd taken my father, my sister and my friends. They'd come and stolen my body — my whole *self*. Now they were taking my home — the last thing that mattered. In my fury; my helpless desperation, I could barely swallow any food.

The doctor finished his coffee. 'I must go out again,' he said, retrieving his hat and coat. 'Don't wait up for me, and don't answer the door to anyone. Or the phone.'

***

I slept badly the first night in Dr. Laforge's spare room, my dreams darkening to nightmare images of Karl and Fritz hulked over me, shearing my father's coat apart and exposing my naked body. Their evil voices chimed in my ears as they ripped the angel pendant from around my neck. Smoke snagged in my throat. I couldn't breathe. A ball of heat shot through me. Flames licked at my bare flesh, hungry and devouring.

A series of distant explosions woke me in a shivering sweat, my cheeks slimy with tears.

'It appears,' Dr. Laforge said, as I joined him in the kitchen. 'Nobody knows who's responsible for the school attack. For the moment.' He nodded towards the window. 'They're all out on the square though, whispering amongst themselves, and glancing suspiciously at each other.'

The doctor then recounted the group's successful Resistance coup in the hour before dawn.

'The Germans got gunpowder from that factory,' he explained. 'We had to stop their supplies.'

'Yes, an explosion did wake me,' I said. 'It must've been the factory blowing up.'

'There will be reprisals, I suppose,' Dr. Laforge went on. 'The Germans absolutely needed that factory to operate, and will surely punish us somehow.' The eyebrows knitted as one. 'But we didn't have a choice. The Allied landing is imminent and we have to cut off all the Germans' lines of communication and transport; stop them sending troops north, to counter the invasion.'

'I wish I could've been there,' I said. 'I hate being cooped up here.'

'Hopefully it will not be for much longer, Céleste.'

I stayed inside Dr. Laforge's flat for the next two days, too fearful of running into Karl and Fritz. If they hadn't already guessed, I was certain they'd only have to glance at me to know the truth.

I kept peering through the window at the villagers down on the square. They were still glancing sideways at each other and gathering in twos and threes, gazing suspiciously at passersby and falling silent when someone else approached. Mothers kept their children by their sides.

On the third day, I ducked out for a few minutes and retrieved Martin's message in Au Cochon Tué. One last time, he'd said. It wasn't reasonable, or sensible, to let him tug at my fragile emotions again, but I was curious to know what he had for me.

'The Germans are still conducting house-to-house searches,' Dr. Laforge said, when he returned in the evening. 'And they've put a message up on the door of the Town Hall, asking anyone with knowledge of the attack to volunteer information. Naturally they're offering a handsome reward.'

'But nobody besides us, and my mother, knows.'

'Let's hope it stays that way,' he said.

***

On the evening of June 6th, I tuned into the BBC on Dr. Laforge's radio. When I heard the broadcast, I sprang from my chair and leapt about like an excited child.

'The Allies have landed! The invasion has begun!'

Dr. Laforge hurried across to the wireless set.

'They said the Americans, Brits, Canadians and Free French airborne troops landed shortly after midnight,' I said. 'Then Allied infantry and armoured divisions on the coast, at six-thirty this morning. They've flung the German armies from the Normandy shore!'

'So this is really it,' Dr. Laforge said with a wide smile. 'The beginning of our long-awaited liberation.'

'Oh yes it must be. Though it still sounds too good; too much of a fairy tale to hope Papa, my sister and my friends will all be home soon.'

Neighbours, who'd already heard it from other neighbours, began shouting the news to each other and soon la place de l'Eglise filled with people kissing each other, wiping away tears of joy and sighing with relief. And when Dr. Laforge and I went outside and joined them, nobody looked at me sideways, or with the least suspicion.

People brought out bottles of homemade alcohol and we raised our glasses and toasted France, and filled ourselves with fresh courage and strength. The Germans were nowhere in sight, no doubt sulking up at L'Auberge, scoffing the requisitioned wine of Lucie-sur-Vionne. Besides, what could they do? They couldn't prove what it was we were celebrating.

And throughout the following day, the radio seemed to

tremble with the thunder of national anthems: *La Marseillaise*, *The Star-spangled Banner*, and *God Save the King*.

So happy celebrating the Allied invasion, and convinced the war was finally over, nobody seemed to give another thought to any retribution the Germans might take for the grenade explosion of Ecole de Filles Jeanne d'Arc.

46

'I'm off into the city for the day,' Dr. Laforge said, as we drank our breakfast coffee. 'Pack your bag, Céleste. It's been almost a week since the explosion and there's been no reprisal. I think we're safe. Nobody has connected the attack to you either, so I'll take you back to Lyon this evening, or tomorrow morning if I stay overnight with Jacqueline.'

'No more rash, unthinking acts,' I said. 'Promise.'

'Besides, keeping you busy in the city might take your mind off what those two did to you,' he said chewing his hunk of bread and jam. 'Instead of sitting here brooding about it. The Allies have landed, and there's still so much to do to stop the German troops travelling north. You might want to go over to Julien and say goodbye to your mother; let her know you'll be in Lyon for some time.'

'Yes, all right, I'll go this afternoon.' Of course I didn't say I would meet Martin Diehl one final time before continuing along through the woods to Julien-sur-Vionne.

Once the doctor left, I cleared the breakfast things, tidied and cleaned the flat and packed my few clothes into the bag my mother had given Dr. Laforge the day she left for Julien.

1145 hours.

Perhaps it was the heavenly weather that made me think everything was going to be better, as I crossed la place de l'Eglise — bold gestures of clouds streaking a sky so blue it seemed to bow down to the horizon and caress the earth. The soft breeze curled the wisteria that flounced across the vestiges of Lucie's stone *vingtain* like a pretty dress, sweeping its bracing perfume over the square.

I waved a greeting to Mr Thimmonier, his gnarly hands planted on aproned hips. I greeted Madame Abraham-Lemoulin in her antiques shop with a cheery, '*Bonjour.*'

'*Salut*, Céleste,' Evelyne Perrault called, from the terrace of Au Cochon Tué, and I raised my arm in a wave.

From the church steps Père Emmanuel gave me a smile, one side of his face dappled light and dark with the shade of the lime tree leaves.

'The Allies are *really* here this time,' Yvon Monbeau was saying to his customers, as I joined the bakery queue for the much sought-after bread. 'Hard to believe, isn't it?'

'We can have faith in the British,' his wife, Ginette, said, and I saw her eyes shine with the longing to see her prisoner-of-war sons again soon.

'*Humph*,' André Copeau's grandfather said. 'Remember what those cursed English did to our Jeanne d'Arc?'

'Oh yes,' Yvon said with a smirk. 'If the Brits hadn't burned Jeanne d'Arc, she would be able to save France today, no doubt!'

'It does seem too good to be true though,' Simon Laforge's wife said. 'We've waited so long for them.'

'Well Hitler did make a big mistake,' said Robert Perrault senior, 'invading Russia, opening a war on two fronts. He only got to be a great man because his enemies were small, but those enemies are no longer small. The man is doomed, Britain's victory certain. And my three grandsons — and your two boys,' he said, waving an arm at the baker, 'can be free again!'

The baguette stowed in my shopping basket, I strode back

towards Saint Antoine's to collect my bicycle, which had been sitting there for almost a week, since that fateful day.

A flurry of small boys dashed around the fountain, shrieking as they flicked water at each other.

'Shouldn't you all be at school?' I said.

'We're home for lunch,' one of them said, droplets of water dripping from his cheeky face.

Miette's two sisters walked with their mother across the square towards me.

'I didn't expect to see you still in Lucie, Céleste,' Madame Dubois said.

'I'm going back to Lyon this evening, or tomorrow.'

'Papa says we're going to win the war after all,' Séverine said.

I smiled at her. 'Yes, I know. Isn't that good news?'

I nodded at Gaspard Bénédict's mother as she scurried home with her perpetually distressed air. None of the villagers had spoken a word to her since Gaspard was found to be a traitor. I felt a pang of sympathy for the woman. After all, it wasn't her fault her son had decided to play that dangerous game.

1200 hours.

The bell of Saint Antoine's chimed, the sun radiating the heat of a midsummer's day as I cycled down the lane to Uncle Claude's farm.

Blue jays and red cardinals darted between the shadowy pear trees and cherry blossoms swayed like snowball puffs. The breeze tugged at the blossoms, as if trying to tear them from their branches, but they held fast, their stems bending with the same trembling kind of grace as a dancer.

I knocked and opened the farmhouse door to the usual smell of curing hay and burning leaves coming from Uncle Claude's pipe. Justin and Gervais, Paulette and Anne-Sophie were eating lunch and greeted me with greasy grins.

'Dr. Laforge had another message from Patrick and Olivier,' I said, joining them at the table. 'They're alive and well.'

The twins clapped their hands together.

'When's Olivier coming back?' Justin said.

'Very soon, I hope,' I said.

'We'll show him we can climb the oak tree higher than him now, eh Justin?' Gervais said with a toothy smirk. 'Even better than you, Céleste.'

'Our meal is far from extravagant,' Uncle Claude said, waving an arm over the mish-mash of watery vegetables. 'But please, join us.'

'I have to leave soon. I'm going back to Lyon this evening, or tomorrow,' I told him, only too aware how little food Claude had for himself and his four growing children. 'I'll eat with you next time.'

'Oh yes, please do,' Anne-Sophie said. 'And come back soon.'

'Keep safe, Céleste,' Uncle Claude said, as he closed the door behind me and I cycled back down the lane.

1220 hours.

I only got as far as the end of the dirt track when I heard the first rumble of engines. I was surprised because vehicles — especially those half-track truck kinds — were unusual. Two of them passed along the road, the soldiers eyeing me with bored, uninterested gazes.

The noon sun caught the glint of the insignia on their uniforms — the Wolfsangel of *Das Reich*'s SS.

Even as I caught sight of that menacing symbol, I felt more curious than worried, and continued cycling behind them, keeping my distance.

The half-track vehicles reached the end of the village and the soldiers got down. Several orders were barked in German and the soldiers marched off in different directions, scanning the vicinity as if they were searching for someone.

I felt the first smatterings of unease. Was it me they'd come for? My first instinct was to run and hide somewhere until they left. I decided to head back to Dr. Laforge's flat, lock myself inside and not answer the door.

1240 hours.

The half-tracks had parked on la place de l'Eglise, the troops scattering in all directions with their unmistakeable walk that no Frenchman could produce — the hammering of boots and the clattering of rifles; a walk that belonged to an arrogant conqueror, trampling across the land of a defeated enemy.

There was not the slightest animosity from the SS, but still I was anxious to reach the doctor's flat, and hurried across the square.

People had started leaving their lunch tables, and standing at their windows and open doors.

'Who are they?' Evelyne asked her husband, from the bar terrace.

'SS,' Robert said, a hand on his wife's arm.

'Why aren't they wearing black then?' his wife said. 'Are you certain it's the SS?'

'Certain, my dear,' Robert said. 'They wear khaki camouflage too. Now come on inside.'

'No reason to be alarmed,' one of the troops said, 'it's a simple identity check. Please come out of your homes and workplaces and assemble on the square.'

Several people came from their houses, dabbing napkins to their lips, mothers holding small children by the hand. I had the key ready to open Dr. Laforge's door when one of the soldiers looked directly at me.

'You too, mam'zelle,' he said. 'Assemble with the others.'

1250 hours.

The sun was burning, the heat oppressive. Although they seemed to be hurrying people up, as if eager to get things over and done with, the troops remained calm, ordering every last person onto the square, reassuring us it was a simple identity check.

Over the next fifteen minutes, the numbers swelled to quite a crowd. In their haste, people had come out as they were, mothers wearing aprons and carrying babies, not bothering to get the pram out. I recognised all of them, huddled in the sparse shade of the lime trees as the bells of Saint Antoine chimed one o'clock.

1305 hours.

By then, families from outlying farms had joined the human column moving towards the square. I saw Uncle Claude, holding the hands of Anne-Sophie and Paulette, Justin and Gervais following, jostling and teasing each other.

The Germans assured us again it was only an identity check. But was it only *my* identity they wanted to check?

I caught Père Emmanuel's eye, giving him a nervous glance. He gave me a thin smile.

'Look, Maman,' Séverine said, pointing to her arm. 'A ladybird.' She started prodding at the little insect, which lifted its delicate, transparent wings.

'Don't you kill it,' Amandine said, wagging a finger at her sister in perfect imitation of their mother. 'It's bad luck to kill one of God's creatures.'

Séverine blew on the ladybird, which must have felt like it was on a lifeboat caught in a storm, and flew off.

The blooming lilacs had attracted an army of honeybees that dived into the flowers, their bodies trembling as they drank. They zoomed around us, and the children shrieked and flapped their arms.

More half-tracks arrived on the square, letting off people I recognised from nearby hamlets. Once the trucks had unloaded they left, only to return shortly after with new passengers, who looked bewildered to see such a crowd.

1330 hours.

The sight of all those familiar faces made me feel a little better. The SS would never go to all the trouble of assembling the entire village and surrounding areas if it was only me they'd come for.

Calm and confident, the soldiers positioned themselves around the perimeter of the square, the red flag with its black swastika flapping above them. Even as they levelled their machine guns at us, nobody seemed truly concerned. After the Allied landing, their caution wasn't the least bit shocking.

In a quiet corner of the square, a stray cat was crouched in the shade of an awning, carrying a bird in its mouth. It dropped its prey onto the cobblestones, plunging its claws into the tender flesh.

The heat was overwhelming, the shade sparse. Conversation became strained. Babies started wailing, and children whined for drinks.

'I want to finish my lunch, Papa,' Anne-Sophie said with a scowl.

'Baby, baby. Little baby wants to finish her lunch,' her brothers needled, dancing about and jabbing fingers at their sister.

'As soon as they've finished checking our papers,' Uncle Claude said, his face tightening in a frown, 'we'll go home and finish lunch.'

'I've got cakes in my oven,' Yvon Monbeau said to one of the soldiers. 'I need to take them out.'

'Don't worry, you'll get back in time for them,' the soldier said with a smirk. But the baker flung his hands up and sighed.

I too was hungry and thirsty, and started to get impatient. Besides, if this went on much longer, it would be too late to get to Julien to see my mother, and I'd miss Martin.

1340 hours.
Some of the soldiers began separating us: men and boys on one side, women and girls on the other. Uncle Claude took his sons by the hand as a soldier pushed Paulette and Anne-Sophie in the direction of the women.

'Papa, Papa!' the little girls cried.

'I'll take care of them,' I called to Claude, taking the girls' hands.

Olivier's uncle dashed me a fearful look as the soldier hustled me off to line up against the church wall with the other women and children.

'Where are you taking my husband?' Ginette Monbeau said.

'What are you doing with them?' Simon Laforge's wife said, holding the hands of her two youngest children.

The SS, chatting and laughing amongst themselves, offered no replies.

1350 hours.

A clipped order was barked in German and the soldiers divided the village men into groups and began marching them down the westbound street, away from the church.

'I want my papa,' Séverine cried, clutching my hand tighter.

Several babies were wailing, and young children complained loudly.

'I'm thirsty.'

'Pee-pee, Maman. I need to do pee-pee.'

I detected the first signs of panic in the women's voices as they tried to calm their children.

'Silence!' an officer snapped. 'No more talking.'

The minutes ticked by. I felt my rising fear, as cloying as the hot summer air that thickened over the square. The children kept crying, their mothers placating them with hushed words.

47

'All into the church!' an officer snapped, and the troops began herding the women and children up the steps of Saint Antoine's. We all fell quiet, and my heartbeat quickened as I held the hands of Anne-Sophie and Paulette and trudged into the house of God. Mothers carried their babies and small children, neighbours and friends helping when there were too many to carry. I felt not a breath of air.

I'd always loved the inside of Saint Antoine's — the rainbow of colours that danced on the walls in the sun, the smell of the candles and the cool, flagstone floor. I was in awe of the painted statues standing in each corner, with their golden shining curves. But all I felt now was a creeping fear.

As the Germans continued herding us into the church, I glanced up at my favourite painting — the long-bearded man in brown robes holding a stick with a bell on the end, a pig sitting at his feet — and said a silent prayer; a few desperate words from a non-believer to a monk who had driven out a demon.

Though I'd never listened to much of Père Emmanuel's Mass, I did find the church instilled a kind of peace inside me and I tried to focus on that, to relieve my ever-growing apprehension.

Crammed inside the church, we bunched together — a huddled, expectant knot of women and children.

'What are they going to do with us?' whispered Miette's

mother, standing beside me with Amandine and Séverine. 'Whatever is this about?'

I shrugged, trying to mask my unease. 'Identity check, so they said.'

'When are they going to check our identities then?' Evelyne Perrault said.

'My husband's cakes will truly be cinders by now,' Ginette Monbeau said.

'And what about my post-office,' Denise said. 'It can't run on its own.'

'Don't be stupid, Denise,' I snapped. 'There's nobody at the post-office. Can't you see the entire village is here?'

'You don't have to get nasty.'

'I'm not. I'm just … this is *very* odd. What are they going to do with us?'

'And where have they taken our husbands?' Simon Laforge's wife said.

'You're right, Céleste,' Madame Abraham-Lemoulin said, standing on the other side of me. 'This looks bad. Very bad.'

After about ten minutes, several soldiers who looked no older than Patrick and Olivier brought a large box into the nave. They placed it close to the choir, the strings that hung from the box trailing on the ground.

'What's in the box, Maman?' Amandine said.

'I haven't the slightest idea, *chérie*,' Madame Dubois said. 'But I suppose we'll know soon enough.'

Several young children skittered towards the box, trying to work out what it was. Their mothers grabbed their hands and pulled them back to their sides.

'Why can't we go home, Céleste?' Paulette said, with a scowl.

I squeezed her hand and tried to keep my voice from shaking. 'Soon. We'll go home soon.'

The troops then proceeded to light the strings that trailed down from the box. Once each string was alight, the Germans stepped back and folded their arms across their chests.

We all stared at the box, waiting for something to happen. The blood pulsed hard through my veins.

The box exploded with a deafening bang. People jumped and cried out. We all looked at each other, the mothers gasping, the children shrieking and crying.

The Germans disappeared as dark smoke began to fill the church. We all started running, half-screaming, half-choking on the smoke-clogged air, tearing wildly to the corners of the church where the air was still breathable. But even as we ran to those parts, the smoke filled the pockets too and many of the women fainted.

I saw the terrified crowd had broken down the side door that gave onto the sacristy. Still clutching Anne-Sophie and Paulette's hands, I followed the surge of women. My breathing short and ragged, I sank down on a step with the girls. My head spun with the smoke, the fear, and with wild, disconnected thoughts of how I might flee the church.

The Germans were back. They must have seen we'd escaped into the sacristy, and their bulk filled the doorway — a barricade obstructing our only possible escape route. Before anyone could scream, or even move, they raised their guns and began firing on us.

I watched, in stunned horror, as Miette's mother fell, a dark hole staining her forehead. Amandine and Séverine fell on top of their mother. I tried to pull them away, but I couldn't budge Amandine and the little girl died on top of her mother, half her head blown away. I retched, pulling Séverine away from the corpses, towards Anne-Sophie and Paulette, standing beside me, rigid with terror.

Everybody was shrieking — one, continuous, curdled wail. Blood spurted and streamed all around me as women and children crumpled to the flagstones, one after the other, those still standing cowering; simply waiting for a bullet to catch them. The smoke stung my eyes so much that tears coursed down my cheeks.

There wasn't a thing I could do. Inside the cramped sacristy, there was nowhere to run, so I dropped to the ground with the dead and dying, dragging the three girls down beside me.

'Don't move, don't make a sound,' I hissed to the girls. And there we stayed, motionless, barely breathing, waiting to die.

I felt Paulette's hand slide from mine, and her little body went limp, a gaping wound exposing her brain. I clamped a hand over her sister's eyes, my terror alone stopping me from being sick.

The Germans kept firing machine-gun rounds. Simon Laforge's wife went down at the same time as her three children, beside Evelyne Perrault, Ginette Monbeau and Denise Grosjean.

More and more dead and wounded fell all around us, on top of us. After several minutes, there was less noise, only fading screams and moans. The smoke and the weight of the bodies pinning me down made it hard to breathe, but through a gap in the splayed limbs I glimpsed the Germans. They had begun piling straw, broken-up pews and chairs in a heap over the pyramid of bodies.

They didn't waste a minute, setting their bonfire alight and retreating several paces where they waited to ensure the fire took hold. Once the flames started crackling, the heat became unbearable and they turned and fled the sacristy.

The fire spread quickly, those still alive either letting out feeble groans or praying. There seemed no way out; no escape from the inferno. Amidst the racket of rising flames and the crack of falling roof tiles, I kept a grip on Anne-Sophie and Séverine knowing without a doubt we would all be dead in a few short, agonising moments.

48

Through the cottony fug of thirst and shock, through the heat of the flames and smoke so dense I could barely see my hands, I felt the first twist of rage. When the Germans took over L'Auberge, I felt they had stolen every last thing from me, apart from my life. Now they were going to take that too. I would not let myself lie down and die for them without the most bitter of fights.

With every bit of strength I could gather, I dragged Séverine and Anne-Sophie from beneath the corpses, trying to find a way out. Amidst the smoke and chaos I couldn't see anything clearly. I was vaguely aware of Madame Abraham's rasping breaths, her shaky fingers gripping the back of my dress.

There was no sign of the SS as we crawled along the flagstones, out of the sacristy and back to the main part of the church. We reached the altar, and I rose to a crouching position behind it, the girls and Madame Abraham still beside me. Through needling smoke, I looked up to the three windows on the curved wall of the apse behind me. Impossible to reach them.

I eyed the stool Père Emmanuel used to light the candles, grabbed it and placed it before the middle window, which was the biggest. I climbed onto the stool and reached up, my fingers curling around the sill. Pure terror, or perhaps my iron will to beat them at their own game, gave me the force to heave myself up onto the ledge.

I turned around and grabbed the outstretched hand of Séverine first, then Anne-Sophie. In turn, I pulled each girl up beside me, then together the three of us lurched through the broken glass to the ground below.

I glanced back up and saw Madame Abraham had followed us. How the old woman had found the strength for such a climb, I would never know, but when she dropped to the ground beside us and lay still, her legs twisted at a strange angle, I was certain the fall had killed her.

'Madame Abraham?' No answer. I patted her cheek softly. She groaned.

'Come on,' I said. 'We've got to move from here. They'll kill us as soon as they see us.'

She moaned again, a grey tangle of hair matting her bone-white face.

'Go, Céleste. Take the little ones. I can't ...' she said, through clenched teeth.

'We haven't done all this,' I said. 'Escaped a burning church, to let them shoot us now.'

Séverine and Anne-Sophie took one of Madame Abraham's arms while I took the other. Our breaths short and ragged we dragged the old woman, her legs dangling limp as a puppet's, towards the garden of Père Emmanuel's presbytery cottage.

We slumped to the ground between the priest's rows of tomato plants. It was only then, as I caught my breath, lying in stunned terror, that the pain came.

'You're bleeding,' Séverine said, pointing to my left arm. I hadn't felt the cracked glass slice through my skin, as I fell through the window. I ripped a strip from the hem of my dress and bound the cut.

Madame Abraham was still not moving but she was at least breathing.

'Where's Papa and my brothers and Paulette?' Anne-Sophie said.

I held the little girl close to me. 'I don't know, *chérie* ... I really don't know.'

Almost immediately, we heard the first of a series of explosions in the direction of the side street down which the SS had herded the men. When I caught sight of the smoke and flames, and smelled the sickly stench of burning flesh, there was no doubt in my mind the village men were suffering the same fate as the women.

Concealed amongst the leafy tomato plants, my breathing slowed and my brain began to function again, and the impact of the Germans' monstrous deed hit me.

Reprisal on the grandest, most unthinkable scale.

I lay there, my eyes shut tight, shaking uncontrollably, aware I was responsible for the whole, evil thing.

49

The stone wall surrounding the presbytery garden was low so I stayed down, crawling across to one side. I peered out through a gap between the stones.

I could see the SS on la place de l'Eglise, piling items looted from homes into the half-tracks. When they finished taking everything they wanted from each house, they calmly set it alight and moved to the next one.

The fires drew people out; those who'd been suspicious of the identity check and had taken refuge in wardrobes and under beds. Those men and women stumbled out, coughing. The SS gunned them down where they stood.

'I'm thirsty,' Anne-Sophie said. Mute with the shock, she hadn't said a word, but then she started to cry. 'Where's my papa?'

Séverine began to cry too. 'I want to go home.'

I put a forefinger to my lips. 'Hush, girls I'll find us some water soon, but we have to stay here for a while, and not move or make a noise. Do you understand?'

The little girls nodded through their quiet sobs.

I crawled across to the well and, crouched over, drew up a pail of water. I poured some into the old tin can with which Père Emmanuel watered his flowers and vegetables.

I gulped a few mouthfuls, refilled the can and crawled back to the others.

Séverine drank the cool water, and passed it to Anne-Sophie.

Madame Abraham still lay motionless, her breathing faster, and shallow. Her face had turned the ghastly hue of ash.

'Madame Abraham.' I knelt beside her and held the can to her lips. 'Open your eyes. Drink some water.'

I knew it was dangerous to let people lapse into unconsciousness. You had to keep them talking, keep them with you. 'Come on,' I insisted. 'Just a sip.'

Her eyes opened to slits. She swallowed a little and slumped back onto the ground.

I tore several more strips from the hem of my grimy dress, pulled a stake from one of the tomato plants, and broke it in half under my foot.

'It's all right,' I said, as I set about splinting her ankles. 'You're going to be all right.'

Once I'd finished with Madame Abraham, I started bathing my own cuts. Blood was oozing from my left arm beneath the makeshift bandage. The little girls sat motionless, staring at me with the uncomprehending innocence of children who could not begin to fathom what had happened in the church. I could not grasp it either and I had no idea what to say to ease their shock or calm their minds.

We must have stayed there two or three hours, amidst the tomato plants, not daring to leave its relative safety. The noise of the pillaging Germans finally died down, and I started to feel heady from the blood loss, the heat and the exhaustion. I sensed too, that Madame Abraham wouldn't last much longer.

I crawled back to the wall and peered out again through the gap. Homes were still burning, smoke surging from the blackened buildings, but there was no sign of any SS uniforms. I scrambled to my feet.

'I think they've gone,' I said. 'Besides, people will have seen the smoke and fires. Word should have reached other villages by now. I'm going out to see if help's on the way.'

'They might still be here,' Séverine said. 'They'll shoot you, if they see you.'

'Madame Abraham needs medical care,' I said. I hated leaving the girls alone with a sick old woman, but what other choice was there? 'Now promise me you and Anne-Sophie will stay here and look after her? I'll come back as soon as I can.'

The girls gave me solemn nods.

I kept low until I reached the gate in the garden wall. Still crouched, I peered between the iron palings. No sign of the SS. I was certain they'd gone.

I clutched my throbbing arm to my side as I dashed around to the front of the church. There was not much left of Saint Antoine's. Most of the roof had caved in, and only parts of the blackened walls still stood. I dared not glance inside.

La place de l'Eglise was a ghost town, the noise and hustle of people oddly absent, smoke drifting aimlessly across the ancient cobblestones.

I hurried up rue Jeanne d'Arc, tearing my eyes from the bullet-ridden corpses flung across the pavement like rubbish. I fought the rising waves of nausea, forcing my quivering legs onward, passed the still-burning buildings. A sob tightened my throat as I watched the homes of my friends burn to the ground, the heat overwhelming me, the smoke making it hard to breathe.

There was still no evidence of any sort of life — SS or surviving villagers — as I crossed rue du Docteur Pierre Laforge. My left arm scalded me, and the bandage had turned rust-red.

I swiped the sweat from my brow and kept on, not really knowing where I should go, my eyes continually scanning the area for SS.

I thought of Martin, waiting for me on the riverbank. Surely he'd have heard about the massacre. Why wasn't he there helping, with the rest of Lucie's garrison — those stationed at L'Auberge? And why were there no other rescuers? Perhaps people were keeping away from Lucie, afraid the SS was still there.

I decided to follow the Vionne River path through the woods

to the nearest village — Julien — to raise the alarm and get help sent. Still gripping my injured arm, I hurried up the hill towards L'Auberge.

Anxious to remain out of sight, I veered off the road to the track that ran in a wide arc around the farmhouse, leading to the woods and the river. I hurried on, continually glancing between the trees into L'Auberge grounds.

I spotted Karl and Fritz amongst the Germans, who were assembling their possessions in the courtyard and loading them into military vehicles. I was not surprised to see them leaving the farm. Lucie was gone; there was no village left to occupy. Perhaps the SS had ordered them out; forbade them from going near the burning village.

I was so intent watching them, I didn't realise at first that Karl's mean cat-eyes had spotted a figure amongst the trees. But when I saw him nudge Fritz and point to me, I bolted off, flying through the woody blur of greens and browns. I soon caught the thud-thud of heavy boots behind me.

My legs were quivering by the time I reached the willow trees that fringed the Vionne. With each step along the path my chest grew tighter, as if the sooty fire flakes still blocked it, threads of flame searing deep into my lungs.

My arm stung so badly I wanted to scream out. The headwind blustered, the heat parching my papery throat even more. I couldn't go on much longer if I didn't get water, but it wasn't safe to stop at the riverbank for even a few seconds.

I reached a familiar oak tree, the one with the twisted trunk, which had always reminded me of two entwined bodies. I ached to rest there, to stop the giddiness that made me want to vomit but I didn't dare slow down or glance behind, for I could hear Karl and Fritz clearly by then. My stomach knotted at the sound of every guttural shriek, each one louder and closer.

I felt I would keel over any second, yet the terror of passing out and waking to the sneering faces of Karl Gottlob and Fritz Frankenheimer urged me on to my special place on the river. My necklace thudded against my breast, and I felt the exhaustion, the thirst, overcome me more with each step.

A gunshot rang out behind me. Or was it the wind? Perhaps only my eardrums, still beating hollow, from the rapid gunfire in the church. On and on it echoed in an endless, evil chime.

The sweet gurgle of water cascading over the ridge into our pool seemed to call out to me. I wanted to slide into the coolness, to feel the maternal arms of the river around me, protecting me from the predators in my shadow.

I eased my pace, aware I was far more familiar with that spot than the Germans, who knew nothing of the old witch's hut where I'd spent my childhood — the shelter that had concealed the Wolfs a lifetime ago.

I stumbled the few steps to the water's edge, cupped my hands and gulped the cool water. More shouts through the trees, the throaty noises growing urgent, louder, as if the wind were carrying the scent of my fear right to their nostrils, and they knew they were closing in on their prey. Karl shouted something to Fritz, and I knew they'd spotted me.

I filled my lungs with air and flung myself into the river, a spatter of bullets peppering the surface of the water around me. I dived deep and swam low, along the riverbed, towards the waterfall. When my lungs reached their limits, I surfaced behind the largest boulder of the pool. And there I stayed, as still as the rock behind which I crouched.

Concealed behind the curtain of water, I watched Fritz and Karl searching the surface of the river, their guns trained on the opposite bank, obviously expecting me to appear on the other side. I still didn't move, and was thankful for the rushing water to mask my pounding heart and my gasping breaths.

From the corner of my eye, I caught a glimpse of someone walking through the willow trees towards us, from the opposite direction. Amidst the high summer foliage I couldn't see who it was at first, but Karl and Fritz must have seen the movement too, because they swivelled around and, convinced it was me, fired at the moving figure.

The person crumpled to the ground, and my breath caught in my throat as I realised, with rising horror, that it was Martin Diehl.

***

Their eyes wide in scarlet faces, Karl and Fritz stood still, wordless at first. When the shock must have hit them — the reality that they'd shot an officer — they began shouting at each other. I couldn't understand their words, but they were obviously arguing. They stomped around in circles, their arms floundering about as if they didn't know what to do. For there was, of course, still me — the fugitive on the run.

From their gestures, I assumed they'd decided to flee, as they swivelled around and hurried back along the track towards L'Auberge.

Once they disappeared from sight, I waded out of the river. Perhaps Martin was only wounded? I could not bring myself to think he might be dead.

I raced to his prone figure and knelt beside him. No rise and swell of his chest. My fingers shook, grappling for his wrist. No pulse. No heartbeat. In that instant of shock and disbelief, I simply grabbed his Luger from its leather holster, clicked a magazine into the butt, and started back along the path.

I caught up to Karl and Fritz in minutes. The strain of all the running had obviously taken its toll on the fat Fritz and he lagged behind Karl, who kept spinning around, frowning, and urging him on.

From behind a willow trunk, I watched them stagger to the river, crouch on the bank and scoop water into their palms.

As they drank, I crept closer, stealing from trunk to trunk, the Luger steady in my damp, gritty hand.

Martin's words rang in my head.

... pull these two knobs backwards, until you see "geladen" which means, "loaded".

The Luger levelled, I sidled the last few steps up to them, both still bent over the gurgling river. I knew the exhausted Fritz would be slower to react, so I shot Karl first, in the back of the head.

Fritz spun around and the next bullet caught him between his piggy eyes. Both Germans lurched forward and fell, with dull splashes, into the river.

I lowered the gun, startled at how easy it had been; astonished at my cold satisfaction. How I'd changed from Gabrielle Fontaine on her first mission at the Antiquaille hospital — the girl who feared she could never kill a soul.

I sank down onto the gravelly shore. I'd felt calm, almost at peace, right before I shot them, but then I shook all over — a numb, emotionless shudder — as if my mind and body were no longer connected.

I scrambled upright and splashed water over my face, swallowed a few gulps and lay back on the smooth stones. The wind cooled my cheeks, and brought a scrap of singed paper floating to the ground beside me. I picked it up, and squinted through the scorch marks, recognising a few broken phrases of the catechism.

I toyed with the scrap of paper, thinking about how things looked. When the Germans found three of their own, murdered, they'd immediately think it smacked of Resistance. There would be more reprisals. I almost laughed. What more could they do? There was nothing, and nobody, left to punish.

But Madame Abraham, Anne-Sophie and Séverine needed help, and any others who might've survived the carnage. Without a backward glance at the corpses floating downstream, I heaved myself off the ground, the pain in my arm lancing me like the stab of a sword, and headed down the path towards Julien-sur-Vionne.

I glanced at Martin lying across the path beside my special

riverbank spot — our spot. A small square parcel lay beside the corpse, as if it had fallen from his pocket. I picked it up, tore off the wrapping and opened the box. My palm flew across my heart as I stared at the diamond ring — the jewel with which Martin had hoped to tempt my brittle emotions.

The sun glinted off the edge of the single gem for, even to my untrained eye, I was certain it was a genuine diamond; no fake square of polished glass that might scratch, and shatter, over time. No, it was an eternal symbol of Martin Diehl's pure emotions; the untarnished love I had not been able to reciprocate.

I snapped the box shut, slid it into my pocket and as I hurried away from the lifeless body, the blood surged through me like the Vionne in a storm, the pain swamping me as if I were caught in a great gaping floodway.

50

Bloodied, filthy and tear-faced, I stumbled into Uncle Félix's shop.

'Thank God,' Maman said, folding me into her arms. 'Thank God.'

'Jesus, Blessed Virgin Mary,' Aunt Maude said. 'We saw the smoke. People are saying the Germans have burned Lucie. Surely that can't be true?'

'I wanted to come straight away,' my mother said, 'to see if you were ...'

'But the mayor forbade us to leave Julien,' Aunt Maude said.

'He said the Germans might still be there,' Uncle Félix said. 'That it could be dangerous. They told us to let the rescue teams go in first.'

My words gushed out in a twittery mumble. 'I need to go back ... M-m ... Abraham, Séverine ... presbytery garden.'

Maman set a cup of herbal tea in front of me. 'Help is being sent,' she said. 'Word of this ... this disaster has spread and your friends will be rescued.'

I sipped the tea, the sting of cognac warming me, and calming my trembling limbs.

'Whatever happened, Céleste?' Aunt Maude said. 'Have the Boche truly burned Lucie? Why would they do such a thing? It's simply unbelievable.'

My aunt's words reverberated against the screams of the

villagers — a continual, tortured wail. The odour of scorched human flesh snagged in my nostrils and made me gag. Numb with the pain, the shock, and twitching with the spasms of guilt, I could no longer speak.

'We'll let Célestine rest now,' Maman said. She sat beside me, dabbed a cloth into a bowl of warm water and started cleansing and disinfecting my cuts. 'Instead of bombarding her with questions. I'm sure she'll tell us everything when she's ready.'

With deft fingers, she stitched the jagged gash on my arm and bound it with a clean bandage. I barely felt the pain of the needle going in and out of my damaged skin.

***

'You know you don't have to go back to Lucie so soon,' Maman said the following morning.

'I want to go … I have to. Don't you see?'

'You won't find any answers, any *absolution*, Célestine,' she said. 'If that's what you're looking for. All that — the reason for such a thing — can only emerge later, once the shock passes.'

'I'm going, Maman.'

With a grim nod my mother helped me climb up into Uncle Félix's trap.

The sun was a fiery orange in a cloudless sky over Lucie. Fat pigeons cooed, swallows wheeled and sang, and sparrows hopped about, unalarmed. The joy of that spring life seemed unreal, offensive even, amidst the desolate scene no words could describe.

Obsessed only with escaping the murderous inferno, I saw it all then, all that remained of people and a village which only the day before had been full of life; everything from which, yesterday, my cocoon of shock had protected me.

Like a silent film in my head, running far too slowly, I watched them all going about their daily lives: Père Emmanuel, Miette's parents and sister, Uncle Claude, Robert and Evelyne Perrault and Ginette and Yvon Monbeau, who would never open their doors to their prisoner-of-war sons.

The faces of Miette and Dr. Laforge too, flashed into my mind. I thought of them going about their work in Lyon, ignorant of what had happened back in Lucie.

The first rescue and salvage teams, many wearing the Red Cross armband, were busy with the gruesome task of recovering bodies. They found Agnes Grattaloup, weak and exhausted, but alive, huddled in her cellar, where she'd taken refuge when the SS arrived. We'd assumed the eccentric old woman hadn't a clue there was a war going on but it was evident she'd known better than the rest of us what it was all about. The rescue workers pulled another handful of survivors from the cellars of their devastated homes — those too fearful to surface yesterday.

It seemed that once the mass execution was over, the SS had gone on a manhunt, systematically shooting down any witnesses. The rescue teams were finding those bodies too, down wells, behind burned-out cars, and shoved into ovens.

There was also a large group of people who had family in Lucie, or those lucky enough to have been away the previous afternoon. Though I was certain those people did not consider themselves fortunate in any way.

They clustered together, walking amongst the smouldering ruins in a kind of unbelieving daze. It seemed they were all caught in that moment between sleeping and waking, when the veil of dreams is about to lift; when you reach out towards the light, relieved that it's all been a nightmare, and force yourself into wakefulness.

The women cried softly. The men remained silent, their heads bowed, and when they came upon their blackened homes, they stared in mute shock.

My fingers folded over my pendant, Maman and I walked amongst the debris of la place de l'Eglise: the black skeletons of the lime trees, the bodies of burnt bicycles, a baby's pram, a child's doll pecked with bullet holes. The ancient gallows posts had survived, untarnished.

The smell of suffering clotted the silent air and I gagged on the stench of burnt flesh, dry retching on the taste of my guilt. I rocked my angel back and forth along Martin's gold chain, trying to feel the familiar comfort from the old bone; to calm my fretful, accusing mind.

Rubble, bits of metal and charred wood littered the broken-down interiors of what had been, just yesterday, warm and lively homes. Several were only partly incinerated, crockery and cutlery still sitting on the table, as if in silent remembrance of a meal begun but never finished.

Every sight stirred in me new shock — a pair of tapestry scissors sitting next to an iron, as if the housewife would be returning to finish her work. In a child's bedroom, a mermaid figurine and a hairbrush sat, undamaged, amidst a charred mess.

Instinctively I grabbed my mother's arm as we came upon the entwined bodies of two children, hand in hand, their cherub faces still wearing their look of innocence.

We picked our way around the debris and up to Saint Antoine's church. On the outside wall, an iron crucifix remained intact. I took a tentative step over the rubble of fallen stones, imagining the bronze organ pipes still ringing out their melancholy sounds, Père Emmanuel's reassuring voice still booming out across the centuries-old flagstones.

From the blackened vestiges, shreds of smoke trailed into the silence. Bands of sunlight speared down through the holes in the roof, specks of dust and soot dancing in the beams. A twittering bird flew in, hovered over the wreckage, flapped its wings and shot back into the sky.

The sun lit up the bullet holes that pocked the walls and marred the white tablet listing Lucie's glorious dead from the Great War. Twisted fragments of the church bell lay where it had fallen beneath the bell tower. I could hardly believe it would never chime out over the village and countryside again — that sound I was born into, something so familiar I'd almost ceased to hear it.

'Look,' I said to my mother. 'The bell was bronze, and it melted. But the altar and the confessional, made of wood, have survived. It makes no sense.'

'Some things are senseless, Célestine.'

In disbelief, we gaped at the blood staining the church flagstones, and at the objects strewn across them: a toy horse, corset stays, hairpins, several nails from clogs.

We stepped back onto la place de l'Eglise, where people were standing alone or in small groups. No longer fearful of the Germans, a deep sadness seemed to hang over them; a sadness that became, as the morning wore on, tinged with the first stirrings of anger.

'I'm going to check on Agnes,' my mother said, nodding in the direction of old Madame Grattaloup who was slumped, alone, against a blackened wall.

I glimpsed Dr. Laforge at the fountain, and made my way over to him.

Two men were speaking with the doctor — René Tallon and Raymond Bollet — Uncle Claude's farmer friends who'd been caught hiding guns. How trivial that all seemed then, being caught hiding guns.

'They herded us into the barn,' René was saying. 'We were all just standing there, nervous and scared, but we still had no notion of what was coming.'

'The SS officer set up his machine gun on a tripod,' Raymond said, running a shaky hand through his hair. 'Other soldiers were standing guard, waiting.'

'Then from outside,' René went on. 'We heard a detonation — obviously the signal to fire. Someone shouted a command and their bullets started mowing us down. Raymond and I were in the middle, all the dead falling on top of us. We didn't move, did we Raymond?'

'Not a single muscle,' Raymond said. 'Even when the soldiers stepped forward to give the coup de grâce to those who might still be alive.'

'I felt my brother take his last breath, on top of me,' René said, his voice breaking up.

'They covered the bodies with straw and kindling,' Raymond said, 'and set fire to the building. Smoke filled the barn but we managed to grope our way out of a small back door that led into another barn. We hid there, in the loft.'

'Then they set that on fire too!' René said. 'So we crawled outdoors and worked our way over walls and gardens till we reached the edge of the village. Behind us, the whole place was burning.'

Apart from their obvious shock, Raymond and René had, miraculously, not suffered the slightest injury. Though I was certain those sole survivors of the barns would be left with far deeper wounds; scars no medicine could heal. Dr. Laforge patted the men on the shoulder, and they moved off with a straggle of people.

The doctor turned to me and took my hand. 'Thank God, Céleste, I couldn't believe it when Madame Abraham told me about your escape from the church.'

'Where is she? And Anne-Sophie and Séverine? Does Miette know what's happened to her family?'

He shook his head. 'Your friend is still unaware of the tragedy. And, for now, Anne-Sophie and Séverine are with a volunteer family in Julien. Many families in other villages have opened their doors to survivors.'

'And Madame Abraham?'

'In hospital,' the doctor said. 'Both ankles fractured, but she's a tough old bird.'

'And the others?' I said.

Dr. Laforge frowned as if he hadn't heard right. 'Others?'

'Yes, everyone — Ginette and Yvon Monbeau, Monsieur Thimmonier, Evelyne and Robert Perrault, Père Emmanuel,

Uncle Claude and his sons and daughter, your brother and his wife …'

'But, Céleste … there are no others.'

'I know,' I said, the tears spilling. 'Of course, I know. I just can't believe it until someone says it aloud. It's my fault, isn't it? All of this is because of me.'

'Don't say such a thing,' Dr. Laforge said. 'There is any number of reasons why they might have done this. When the Allies landed, everybody thought the war was over,' he continued in a hushed tone. 'But the harsh fact, Céleste, is that these are the most dangerous of times. The Germans are hair-trigger edgy.'

'Yes, but —'

He held up a hand. 'It might be reprisal for the gunpowder factory we blew up, or some generalised punishment for Lucie being an effective Resistance centre for the past year. It was the deed of an army in panic, caught in a race against time by the advancing Allies, harried by Maquisards. Out of contact with their superiors, they too behaved like terrorists.'

'But I'll never know, will I?' I said. 'Never know for certain I haven't destroyed our village; murdered all our people?'

'There's no point thinking about who might be at fault,' he said. 'After this …' He waved an arm across the square. 'This evil massacre, we have far more to worry about.'

I nodded towards his burnt-out rooms and home, and the place where Simon's chemist had once stood; where he, his wife, and three children had lived. 'What will you do now? Where will you go? Back to Lyon with Jacqueline? Maybe I should come with you? I can't bear the thought of staying here.'

'You'll return to Lyon later, Céleste. Once I've …' The one eyebrow knotted. 'Once I've started to digest all of this.'

He nodded at my mother, walking back with Uncle Félix. 'Go back to Julien. Let Marinette take care of you; let her help assuage this self-reproach you've burdened yourself with.'

'I'm taking you home now, Céleste,' Uncle Félix said, his hand on my arm. 'You need to rest.'

'I must go to the farm first,' my mother said. 'To see if L'Auberge is ...'

'But the Germans are there,' Dr. Laforge said. 'They requisitioned it, after the school explosion. You knew that, Marinette.'

'They've gone,' I said. 'I saw them leaving yesterday.'

I said nothing about the deaths of Karl and Fritz, or Martin. Someday I might tell my mother but there was far too much else to take in that day.

'I'll take you up to the farm,' Uncle Félix said.

I winced, cradling my injured arm, as my mother helped me climb into the trap. My uncle took the reins and we headed off up the hill, away from the smouldering ruins.

As the horse's hooves clomped away, the faces of the people I would never see again swam through my mind, their voices, their laughter and their smells: the sweet aroma of Uncle Claude's pipe, the rough and tumble noise of his children. Everything swept away in a few horrific hours, all perhaps, because vengeance had consumed my mind. I couldn't help thinking Dr. Laforge was simply trying to make me feel better, inventing alternative reasons for the carnage.

As the horse struggled up the hill to L'Auberge, I gathered up every one of those farms, shops and homes — the two thousand-year old village of Lucie-sur-Vionne — firmly, and forever, into my mind and my heart.

***

From the empty bottles strewn about, the splintered furniture, the cracked food jars lying on their side, it was obvious the Germans' time at L'Auberge had been one great orgy of drinking and eating. There was not a single animal left, not one vegetable, plant or flower remaining in the trampled kitchen garden. The orchard was a wreck too, as if the Germans had deliberately destroyed whatever they hadn't taken with them. My mother and I left Uncle Félix checking the outhouses, while we tramped up the steps and inside.

Maman stared at her muddied, scuffed tiles and parquet floors; at the pictures in the living room hanging sideways or lying, their frames cracked, on the floor. It was easy to sympathise with her distress, at the devastation of her usually neat and clean home.

I touched her arm. 'I'm sorry … so sorry. It was my fault they came to L'Auberge. If I hadn't … everything is my fault. But I'll clean it all up, every last bit of this mess.'

My mother said nothing; she simply shook her head and kept gazing about her.

My heart heavy, I plodded upstairs and attempted to climb the attic ladder but my injured arm was useless, and I could not know if Max's paintings were safe. I returned to the kitchen, and heard Maman's shriek, from her herbal room.

They'd smashed every bottle, jar and container, the contents leaking across the floor in one great mangle of liquid, glass and mulched plant. She stood amidst the mess, one hand fussing with her chignon, the other clamped over her mouth.

'Oh God no …' I clutched my wounded arm, which ached even more. 'I'm sor —'

'Don't keep apologising, Célestine. I do understand you only did what you felt you had to … up at the school. I know you had to do something — anything — not to end up like your embittered mother.'

'Still, I never thought the Germans would … But I'll fix it, Maman. I'll help you gather more stocks. You'll see, one day I'll make it the same again.'

'At least they didn't find my stash,' she said, nodding at the intact parquetry floor. 'It seems we'll need every last franc to repair this damage.'

Uncle Félix appeared in the kitchen.

'We'll get the old place right again, Marinette.'

'Yes we will, Maman.'

My mother nodded. 'L'Auberge des Anges has survived uprisings, revolutions, war and every caprice of nature,' she said. 'It has been our family home for centuries. These walls of stone, their legends and secrets, *are* our family. Without it, we have nothing.' She made a move towards the door, to take an apron from the hook. 'I'm not about to let it crumble in the face of a few Nazi thugs. We'll start cleaning up right now.'

Uncle Félix laid a hand on her arm. 'Not now, Marinette. Céleste needs to rest and there is so much else ...' he waved an arm in the direction of Lucie, 'so much more to deal with. We'll come back another day.'

We climbed back into the trap and rode away, back to Julien. The Germans may have devastated L'Auberge but it was still there, perched on the hill like a great timeless being, its stony face twisted in defiant scorn at the cruelty of mankind that had destroyed an entire village.

Summer 1944 – Summer 1946

51

It was a hot June morning, two days after the massacre, the wind gusting in from the Massif Central. The chestnut trees on the square of Julien swayed like a troupe of mad dancers, as two thin figures plodded into Uncle Félix's clog shop, clots of hair matting their sun-bronzed cheeks.

Olivier's face seemed twisted in an odd shape and, in an instant, I saw that he knew. I spread my arms to him. He collapsed against me and, through the thin layer of flesh, I felt his bones shudder with the sobs.

'We heard,' Patrick said. 'I imagine the whole of France knows about this.' He clamped a hand on his friend's shoulder. 'He's been all right, up till now ...'

'I'm so sorry,' I said. 'It's beyond evil.'

Of course, I didn't mention the part I might have played in that evil, despite Dr. Laforge assuring me the carnage was most likely nothing to do with my pathetic act of revenge. He claimed newspapers like *Libération*, *Résistance* and *La Marseillaise* were publicising the massacre as a Nazi reprisal for Resistance activities, and that that should soothe my conscience. He even said people were calling me a heroine. A heroine! That only heightened the guilt that shadowed my every move.

There was no escape in sleep either, because it entered my dreams; dreams which became nightmares, which startled me into wakefulness and left me feeling exhausted, my heart beating fast. As I bolted upright in the bed, bathed in an icy sweat, my mother would hurry into the room and hold a beaker of something sweet to my lips.

'You cried out again,' she'd say. 'Drink this, you'll feel better.' But I didn't feel better — not better at all. I wouldn't feel better until I could, somehow, gouge the guilt from my heart and my skull.

Patrick and Olivier quickly became heroes. Julien-sur-Vionne buzzed with talk of the brave Maquisards, and the villagers — proud as if they were their own sons — patted their shoulders and shook their hands when they walked past them on the square.

That they'd managed to avoid German bullets fed the peoples' craving for miracles and boosted their sense of justice. It seemed all the mothers, like Aunt Maude, who still had no news of their imprisoned sons, felt new hope beat within their breasts.

***

On a sultry August morning two months later, the Allies crossed the Seine River, bringing the Allied invasion to a successful close. The day Lyon was liberated — 2nd September — Maman proclaimed that since the city was free, we would all return to L'Auberge des Anges and free our home from the final bonds of its Nazi grip.

In the wake of the massacre, my mother had gathered Anne-Sophie Primrose and Séverine Dubois beneath her newly-spread maternal wings. She welcomed not only the two five-year old survivors to L'Auberge's hearth, but Olivier too, and Séverine's sister, Miette.

'She takes care of those kids better than she ever took care of us,' Patrick said. 'She even seems to be enjoying mothering them. Whatever happened to change her?'

I shrugged, smiling too, at that side of her motherhood

we'd rarely seen. I'd not told my brother about a German army deserter named Axel, or my own bitter secret. I sensed they were things Maman and I would keep between us.

Besides, after the darkness that had struck Lucie-sur-Vionne, Karl and Fritz's attack had paled against the shocking tragedy my friends had suffered.

Even as the cold hard voice of reason told Miette otherwise, she still clung to the hope that the bodies of her sister, parents and grandparents would be identified, but we both knew they'd simply been piled together in a mass grave with all the other dead of Lucie. She told me how she and Séverine felt like stray dogs; and how from one day to the next there was suddenly nobody to sit with in the evenings, at midday, on weekends.

I stayed close to her, trying to scrape together comforting words, but I never knew what to say to help ease the pain that ploughed creases into my friend's face. There were no words for what had happened to our village. I think we were still suffering from the shock, the tragedy too fresh in our minds; the spirits of the dead still trapped in their charred homes.

Throughout those autumn months, during which I turned twenty-one, the leaves fading to yellow, crimson and ochre, and falling to the damp ground, many willing hands worked in L'Auberge kitchen garden, dragging down tangles of mistletoe, and pruning the orchard trees. It seemed we were all as determined as my mother to restore the farm to the thriving, homely place it had once been.

The silence about the fates of Félicité, Papa and the Wolfs stretched into the short bleak days of December and January. As a cold numbness descended from the Monts du Lyonnais, the hillsides thick cotton-wool beds, we scrubbed L'Auberge, scouring away every last trace of the occupier. We repainted and hung wallpaper, and Patrick used his carpentry skills to mend and replace the furniture the Germans had either burned or broken.

Throughout the iciest part of winter, the scent of woodsmoke in our nostrils, we gathered around the fireplace and Patrick and Olivier regaled us with tales of their wild Maquis days. I think they made up half the stories, simply to keep our anguished minds off those absent from the fireside, but they spoke with such excitement that I wondered if they didn't miss the action, the adventure and the danger.

One morning in early March the new spring birdsong startled me from a dream of Martin Diehl and me standing side by side, skimming stones from the gravelly shore of the Vionne. It almost escaped me but I clutched onto the images, holding them fast in my fisted hand, beneath the eiderdown. I lay there, thinking about him, then I rolled back the covers, flung the window open and inhaled the fragrant scents.

Winter had retreated across the hills for another year and I looked out onto the tulips, crocuses and daffodils awakening from their earthy beds and trembling in the breeze. Beyond the splash of spring colour, the fields glittered silvery-green with morning dew. The birds continued to shriek, competing with the bleat of young goats, the squeak of piglets from their beds of hay, and the neigh of the new horse.

I glimpsed little Anne-Sophie and Séverine in the meadow, squealing in delight as they plucked young dandelion leaves from the moist earth — for Maman's *pissenlit* jam no doubt.

'Eight hundred,' Anne-Sophie said to her little friend. 'Not one more, not one less, otherwise the jam will be ruined.' I smiled at my mother's words falling from her innocent lips.

The spring days lengthened, and in May of 1945 we finally had the first news of the deportees.

***

'Come down, girls,' I called to Anne-Sophie and Séverine, perched on a high branch of the poplar tree. 'It's dangerous; you'll fall and hurt yourselves.'

Patrick and Olivier looked up from the stakes they were sawing to build a new hen house. 'Dangerous?' Patrick said with a grin. 'As if that ever stopped you.'

'Thank God she was so determined to climb trees better than us,' Olivier said, giving me a wink. 'Or she'd never have got herself, or anybody, out of … of that inferno.'

Crouched over, tending her infant herbs and flowers, my mother glanced up. 'Let the girls be, Célestine. Hounding children only makes them more determined to chase after what's forbidden.'

I ignored Maman's smirk, as Dr. Laforge's Traction pulled up at the gateway of L'Auberge. The doctor opened the back door and helped two figures from the car.

My mother stood and wiped an arm across her brow, streaking it with soil. I ran across the cobblestones. So ghostly and fragile were the two figures, I feared they'd break at the slightest touch, and I had to stop myself flinging myself at them and showering them with kisses.

'Céleste.' Sabine's voice was little more than a ragged whisper. Beside her, Talia seemed to stare straight through us, as if not seeing anything at all. The girl hugged a scrap of paper to her chest.

'We could never return to Julien-sur-Vionne,' Sabine said to my mother. 'The memories … you understand. My daughter and I will live in one of the village houses, once they've finished building the new Lucie-sur-Vionne.'

I hated being reminded of the massacre, of which we rarely spoke those days; to recall that terrible afternoon, a part of me still convinced I had taken the lives of five hundred and six people.

The handful who'd escaped the carnage were temporarily housed in make-shift barrack-huts — ghost-town guardians existing in minimum comfort, for, with the widespread destruction of war, humanitarian help was almost impossible. A committee was busy planning the new Lucie-sur-Vionne, to be constructed close to the original village, the charred ruins of which would be preserved as a memorial. At first I could hardly believe any sort of new world could be born from that burnt-out cadaver; that any kind of life could spring from such bloodstained earth, but then I saw how important it was to freeze the terrible afternoon of June 8th in time. A testament to our suffering under the German occupation, so future generations would never forget.

My mother kept wiping her palms down her apron. 'You and Talia are welcome at L'Auberge for as long as you wish.'

I wrapped my arms around Talia and gave her a gentle hug. 'I'm so happy to see you.'

Talia stared at me from sombre, vaulted eyes. She kept clutching the sheet of paper to her chest, without uttering a word.

'Talia fell silent one day,' Sabine said. 'I haven't heard the sound of my daughter's voice for over a year. The sanatorium doctor said it was the shock. He said she may never speak again.'

'I have something that might help,' Maman said. 'In my special room.'

As my mother gently pushed dark strands of frizzy hair from Talia's eyes, my heart ached for the haunted little creature who bore not the slightest resemblance to the talkative, bright-eyed girl we'd known.

'I tried to find out about you, Sabine,' I said. 'And ... and the others. I went back to the prefecture over and over but they couldn't tell me anything.'

'They told us people were trickling back,' Patrick said. 'That they were being taken to the Hôtel Lutétia in Paris but it might take a long time for them all to return.'

'We saw photographs,' I said. 'Terrible pictures, in *Le Figaro*. It seemed the rumours we'd heard were true. We thought ... '

'What of your husband, and your boy?' Maman asked.

'My little Jacob.' Sabine shook her head and looked away. She didn't cry, and I thought perhaps she'd already used up every last tear.

'My husband was taken on a different train,' she said. 'I do not know where he ...'

'Do you know about ...' Patrick took a breath. '... about anyone else?' I was certain my brother was as anxious as I to know about our sister but he too, was afraid to say her name.

'Talia has something for you,' Sabine said, laying a hand on her daughter's arm. 'A picture she painted while we were at the sanatorium.'

Talia pushed her paper into my hands. Instinctively, I gripped my mother's arm as I looked down at the little girl's painting of a golden-winged creature in a flowing robe. A halo circled the dark hair, and the face was tilted skyward, gazing into a great, gleaming sun. In the bottom right-hand corner, Talia had printed her name, just as Max had done.

I read the caption beneath her name: *Sister Marie-Félicité. The Wolfs' angel.*

I kept a grip on my mother's arm, afraid I would pass out.

'It's the most beautiful painting ever, Talia,' Maman said, and I caught the sound of the sob that snagged in her throat.

'She was much weakened,' Sabine said. 'Like the rest of us. But she found strength in her soul, in her beliefs, to give us all comfort. The courage to go on. They were to send me to ...' She took a breath and focussed her dark, sad eyes on us. 'Marie-Félicité took my place, sacrificed herself to save a little girl's mother.' She cast a glance at Talia, standing motionless beside her.

'March thirtieth, it was,' Sabine said her voice dropping to a reverent kind of whisper. 'Our Good Friday angel.'

***

It was a warm overcast day towards the end of May when the tramp shuffled beneath the wooden gateway of L'Auberge. Anne-

Sophie and Séverine were feeding carrots to the baby goats whose mothers Miette and I were milking. Out in the orchard, the strawberries were fat and almost ripe, the fruit trees in full blossom. Maman was working in her kitchen garden, arranging her plants in ordered rows, each one bearing its own nametag as it either reached for the sky or crawled along the earth. The breeze carried the smell of the lavender bushes, and the citrusy-mint perfume of the lemon balm, across the cobbles.

My mother must have seen the tramp too, for she came around through the gate and into the courtyard, the wind lifting the hem of her dress and snatching her herbal scent.

I stopped my milking and eyed the tramp's long, straggly hair, his unkempt beard and hunched-over frame. As he crossed the courtyard, a dagger of sunlight pierced the clouds and I saw he was filthy, and painfully thin.

Maman was walking across the cobblestones towards the man, wiping her hands down her apron and patting her chignon.

'You'll see,' I said to Miette. 'My mother will chase that tramp away quick smart.'

'Maybe he's a prisoner of war on his way home?' Miette said. 'The government *is* encouraging us all to receive returning workers with open arms, whether they are family or not.'

'Oh yes! While that same government doesn't even give most of them a fresh set of clothes or a homeward bound train ticket,' I said. 'It's scandalous.'

My mother was hurrying to the tramp, who spread his arms wide.

In all the years before they'd sent Papa to Germany, I couldn't recall seeing my parents touch each other, but then they hugged and kissed like impatient young lovers. For the first time ever, I think, I heard the sound of my mother's laugh. A real laugh, from the heart.

52

On a scorching summer day of 1946 I married Olivier Primrose. It was a double wedding, with Patrick and Juliette Dubois.

Miette insisted the ceremony take place in the charred remains of Saint Antoine's church. 'So my mother, and Amandine, will be with us,' she said. 'And so many of our friends.'

When Rachel Abraham had learned of the planned nuptials, she limped up to L'Auberge from her home in the new Lucie-sur-Vionne and presented my mother with a bolt of cream-coloured cloth and a skein of exquisite antique lace, from which Maman fashioned two beautiful gowns.

Aunt Maude and Uncle Félix arrived in the trap from Julien, with my cousins, Jules and Paul.

'Come on, Félicité,' my father said. 'We'll be late for the wedding. You know Céleste's getting married today.' His face spread in a silly grin, his arms stretched wide towards his beloved invisible daughter. 'And your mother's prepared such a feast. You'll have to feed yourself up, look at you, how much weight you've lost. Oh what lovely days we're going to spend together, Félicité, now the war is over.'

My father never uttered a word about those lost years, and we heard the Germans had allowed prisoners to send letters home only until July of 1943, to boost morale and control the anxiety of those back home. After that, they'd forbidden any correspondence.

He'd been back from the labour camp only a few days when we noticed his mind had gone astray. The visions of Félicité began as soon as we told him how his daughter died a heroine, and he began to resurrect treasured memories, recalling certain words she'd said, gestures made with a little girl's hand. He spoke of the pink smock she wore as a child, and the way she cried and held out her arms to him when she'd been stung by nettles.

But for the most part he was still lucid, quite aware his daughter was gone, as he was then, as the wedding party stood on la place de l'Eglise, before the ruins of Saint Antoine's church.

'She came from a different world,' he said to Maman, clamping his wrinkled, stick-thin arms across his chest. 'People talk about Heaven, but they only think about this world. Saints like her are sent here to make up for our sins. Félicité came from God and she must be very happy now.'

His shoulders heaved, tears coursing down his cheeks which he swiped at angrily. He hid his face in his cupped hands and my mother boosted him up as he bent into her shoulder.

Between those imaginary sightings and conversations with Félicité, my father spent most of his days staring at nothing with a bored, milky gaze, even more so when he was forced to stop working the wood.

We learned that failing eyesight was a common problem for those who'd worked in the *Reich* rayon factories. While it was important for manufacturing German army uniforms, the workers had inhaled volatile carbon disulphide, increasing their chances of heart disease, toxic effects to the nervous system and serious eye problems.

So Papa simply sat in the same chair in the kitchen, staring at his hands, which he turned over and over — the wood carver's hands in which something unique and splendid had lived, and died. Oh yes, we were one of the lucky families. Our father had made it home from the terrible German labour camps in which countless had perished. He had survived!

Olivier's parents also came for the wedding. They'd learned of the Lucie tragedy while still in London, but had no wish to return to the scene of their devastated home, or the painful reminders of Uncle Claude, Justin and Gervais, and little Paulette.

'We've bought a home down south,' Olivier's father, Edward Primrose, told us.

'But we understand why Olivier is staying,' his mother said. 'He has his roots here; everything he knows and loves. And now he has you too, Céleste, but I hope you'll both visit often.'

As I stood in the ghost-like silence of la place de l'Eglise, Miette and I swathed in our elegant gowns, the sun and shade painting our bare shoulders, I couldn't help recalling how it was before. I saw the leafy lime trees, and the blooming roses. I heard the clatter of familiar footsteps on the cobblestones, the trickle of the fountain, the creaking of wheelbarrows, the *bawk-bawk-bawk* of hens.

I lifted my arm in a wave, as Dr. Etienne Laforge arrived with his sister, Jacqueline. Pierre and Antoine were with them too, released from prison after the liberation, and continuing their law degrees.

Jacqueline Laforge's reputation as an ardent women's rights worker was widely known. I pored over her magazine and newspaper articles and attended the meetings and demonstrations she led in the city. She still drank and smoked like a man, and occasionally came to L'Auberge for a Sunday picnic with her brother, who continued his doctor's practice from one of the new homes of Lucie.

All the guests had arrived, and we moved across to the vestiges of Saint-Antoine's. Summer heat filling the blackened chamber, I stood with Olivier, Patrick, Miette, and the girls — Séverine, Anne-Sophie and Talia — proudly holding their bright posies.

The priest came from the church they were building in the new Lucie, and while his sermon was pleasant, it was the soothing, learned voice of Père Emmanuel I heard booming from where the pulpit once stood.

The ceremony over, I let Olivier's hand go and walked across to the three windows on the apse wall, behind the altar. I knelt down before the largest one and bowed my head. I didn't attempt to pray; I simply placed my bouquet of red roses and sunflowers, sprinkled with baby's breath, against the blackened wall.

'For you, Sister Marie-Félicité,' I whispered. 'Our bride of Christ.'

***

With Sabine and Madame Abraham's help, my mother had prepared a feast at L'Auberge.

It had been stiflingly hot all day, and we only started to breathe easily as the sun cast its final orange glow across the Monts du Lyonnais. The sweet-smelling dusk dropped and Maman threw the doors and windows open, welcoming in the night freshness.

My mother's garden was at its most beautiful. The heat had withered the daisies and carnations, but around the well the cluster of rose bushes was in full bloom, their sugary scent splayed across the cobblestones.

Amidst the racket of crickets and the laughter and chatter of my friends and family, my new husband drew me close and kissed me. He lifted my angel pendant from where it lay against the laced edge of my wedding gown.

'Let's hope there'll soon be someone to hand this down to.'

'Not *too* soon,' I said with a smile. 'You know I need to finish my studies and get a job. I might be a wife now, Olivier, but I'm still a free woman!'

He laughed. 'And so you'll always be, I fear.'

I tilted my face to the moon, which was rising like a gigantic blood-orange in the sky. One of the stars glowed brighter and larger than the others, and winked at me. As the light disappeared and I lowered my eyes from that golden crown, I had no regrets, convinced the dark-headed childhood friend by my side was the perfect husband.

My mother brought the cake out, a three-tiered creation layered with cream and edged in raspberries and redcurrants.

'I want to cut it,' Anne-Sophie said.

'No me, let me,' Séverine said.

As usual, Talia watched from a distance in wide-eyed silence. It seemed nobody dared tempt her to speak, perhaps for fear of causing more damage, if that were possible. At least she'd joined us today instead of taking refuge in the attic, hunched over her father's paintings.

'Don't bicker, girls,' Maman said. 'You'll both have a turn cutting the cake.'

Anne-Sophie and Séverine clapped their hands but Talia remained wordless, though I did catch a glimmer in those sad pearl-grey eyes as the girl turned to her mother.

Clad in a billowy skirt and ballet shoes, her hair shining blue-black in the moonlight, Sabine glided across the grass towards us. Nobody uttered a sound as she clasped her hands in prayer position close to her heart and fixed her eyes on her daughter.

My father must have known about Sabine's show, because a silly grin lit his face as he stood over the gramophone player.

'When you're ready,' he said to Sabine. 'Céleste, go and call your sister, she'll love this.'

Maman's brow creased and I patted the chair next to me.

'Félicité is already here, Papa, all set to enjoy the show. Why don't you put the music on, then come and sit next to me?'

Sabine gave the slightest nod and the first melodious notes struck the night air. Her head extended high and proud, she began to dance, each practised step light, and liquid as a high-running spring river.

'What's the music?' I whispered to Madame Abraham, as Sabine hovered over the sun-warmed grass.

'It's Swan Lake,' she said. 'The story of a princess turned into a swan by an evil sorcerer's curse.'

We watched in enchanted silence — Sabine's languid arm gestures, and the way she balanced on her tiptoes and pirouetted like a spinning top. The music grew louder, faster, as if it were rolling across the garden, over the cobblestones and echoing deep through the secret valleys and the frill of trees that looked like hooded nuns shuffling into the woods.

The music began to fade. Sabine raised her arms and slid to the earth in a final, graceful arch.

Talia was the first to clap. Like a thousand stars from the summer night sky shining on her at once, a smile lit her face.

'Maman's the best ballerina in all the world,' she said.

The applause stopped. All eyes turned to Talia.

'Well, I never,' Papa said. 'The child's come home to us.'

He began pouring half-finger doses of Maman's *confiture de vieux garçon* into the *digestif* glasses.

'Why's it called old boy's jam?' Séverine asked, sniffing at the liqueur in her sister's glass. 'What's in it?'

'Just a bit of fruit left over after the jam,' Maman said. 'Strawberries, raspberries, cherries, plums. All soaked in cognac.'

Our faces glowing in the moonlight, the smoky perfume of lime-blossom, lavender, oak and chestnut bark filling our nostrils, my father lifted his glass.

'To the happy couples,' he said.

'Happy couples,' everyone chanted.

We lifted our glasses to the sky, from where the sun would rise tomorrow over Mont Blanc, flinging its broad rays across the Monts du Lyonnais; from where the wind and the birds would glide across the fields and woods, and from where the Vionne River would spring from the hills and carve its timeless path through the valley.

We drank to the glory of people walking from one place to another in freedom.

I made a silent toast to that other person who was gone too; the one whose diamond ring and photo were gathering dust in a little wooden box, the corners curling with the winter damp, the handsome features fading so that they'd become so hazy I could no longer define the face.

'To our friends and loved ones,' Maman said. 'Who will never leave us.'

Nobody spoke as we raised our glasses to Sister Marie-Félicité; to Max and Jacob Wolf.

We rarely mentioned them those days. Nor did we speak about the people who'd perished in the Lucie massacre. It was as if none of us, besides my father whose tortured mind gave him no choice, wanted to linger in our tragic pasts, and we simply carried our individual burdens of grief; our guilty millstones, close to our hearts.

Author's Note

Oradour-sur-Glane

The idea for *Wolfsangel*, and the factual event upon which the Lucie-sur-Vionne massacre is based, came to me when I visited the memorial site of the original village of Oradour-sur-Glane, a commune in the Limousin region of west-central France.

On 10th June 1944, four days after the Allied landings in Normandy, SS troops encircled the village and rounded up its inhabitants. In the marketplace they divided the men from the women and children. The men were marched off to barns and shot. Only five of the 186 male civilians survived, by staying — partly covered by dead bodies — in the barn and pretending to be dead. The SS set the barn alight fifteen minutes after the execution to cover the tracks of their massacre.

The soldiers locked the women and children in the church, shot them, and set the building (and then the rest of the town) on fire. Two women and one child survived. One was 47-year-old Marguerite Rouffanche. She hauled herself out of a window behind the altar, followed by a young woman and child. German soldiers shot all three of them, killing the woman and child and wounding Rouffanche, who escaped into nearby foliage where she stayed until she was rescued the following day.

Those residents of Oradour who had been away for the day, or had managed to escape the roundup, returned to a blackened scene of horror, carnage and devastation. Those moments of unthinkable atrocity obliterated the lives of many and broke those of the few survivors. The fact that so few survived the savage slaughter is a testimony to the efficiency of the German plan. Moreover, the reasons why the SS committed such a crime against humanity have never been determined. Some of them were brought to trial, either in Bordeaux or Berlin, the others escaped retribution. Among German crimes of the Second World War, the Oradour-sur-Glane massacre of 642 men, women and children is one of the most notorious.

A new village was constructed on a nearby site, but on the orders of the French president, Charles de Gaulle, the original site was maintained as a permanent memorial. He wanted the ruins to be preserved so that future generations might see, realise and never forget where such evil folly may lead. These ruins demand respect and sorrow of all who visit them.

If you would like to learn more about the true story behind the book, please visit the *Wolfsangel* page of my website: www. lizaperrat.com

Elise Rivet

The character of Félicité Roussel is based on Elise Rivet, a Roman Catholic nun who became Mother Superior in 1933. She concealed refugees from the Gestapo in her convent, and stored weapons and ammunition for the Resistance movement. Eventually arrested by the Gestapo, she was taken to the Montluc Prison in Lyon, and shipped to Ravensbrück concentration camp. On 30 March 1945, only weeks before the war ended, she volunteered to go to the gas chambers in the place of a young mother. In 1961 the French government honoured her with her portrait on a postage stamp. A street bearing her name (rue Mère Elise Rivet) was inaugurated in Brignais (Lyon) on December 2, 1979. In 1977, she was posthumously awarded the *Médaille des Justes* and in 1999, the Salle Elise Rivet was named for her at the *Institut des Sciences de L'Homme* in Lyon.

Angel-maker

Marie-Louise Giraud (November 17, 1903 – July 30, 1943) was a 39-year old housewife, mother and laundress who became one of the last women to be guillotined in France. Giraud was a convicted abortionist in 1940s Nazi occupied France, executed on July 30, 1943 for having performed 27 abortions in the Cherbourg area. She was the only *faiseuse d'anges* (angel-maker) to be executed for this reason. Her story was dramatised in the 1988 movie *Story of Women*, directed by Claude Chabrol.

Despite these historical facts, this novel is a work of fiction; a work that combines the actual with the invented. All incidents and dialogue and all characters, with the exception of some well-known historical figures, are products of the author's imagination and are not to be construed as real. Where real-life historical figures appear, the situations, incidents and dialogues concerning those persons are fictional and are not intended to depict actual events or to change the fictional nature of the work. In all other respects, any resemblance to persons living or dead is entirely coincidental.

Acknowledgements

With grateful thanks to the writers and readers who helped shape this novel: JD Smith, Gillian Hamer, JJMarsh, Catriona Troth and Sheila Bugler (Triskele Books); Lorraine Mace, Barbara Scott-Emmett, Tricia Gilbey, Claire Whatley, Marlene Brown (Writing Asylum); Pauline O'Hare for the Barry's tea and for always being there; Judith Murdoch for her wisdom and expert editorial advice; Perry Iles for his editorial and proofreading expertise; Claire Morgan, Debra Prichard, and Gwenda Lansbury for their input on early drafts; Kari Chevalier for her final-draft comments and help with the cover; Guy Dufeu (French Resistance member) who agreed to be interviewed; JD Smith for her wonderful cover design; the very helpful people from *L'Araire* (historical research group of Messimy, France); and Jean-Yves, Camille, Mathilde and Etienne Perrat for their infinite patience with an absent wife and mother.

Thank you for reading
a Triskele Book

Enjoyed *Wolfsangel*? Here's what you can do next.

If you loved the book and would like to help other readers find Triskele Books, please write a short review on the page where you bought the book. Your help in spreading the word is much appreciated and reviews make a huge difference to helping new readers find good books.

More novels from Triskele Books are coming soon. You can sign up to be notified of the next release and other news here: http://www.triskelebooks.co.uk

 If you are a writer and would like more information on writing and publishing, visit www.triskelebooks.blogspot.com and www. wordswithjam.co.uk, which are packed with author and industry professional interviews, links to articles on writing, reading, libraries, the publishing industry and indie-publishing.

Connect with us:
Email admin@triskelebooks.co.uk
Twitter @TriskeleBooks
Facebook www.facebook.com/triskelebooks

Other Novels by Liza Perrat
Spirit of Lost Angels

First book of *L'Auberge des Anges* series.

Her mother executed for witchcraft, her father dead at the hand of a noble, Victoire Charpentier vows to rise above her impoverished peasant roots.

Forced to leave her village of Lucie-sur-Vionne for domestic work in the capital, Victoire suffers gruesome abuse under the *ancien régime* of 18th century Paris.

Imprisoned in France's most pitiless madhouse — *La Salpêtrière* asylum — Victoire becomes desperate and helpless, until she meets fellow prisoner Jeanne de Valois, infamous conwoman of the diamond necklace affair. With the help of the ruthless and charismatic countess who helped hasten Queen Marie Antoinette to the guillotine, Victoire carves out a new life for herself.

Enmeshed in the fever of pre-revolutionary Paris, Victoire must find the strength to join the revolutionary force storming the Bastille. Is she brave enough to help overthrow the diabolical aristocracy?

As *Spirit of Lost Angels* traces Victoire's journey, it follows too the journey of an angel talisman through generations of the Charpentier family. Victoire lives in the hope her angel pendant will one day renew the link with a special person in her life.

Amidst the tumult of the French revolution drama, the women of *Spirit of Lost Angels* face tragedy and betrayal in a world where their gift can be their curse.

Spirit of Lost Angels listed on "Best of 2012" sites
http://darleneelizabethwilliamsauthor.com/blog/2012-top-10-historical-fiction-novels/

http://abookishaffair.blogspot.fr/2012/12/best-books-of-2012.html

http://thequeensquillreview.com/2012/12/10/holiday-picks-from-the-queens-quill/

Shortlisted Writing Magazine Self-Publishing Awards 2013
http://lizaperrat.blogspot.fr/2013/06/spirit-of-lost-angels-shortlisted.html

Winner EFestival of Words 2013, Best Historical Fiction category
http://www.efestivalofwords.com/congratulations-to-the-2013-winners-t473.html

Recommended at the 2013 Historical Novel Conference in "Off the Beaten Path" recommendations
http://thequeensquillreview.com/2013/06/26/the-mammoth-list-of-off-the-beaten-path-book-recommendations-brought-to-you-by-our-hns-conference-panel/

Indie Book of the Day Award, 13th July, 2013
http://indiebookoftheday.com/spirit-of-lost-angels-by-liza-perrat/

Coming next in
L'Auberge des Anges series …
Midwife Héloïse –
Blood Rose Angel

1348. A bone-carved angel talisman — family heirloom, evil curse, holy relic. And Héloïse Dumortier, the midwife-healer woman who wears it — heretic, Devil's servant, saint.

When the Black Plague arrives, sweeping across France, the superstitious villagers begin to ask who or what is to blame for this pestilence. Fire and foul winds from the East, or the stinking miasmas of stagnant lakes? Is it some malign conjunction of the planets, or God's wrath against sinners? Perhaps it is the curse of a mere woman.

Amidst the terror, grief and contagion, Héloïse must find the courage and compassion to care for birthing women and plague-stricken victims. She must also fight against those who accuse her.

Also from Triskele Books

OVERLORD

My name is Zabdas: once a slave; now a warrior, grandfather and servant. I call Syria home. I shall tell you the story of my Zenobia: Warrior Queen of Palmyra, Protector of the East, Conqueror of Desert Lands ...

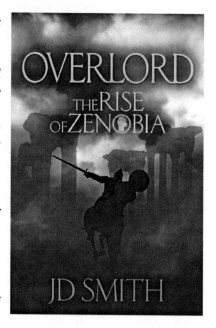

The Roman Empire is close to collapse. Odenathus of Palmyra holds the Syrian frontier and its vital trade routes against Persian invasion. A client king in a forgotten land, starved of reinforcements, Odenathus calls upon an old friend, Julius, to face an older enemy: the Tanukh.

Julius believes Syria should break free of Rome and declare independence. But his daughter's beliefs are stronger still. Zenobia is determined to realise her father's dream.

And turn traitor to Rome ...

Also from Triskele Books

GHOST TOWN

1981. Coventry, city of Two Tone and Ska, is riven with battles between skinheads and young Asians.

Photographer Baz—'too desi to be gora, too Paki to be white'—is capturing the conflict on film.

Unemployed graduate Maia—serial champion of liberal causes—is pregnant with a mixed-race child.

Neither can afford to let the racists win. They must take a stand.

A stand that will cost lives.

Also from Triskele Books

The Open Arms of the Sea by Jasper Dorgan
The Charter by Gillian Hamer
Closure by Gillian E Hamer
Complicit by Gillian E Hamer
Behind Closed Doors by JJ Marsh
Raw Material by JJ Marsh
Tread Softly by JJ Marsh
Spirit of Lost Angels by Liza Perrat
Tristan and Iseult by JD Smith
Overlord by JD Smith
Gift of the Raven by Catriona Troth
Ghost Town by Catriona Troth

Bibliography

Many fictional and factual books, movies and other material helped create the atmosphere of *Wolfsangel*.

Aubrac, Lucie: Outwitting the Gestapo
Braddon, Russell: Nancy Wake
Farmer, Sarah: Martyred Village
Gildea, Robert: Marianne in Chains
Gille, Elisabeth: Shadows of a Childhood
Hébras, Robert: Oradour-Sur-Glane, The Tragedy Hour by Hour
Humbert, Agnes: Résistance
Némirovsky, Irène: Suite Française
Ousby, Ian: Occupation – The Ordeal of France 1940 – 1944
Schnur, Steven: The Shadow Children
Tickell, Jerrard: Odette – Secret Agent, Prisoner, Survivor
"Vercours" (Anonymous): The Silence of the Sea
Vinen, Richard: The Unfree French – Life under the Occupation
Walters, Anne-Marie: Moondrop to Gascony
L'Araire (*Groupe de Recherche sur l'histoire, l'archéologie et le folklore du Pays Lyonnais*) booklets:
Foires et Marchés en Pays Lyonnais: N° 148 — March, 2007
Soins et Santé en Pays Lyonnais: N° 157 — June, 2009

About the Author

Liza grew up in Wollongong, Australia, where she worked as a general nurse and midwife. She has been living in rural France for the past twenty years, working as a medical translator and a novelist.

CPSIA information can be obtained at www.ICGtesting.com
Printed in the USA
LVOW12s1209251013

358466LV00003B/78/P